LOVER ENSHRINED

BY J. R. WARD

J. R. WARD

LOVER
ENSHRINED

A NOVEL OF THE BLACK DAGGER BROTHERHOOD

 NEW AMERICAN LIBRARY

New American Library
Published by the Penguin Group
Penguin Group (USA) LLC, 375 Hudson Street,
New York, New York 10014

USA | Canada | UK | Ireland | Australia | New Zealand | India | South Africa | China
penguin.com
A Penguin Random House Company

Published by New American Library, a division of Penguin Group (USA) LLC. Previously published
in a Signet edition.

First New American Library Printing, February 2014

 REGISTERED TRADEMARK—MARCA REGISTRADA

NEW AMERICAN LIBRARY HARDCOVER ISBN: 978-0-451-46602-0

Printed in the United States of America
1   3   5   7   9   10   8   6   4   2

Set in Garamond
Designed by Patrice Sheridan

Dedicated to: *You.*
You were a total gentleman and a relief.
And I believe that joy becomes you—
you most certainly deserve it.

ACKNOWLEDGMENTS

With immense gratitude to the readers
of the Black Dagger Brotherhood
and a shout-out to the Cellies!

Thank you so very much:
Karen Solem, Kara Cesare, Claire Zion, Kara Welsh.

Thank you, S-Byte and Ventrue and Loop and Opal for everything
you do out of the goodness of your hearts!

As always with gratitude to my Executive Committee:
Sue Grafton, Dr. Jessica Andersen, and Betsey Vaughan.
And with much respect to the incomparable
Suzanne Brockmann.

To DLB—RESPECT love u xxx mummy
To NTM—as always, with love and gratitude. You are indeed a
prince amongst men.
PS—is there anything you can't find?

To LeElla Scott—are we there yet? are we there yet?
are we there yet?
Remmy, cruise control is our friend and we are nothing without
LeSunshine.
Love to you, my bestie.

To Kaylie—welcome to the world, baby girl.
You have a spectacular mother—she's absolutely my Idol,
and not just because she keeps me in hair care products.

ACKNOWLEDGMENTS

To Bub—thanks for *schwasted*!

None of this would be possible without:
my loving husband,
who is my adviser and caretaker and visionary,
my wonderful mother, who has given me so much love I couldn't
possibly ever repay her,
my family (both those of blood and those by adoption),
and my dearest friends.
Oh, and the better half of WriterDog, of course.

GLOSSARY OF TERMS AND PROPER NOUNS

abstrux nohtrum (n.) Private guard with license to kill who is appointed to his or her position by the king.

ahvenge (v.) Act of mortal retribution, carried out typically by a male loved one.

Black Dagger Brotherhood (pr. n.) Highly trained vampire warriors who protect their species against the Lessening Society. As a result of selective breeding within the race, Brothers possess immense physical and mental strength, as well as rapid healing capabilities. They are not siblings for the most part, and are inducted into the Brotherhood upon nomination by the Brothers. Aggressive, self-reliant, and secretive by nature, they exist apart from civilians, having little contact with members of the other classes except when they need to feed. They are the subjects of legend and the objects of reverence within the vampire world. They may be killed only by the most serious of wounds, e.g., a gunshot or stab to the heart, etc.

blood slave (n.) Male or female vampire who has been subjugated to serve the blood needs of another. The practice of keeping blood slaves has recently been outlawed.

chrih (n.) Symbol of honorable death in the Old Language.

the Chosen (n.) Female vampires who have been bred to serve the Scribe Virgin. They are considered members of the aristocracy, though they are spiritually rather than temporally focused. They

have little or no interaction with males, but can be mated to
Brothers at the Scribe Virgin's direction to propagate their class.
Some have the ability to prognosticate. In the past, they were
used to meet the blood needs of unmated members of the Brotherhood, and that practice has been reinstated by the Brothers.

cohntehst (n.) Conflict between two males competing for the right
to be a female's mate.

doggen (n.) Member of the servant class within the vampire world.
Doggen have old, conservative traditions about service to their
superiors, following a formal code of dress and behavior. They
are able to go out during the day, but they age relatively quickly.
Life expectancy is approximately five hundred years.

Dhunhd (pr. n.) Hell.

ehros (n.) A Chosen trained in the matter of sexual arts.

exhile dhoble (n.) The evil or cursed twin, the one born second.

the Fade (pr. n.) Nontemporal realm where the dead reunite with
their loved ones and pass eternity.

First Family (pr. n.) The king and queen of the vampires, and any
children they may have.

ghardian (n.) Custodian of an individual. There are varying degrees
of *ghardians*, with the most powerful being that of a *sehcluded*
female.

glymera (n.) The social core of the aristocracy, roughly equivalent to
Regency England's ton.

hellren (n.) Male vampire who has been mated to a female. Males
may take more than one female as mate.

leahdyre (n.) A person of power and influence.

leelan (adj.) A term of endearment loosely translated as "dearest
one."

Lessening Society (pr. n.) Order of slayers convened by the Omega
for the purpose of eradicating the vampire species.

lesser (n.) De-souled human who targets vampires for extermination
as a member of the Lessening Society. *Lessers* must be stabbed

through the chest in order to be killed; otherwise they are ageless. They do not eat or drink and are impotent. Over time, their hair, skin, and irises lose pigmentation until they are blond, blushless, and pale eyed. They smell like baby powder. Inducted into the society by the Omega, they retain a ceramic jar thereafter into which their heart was placed after it was removed.

lewlhen (n.) Gift.

lheage (n.) A term of respect used by a sexual submissive to refer to her dominant.

mahmen (n.) Mother. Used both as an identifier and a term of affection.

mhis (n.) The masking of a given physical environment; the creation of a field of illusion.

nalla (n. f.) or *nallum* (n. m.) Beloved.

needing period (n.) Female vampire's time of fertility, generally lasting for two days and accompanied by intense sexual cravings. Occurs approximately five years after a female's transition and then once a decade thereafter. All males respond to some degree if they are around a female in her need. It can be a dangerous time, with conflicts and fights breaking out between competing males, particularly if the female is not mated.

newling (n.) A virgin.

the Omega (pr. n.) Malevolent, mystical figure who has targeted the vampires for extinction out of resentment directed toward the Scribe Virgin. Exists in a nontemporal realm and has extensive powers, though not the power of creation.

phearsom (adj.) Term referring to the potency of a male's sexual organs. Literal translation something close to "worthy of entering a female."

princeps (n.) Highest level of the vampire aristocracy, second only to members of the First Family or the Scribe Virgin's Chosen. Must be born to the title; it may not be conferred.

pyrocant (n.) Refers to a critical weakness in an individual. The weakness can be internal, such as an addiction, or external, such as a lover.

rahlman (n.) Savior.

rythe (n.) Ritual manner of assuaging honor granted by one who has offended another. If accepted, the offended chooses a weapon and strikes the offender, who presents him- or herself without defenses.

the Scribe Virgin (pr. n.) Mystical force who is counselor to the king as well as the keeper of vampire archives and the dispenser of privileges. Exists in a nontemporal realm and has extensive powers. Capable of a single act of creation, which she expended to bring the vampires into existence.

sehclusion (n.) Status conferred by the king upon a female of the aristocracy as a result of a petition by the female's family. Places the female under the sole direction of her *ghardian*, typically the eldest male in her household. Her *ghardian* then has the legal right to determine all manner of her life, restricting at will any and all interactions she has with the world.

shellan (n.) Female vampire who has been mated to a male. Females generally do not take more than one mate due to the highly territorial nature of bonded males.

symphath (n.) Subspecies within the vampire race characterized by the ability and desire to manipulate emotions in others (for the purposes of an energy exchange), among other traits. Historically, they have been discriminated against and, during certain eras, hunted by vampires. They are near to extinction.

the Tomb (pr. n.) Sacred vault of the Black Dagger Brotherhood. Used as a ceremonial site as well as a storage facility for the jars of *lessers*. Ceremonies performed there include inductions, funerals, and disciplinary actions against Brothers. No one may enter except for members of the Brotherhood, the Scribe Virgin, or candidates for induction.

trahyner (n.) Word used between males of mutual respect and affection. Translated loosely as "beloved friend."

transition (n.) Critical moment in a vampire's life when he or she transforms into an adult. Thereafter, they must drink the blood of the opposite sex to survive and are unable to withstand sunlight. Occurs generally in the mid-twenties. Some vampires do not survive their transitions, males in particular. Prior to their transitions, vampires are physically weak, sexually unaware and unresponsive, and unable to dematerialize.

vampire (n.) Member of a species separate from that of Homo sapiens. Vampires must drink the blood of the opposite sex to survive. Human blood will keep them alive, though the strength does not last long. Following their transitions, which occur in their mid-twenties, they are unable to go out into sunlight and must feed from the vein regularly. Vampires cannot "convert" humans through a bite or transfer of blood, though they are in rare cases able to breed with the other species. Vampires can dematerialize at will, though they must be able to calm themselves and concentrate to do so and may not carry anything heavy with them. They are able to strip the memories of humans, provided such memories are short-term. Some vampires are able to read minds. Life expectancy is upward of a thousand years, or in some cases even longer.

wahlker (n.) An individual who has died and returned to the living from the Fade. They are accorded great respect and are revered for their travails.

whard (n.) Equivalent of a godfather or godmother to an individual.

LOVER ENSHRINED

PROLOGUE

Twenty-five years, three months, four days,
eleven hours, eight minutes, and thirty-four seconds ago . . .

Time was not, in fact, a draining loss into the infinite. Up until the very second of the present, it was malleable, not fixed. Clay, not concrete.

Which was something for which the Omega was grateful. If time had been fixed, he would not be holding his newborn son in his arms.

Children had never been his goal. And yet in this moment, he was transformed.

"Is the mother dead?" he asked as his *Fore-lesser* came down the stairs. Funny, if you had asked the slayer what year he thought it was, he would have said 1983. And he would have been correct, in a way.

The *Fore-lesser* nodded. "She didn't survive the birth."

"Vampires rarely do. It's one of their few virtues." And in this case apropos. Killing the mother after she had served him so well seemed ungracious.

"What do you want me to do with her body?"

The Omega watched as his son reached out and grabbed hold of his thumb. The grip was strong. "How odd."

"What?"

It was hard to put into words what he was feeling. Or perhaps that was the point. He hadn't expected to feel anything.

His son was supposed to be a defensive reaction to the Destroyer Prophecy, a calculated response in the war against the vampires, a strategy to ensure the Omega survived. His son would do battle in a new way and kill off that race of savages before the Destroyer chipped away at the Omega's being until there was nothing left.

Up until this moment, the plan had been executed flawlessly, starting with the abduction of the female vampire the Omega had inseminated and ending here with this new arrival in the world.

The infant looked up at him, budding mouth working. He smelled sweet, but not because he was a *lesser*.

The Omega didn't want to let him go, suddenly. This young in his arms was a miracle, a living, breathing loophole. The Omega had not been granted the act of creation as his sister had, but reproduction had not been denied him. He might not have been able to bring a whole new race into being. But he could bring a part of himself forward from the genetic pool.

And he had.

"Master?" the *Fore-lesser* said.

He really did not want to let the baby go, but to have this work, his son had to live with the enemy, be raised as one among them. His son had to know their language and their culture and their ways.

His son had to know where they lived so he could go and slaughter them.

The Omega forced himself to give the infant over to his *Fore-lesser*. "Leave him at the gathering place I forbade you to sack. Swaddle him and leave him, and when you return here I shall draw you forth unto me."

Whereupon you shall die as I so will it, the Omega finished to himself.

There could be no leaks. No mistakes.

As the *Fore-lesser* did some fawning, which would have interested the Omega at any other time, the sun came up over the cornfields of Caldwell, New York. From upstairs, a soft fizzling sound bloomed into a full-blown fire, the burning smell announcing the incineration of the female's body along with all the blood on that bed.

Which was just lovely. Tidiness mattered, and this farmhouse was brand-new, built especially for the son's birth.

"Go," the Omega commanded. "Go and carry out your duty."

The *Fore-lesser* left with the infant, and as the Omega watched the door shut, he yearned for his offspring. Positively ached for the boy.

The solution for his angst was at hand, however. The Omega willed himself into the air and catapulted what corporeal form he had to the "present," to the very living room he was in.

The change in time registered in a rapid aging of the house around him. Wallpaper faded and peeled off in lazy strips. Furniture ratted and became worn in patterns consistent with over two decades of use. The ceiling dulled from bright white to dingy yellow, as if smokers had been exhaling for years. Floorboards curled up at the corners of the hallway.

In the back of the house, he heard two humans arguing.

The Omega drifted down to the filthy, wilted kitchen that merely seconds ago had been shiny as the day it had been built.

As he came into the room, the man and the woman stopped their fighting, freezing with shock. And he got on with the tedious business of emptying the farmhouse of prying eyes.

His son was returning unto the fold. And the Omega needed to see him almost more than he needed to put him to use.

As the evil touched the center of his chest, he felt empty and thought of his sister. She had brought forth into the world a new race, a race engineered through a combination of her will and the biology that was available. She'd been so proud of herself.

Their father had, as well.

The Omega had started to kill the vampires just to spite them both, but had quickly learned he fed off deeds of evil. Their father couldn't stop him, of course, because, as it turned out, the Omega's deeds—nay, his very existence—were necessary to balance his sister's goodness.

Balance had to be maintained. It was his sister's core principle, the justification for the Omega, and their father's mandate from his father. The very basis of the world.

And so it was that the Scribe Virgin suffered and the Omega drew his satisfaction. With each death wrought on her race she hurt, and well he knew it. The brother had always been able to feel the sister.

Now, though, that was even truer.

As the Omega pictured his son out there in the world, he worried about the boy. Hoped that the twenty-plus years had been easy for him. But that was a proper parent, was it not. Parents were supposed to have concern over their offspring and nurture them and protect them. Whatever your core was, whether it be virtue or sin, you wanted the best for what you had brought forth into the world.

It was stunning to find that he had something in common with his sister, after all . . . a shock to know that they both wanted what children they begot to survive and thrive.

The Omega looked at the bodies of the humans he had just laid to waste.

Of course, that was a mutually exclusive proposition, wasn't it.

ONE

The wizard had returned.

Phury closed his eyes and let his head fall back against his headboard. Ah, hell, what was he saying. The wizard had never left.

Mate, sometimes you take the piss out of me, the dark voice in his head drawled. *You truly do. After all we've been together?*

All they'd been together . . . wasn't that the truth.

The wizard was the cause of Phury's driving need for red smoke, always in his head, always hammering about what he hadn't done, what he should have done, what he could have done better.

Shoulda. Woulda. Coulda.

Cute rhyme. The reality was that one of the Ring-wraiths from *The Lord of the Rings* drove him to the red smoke sure as if the bastard hog-tied him and threw him in the back of a car.

Actually, mate, you'd be the front bumper.

Exactly.

In his mind's eye, the wizard appeared in the form of a Ring-wraith standing in the midst of a vast gray wasteland of skulls and bones. In its proper British accent, the bastard made sure that Phury never forgot his failures, the pounding litany causing him to light up again and again just so he didn't go into his gun closet and eat the muzzle of a forty.

You didn't save him. You didn't save them. The curse was brought upon them all by you. The fault is yours . . . the fault is yours. . . .

Phury reached for another blunt and lit it with his gold lighter.

He was what they called in the Old Country the *exhile dhoble.*

The second twin. The evil twin.

Born three minutes after Zsadist, Phury's live birth had brought the curse of imbalance to the family. Two noble sons, both born breathing, was too much good fortune, and sure enough, balance had been wrought: Within months, his twin had been stolen from the family, sold into slavery, and abused for a century in every manner possible.

Thanks to his sick bitch mistress, Zsadist was scarred on his face and his back and his wrists and neck. Scarred worse on the inside.

Phury opened his eyes. Rescuing his twin's physical body hadn't gone far enough; it had taken the miracle of Bella to resurrect Z's soul, and now she was in danger. If they lost her . . .

Then all is proper and the balance remains intact for the next generation, the wizard said. *You don't honestly think your twin will reap the blessing of a live birth? You shall have children beyond measure. He shall have none. That is the way of the balance.*

Oh, and I'm taking his shellan, *too, did I mention that?*

Phury picked up the remote and turned up *"Che Gelida Manina."*

Didn't work. The wizard liked Puccini. The Ring-wraith just started to waltz around the field of skeletons, its boots crushing what was underfoot, its heavy arms swaying with elegance, its black shredded robes like the mane of a stallion throwing its regal head. Against a vast horizon of soulless gray, the wizard waltzed and laughed.

So. Fucked. Up.

Without looking, Phury reached over to the bedside table for his bag of red smoke and his rolling papers. He didn't have to measure the distance. He was the rabbit who knew where its pellets were.

While the wizard whooped it up to *La Bohème*, Phury rolled up two fatties so he could keep his chain going, and he smoked while he readied his reinforcements. As he exhaled, what left his lips smelled like coffee and chocolate, but to put a dull on the wizard, he would have used the stuff even if it had been like burning trash in the nose.

Hell, he was getting to the point where lighting up a whole fucking Dumpster would have been fine and dandy if it could get him some peace.

I can't believe you don't value our relationship more, the wizard said.

Phury focused on the drawing in his lap, the one he'd been working on for the last half hour. After he did a quick catch-up review, he dipped the tip of his quill into the sterling silver pot he had balanced against his hip. The pool of ink inside looked like the blood of his enemies, with its dense, oily sheen. On the paper, though, it was a deep reddish brown, not a vile black.

He would never use black to depict someone he loved. Bad luck.

Besides, the sanguinary ink was precisely the color of the highlights in Bella's mahogany hair. So it fit his subject.

Phury carefully shaded the sweep of her perfect nose, the fine lashes of the quill crisscrossing one another until the density was correct.

Ink drawing was a lot like life: One mistake and the whole thing was ruined.

Damn it. Bella's eye wasn't quite up to par.

Curling his forearm around so he didn't drag his wrist through the new ink he'd laid, he tried to fix what was wrong, shaping the lower lid so the curve of it was more angled. His strokes marked up the sheet of Crane paper nicely enough. But the eye still wasn't working.

Yeah, not right, and he should know, considering how much time he'd spent drawing her over the last eight months.

The wizard paused in mid-plié and pointed out that this pen-and-ink routine was a shitty thing to do. Drawing your twin's pregnant *shellan*. Honestly.

Only a right sodding bastard would get fixated on a female who was taken by his twin. And yet you have. You must be so proud of yourself, mate.

Yeah, the wizard had always had a British accent for some reason.

Phury took another drag and tilted his head to the side to see if a change in viewing angle would help. Nope. Still not right. And neither was the hair, actually. For some reason he'd drawn Bella's long, dark hair in a chignon, with wisps tickling her cheeks. She always wore it down.

Whatever. She was beyond lovely anyway, and the rest of her face was as he usually depicted her: Her loving stare was to the right, her lashes silhouetted, her gaze showing a combination of warmth and devotion.

Zsadist sat to her right at meals. So that his fighting hand was free.

Phury never drew her with her eyes looking out at him. Which made sense. In real life, he never drew her stare, either. She was in love with his twin, and he wouldn't have changed that, not for all his longing for her.

The scope of his drawing ran from the top of her chignon to the top of her shoulders. He never drew her pregnant belly. Pregnant females were never depicted from the breastbone down. Again, bad luck. As well as a reminder of what he feared most.

Deaths on the birthing bed were common.

Phury ran his fingertips down her face, avoiding that nose, where the ink was still drying. She was lovely, even with the eye that wasn't right, and the hair that was different, and the lips that were less full.

This was done. Time to start another.

Moving down to the base of the drawing, he started the curl of the ivy at the curve of her shoulder. First one leaf, then a growing

stem . . . now more leaves, curling and thickening, covering up her neck, crowding against her jaw, lipping up to her mouth, unfurling over her cheeks.

Back and forth to the ink jar. Ivy overtaking her. Ivy covering the tracks of his quill, hiding his heart and the sin that lived in it.

It was hardest for him to cover her nose. That was always the last thing he did, and when he could avoid it no longer, he felt his lungs burn as if it were him who would no longer be free to breathe.

When the ivy had won out over the image, Phury wadded up the paper and tossed it into the brass wastepaper basket across his bedroom.

What month was it now . . . August? Yeah, August. Which would be . . . She had a good year left of the pregnancy, assuming she could hold it. Like a lot of females, she was already on bed rest because preterm labor was a big concern.

Stabbing out the tail end of his blunt, he reached for one of the two he'd just made and realized he'd smoked them.

Stretching out his one whole leg, he put his lap easel to the side and brought his survival kit back over: a plastic Baggie of red smoke, a thin packet of rolling papers, and his chunky gold lighter. It was the work of a moment to roll up a freshie, and as he drew in the first hit, he measured his stash.

Shit, it was thin. Very thin.

The steel shutters rising from the windows calmed him out. Night, in all its sunless glory, had fallen, the arrival bringing freedom from the Brotherhood's mansion . . . and the ability to get to his dealer, Rehvenge.

Shifting the leg that had no foot or calf off the bed, he reached for his prosthesis, plugged it on below his right knee, and stood up. He was toasted enough so the air around him felt like something he had to wade through and the window he headed toward seemed miles away. But it was all good. He was comforted by the familiar haze, eased by the sensation of floating as he walked naked across his room.

The garden down below was resplendent, lit by the glow from the library's bank of French doors.

This was what a back vista should look like, he thought. All the flowers blooming with health, the fruit trees fat with pears and apples, the pathways clear, the boxwood clipped.

It was not like the one he had grown up with. Not at all.

Right beneath his window, the tea roses were in full bloom, their fat, rainbow-hued heads held up proudly on their thorned spines. The roses brought his train of thought to another female.

As Phury inhaled again, he pictured his female, the one who he rightfully should be drawing . . . the one who, according to law and custom, he should be doing a hell of a lot more to than sketching.

The Chosen Cormia. His First Mate.

Among forty.

Man, how the hell had he ended up Primale to the Chosen?

I told you, the wizard answered. *You're going to have children beyond measure, all of whom shall have the enduring joy of looking up to a father whose only accomplishment has been letting everyone around him down.*

Okay, nasty as the bastard could be, that was a hard point to argue. He hadn't mated with Cormia as ritual required. He hadn't been back to the Other Side to see the Directrix. He hadn't met the other thirty-nine females he was supposed to lay with and impregnate.

Phury smoked harder, the weight of those big-ass nothings landing on his head, flaming boulders launched by the wizard.

The wizard had excellent trajectory. Then again, he'd had a lot of practice.

Well, now, mate, you're an easy target. That's all there is about that.

At least Cormia wasn't complaining about the dereliction of duties. She hadn't wanted to be First Mate, had been forced into the role: On the day of the ritual, she'd had to be tied down on the ceremonial bed, splayed out for his use like an animal, utterly terrified.

The moment he'd seen her he'd gone into his default setting, which was full savior mode. He'd brought her here to the Black Dagger Brotherhood's mansion and put her in the bedroom next to his. Tradition or not, there was no way in hell he was forcing himself on a female, and he figured that if they had some space and time to get to know each other it would be easier.

Yeah . . . *no.* Cormia had kept to herself, while he went about his daily business of trying to keep from imploding. Over the last five months, they were no closer to each other or a bed. Cormia rarely spoke and showed her face only at meals. If she went outside of her room, it was just to the library for books.

In her long white robe, she was more like a jasmine-scented shadow than anything made of flesh and bone.

The shameful truth of it was, though, he was okay with the way things were. He'd thought he'd been fully aware of the sexual commitment he was making when he took Vishous's place as the Primale, but the reality was far more daunting than the concept had been. Forty females. Forty.

Four-oh.

He must have lost his damn mind when he stepped in for V. God knew, his one shot at trying to lose his virginity hadn't been a party—and that had even been with a professional. Although maybe trying things out with a whore had been part of the problem.

But who the hell else did he have to go to? He was a two-hundred-year-old clueless celibate. How was he supposed to climb on top of lovely, fragile Cormia, pound into her until he came, and then high-tail it to the Chosen's Sanctuary and make like Bill Paxton in *Big Love*?

What the *hell* had he been thinking?

Phury put his blunt between his lips and jacked up the window. As the summer night's thick perfume rolled into his room, he refocused on the roses. He'd caught Cormia with one the other day, one she'd evidently taken from the bouquet Fritz kept in the second-floor sitting room. She'd been poised next to the vase, the pale lavender

rose between two of her long fingers, her head bent down to the bud, her nose hovering over the fat bloom. Her blond hair, which was as always up in a twist on her head, had let loose delicate wisps that fell forward and curved in a natural curl. Just like the rose's petals.

She'd jumped when she caught him staring at her, put the rose back, and quickly gone to her room, the door shutting without a sound.

He knew he couldn't keep her here forever, away from all she was familiar with and all that she was. And they had to complete the sexual ceremony. That was the deal he'd made, and that was the role that she'd told him, no matter how scared she'd been at first, she was prepared to fulfill.

He looked over to his bureau, to a heavy gold medallion that was the size of a large fountain pen. Marked with an ancient version of the Old Language, it was the symbol of the Primale: not just the key to all the buildings on the Other Side, but the calling card of the male who was in charge of the Chosen.

The strength of the race, as the Primale was known.

The medallion had rung again today as it had rung before. Whenever the Directrix wanted him, the thing vibrated, and theoretically he was supposed to poof his ass to what should have been his home, the Sanctuary. He'd ignored the summons. As he had the other two.

He didn't want to hear what he already knew: Five months without sealing the deal on the Primale ceremony was pushing it.

He thought of Cormia holed up in that guest room next door, keeping to herself. No one to talk to. Away from her sisters. He'd tried to reach out to her, but he made her jumpy as hell. Understandably.

God, he had no idea how she passed the hours without going mad. She needed a friend. Everyone needed friends.

Not everyone deserves them, however, the wizard pointed out.

Phury turned and headed for the shower. As he passed by the wastepaper basket, he stopped. His drawing had begun to unravel from the ball he'd wadded it into, and within the crinkled mess, he saw the ivy overlay he'd added. For a split second, he remembered what was underneath, recalled the upswept hair and the wisps that fell on a smooth cheek. Wisps that had the same curl as a rose's petals.

Shaking his head, he kept going. Cormia was lovely, but—

Wanting her would be appropriate, the wizard finished. *So why in a million years would you go down that road. Might ruin your* perfect *record of accomplishments.*

Oh, wait, that would be fuckups, mate. Wouldn't it.

Phury cranked up Puccini and hit the shower.

TWO

As the shutters lifted for the night, Cormia was very busy. Sitting cross-legged on the Oriental rug in her bedroom, she was fishing around in a crystal bowl of water, chasing peas. The legumes were hard as pebbles when Fritz brought them to her, but after they soaked for a while, they became soft enough to use.

When she'd captured one, she reached to the left and took a toothpick from a little white box that read, in red English letters, SIMMONS'S TOOTHPICKS, 500 COUNT.

She took the pea and pushed it onto the end of the pick, then took another pea and another pick, and did the same until a right angle was formed. She kept going, creating first a square, and then a three-dimensional box. Satisfied, she bent forward and attached it to one of its brethren, capping off the final corner in a four-sided base structure about five feet in diameter. Now she would go upward, building floors of the latticework.

The picks were all the same, identical slices of wood, and the peas were all alike, round and green. Both reminded her of where she was from. Sameness mattered in the Chosen's nontemporal Sanctuary. Sameness was the most important thing.

Very little was alike here on this side.

She'd first seen the toothpicks downstairs after the meals, when the Brother Rhage and the Brother Butch would take them out of a slender silver box as they left the dining room. For no good reason, one evening she'd taken a number of them on her way back to her room. She'd tried putting one in her mouth, but hadn't liked the dry, woody taste. Not sure what else to do with them, she'd laid out the picks on the bedside table and arranged them together so that they formed shapes.

Fritz, the butler, had come in to clean, noticed her machinations, and returned some time later with a bowl of peas soaking in warm water. He'd shown her how to make the system work. Pea between two picks. Then add another section and another and another, and before you knew it you had something worth seeing.

As her designs got bigger and more ambitious, she'd taken to planning out in advance all the angles and the elevations to reduce errors. She'd also started working on the floor so she had more space.

Leaning forward, she checked the drawing she'd done before she'd started, the one she used to guide her. Next layer would decrease in size, as would the one after that. Then she would add a tower.

Color would be good, she thought. But how to work it into the structure?

Ah, color. The liberation of the eye.

Being on this side had its challenges, but one thing she absolutely loved were all the colors. In the Chosen's Sanctuary, everything was white: from the grass to the trees to the temples to the food and drink to the devotional books.

With a wince of guilt, she glanced over to her sacred texts. It was hard to argue that she'd been worshiping the Scribe Virgin at her little cathedral of peas and picks.

Nurturing the self was not the goal of the Chosen. It was a sacrilege.

And the visit earlier from the Chosen's Directrix should have reminded her of that.

Dearest Virgin Scribe, she didn't want to think about that.

Getting up, she waited for her light-headedness to clear, then went to a window. Down below were the tea roses, and she noted each of the bushes, checking for new buds and petals that had dropped and fresh leaves.

Time was passing. She could tell by the way the plants changed, their cycle of budding lasting three or four days for each bloom.

Yet another thing to get used to. On the Other Side, there was no time. There were rhythms of rituals and eating and baths, but no alternation of day or night, no hourly measure, no change of season. Time and existence were static just as the air was, just as the light was, just as the landscape was.

On this side, she'd had to learn that there were minutes and hours and days and weeks and months and years. Clocks and calendars were used to mark the passings, and she'd figured out how to read them, just as she'd come to understand the cycles of this world and the people in it.

Out on the terrace, a *doggen* came into view. He had a pair of shears and a large red bucket and he went along the bushes, clipping them into place.

She thought of the rolling white lawns of the Sanctuary. And the unmoving white trees. And the white flowers that were always in bloom. On the Other Side, everything was frozen in its proper place so there was no trimming needed, no mowing, never any change.

Those who breathed the still air were likewise frozen even as they moved, living and yet not living.

Although the Chosen did age, didn't they. And they did die.

She glanced over her shoulder to a bureau that had empty drawers. The scroll the Directrix had come to deliver sat on its glossy top.

The Chosen Amalya, as Directrix, was issuer of such birth recognitions and had appeared to complete her duty.

Had Cormia been over on the Other Side, there would have been a ceremony as well. Although not for her, of course. The individual whose birth it was received no special due, as there was no self on the Other Side. Only the whole.

To think for yourself, to think of yourself, was blasphemy.

She'd always been a secret sinner. She'd always had errant ideas and distractions and drives. All of which went nowhere.

Cormia brought her hand up and put it on the windowpane. The glass she stared through was thinner than her pinkie, as clear as air, hardly any barrier at all. She'd wanted to go down to the flowers for quite a while now, but was waiting for . . . she did not know what.

When she had first come to this place, she'd been racked by sensory overload. There were all kinds of things she didn't recognize, like torches that were plugged into the walls that you had to switch on for light, and machines that did things like wash dishes or keep food cold or create images on a little screen. There were boxes that chimed with every hour, and metal vehicles that carried people around, and things you ran back and forth across floors that whirred and cleaned.

There were more colors here than in all the jewels in the treasury. Smells as well, both good and bad.

Everything was so different, and so were the people. Where she was from, there were no males, and her sisters were interchangeable: All Chosen wore the same white robe and twisted their hair up in the same way and had a single teardrop pearl around their necks. They all walked and talked in the identical quiet manner and did the same thing at the same time. Here? Chaos. The Brothers and their *shellans* wore different clothes and they conversed and laughed in separate, identifiable patterns. They liked certain foods, but not others, and some slept late and others didn't sleep at all. Some were funny, some were fierce, some were . . . beautiful.

One was definitely beautiful.

Bella was beautiful.

Especially in the Primale's eyes.

As the clock started to chime, Cormia tucked her arms in close to her body. Meals were a torture, giving her a taste of what it was going to be like when she and the Primale returned to the Sanctuary.

And he looked upon the faces of her sisters with similar admiration and pleasure.

Talk about change. In the beginning she had been terrified of the Primale. Now, after five months, she didn't want to share him.

With his mane of multicolored hair, and his yellow eyes, and his silky, low voice, he was a spectacular male in his mating prime. But that wasn't what really compelled her. He was the epitome of all that she knew to be of worth: He was focused always on others, never on himself. At the dinner table, he was the one who inquired after each and every person, following up about injuries and stomach upsets and anxieties large and small. He never demanded any attention for himself. Never drew the conversation to something of his. Was endlessly supportive.

If there was a hard job, he volunteered for it. If there was an errand, he wanted to run it. If Fritz staggered under the weight of a platter, the Primale was the first out of his chair to help. From all that she'd overheard at the table, he was a fighter for the race and a teacher of the trainees and a good, good friend to everyone.

He truly was the proper example of the selfless virtues of the Chosen, the perfect Primale. And somewhere in the seconds and hours and days and months of her stay here, she had veered from the path of duty into the messy forest of choice. She now wanted to be with him. There was no *had to*, *must do*, *need to*.

But she wanted him to herself.

Which made her a heretic.

Next door to her, the gorgeous music the Primale always played when he was in his room cut off. Which meant he was heading down for First Meal.

The sound of a knock on her door made her jump and twirl around. As her robe settled against her legs, she caught the scent of red smoke drifting into her room.

The Primale had come for her?

She quickly checked her chignon and tucked some of the stray hairs behind her ears. When she opened the door a crack, she stole a glance up into his face before she bowed to him.

Oh, dearest Virgin Scribe . . . the Primale was too glorious to stare at for long. His eyes were yellow as citrines, his skin a warm golden brown, his long hair a spectacular mélange of color, from the palest of blond to deep mahogany to warm copper.

He bowed in a short, quick body bob, a formality she knew he disliked. He did it for her, though, because no matter how many times he told her not to be formal, she couldn't stop herself.

"Listen, I've been thinking," he said.

In the hesitation that followed, she worried that the Directrix had been to see him. Everyone in the Sanctuary was waiting for the ceremony to be completed, and all were aware it hadn't been yet. She was beginning to feel an urgency that had nothing to do with her attraction to him. The weight of tradition was growing heavier with each passing day.

He cleared his throat. "We've been here for a while, and I know the transition's been tough. I was thinking you must be a little lonely and that you might like some company."

Cormia brought her hand to her neck. This was good. It was time for them to be together. In the beginning, she hadn't been ready for him. Now she was.

"I really think it would be good for you," he said in his beautiful voice, "to have some company."

She bowed low. "Thank you, Your Grace. I agree."

"Great. I have someone in mind."

Cormia straightened slowly. *Someone?*

*   *   *

John Matthew always slept naked.

Well, at least ever since his transition, he slept naked.

It saved on laundry.

With a groan, he reached between his legs and palmed his rock-hard erection. The thing had woken him up as usual, an alarm clock as reliable and stiff off the ground as Big Fucking Ben.

It had a snooze button, too. If he took care of the thing, he could rest another twenty minutes or so before it got up to stuff again. Typically the routine was three times before he left the bed and once more in the shower.

And to think he'd once wished for this.

Focusing on unattractive thoughts didn't help, and though he suspected getting off actually made the drive worse, denying his cock wasn't an option: When he'd backed off a couple months ago as a test pattern, within twelve hours he'd been ready to fuck a tree, he was so horny.

Was there any such thing as anti-Viagra? Cialis Reversailis? Limpicillin?

Rolling onto his back, he shifted one leg out to the side, pushed the covers off his body, and started stroking himself. This was his preferred position, although if he came really hard he curled over onto his right side in the middle of the orgasm.

As a pretrans, he'd always wanted an erection, because he'd figured that getting hard would make him a man. The reality hadn't worked out that way. Sure, with his enormous body and his innate fighting skills and this permarousal he had going on, he was flying the he-man flag and then some on the outside.

Inside, he still felt as small as he'd ever been.

He arched his back and pumped up into his hand with his hips. God . . . it felt good, though. Every time this felt good . . . as long as it was his palm doing the pneumatics. The one and only time a female had touched him, his erection had deflated faster than his ego.

So actually, he had his anti-Viagra: another person.

But now was not the time to rehash his bad past. His cock was getting ready to go off; he could tell by the numbness. Right before he came the thing went dull for a couple of strokes, and that was what was happening now as his hand moved up and down the wet shaft.

Oh, yeah . . . here it comes. . . . The tension in his balls tightened into a twisted cable and his hips rocked uncontrollably and his lips parted so he could pant easier . . . and as if all that wasn't enough, his brain anted into the action.

No . . . fuck . . . no, not her again, please not—

Shit, too late. In the midst of the swirling sex, his mind latched onto the one thing that was guaranteed to make him multiple it: a leather-clad female with a man's haircut and shoulders tight as a prizefighter's.

Xhex.

On a soundless bark of air, John flipped onto his side and started to come. The orgasm went on and on as he fantasized about the two of them having sex in one of the bathrooms at the club she was head of security for. And as long as the images shot around his brain, his body wouldn't stop releasing. He could literally keep it up for ten minutes straight until he was covered with what came out of his cock and his sheets were totally wet.

He tried to corral his thoughts, tried to get a rein on things . . . but failed. He just kept coming, his hand stroking, his heart pounding, his breath choked in his throat as he pictured the two of them together. Good thing he'd been born without a voice box or the Brotherhood's whole mansion would know exactly what he was doing over and over and over again.

Things quieted down only after he forcibly removed his hand from his cock. As his body slowed its roll, he lay in a limp heap, breathing into his pillow, sweat and other stuff drying on his skin.

Nice wake-up call. Nice little exercise sesh. Nice way to kill some time. But ultimately hollow.

For no particular reason, his eyes wandered and settled on the bedside table. If he were to open the drawer, which he never did, he would find two things: a bloodred box about the size of a fist and an old leather diary. Inside the box was a heavy gold signet ring bearing the crest of his lineage as the son of the Black Dagger warrior Darius, son of Marklon. The antique journal contained his father's private thoughts from a two-year period of his life. Also given as a gift.

John had never put on the ring and he had never read the entries.

There were a lot of reasons, but the main one for shutting both away was that the male he considered his father was not Darius. It was another Brother. A Brother who had been MIA for eight months now.

If he was going to wear any ring, it would be one with Tohrment, son of Hharm's crest on it. As a way to honor the male who had meant so much to him in such a short time.

But that wasn't happening. Tohr was likely dead, no matter what Wrath said, and in any event had never been his father.

Not wanting to sink into a mood, John pushed himself up off the mattress and lurched into the bathroom. The shower helped focus him, and so did getting dressed.

The trainee class wasn't meeting tonight, so he was going to log some more hours down in the office and then meet up with Qhuinn and Blay. He was hoping there was a lot of paperwork to do. He wasn't looking forward to seeing his best friends tonight.

The three of them were going across town to the . . . God, to the mall.

It was Qhuinn's idea. As most of them were. According to the guy, John's wardrobe needed a style injection.

John looked down at his Levi's and his white Hanes T-shirt. The only flash he sported was his running shoes: a pair of Nike Air Maxes in black. And even they weren't very flashy.

Maybe Qhuinn had a point that John was a fashion victim, but come on. Who did he have to impress?

The word that popped into his head had him cursing and rearranging himself: *Xhex.*

Someone knocked on his door. "John? You there?"

John quickly tucked in the T-shirt and wondered why Phury would be seeking him out. He'd been keeping up with his studies and doing well on the hand-to-hand. Maybe it was about the work he did in the office?

John opened the door. *Hi,* he signed in American Sign Language.

"Hey. How's you?" John nodded and then frowned as the Brother switched into ASL. *I was wondering if you might do me a favor.*

Anything.

Cormia is . . . well, she's had some challenges being on this side. I think it would be great if she had someone to spend a little time with, you know . . . someone who's tight in the head and low-key. Uncomplicated. So, do you think you could do the honors? Just talk to her or take her around the house or . . . whatever. I'd do it but . . .

It's complicated, John finished in his head.

It's complicated, Phury signed.

An image of the silent blond Chosen popped into John's mind. He'd watched Cormia and Phury studiously not look at each other for the past few months, and had wondered—like everyone else, no doubt—whether they'd sealed the deal.

John didn't think so. They were far, far too awkward still.

Would you mind, Phury signed. *I figure she must have questions or . . . I don't know, things to talk about.*

Truthfully, the Chosen didn't seem as if she wanted to be hung out with. She always kept her head down at meals and never said a thing while she ate only food that was white. But if Phury asked, how could John say no? The Brother always helped him on his fighting stances and answered questions outside of the classroom and was the type of person you wanted to do nice things for because he was kind to everyone.

Sure, John replied. *I'd be happy to.*

Thanks. Phury clapped him on the shoulder with satisfaction, like he'd plugged a hole. *I'll tell her to meet you in the library after First Meal.*

John looked down at what he was wearing. He wasn't sure the jeans routine was fancy enough, but his closet was only stuffed with more of the same.

Maybe it was a good thing he and his boys were malling it. And too bad they hadn't gone already.

THREE

The tradition in the Lessening Society was that once you were inducted, you were known only by the first letter of your last name.

Mr. D should have been known as Mr. R. R as in Roberts. Thing was, the identity he'd been using when he'd been recruited had been Delancy. So Mr. D he had become, and he'd been known by that for the last thirty years.

Weren't no nevermind, though. Names never did matter none.

Mr. D downshifted as he headed into a turn on Route 22, but going into third didn't help him pull through the curve much. The Ford Focus had getup like a ninety-year-old. Kinda smelt like mothballs and flaky skin, too.

Caldwell, New York's farm alley was a stretch of about fifty miles of cornfields and cow pastures and while he putt-putt-putted through it, he found himself thinking about pitchforks. He'd killed his first

person with one. Back in Texas when he was fourteen. His cousin, Big Tommy.

Mr. D had been right proud of himself for getting away with that murder. Being small and appearing defenseless had been the ticket. Good ol' Big Tommy had been a roughneck, with ham hands and a mean streak, so when Mr. D had run screaming to his mama with a beat-in face, everyone had believed his cuz had been in a killing rage and deserved what he'd got. Hah. Mr. D had tracked Big Tommy into the barn and riled him up but good for to get himself the fat lip and black eye necessary to argue self-defense. Then he'd taken the pitchfork he'd propped up against a stall beforehand and gotten to work.

He'd just wanted to know what it felt like to kill a human. The cats and the possums and the raccoons he'd trapped and tortured had been okay, but they weren't no human.

The deed was harder to do than he'd thought. In the movies, pitchforks just went right into people like a spoon to soup, but that was a lie. The tines of the thing had got tangled in Big Tommy's ribs so bad to where Mr. D had had to brace his foot on his cousin's hip to get the leverage to yank the fork out. Second thrust had gone into the stomach, but got jammed again. Probably in the spine. More with the foot bracing. By the time Big Tommy stopped baying like a wounded pig, Mr. D was puffing the sweet, hay-dust air of the barn like there was too little of it to go around.

But it hadn't been no total bust. Mr. D had really liked the changing expressions on his cousin's face. First there had been anger, the stuff that got Mr. D hit. Then disbelief. Then horror and terror at the end. As Big Tommy had coughed up blood and gasped, his eyes had peeled with righteous fear, the kind your mama always wanted you to have for the Lord. Mr. D, the runt of the family, the little guy, had felt seven feet tall.

It had been his first taste of power and he'd wanted it again, but the police had come and there had been a lot of talk in town and he'd forced himself to be good. A couple of years passed before he did something like that again. Working at a meat-processing plant had done right by his knife skills, and when he was ready, he'd used the Big Tommy kind of setup again: bar fight with a bulldozer of a man. He'd madded up the bastard, then lured him over to a dark corner. A screwdriver, and not the kind you drank, did the job.

Things had been more complicated than with Big Tommy. Once Mr. D had started in on the bulldozer guy, he hadn't been able to stop. And it was harder to pull self-defense out your pocket when the body done been stabbed seven times, dragged out behind a car, and dismembered like a machine that were broke.

Packing the dead guy into some Heftys, Mr. D'd taken his little buddy on a road trip, heading north. He'd used the guy's own Pinto for to make the miles, and when the body started to smell, he'd found what passed for a hill in rural Mississippi, set the car on the incline facing backward, and given the front bumper a push. The trunk with its stinking cargo had gone smack into a tree. The bomb burst had sure been exciting.

After that he'd hitchhiked to Tennessee and then hung around doing odd jobs for room and board. He'd killed two more men before drifting up to North Carolina, where he'd almost been caught in the act.

His targets were always big, beefy assholes. And that was how he'd come to be a *lesser*. He'd targeted one of the Lessening Society's members, and when he'd nearly killed the guy in spite of his size, the slayer had been so impressed he'd asked Mr. D to join up and go after the vampires.

Seemed like a good deal. Once he'd gotten over the whole good-dog-was-this-for-reals.

After his induction, Mr. D had been stationed in Connecticut, but he'd moved to Caldie about two years ago, when Mr. X, the then-*Fore-lesser*, had tugged in the Society's reins a little.

In thirty years, Mr. D hadn't been called by the Omega.

That had changed a couple hours ago.

The summons had come in the form of a dream when he'd been sleeping, and he hadn't needed his mama's manners to get him to RSVP in the yes. But he had to wonder if he was going to live through the night.

Things weren't going so good in the Lessening Society. Not since the prophesied Destroyer had pulled his horse into the barn.

The Destroyer had been a human cop, from what Mr. D had heard. A human cop with vampire blood in him who had been tinkered with by the Omega to real bad results. And, of course, the Black Dagger Brotherhood took the guy on and used him but good. They weren't no dummies.

Because a kill by the Destroyer was not just one less slayer.

If the Destroyer got you, he took the piece of the Omega that was in you and drew it into himself. Instead of the eternal paradise you was promised when you joined the Society, you ended up stuck in that man. And with each slayer what got destroyed, a piece of the Omega was lost forever.

Before, if you fought the Brothers, the worst that could happen was you went to heaven. Now? More often than not you got left half-dead until the Destroyer could come by and inhale you into ash and cheat you out of your rightful eternity.

So things had been right tense lately. The Omega had been nastier than usual, the slayers were prickly from looking over their shoulders, and new membership was at an all-time low because everyone was so worried about saving their own skin that they weren't looking for new blood.

And there had been a lot of turnover of *Fore-lessers*. Although that had always been the case.

Mr. D hung a right on to RR 149 and went three miles down to the next RR, the sign of which had been flattened, probably by a baseball bat. The winding road was just a footpath frosted with potholes, and he had to slow down or his guts milk-shaked it: The car had suspension like you'd find on a toaster oven. Which weren't none.

One bad thing about the Lessening Society was they gave you POSs to drive.

Bass Pond Lane . . . he was looking for Bass Pond La— There it was. He wrenched the wheel, stomped the brake, and just made it onto the road.

With no streetlights, he blew right by the shitty, overgrown yard he was looking for and had to throw the clunker into reverse and backpedal. The farmhouse was worse off than the Focus, nothing but a loose-roofed, barely sided rat hole choked with New York State's equivalent of kudzu: poison ivy.

Parking on the road because there was no driveway, Mr. D got out and adjusted his cowboy hat. The house reminded him of back home, what with the tarpaper that showed and the sprung windows and the poorman's lawn of weeds. Hard to believe his fat, house-bound mother and his worn-out farmer father weren't in there waiting for him.

They musta passed a while ago, he thought as he walked over. He'd been the youngest of their seven kids, and both had been smokers.

The screen door had almost no screen and a frame that was rusted out. When he opened the thing, it squealed like a stuck pig, squealed like Big Tommy, just like the one back home had. Knocking on the second door didn't get him no answer, so he took off his cowboy hat and pushed into the house, using his hip and his shoulder to bust free the lock.

Inside smelled like cigarette smoke, mold, and death. The first two were stale. The death was fresh, the kind of juicy, fruity stuff that made you want to go out and kill something so you could join the party.

And there was another smell. The lingering sweet scent in the air told him the Omega had been here recently. Either that or another slayer.

With his hat in his hands, he walked through the dark front rooms and into the kitchen in the back. That was where the bodies was. Two of them on their stomachs. He couldn't tell the sex of either because they'd been decapitated and no one was in a dress, but the pools of blood from where their heads should have been mingled, kind of like they was holding hands.

It was real sweet, actually.

He glanced across the room, to the black stain on the wall between the harvest gold fridge and the spindly Formica-topped table. The bomb burst meant a fellow slayer had bit it and bit it hard at the hand of the Omega. Evidently the master had fired another *Fore-lesser*.

Mr. D stepped over the bodies and cracked the fridge. *Lessers* didn't eat, but he was curious what the couple had in there. Huh. More memories. There was an open package of Oscar Mayer bologna, and they were almost out of mayo.

Not that they had to worry about making sandwiches no more.

He closed the fridge and leaned back against the—

The temperature in the house dropped by twenty degrees, like someone had cranked a central-air unit on so the dial read, *Freeze Your Nuts Off.* The wind followed, roughing up the still summer night, gathering in force until the farmhouse groaned.

The Omega.

Mr. D came to attention just as the front door blew open. What came down the hall was an inky mist, fluid and transparent, rolling along the floorboards. It coalesced in front of Mr. D, rising up into a male form.

"Master," Mr. D said as he bowed at the waist and his black blood raced in his veins out of fear and love.

The Omega's voice came from a vast distance and carried an electronic cadence with static. "I am appointing you *Fore-lesser.*"

Mr. D's breath caught. This was the highest honor, the single most powerful position in the Lessening Society. He'd never even hoped for it. And maybe he could actually hang for a spell in the job. "Thank—"

The Omega misted forward and blanketed Mr. D's body like a coating of tar. As pain took the place of every bone in his body, Mr. D felt himself get spun around and pushed face-first into the counter, his hat flying from his hands. The Omega took control, and things happened that Mr. D would never have consented to.

There was no consent in the Society, though. You had only one yes, and that was the one that got you into it. Everything else that came after, you had no control over.

When what seemed like centuries passed, the Omega stepped out of Mr. D's body and clothed himself, a white robe covering him from head to foot. With ladylike elegance, the evil arranged his lapels, his claws having disappeared.

Or maybe they'd just been worn to stubs after all the ripping and tearing.

Weak and leaking, Mr. D sagged against the pitted countertop. He wanted to get dressed, but there wasn't much left of his clothes.

"Events have come to a head," the Omega pronounced. "The incubation is done. It is time now to shed the cocoon."

"Yes, suh." As if there was another answer? "How can I serve you?"

"Your task is to bring this male to me." The Omega extended his hand palm up and an image appeared, hovering in the air.

Mr. D studied the face, anxiety kicking his brain into high gear. For sure, he needed more details than this translucent mug shot. "Where do I find him?"

"He was born here and he lives among the vampires in Caldwell." The Omega's voice was out of a sci-fi movie, echoing with eerie displacement. "He is newly transitioned by but months. They believe him to be their own."

Well, that sure did narrow it down.

"You may marshal the others," the Omega said. "But he must be taken alive. If anyone kills him, you shall be accountable unto me."

The Omega leaned to the side and put his palm to the wallpaper next to the black bomb burst. The image of the civilian, imprinted on the stretch of faded yellow flowers, burned there.

The Omega tilted his head and gazed at the image. Then, with a gentle, elegant hand, he caressed the face. "He is special, this one. Find him. Bring him back here. Do this with haste."

The *or else* didn't have to be said.

As the evil disappeared, Mr. D bent down and picked up his cowboy hat. Fortunately, it hadn't been crushed or stained.

Rubbing his eyes, he counted the ways he was in it up to his buckle. A vampire male somewhere in Caldwell. It was gonna be like looking for a blade of grass in an acre of meadow.

Picking up a paring knife from the counter, he used the thing to cut around the image on the wallpaper. Peeling the sheet off carefully, he studied the face.

Vampires were secretive for two reasons: They didn't want humans interfering none with their race, and they knew that the *lessers* were after them. They did go out in public, though, especially the newly transitioned males. Aggressive and reckless, the young ones hit the seedier parts of Caldwell's downtown because there were humans to have sex with and fights to get into and all kinds of fun things to snort and drink and smoke.

Downtown. He'd get a squad together and head to the bars downtown. Even if they didn't find the male right away, the vampire community was a small one. Other civilians were bound to know their target, and information gathering was one of Mr. D's strengths.

To heck and gone with truth serum. Give him a claw hammer and a length of chain, and he was a machine with getting a pair of lips to babble.

Mr. D dragged his sorry, too-used body upstairs and took a careful shower in the dead people's shitty bathroom. When he was done, he changed into a pair of overalls and a button-down, which were naturally too big for him. After he rolled up the shirt cuffs and cut three inches off the legs of the pants, he combed his white hair flat to his skull. Before he left the room, he put on some Old Spice from the guy's bureau. The stuff was mostly alcohol, like the bottle had been sitting there for a while, but Mr. D liked to be classy.

Back downstairs, he swung through the kitchen and picked up the strip of wallpaper with the male's face on it. Eating up the features with his eyes, he found himself getting bluetick hound dog excited even though he was still aching all over.

The hunt was on and he knew who else to use. There was a crew of five *lessers* who he'd worked with on and off during the past couple years. They were good guys. Well, *good* was probably the wrong word. But he could deal with them, and now that he was *Fore-lesser* he could give them orders.

On his way out the front door, he tugged his hat into place and tipped the brim to the dead people. "See y'all later."

Qhuinn walked into his father's study in a bad mood, and he sure as hell didn't expect to leave feeling all glowy and shit.

And there you go. The second he entered the room, his father let one side of the *Wall Street Journal* flop loose so he could press his knuckles to his mouth, then touch each side of his throat. A quick phrase in the Old Language came out in a mutter, then the paper was back up in place.

"Do you need me for the gala," Qhuinn said.

"Didn't one of the *doggen* tell you?"

"No."

"I told them to tell you."

"So that would be a no, then." Like asking the question in the first place, he pressed for the answer just to be a pain in the ass.

"I don't understand why they didn't tell you." His father uncrossed then recrossed his legs, the crease in his slacks as sharp as the lip on his glass of sherry. "I really only want to have to communicate things once. I don't believe that is too much—"

"You're not going to say it to me, are you?"

"—to ask. I mean, honestly, the job of a servant is self-evident. Their purpose is to serve, and I really don't like repeating myself."

His father's free foot tapped at the air. His tasseled loafers were, as always, by Cole Haan: pricey, but no more showy than an aristocratic whisper.

Qhuinn looked down at his New Rocks. The treaded soles were two inches thick at the ball of his foot and three inches at his heel. The black leather went up to the base of his calves and was crisscrossed by laces and three boss chrome buckles.

Back when he'd been getting an allowance, before his change hadn't cured his defect, he'd saved up for months to get these mean-ass motherfucking shitkickers, and he'd bought them as soon as he could after his change. They were his prezzie to himself for living through his transition, because he knew better than to expect anything from the parents.

His father's eyes had nearly popped out of his establishment skull when Qhuinn had worn them to First Meal.

"Was there something else," his father said from behind the *WSJ*.

"Nah. I'll get good and ghost. Don't you worry."

God knew he'd done it before at official functions, although really, who were they kidding? The *glymera* was fully aware of him and his little "problem," and those cob-assed snobs were like elephants. They never forgot.

"By the way, your cousin Lash has a new job," his father murmured. "At Havers's clinic. Lash fancies becoming a doctor and is interning after his classes." The newspaper flipped around and his father's face briefly appeared . . . which was a curious killer, because Qhuinn caught the wistful cast to his old man's eyes. "Lash is such a source of pride for his father. A worthy successor to the family mantle."

Qhuinn glanced at his father's left hand. On the forefinger, taking up all the space beneath the big knuckle, was a solid gold ring bearing the family's crest.

All the young males from the aristocracy got one after they went through their transitions, and Qhuinn's best friends both had theirs. Blay wore his all the time except when fighting or out downtown, and John Matthew had been given one, although he didn't put it on. They weren't the only ones with the flashy paperweights, either. In their training class at the Brotherhood's compound, one by one the trainees were going through the change and showing up with a signet ring on their finger.

Family crest pressed into ten ounces of gold: five thousand dollars.

Getting it from your father when you became a true male: priceless.

Qhuinn's transition had occurred about five months ago. He'd stopped waiting for his ring four months, three weeks, six days, and two hours ago.

Roughly.

Man, in spite of the friction between him and his dad, he'd never thought he wouldn't get one. But surprise! New way to feel out of the fold.

There was another rustle of the paper and this one was impatient, as if his father were shooing a fly away from his hamburger. Although, of course, he didn't eat hamburgers, because they were too common.

"I'm going to have to talk to that *doggen*," his father said.

Qhuinn shut the door on his way out, and when he turned to go down the hall, he nearly bumped into a *doggen* who was coming from the library next door. The uniformed maid leaped back, kissed her knuckles, and tapped the veins running up her throat.

As she scampered off, muttering the same phrase his father had, Qhuinn stepped up to an antique mirror that hung on the silk-covered wall. Even with the ripples in the leaded glass and the blackened flecks where the reflective part had flaked off, his problem was obvious.

His mother had gray eyes. His father had gray eyes. His brother and sister had gray eyes.

Qhuinn had one blue eye and one green eye.

Now, there were blue and green eyes in the bloodline, of course. Just not one of each in the same person, and what do you know, deviation was not divine. The aristocracy refused to deal with defects, and Qhuinn's folks were not only firmly entrenched in the *glymera*, as both were from the six founding families, but his father had even been *leahdyre* of the Princeps Council.

Everyone had hoped his transition would cure the problem, and either blue or green would have been acceptable. Yeah, well, *denied*. Qhuinn came out of his change with a big body and a pair of fangs and a craving for sex . . . and one blue eye and one green eye.

What a night. It had been the first and only time his father had lost it. The first and only time Qhuinn had ever been struck. And since then, no one in the family or on the staff had met his stare.

As he headed out for the night, he didn't bother to say good-bye to his mother. Or to his older brother or sister.

He'd been sidelined in this family since the moment of his birth, set apart from them, benched by some kind of genetic injury. The only saving grace to his pitiable existence, according to the race's value system, was the fact that there were two healthy, normal young in the family, and that the oldest male, his brother, was considered acceptable for breeding.

Qhuinn always thought his parents should have stopped at two, that to try for three healthy children was too much of a gamble with fate. He couldn't change the hand that had been dealt, though. Couldn't stop himself from wishing things were different, either.

Couldn't keep from caring.

Even though the gala would just be a bunch of stuffy types wearing gowns and penguin suits, he wanted to be with his family during the *glymera*'s big end-of-summer ball. He wanted to stand shoulder-to-shoulder with his brother and be counted for once in his life. He wanted to dress up like everyone else and wear his gold ring and maybe dance with some of the high-bred, unmated females. In the glittering crowd of the aristocracy, he wanted to be acknowledged as a citizen, as one among them, as a male, not a genetic embarrassment.

Not going to happen. As far as the *glymera* were concerned, he was less than an animal, no more suitable for sex than a dog.

Only thing missing was a collar, he thought, as he dematerialized to Blay's.

FOUR

ver to the east, in the Brotherhood's mansion, Cormia waited in the library for the Primale and whoever it was he thought she should spend time with. As she paced from couch to club chair and back, she heard the Brothers talking in the foyer, discussing some upcoming fete of the *glymera's*.

The Brother Rhage's voice boomed. "That bunch of self-serving, prejudicial, light-in-the-loafer—"

"Watch the loafer references," the Brother Butch cut in. "I have some on."

"—parasitic, shortsighted motherfuckers—"

"Tell us how you really feel," someone else said.

"—can take their *fakakta* ball and blow it out their asses."

The king's laugh was low. "Good thing you're not a diplomat, Hollywood."

"Oh, you gotta let me send a message. Better yet, let's have my beast go as an emissary. I'll have him rip up the place. Serve those bastards right for how they've treated Marissa."

"You know," Butch announced, "I've always thought you had half a brain. In spite of what everyone else has said."

Cormia stopped pacing as the Primale appeared in the library's entrance, a glass of port in his hand. He was dressed in what he usually wore to First Meal when he wasn't teaching: a pair of perfectly tailored slacks, cream tonight; a silk shirt, black per normal; and a black belt, the buckle of which was an elongated, golden H. His square-toed shoes were buffed to a shine and bore the same H as the belt.

Hermès, she thought she'd overheard him say at one meal.

His hair was loose, the waves breaking on his heavy shoulders, some in the front, some down the back. He smelled of what the Brothers called aftershave, as well as the coffee-scented smoke that lingered in his bedroom.

She knew precisely how his bedroom smelled. She had spent a single day lying beside him in his room, and everything about the experience had been unforgettable.

Although now was not the time to remember what had happened between them in that big bed of his when he'd been asleep. Hard enough to be in his company with a whole room between them and people out in the foyer. To add those moments when he'd pressed his naked body to hers—

"Did you enjoy your dinner?" he asked, taking a sip from his glass.

"Yes, indeed. And you, Your Grace?"

He was about to reply when John Matthew appeared behind him.

The Primale turned to the young male and smiled. "Hey, my man. Glad you're here."

John Matthew looked across the library at her and lifted his hand in greeting.

She was relieved by the choice. She didn't know John any more than she knew the others, but he was quiet during meals. Which made his size not quite as intimidating as it would have been if he'd been loud.

She bowed to him. "Your Grace."

As she straightened, she felt his eyes on her and she wondered what he saw. Female or Chosen?

What an odd thought.

"Well, you two visit." The Primale's brilliant golden eyes shifted her way. "I'm on duty tonight, so I'll be out."

Fighting, she thought, with a stab of fear.

She wanted to rush over to him and tell him to be safe, but that was not her place, was it? She was barely his First Mate, for one thing. For another, he was the strength of the race and hardly needed her concern.

The Primale clapped John Matthew on the shoulder, nodded at her, and left.

Cormia leaned to the side so she could watch the Primale going up the staircase. His gait was smooth as he went along, in spite of his missing limb and his prosthesis. He was so tall and proud and lovely, and she hated that it would be hours before he would return.

When she glanced back, John Matthew was over at the desk, taking out a small pad and a pen. As he wrote, he held the paper close to his chest, his big hands curling up. He looked much younger than the size of his body suggested while he labored over his letters.

She'd seen him communicate with his hands on those rare occasions he had something to say at the table, and it dawned on her that perhaps he was a mute.

He turned the pad to her with a wince, as if he were not impressed with what he'd written. *Do you like to read? This library has lots of good books.*

She looked up into his eyes. What a lovely blue color they were. "What is the difficulty of your voice? If I may ask."

No difficulty. I took a vow of silence.

Ah . . . she remembered. The Chosen Layla had said he'd taken such a pledge.

"I see you using your hands to talk," she said.

American Sign Language, he wrote.

"It's an elegant way of communicating."

It gets the job done. He wrote some more and then flashed the pad again. *I've heard the Other Side is very different. Is it true it's all white?*

She lifted the skirting of her robe as if to give an example of what is was like where she was from. "Yes. White is all we have." She frowned. "All we need, rather."

Do you have electricity?

"We have candles, and we do things by hand."

Sounds old-fashioned.

She wasn't sure what he meant by that. "Is that bad?"

He shook his head. *I think it's cool.*

She knew the term from the dinner table, but still didn't understand why temperature would have anything to do with an apparently positive value judgment.

"It's all I know." She went over to one of the tall, narrow doors that had glass panes. "Well, until now."

Her roses were so close, she thought.

John whistled, and she looked over her shoulder at the pad he was holding face-out. *Do you like it here at all?* he'd written. *And please know you can tell me you don't. I won't judge.*

She fingered her robe. "I feel so different from everyone. I am lost in the conversations, though I speak the language."

There was a long silence. When she glanced back at John, he was writing, his hand pausing every once in a while, as if he were choosing a word. He crossed something out. Wrote some more. When he was finished, he gave the pad to her.

I know what that's like. Because I'm a mute, I feel out of place a lot of the time. It's better since my transition, but it still happens. No one

judges you here, though. We all like you, and we're glad you're in the house.

She read the paragraph twice. She wasn't sure how to respond to the last part. She'd assumed she was tolerated because the Primale had brought her in.

"But . . . Your Grace, I thought you had assumed the mantle of silence?" As he flushed, she said, "I'm sorry, that's not my concern."

He wrote and then showed her his words. *I was born without a voice box.* The next sentence was crossed out, but she was able to get the gist. He'd written something like, *But I still fight well and I'm smart and everything.*

She could understand the subterfuge. The Chosen, like the *glymera*, valued physical perfection as evidence of proper breeding and the strength of the race's genes. Many would have viewed his silence as a deficiency, and even the Chosen could be cruel to those they viewed as beneath them.

Cormia reached out and put her hand on his forearm. "I think not all things have to be spoken to be understood. And it is well obvious you are fit and strong."

His cheeks bloomed with color, his head dropping to hide his eyes.

Cormia smiled. It seemed perverse that she should relax in the face of his getting awkward, but somehow she felt as though they were on more level footing.

"How long have you been here?" she asked.

Emotion flickered across his face as he went back to the pad. *Eight months or so. They took me in because I had no family. My father was killed.*

"I am so sorry for your loss. Tell me . . . do you stay because you like it here?"

There was a long pause. Then he wrote slowly. When he flashed

her the pad, it said, *I like it no more or less than I would any other house.*

"Which makes you displaced like me," she murmured. "Here but not here."

He nodded, then smiled, revealing bright white fangs.

Cormia couldn't help but return the expression on his handsome face.

Back at the Sanctuary, everyone had been like her. Here? No one was at all. Until now.

So do you have any questions you'd like to ask about stuff? he wrote. *The house? The staff? Phury said you might have some.*

Questions . . . oh, she could think of a few. For instance, how long had the Primale been in love with Bella? Had there ever been any feelings on her side? Had the two of them ever lain together?

Her eyes focused on the books. "I don't have any questions right now." For no particular reason, she added, "I just finished Choderlos de Laclos's *Les Liaisons Dangereuses.*"

They made that into a movie. Sarah Michelle Gellar and Ryan Phillippe and Reese Witherspoon.

"A movie? And who are all those people?"

He wrote for quite a while. *You know television, right? That flat panel in the billiards room? Well, movies are on an even bigger screen, and the people in them are called actors. They pretend to be people. Those three are actors. Actually, they're all actors, when they're on TV or in the movies. Well, most of them.*

"I've only glanced into the billiards room. I haven't been in it." There was a curious shame to admitting how little she'd ventured out. "Is television the glowing box with the pictures?"

That's the one. I can show you how it works if you like?

"Please."

They went out of the library into the magical, rainbowed foyer of

the mansion, and as always, Cormia glanced up to the ceiling, which floated three stories above the mosaic floor. The scene depicted far above was of warriors mounted on great steeds, all of them going off to fight. The colors were outrageously bright, the figures majestic and strong, the background a brilliant blue with white clouds.

There was one particular fighter with blond-streaked hair that she had to measure every time she passed through. She had to make sure he was all right, even though that was ridiculous. The figures never moved. Their fight was always on the verge, never in the actuality.

Unlike the Brotherhood's. Unlike the Primale's.

John Matthew led the way into the dark green room that was across from where meals were taken. The Brothers spent a lot of time here; she'd often hear their voices drifting out, marked by soft cracking noises, the source of which she couldn't identify. John solved that mystery, though. As he passed by a flat table that had a green felt covering, he took one of the many multicolored balls on its surface and sent it rolling across the way. When it ran into one of its mates, the quiet knocking explained the sound.

John stopped in front of an upright gray canvas and picked up a slim black unit. All at once an image popped up in full color and sound came from everywhere. Cormia jumped back as a roar filled the room and bulletlike objects rushed by.

John steadied her as the din gradually faded, and then he wrote on his pad. *Sorry, I turned the sound down. This is NASCAR racing. There are people in the cars and they go around the track. The fastest wins.*

Cormia approached the image and touched it with hesitation. All she felt was a flat, clothlike stretch. She looked behind the screen. Nothing but wall.

"Amazing."

John nodded and put out the slim unit to her, jogging it up and down as if encouraging her to take it. After he showed her what to

push among the multitude of buttons, he stepped back. Cormia pointed the thing at the moving pictures . . . and made the images change. Again and again. There seemed to be an endless number of them.

"No vampires, though," she murmured, as yet another broad-daylight setting appeared. "This is just for humans."

We watch it too, though. You get vampires in movies—just not good ones usually. The films or the vampires.

Cormia slowly sank down onto the sofa in front of the television, and John followed suit in a chair next to her. The endless variation was enthralling, and John narrated each "channel" with notes to her. She didn't know how long they sat together, but he didn't seem impatient.

What channels did the Primale watch, she wondered.

Eventually, John showed her how to turn the images off. Flushed from excitement, she looked toward the glass doors.

"Is it safe outdoors?" she asked.

Very. There's a huge retaining wall surrounding the compound, plus security cameras are everywhere. Even better, we're insulated by mhis. *No* lesser *has ever gotten in here, and none ever will—oh, and the squirrels and deer are harmless.*

"I'd like to go outside."

And I'd be happy to take you.

John tucked the pad under his arm and went over to one of the sets of glass doors. After he unlatched the brass lock, he swung one half of the pair wide with a gallant sweep of his arm.

The warm air that rushed in smelled different from that which was in the house. This was rich. Complex. Sultry with its garden bouquet and humid warmth.

Cormia got up from the couch and approached John. Beyond the terrace, the landscaped gardens she'd stared at from afar for so long stretched out over what seemed to be a vast distance. With its color-ful flowers and blooming trees, the vista was nothing like the mono-

chromatic expanse of the Sanctuary, but it was just as perfect, just as lovely.

"It's the day of my birthing," she said for no particular reason.

John smiled and clapped. Then he wrote, *I should have gotten you a present.*

"Present?"

You know, a gift. For you.

Cormia leaned her body out and craned her head back. The sky above was a dark satin blue with twinkling lights marking its folds. Wondrous, she thought. Simply wondrous.

"This is a gift."

They stepped out of the house together. The flat stones of the terrace were chilly under her bare feet, but the air was warm as bathwater, and she loved the contrast.

"Oh . . ." She breathed in deep. "How lovely . . ."

Turning round and round, she looked at it all: The majestic mountain of the mansion. The fluffy, dark heads of the trees. The rolling lawn. The flowers in their orderly sections.

The breeze that swept over it all was gentle as a breath, carrying a fragrance too complex and heady to label.

John let her lead, her cautious steps carrying them closer to the roses.

When she got to them, she reached out and petted the fragile petals of a mature rose as big as her palm. Then she bent down and inhaled its perfume.

As she straightened, she started to laugh. For no reason at all. It was just . . . her heart had abruptly taken wing and was soaring in her chest, the lethargy that had been plaguing her for the past month lifting in the face of a bright surge of energy.

It was the day of her birthing and she was outside.

She glanced at John and found him staring at her, a little smile on his face. He knew, she thought. He knew what she was feeling.

"I want to run."

He swept his arm toward the lawn.

Cormia didn't let herself think about the dangers of the unknown or the dignity that Chosen were supposed to wear along with their white robing. Casting aside the great weight of propriety, she hiked up her white robe and tore off as fast as her legs could carry her. The springy grass cushioned her feet and her hair feathered out behind her and the air on her face rushed by.

Though she remained earthbound, the freedom in her soul made her fly.

FIVE

Downtown in the club and drug district, Phury was flying through an alley off Tenth Street, his shitkickers pounding the ratty pavement, his black windbreaker flapping behind him. About fifteen yards ahead of him was a *lesser*, and given their positions, technically Phury was in pursuit. In reality, the slayer wasn't trying to get away with all this heel kicking. The bastard wanted to get deep enough into the shadows so that the two of them could fight, and Phury was so on board that train.

Rule number one in the war between the Brotherhood and the Lessening Society: no roughhousing around humans. Neither side needed the hassle.

That was about the only rule.

The sweet smell of baby powder wafted back to Phury, the wake of his enemy one hell of a nose-cloying nasty. It was so worth the stink, though, because this was going to be a good fight. The slayer he was after had hair that was fish-belly white—which meant the guy had been in the Society a long time: For reasons that were unknown, all *lessers* faded to pale over time, losing their individual hair, eye, and skin coloration as they gained experience in hunting and killing innocent vampires.

Great trade-off. The more you murdered, the more you looked like a corpse.

Dodging a Dumpster and jumping over what he hoped was a pile of rags and not a dead homeless human, he figured in another fifty yards he and his *lesser* buddy were going to hit pay dirt for privacy. The bowel of the alley was an unlighted dead end, bracketed by windowless brick buildings and—

There were a pair of humans in it.

Phury and his slayer stopped short in the face of the buzz kill. Keeping a healthy distance from each other, they assessed the sitch as the two human men looked over.

"Get the fuck out of here," the one on the left said.

Okay, this was obviously a case of *dealus interruptus*.

And the guy to the right was definitely on the buy side of the exchange, and not just because he wasn't trying to take control of the intrusion. The mangy bastard was twitchy in his dirty pants, his fevery eyes wide, his sallow skin waxed out and spotted with acne. Most telling, though, was that he went back to focusing on his dealer's jacket pockets, not at all worried about the possibility of getting capped by Phury or the slayer.

Nah, his biggie was about getting his next fix, and he was clearly terrified he'd have to go home without what he needed.

Phury swallowed hard as he watched those empty-house eyes bounce around. God, he'd just had that stinging panic . . . had tangoed with it right before the shutters had gone up for the night back at home.

The drug dealer put one of his hands to the small of his back. "I said, get out of here."

Fuck. If the asshole pulled out a gun, all hell was going to break

loose because . . . Okay, right, the slayer was also reaching into his jacket. With a curse, Phury joined the party by putting his palm to the butt of the SIG at his hip.

The drug dealer paused, clearly realizing everyone had lead accessories. After doing some sort of risk evaluation, the guy put a pair of empty hands out in front of him.

"On second thought, maybe I'll just take off."

"Good choice," the *lesser* drawled.

The addict didn't think that was such a hot idea. "No, oh, no . . . no, I need—"

"Later." The dealer buttoned up his jacket like a storekeeper would lock up a shop.

And it happened so fast, you couldn't have stopped it. From out of nowhere, the addict brought out a box cutter and with a messy, more-luck-than-skill slash, he sliced the dealer's throat wide-open. As blood went everywhere, the buyer busted the dealer's shop apart, going through jacket pockets and stuffing cellophane packets into his beat-to-shit jeans. When the raid was over, he tore off like a rat, hunched over, scampering, too juiced with his lottery win to bother with the two bona fide killers who were in his path.

No doubt the *lesser* let him go just to clear the field so the real fighting could begin.

Phury let the human go because he felt like he was looking into a mirror.

The rank joy on the addict's face was a total head nailer. The guy was clearly on the express train to one hell of a bender, and the fact that it was a free fix was only a small part of the buzz. The real boon was the lush ecstasy of super-surplus.

Phury knew that orgasmic rush. He got it every time he locked himself in his bedroom with a big fat pouch of red smoke and a fresh pack of rolling papers.

He . . . was jealous. He was so—

The length of steel chain caught him on the side of the throat and wrapped itself around his neck, a metal snake with one hell of a tail recoil. As the *lesser* yanked, the links dug in and cut off all kinds of things: breathing, circulation, voice.

Phury's center of gravity shifted from his hips to his shoulders, and he fell forward, throwing out his hands to keep from face-planting it into the pavement. As he landed on all fours, he got a brief, vivid eyeful of the drug dealer, who was gurgling like a coffee-pot ten feet away.

The dealer reached out a hand, his bloody lips working slowly. *Help me . . . help me. . . .*

The *lesser's* boot hit Phury's head like it was a soccer ball, the cracking impact sending the world spinning round and round as Phury's body did the dreidel. He ended up flush against the drug dealer, the dying man's deadweight stopping his roll.

Phury blinked and gasped. Up above, the glow of the city canceled out much of the galaxy's stars, but didn't touch the ones that were doing laps in his vision.

There was a choking gasp next to him, and for a split second he shuffled his dazed eyes next door. The drug dealer was doing a meet and greet with the Grim Reaper, his last breaths escaping through the gaping second mouth at the front of his throat. The guy smelled like crack, as if he were a user as well as a peddler.

This is my world, Phury thought. This world of Baggies and wads of cash and using and worrying about the next fix consumed more of his time than even the Brotherhood's mission.

The wizard popped into his mind, standing like Atlas in that field of bones. *Damn right it's your world, ya fried daft bastard. And I am your king.*

The *lesser* hauled on the chain, cutting off the wizard and making the stars in Phury's head even brighter.

If he didn't get back in the game here, asphyxiation was going to be his best and only friend.

Bringing his hands up to the links, he gripped the fuckers in two

thick fists, jacked into a tuck position, and roped his prosthetic leg around the steel leash. Using the foot for leverage, he pushed against the links that ran under the sole of his shitkicker and created some slack so he could breathe.

The slayer leaned back like a waterskier, and the prosthesis weakened under the pressure, the angle of his fake foot changing. With a quick unhook, Phury freed his leg from the chain, dropped the slack on his end and braced his neck and shoulders. As the slayer went flying against the brick wall of a Valu-rite Dry Cleaners, the undead's force and body weight yanked Phury up off the ground.

For a split second the chain went loose.

It was just enough for Phury to spin around, get the thing off his neck, and palm a dagger.

The *lesser* was stunned from getting body-slammed by the building, and Phury took advantage of his struck-stupids, lancing forward with his blade. The steel-composite tip and shaft went deep into the *lesser's* soft, empty gut, springing a leak that ran glossy and black.

The slayer looked down in confusion, as if the rules of the game had changed in the middle and no one had told him. His white hands came up to stem the flow of sweet, evil blood and got nowhere against the deluge.

Phury wiped his mouth with the back of his sleeve, as a tingling anticipation lit him up from the inside.

The *lesser* took one look at his face and lost his out-of-it expression. Fear seeped into his pale features.

"You're the one . . ." the slayer whispered as his knees went wonky. "The torturer."

Phury's can't-waits faded a little. "What?"

"Heard . . . about you. Mauls first . . . then kills."

He had a reputation in the Lessening Society? Well, duh. He'd been making messes of *lessers* for a couple of months now.

"How do you know that's me?"

"By the way . . . you're . . . smiling."

As the slayer slid down onto the pavement, Phury became aware of the gruesome grin he was sporting.

Hard to know what was more horrific: that it was there or that he hadn't noticed.

Suddenly, the *lesser*'s pupils shot to the left. "Thank . . . fuck."

Phury froze as a gun muzzle pressed against his left kidney and a fresh wave of baby powder shot into his nose.

Not more than five blocks to the east, in his private office at Zero-Sum, Rehvenge, aka the Reverend, cursed. He hated the incontinent ones. *Hated* them.

The human man dangling in front of his desk had just pissed in his pants, the stain showing up as a dark blue circle at the crotch of his distressed Z Brands.

Looked like someone had nailed him in the hey-nanny-nannies with a wet sponge.

"Oh, for God's sake." Rehv shook his head at his private guard of Moors, the ones who were playing hanger to the piece of shit. Trez and iAm both sported the same disgusted expressions that he did.

Only saving grace, Rehv supposed, was that the guy's pair of Doc Martens seemed to function okay as a pair of punch bowls. Nothing was dripping.

"What'd I do?" the guy squeaked, the pitch of his voice suggesting his balls were somewhere north of his wet boxers. Any higher and he could have been a contralto. "I didn't do noth—"

Rehv cut the denial off. "Chrissy showed up with a busted lip and black-and-blues. Again."

"You think I did that? Come on, the girl whores out for you. It could have been any—"

Trez raised an objection to the testimony, cranking the man's hand into a ball and squeezing the forced fist like an orange.

As the defendant's bark of pain trailed off to a whimper, Rehv idly picked up a sterling-silver envelope opener. The thing was shaped

like a sword, and he tested the point with his forefinger, quickly licking off the dot of blood it left behind.

"When you applied for work here," he said, "you gave an address of Thirteen-eleven Twenty-third Street. Which is Chrissy's addy, too. You arrive and leave at the end of the night together." As the guy popped open his piehole, Rehv held his hand up. "Yes, I'm aware that's not dispositive. But you see that ring on your hand— Wait, why are you trying to put your arm behind your back? Trez, you mind helping him plant that palm of his on my real estate over here?"

As Rehv tapped the tip of the opener on his desk, Trez muscled the beefy human over like the guy weighed nothing more than a laundry bag. With absolutely no effort at all, he flattened the bastard's hand out in front of Rehv and held it in place.

Rehv leaned forward and traced a Caldwell High School class ring with the opener. "Yeah, see, she's got a funny mark on her cheek. When I first saw it, I wondered what it was. It's this ring, isn't it? You backhanded her, didn't you. Caught her in her face with this."

As the guy sputtered like a bass boat, Rehv ran another little circle around the blue stone of the ring, then took the razor-sharp point and stroked the man's fingers one by one, from the bony knuckles on the hand to the flat nail beds at the ends.

The two biggest knuckles were bruised, the pale skin purple and swollen.

"Looks like you didn't just backhand her," Rehv murmured, still petting the man's fingers with the opener.

"She asked for—"

Rehv's fist pounded into his desk so hard, his multiline office phone did a jump and scramble, the receiver bouncing free of the cradle.

"Don't you *dare* finish that sentence." Rehv fought not to bare his fangs as they punched out into his mouth. "Or so help me God I will feed you your own balls right now."

The ass-wipe went inanimate as a subtle *beep-beep-beep* replaced the phone's dial tone. iAm, cool as always, calmly reached forward and replaced the receiver.

As a bead of sweat dripped off the human's nose and landed on the back of his hand, Rehv smoothed out his anger.

"Right. Where were we before you almost got yourself castrated? Oh, yeah. Hands . . . we were talking about hands. Funny, I don't know what we would do without two. I mean, you couldn't drive a stick-shift car, for example. And you have a stick, don't you? Yeah, I've seen that tripped-out Acura you tool around in. Nice car."

Rehv laid his own hand down on the glossy wood, right next to the guy's, and as he made comparisons, he pointed to the salient distinctions with the envelope opener.

"My hand's bigger than yours in length . . . and width. Fingers are longer. My veins stand out more. You have a tattoo of . . . what is that at the base of your thumb? Some kind of . . . ah, the Chinese symbol for strength. Yeah, my tats are elsewhere. What else, now . . . your skin's lighter. Damn, you white boys really need to think about tanning. You look like death without some UVs."

As Rehv glanced up, he thought of the past, of his mother and her collections of bruises. It had taken him far, far too long to do right by her.

"You know the biggest diff between you and me?" he said. "See . . . my knuckles aren't bruised from beating a woman."

In a quick move, he drew the envelope opener up and slashed it down so hard the tip didn't just go through flesh; it penetrated the teak of the desk.

The hand he stabbed was his own.

As the human screamed, Rehv didn't feel a thing.

"Don't you dare pass out, you fucking lightweight," Rehv spat as the asshole's eyes started to roll. "You're going to watch this carefully so you remember my message."

Rehv yanked the opener free of the desk by jacking up his palm

so that it caught the scabbard and popped the blade out. Putting his hand up where the man could watch, he twisted the opener back and forth with grim precision, creating a portal in his skin and bones, widening the puncture into a little window. When he was finished, he withdrew the blade and put it carefully beside the phone.

As blood dripped down the inside of his sleeve and pooled at his elbow, he looked at the man through the hole. "I'll be watching you. Everywhere. All the time. She turns up with another 'bruise' from 'falling down in the shower' and I'm going to mark you up like a calendar, feel me?"

The man jerked to the side and threw up down his pant leg.

Rehv cursed. He should have known something like that was coming. Fucking pansy-ass bully bastard.

And good thing this fool with the partially digested pasta dripping onto his piss-laden Doc Martens didn't know what Rehv was really capable of. This human, like all the other humans in the club, had no idea the boss of ZeroSum was not just a vampire, but a *symphath*. Motherfucker would have shit himself, and what a mess that would have been. It was already wet-obvious he wasn't sporting Depends.

"Your car is now mine," Rehv said as he reached over to the phone and dialed housekeeping. "Consider it repayment plus interest and penalties on the cash you've been skimming from my bar. You're fired for that, and for side-dealing H in my private zip code. PS, next time you try to crop off someone else's turf? Don't mark your packs with the same eagle you wear on your fucking jacket. Makes it too easy to figure out who the rogue dealer was. Oh, and like I said, that lady of mine had better not show up with so much as a chipped nail or I'll be coming for a visit. Now, get the fuck out of my office and don't ever come in this club again."

The guy was so shell-shocked, he didn't argue as he was frog-marched toward the door.

Rehv slammed his bloodied fist into the desk again to get every-one's attention.

The Moors halted and so did the meat. The human was the only one who looked over his shoulder, and there was absolute terror in his eyes.

"One. Last. Thing." Rehv smiled tightly, keeping his sharp canines to himself. "If Chrissy quits, I'm going to assume it's because you forced her to, and I will come after you for my pecuniary losses." Rehv leaned forward. "And bear in mind, I don't need the money, but I'm a sadist, so I get a hard-on hurting people. Next time, I'll be taking my piece out of your hide, not your wallet or what's parked in your driveway. Keys? Trez?"

The Moor crammed his hand into the back pocket of the guy's Z Brands and tossed over a key chain.

"Don't worry about getting me the title," Rehv said as he caught it. "Where your Ass-cura is ending up, we don't need paperwork to transfer ownership. Bye for now."

As the door shut behind the drama, Rehv glanced at the key ring. The tag hanging off of it read, SUNY NEW PALTZ.

"What?" he said without looking up.

Xhex's voice was low, seeping out from the dark corner of the office, where she always watched fun and games go down. "If he does it one more time, I want to take care of it."

Rehv fisted the keys and leaned back in his chair. Even if he said no, if Chrissy got cracked again his chief of security would probably roll out a beat-down anyway. Xhex was not like his other employees. Xhex wasn't like anybody.

Well, that wasn't entirely true. She was like him. Half *symphath*.

Or half sociopath, as was the case.

"You watch the girl," he said to her. "If that sonofabitch gets busy with his class ring again, we'll do a coin toss for who gets to fuck him up."

"I watch all your girls." Xhex walked over to the door, moving with smooth power. She was built like a male, tall and muscular, but she wasn't coarse. In spite of her Annie Lennox haircut and her tight

body, she wasn't some bulky she-male bitchsicle in her standard uniform of black muscle shirt and black leathers. No, Xhex was lethal in the elegant way of a blade: quick, decisive, sleek.

And like all daggers she loved drawing blood.

"It's the first Tuesday of the month," she said as she put her hand on the door.

As if he didn't know. "I'm leaving in a half hour."

The door opened and closed, the sound of the club on the other side flaring, then getting cut off.

Rehv lifted his palm. The blood flow was already stopping, and the hole would be closed in another twenty minutes. By midnight nothing would show of the penetration.

He thought of the moment when he'd impaled himself. To feel nothing of your body was an odd kind of paralysis. Although you moved, you didn't recognize the weight of the clothes on your back or whether your shoes were too tight or if the ground beneath your feet was uneven or slippery.

He missed his body, but either he took the dopamine and dealt with the side effects or he tangoed with his evil side. And that was one MMA fight he wasn't sure he could win.

Rehv palmed his cane and carefully eased himself up out of his chair. As a result of his numbness, balance was a bitch and gravity wasn't his friend, so the trip over to the panel on the wall took longer than it should have. When he got over to it, he placed his palm on a raised square and a door-sized panel slid back, all *Star Trek* and shit.

The black bedroom-and-bath suite that was revealed was one of his three crash pads, and for some reason it had the best shower. Probably because with only a couple hundred square feet, the whole place could go tropical just by running the damn thing.

And when you were cold all the time, that was a serious value-add.

Stripping off his clothes and starting the water, he did a quick shave while he waited for the spray to get nuclear hot. While he ran the razor down his cheeks, the male staring back at him was the same as always. Cropped Mohawk. Amethyst eyes. Tattoos on his chest and abs. Long cock lying loose between his legs.

He thought about where he had to go tonight and his vision changed, a red haze gradually replacing all the colors of his sight. He wasn't surprised. Violence had a way of coaxing his evil nature free, like food laid out to the starved, and he'd had only a sweet lick of the plate back in his office just now.

Under normal circumstances, it would be time for more dopamine. His chemical savior kept the worst of his *symphath* urges at bay, swapping them for hypothermia and impotence and numbness. The side effects sucked, but you had to do what you had to do, and lies required upkeep.

As well as performance.

His blackmailer demanded performance.

Palming his cock, like he could protect it from what it was going to have to do later tonight, he went over and tested the water. Even though steam was thickening the air until he felt like he was breathing cream, the shit wasn't hot enough. It never was.

He rubbed his eyes with his free hand. The red in his vision persisted, but it was a good thing. Better to meet his blackmailer on like terms. Evil to evil. *Symphath* to *symphath*.

Rehv stepped under the spray, the blood that he'd spilled washing away. As he soaped up his skin, he felt dirty already, totally unclean. The feeling was just going to be worse by the time dawn came.

Yeah . . . he knew precisely why his working girls steamed up their locker room at the end of their shifts. Whores loved hot water. Soap and hot water. Sometimes that and a washcloth were all that got you through the night.

SIX

John tracked Cormia with his eyes as she raced and twirled over the grass, her white robing flowing behind her, part flag, part wing. He didn't know that Chosen were allowed to run around all willy-nilly in their bare feet, and had the feeling that she was breaking rules.

Well, good for her. And beautiful for him to watch. With her joy, she was in the night but not part of the darkness, a firefly, a brilliant dancing spot against the forest's dense horizon.

Phury should see this, John thought.

His phone went off with a beep and he took it out of his pocket. The text from Qhuinn read: *can u gt fritz 2 t8 u 2 blays now? wr redy.* He hit his buddy back: *yup.*

He put the BlackBerry away and wished like hell he could dematerialize. You were supposed to try it for the first time a couple weeks after your transition, and Blay and Qhuinn had had no problem with the up and disappearing. Him? It was like when he'd started training and was always slowest and weakest and worst. All you had to do was concentrate on where you wanted to go and will yourself there. At least in theory. Him? He'd just spent a lot of time with his eyes shut and his face twisted up like a shar-pei's, trying to force his molecules across his room, staying exactly where he was. He'd heard it could sometimes take up to a year after your transition before you could pull it off, but maybe it was something he'd never be able to do.

In which case, he needed to get a fricking driver's license. He felt twelve with all the can-you-take-me-theres. Fritz was a great chauffeur, but come on. John wanted to be a man, not *doggen* cargo.

Cormia circled around and came back toward the house. As she stopped in front of him, her robe looked as if it wanted to keep going, the folds swaying forward before settling on her body. She was breathing fast and her cheeks were cherry red and her smile was bigger than the full moon.

God, with her blond hair all loose and her pretty flush, she was the perfect summer girl. He could so picture her in a field on a gingham blanket, eating apple pie next to a dewy pitcher of lemonade . . . wearing a red-and-white bikini.

Okay, that felt wrong.

"I like it outside," she said.

The outside likes you, he wrote, then showed her.

"I wish I had come here sooner." She looked over the roses that were growing around the terrace. As her hand crept onto her neck, he had a feeling that she wanted to touch them, but her bridle of reserve was returning.

He cleared his throat so she would glance over. *You can pick one if you like,* he wrote.

"I . . . I believe I would."

She approached the roses like they were deer that might spook, her hands by her sides, her bare feet slow over the slate. She went right for the pale lavender ones, bypassing the bolder red and yellow buds.

He was writing, *Be careful of thorns*, when she reached forward, yelped, and yanked back her hand. A drop of blood formed on the tip of her finger, the dim glow of the night making it look black on her white skin.

Before he knew what he was doing, John leaned down and put his mouth to work. He sucked quick and licked quicker, stunned by what he was doing as well as how delicious it was.

In the back of his mind, he realized he needed to feed.

Shit.

As he straightened, she stared at him wide-eyed and frozen. Double shit.

I'm sorry, he scribbled. *I didn't want it to get on your robe.*

Liar. He'd wanted to know what she tasted like.

"I . . ."

Pick your rose, just be careful of the thorns.

She nodded and gave it another shot, partially, he suspected, because she wanted to get her flower and partially to fill the awkward silence he'd created.

The rose she chose was a perfect specimen, just on the verge of blooming, a silver-purple spear with the potential of being the size of a grapefruit.

"Thank you," she said. He was about to you're-welcome her when he realized she was talking to the mother plant, not him.

Cormia turned to him. "The other flowers were in glass houses with water."

Let's go get you a vase, he wrote. *That's what they're called here.*

She nodded and started for the French doors that led into the billiards room. Just as she stepped through, she looked back outside. Her eyes held on to the garden as if it were a lover she would never see again.

We can do more of this sometime, he wrote on his pad. *If you'd like?*

Her quick nod was a relief, considering what he'd just done. "I would like that."

Maybe we could watch a movie, too. Upstairs in the theater.

"Theater?"

He shut the doors behind them. *It's a room that's specially made for watching stuff.*

"Can we see the movie now?"

The strong tone to her voice made him recalibrate his impression of her a little. The soft-spoken reserve might just be training, he decided, and not personality.

I have to go out. But we could tomorrow night?

"Good. We will do that after First Meal."

Okay, the meekness was definitely not personality. Which made him wonder how she handled the whole Chosen thing. *I have class, but we could do it after that?*

"Yes. And I should like to learn more about everything here." Her smile lit up the billiards room sure as a roaring fire, and as she pivoted around on one foot he thought of those pretty pop-up ballerinas in jewelry boxes.

Well, I'm up for teaching you, he wrote.

She came to a stop, her loosened hair swinging. "Thank you, John Matthew. You shall be a fine teacher."

As she looked up at him, he saw her colors more than her face or her body: that red in her cheeks and lips, the lavender of the flower in her hand, the brilliant pale green of her eyes, the buttercup yellow of her hair.

For no good reason, he thought of Xhex. Xhex was a thunderstorm, made up of hues of black and iron gray, power leashed but no less lethal for its control. Cormia was a sunny day cast in a rainbow of brightness, warmth realized.

He put his hand over his heart and bowed to her, then left. As he started up for his room, he wondered whether he liked the storm or the sunshine better.

Then realized neither was his for the taking, so what did it matter.

*　　*　　*

Standing in the alley with his nine pressed into the liver of a Brother, Mr. D was barn-cat alert. He would have much rather put the business end of his weapon to the vampire's temple, but that would have required a stepladder. Honest to heaven, the bastards were huge.

Made big ol' cousin Tommy seem no taller than a can of Bud. And just as crushable.

"You got hair like a girl," Mr. D said.

"And you smell like bubble bath. At least I can get a trim."

"I'm wearing Old Spice."

"Next time try something stronger. Like horse manure."

Mr. D pressed the muzzle in harder. "I want you on your knees. Hands behind your back, head down."

He stayed right where he was while the Brother complied, making no move to get out his steel cuffs. Sissy shit on his silo notwithstanding, this vampire was not the kind of thing you wanted getting away from you, and not just because a Brother captured was a feat for the history books. Mr. D had a rattler by the tail, and well he knew it.

Reaching into his belt to get his wristies, he—

The tide turned quick as a twitch.

The Brother spun around on one knee and punched a palm up into the muzzle of the gun. Mr. D pulled the trigger on reflex and the bullet kicked out to the sky, flying uselessly to heaven.

Before the popping sound stopped echoing, Mr. D was on his back on the ground, doing the dazed and confused, his cowboy hat once again off his head as he was overcome.

The Brother's eyes were dead as he stared down, lifeless in a way that their bright yellow color couldn't change. But then it made sense. No one in his right mind would pull a spin deflection when he was on his knees like that. Unless he was already flatlined.

The Brother lifted his fist over his head.

Sure 'nuff, this was going to hurt.

Mr. D moved fast, slipping free of the hold on his shoulder and twisting to the side. In a quick jab, he kicked both feet into the right calve of the Brother.

There was a snapping sound and . . . holy shit, a part of a leg went flying. The Brother teetered, his leathers going loose from the knee down on that side, but there was no time to do a lot of *what-the-fuck–ing*. The big bastard fell over, crumbling like a building.

Mr. D scampered out of the way, then jumped on the wreckage, damn sure that if he didn't take control of the ground game he would be eating his own chitlins. He threw a leg over the Brother, grabbed a fist full of that sissy hair, and yanked back hard as he went for his knife.

Didn't make it. The Brother done went bronco on him, popping off the pavement and rearing up. Mr. D latched on with his legs and threw an arm around a neck thick as his thigh—

In a flash, the earth tilted wildly and—*fuck*—the Brother turtled 'round and fell backward, turning Mr. D into a mattress.

It was like having a granite slab fall on your chest.

Mr. D was knocked stupid for a split second, and the Brother grabbed the advantage, shifting to the side and using his elbow as a gut ram. As Mr. D grunted and started to heave, there was a flash of a black dagger being unsheathed, then the Brother rose up onto his knees.

Mr. D braced himself to get stabbed, thinking that he'd had less than three hours of being the *Fore-lesser*, and wasn't that a sorry showin'.

But instead of getting stuck in the heart, Mr. D felt his shirt get pulled out of the waistband of his pants. As his belly flashed white in the night, he looked up in horror.

This was the Brother who liked to slice before he killed. Which meant there was no simple death a-comin'. This was going to be a long, bloody process. Sure, it wasn't the Destroyer, but this bastard was going to make Mr. D work for his ride to the Pearly Gates.

And *lessers* might be dead, but they felt pain like everyone else did.

Phury should have been catching his breath and finding his lower leg, not getting ready to go Sweeney Todd on the pint-sized slayer. God, you'd think his near miss with that bullet with his name on it would have juiced him to close the deal and get the fuck out of the alley before more of the enemy showed.

Nope. As he exposed the *lesser's* stomach, he was both frozen to the core and animated by heat, buzzing as if he were walking into his room with a bag full of red smoke and nowhere to go for ten hours.

He was like the addict who'd run away, all I've-won-the-lottery high.

The wizard's voice cut into the anticipation, as if the excitement had drawn the wraith like spoiled meat. *This butchering thing is one bloody way to distinguish yourself, but then, being a mere rank failure is a bit pedestrian, isn't it. And you were from a noble family until you ruined them. So bash on, mate.*

Phury focused on the undulating skin he'd revealed and let the feel of the dagger in his hand and the paralytic, bracing terror of the *lesser* seep into him. As his mind calmed, Phury smiled. This time was his. He owned this. There would be, for however long it took him to do what he wanted to this evil, peace from the chaos of the wizard's voice.

In doing this damage, he healed himself. If only for a short while.

He brought the black dagger to the *lesser's* skin and—

"Don't you fucking dare."

Phury looked over his shoulder. His twin was standing in the mouth of the alley, a big black shadow with a skull trim. Zsadist's face wasn't visible, but you didn't need to eyeball a furrowed brow to know the drill. The pissed-off came off him in waves.

Phury closed his eyes and fought a vicious anger. Goddamn it, he was being robbed. He was absolutely being robbed.

In a quick flash, he thought of the number of times Zsadist had demanded that he beat him, beat him until Z's face ran with blood. And the Brother thought this shit with a *lesser* was wrong? What the fuck? The slayer had no doubt killed his fair share of innocent vampires. How was this worse than asking your blooded brother to pound you to a pulp, even though you knew it made him sick to his stomach and it scrambled his brains for days afterward?

"Get out of here," Phury said, tightening his hold on the *lesser* as he squirmed. "This is my biz. Not yours."

"The fuck it's not my biz. And you told me you would stop."

"Turn around and walk away, Z."

"So you can get cracked when backup comes?"

The slayer in Phury's grip heaved to get free, and he was so small and wiry it almost worked. Oh, hell no, Phury thought, he wasn't losing his prize. Before he knew what he was doing, he plowed the dagger into the thing's belly and dragged the blade through its intestinal playing field.

The *lesser* screamed louder than Zsadist cursed, and in that moment, Phury didn't feel bad about either noise. He was sick to fucking death of everything, including himself.

Attaboy, the wizard whispered. *Just where I like you.*

Zsadist was on him in the next breath, yanking the dagger out of his hand and throwing it across the alley. While the *lesser* passed out cold, Phury shot to his feet to confront his twin.

Problem was, he didn't have his lower leg.

As he fell hard against the bricks, he knew he must look like a drunk, and that pissed him off even more.

Z picked up his prosthesis and tossed it across the alley. "Put that the fuck back on."

Phury caught the thing with one hand and let himself slide down the cool, raspy exterior of the dry cleaner's building.

Shit. Busted. So fucking busted, he thought. And now he was going to have to deal with his brothers crawling all over him.

Why couldn't Z have just gone down another alley? Or this one at another time?

Damn it, he needed this, Phury thought. Because if he didn't let out some of his rage, he was going to go fucking mad, and if Z, after all his masochistic bullshit, couldn't understand that? Fuck. Him.

Zsadist unsheathed his dagger, stabbed the first *lesser* back to the Omega, and then just stood over the burn spot.

"Shit of ten horses," his twin said in the Old Language.

"The new aftershave of the *lessers*," Phury muttered, rubbing his eyes.

"I think y'all need to think 'bout this here," a strangled Texas twang pronounced.

As Z spun around, Phury lifted his head. The little *lesser* had his gun again and was pointing it at Phury while staring at Z.

Z's response was to level his SIG at the slayer.

"W'all are in some bind," the thing said as it bent down with a groan and picked up a cowboy hat. It arranged the Stetson on its head, then went back to holding its stomach in. "See, if you shoot me, my hand's gonna tighten on the trigger and I'm gonna pop your friend here. If I shoot him, you're gonna lead me up." The *lesser* took a deep breath and released it on another groan. "I do believe this is a standoff, and we don't have all night. One shot's already gone off, and who knows who heard it."

The Texas bastard was right. Downtown Caldwell after midnight was not Death Valley at high noon. There were folks around, and not all were of the drugged-out human variety. There were also cops. And civilian vampires. And other *lessers*. Sure, the alley was secluded, but it offered only relative privacy.

Way to go, mate, the wizard said.

"Shit," Phury cursed.

"Yes, suh," the slayer murmured. "I do believe that is where we be."

As if on cue, police sirens flared up and grew closer.

No one moved, even when the patrol car swung around the corner and came barreling down the alley. Yup, someone had heard the

shot when Phury and John Wayne-ette had been going at it, and whoever it was had let his fingers do the walking.

The frozen tableau between the buildings was spotlit by the police car as the thing heaved to a stop with a screech.

Two doors were thrown open. "Drop your weapons!"

The *lesser*'s drawl was soft as the summer night air. "Y'all can take care of this for us, can't you?"

"I'd rather cap your ass," Z shot back.

"Drop your weapons or we will shoot!"

Phury stepped up to the plate, willing the humans into a semi–dream state and making the one on the right duck into the car and turn off the headlights.

"Much obliged," the *lesser* said as he started to shuffle down the alley. He kept his back to the building and its eyes on Zsadist and its gun on Phury. As the thing went past the cops, it took the gun from the officer it was closest to, peeling what was undoubtedly a nine-millimeter right out of the woman's unresisting hand.

The slayer leveled that gun at Z. With both arms busy, its black blood positively streamed out of its gut. "I would shoot y'all, but then your little mind-control games wouldn't work on this here matched set of Caldwell's finest. Guess I'm going to have to be good."

"Goddamn it." Z's weight shifted back and forth on his feet, like he wanted to haul ass.

"Please don't take the Lord's name in vain," the slayer said when it got to the corner the police had come around. "And have a good evenin', gentlemen."

The little guy was gone quick, not even his footsteps sounding out as he tore off.

Phury willed the cops back into their patrol car and made the female one call into the station and report that their investigation showed no altercations or public disturbances in the alley. But that

missing gun . . . that was straight-up trouble. Goddamn slayer. No memory imprint could solve the fact that there was a nine missing.

"Give her your gun," he told Zsadist.

His twin popped the sleeve of bullets out as he went over. He didn't wipe the weapon before he dropped it in the woman's lap. No reason to. Vampires left no identifying fingerprints.

"She'll be lucky if she doesn't lose her mind over this," Z said.

Yup. It wasn't her gun and it was emptied. Phury did the best he could, giving her a memory of buying this new piece and trying it out and tossing the clip because the bullets were faulty. Not a great cover. Especially considering that all the Brotherhood's guns had the serial numbers removed.

Phury willed the officer who was behind the wheel to throw the squad car in reverse and back out of the alley. The destination? Station house for a coffee break.

When they were alone, Z cranked his head around and met Phury in the eye. "Do you want to wake up dead."

Phury checked over his prosthesis. It was undamaged, at least for regular use, just knocked free from where it plugged in under his knee. It was not safe to fight with, though.

Pushing up the pant leg of his leathers, he reattached it, then stood up. "I'm going home."

"Did you hear me?"

"Yeah. I did." He met his twin's eyes and thought it was a helluva question for the guy to ask. Z's death wish had been his operating principle up until he met Bella. Which was, comparably, like ten minutes ago.

Z's brows came down over a stare gone black. "Go straight home."

"Yeah. Right home. You got it."

As he turned away, Z said roughly, "Haven't you forgotten something?"

Phury thought about all the times he had chased after Zsadist, desperate to save the Brother from killing himself or killing someone else. He thought about the days he couldn't sleep for wondering whether Z was going to make it because he refused to drink from female vampires and insisted on getting by on human blood. He thought of the aching sadness he had every time he looked at his twin's ruined face.

Then he thought of the night he'd faced off at his own mirror and cut off his hair and dragged a blade down his own forehead and his own cheek so he could look like Z . . . so he could take his twin's place and be at the mercy of a *lesser*'s sadistic vengeance.

He thought of the leg he'd shot off to save them both.

Phury looked over his shoulder. "No. I remember everything. All of it."

With no remorse whatsoever, he dematerialized and reassumed form on Trade Street.

Facing off at ZeroSum, his heart and his head screaming, he was called forth to cross the road like he'd been chosen for this mission of self-destruction, tapped on the shoulder, beckoned forward by the bony forefinger of his addiction.

He couldn't fight the invite. Worse, he didn't want to.

As he approached the club's front doors, his feet—the real one and the one made of titanium—were serving the wizard's mission. The pair of them took him right in the front door and past the VIP area's security guard and by the tables of highfliers to the back, to Rehvenge's office.

The Moors nodded and one of them talked into his watch. While waiting, Phury knew damn well he was stuck in an endless loop, going around and around like the head of a drill, digging farther and farther underground. With each new level that he sank to, he tapped into deeper and richer veins of poisonous ore, ones that spidered up through the bedrock of his life and enticed him down even farther. He was heading for the source, for the consummation with hell that was his ultimate destination, and each lower plateau was his malignant encouragement.

The Moor on the right, Trez, nodded and opened the door to the black cave. Here was where little bits of Hades were dealt out in cellophane Baggies, and Phury went in with twitchy impatience.

Rehvenge came out of a pocket door, his amethyst stare shrewd and slightly disappointed.

"Your usual gone already?" he asked quietly.

The sin-eater knew him so well, Phury thought.

"It's *symphath*, remmy?" Rehv slowly went to his desk, relying on his cane. "Sin-eater's such an ugly degradation. And I don't need my bad side to know where you're at. So how much is it going to be tonight?"

The male unbuttoned his flawless double-breasted black jacket and lowered himself into a black leather chair. His low-cut Mohawk glistened as if he'd just gotten out of the shower, and he smelled good, a combination of Cartier for Men and some kind of spicy shampoo.

Phury thought of the other dealer, the one who had died back in that alley just now, the one who had bled out while reaching for help that never came. That Rehv was dressed like something off of Fifth Avenue didn't change what he was.

Phury looked down at himself. And realized that his clothes didn't alter what he was either.

Shit . . . one of his daggers was missing.

He'd left it back in the alley.

"The usual," he said, taking a thousand dollars out of his pocket. "Just the usual."

SEVEN

Upstairs in her bloodred bedroom, Cormia couldn't shake the conviction that by going outside, she had triggered a chain of events, the culmination of which she couldn't begin to guess at. She only knew that destiny's hands were moving things around behind her stage's velvet curtain, and when the two halves opened again, something new was going to be revealed.

She wasn't sure she trusted fate to have the next act in the play be one she would enjoy. But she was stuck in the audience with nowhere to go.

Except that wasn't entirely true, was it.

Going to her door, she cracked it open and looked down the Oriental runner to the head of the grand staircase.

The hall of statues was off to the right.

Every time she came to the second floor, she caught a glimpse of the elegant figures in their windowed corridor and was fascinated. In

their formality and their frozen bodies and their white robes, they reminded her of the Sanctuary.

In their nudity and their maleness, they were utterly foreign.

If she could go outside, she could go down and see the statues up close. She absolutely could.

Whispering down the runner in her bare feet, she passed the Primale's bedroom, then Rhage and Mary's. The king's study, which was at the top of the stairway, was closed off, and the foyer far below was empty.

As she rounded the corner, the statues stretched out for what seemed like forever. Positioned to the left, they were illuminated from above by inset lights and separated one from another by arching windows. On the right, opposite every other window, there were doors that she assumed opened into more bedrooms.

Interesting. If she had designed the house, she would have put the bedrooms on the window side so they would have enjoyed the benefit of garden views. As it was now, if she had triangulated the layout of the mansion correctly, the bedrooms overlooked the opposite wing, the one that bracketed the far side of the front courtyard. Attractive, true, but better to have architectural landscapes in hallways and vistas of gardens and mountains in bedrooms. At least, in her opinion.

Cormia frowned. She'd been having odd thoughts like that lately. Thoughts about things and people and even prayers that weren't always of an approving nature. The random opinions made her uneasy, but she couldn't stop them.

Trying not to dwell on where they came from or what they meant, she made the corner and faced off at the hallway.

The first statue was of a young male—a human male, going by its size—who was draped in rich folds of robing that ran from his right shoulder to his left hip. His eyes were trained on the middle ground, and his face was composed, neither sad nor happy. His chest was broad, his upper arms strong yet sleek, his belly flat and ribbed.

The next statue was similar, only his limbs were arranged differently. And the next was in yet another position. The fourth as well . . . except that one was fully nude.

Instinct made her want to rush by. Curiosity demanded that she stop and stare.

He was beautiful in his nakedness.

She looked over her shoulder. No one was around.

Reaching out, she touched the neck of the statue. The marble was warm, which was a shock, but then she realized the spotlight up above was its heat source.

She thought of the Primale.

They had spent one day in the same bed, that first day she was here with him. She had had to ask if she could join him in his room and lie beside him, and as they had stretched out beneath the sheets, awkwardness had been a blanket of thistles over them both.

But then she had fallen asleep . . . only to wake up to a huge male body pushing into her, a hard, warm length against her hip. She had been too stunned to do anything but acquiesce as, without words, the Primale had stripped her robing from her body and replaced it with his own skin and the weight of his strength.

Indeed, speech was not always necessary.

With a slow caress, she ran her fingertips down the statue's warm marble chest, pausing at the nipple on its flat base of muscle. Down farther, the ribs and stomach were a lovely pattern of undulations. Smooth, so smooth.

The Primale's skin was just as smooth.

Her heart beat hard as she reached to the statue's hip.

The tingling heat she felt wasn't about the stone in front of her. In her mind, it was the Primale she was touching. It was his body that was beneath her fingers. It was his sex and not the statue's that called her.

Her hand drifted down farther until it hovered right on the top of the male's pubic bone.

The sound of someone bursting into the mansion ricocheted up from the foyer.

Cormia jumped back from the statue so fast she tripped on the hem of her robe.

As heavy footfalls stormed to the stairway and pounded up to the second floor, she took cover in a window's alcove and peeked around the corner.

The Brother Zsadist appeared at the head of the stairs. He was dressed for fighting, with daggers on his chest and a gun on his hip—and by the hard set of his jaw it looked like he was still in combat.

After the male stalked out of sight, she heard knocking on what had to be the doors of the king's study.

Moving silently, Cormia went down the hall, pausing at the corner next to where the Brother was.

There was a barking command, and then the door open and shut.

The king's voice resonated through the wall she leaned against. "Not having fun tonight, Z? You look like someone's shit on your front lawn."

The Brother Zsadist's words were dark. "Has Phury been home yet?"

"Tonight? Not that I know of."

"Fucking bastard. He said he was going home."

"Your twin says a lot of things. Why don't you four-one-one me on the current drama bomb?"

Flattening herself in hopes of being less visible, she prayed that no one came down the corridor. What had the Primale done?

"I caught him making California rolls out of *lessers*."

The king cursed. "I thought he told you he was going to stop."

"He did."

There was a groan, as if the king were rubbing his eyes or maybe his temples. "So what exactly did you walk into?"

There was a long pause.

The king's voice dropped even lower. "Z, my man, talk to me. I gotta know what I'm dealing with if I'm going to do anything about him."

"Fine. I found him with two *lessers*. His leg was knocked off, and he had a burn mark around his neck like he'd been strangled with a length of chain. He was leaning over a slayer's belly with a dagger in his hand. Goddamn it . . . he wasn't aware of his surroundings at all. Didn't look up at me until I said something. I could have been another fucking *lesser*, and if I had been? He'd either be getting tortured right now or he'd be deader than dead."

"What the *fuck* am I going to do with this guy?"

Z's voice took on a tight tone. "I don't want him kicked out."

"Not your call. And don't look at me like that—I'm still your boss, you hotheaded SOB." There was a pause. "Shit, I'm beginning to think your twin needs to be airmailed to a goddamned shrink. He's a danger to himself and others. Did you say anything to him?"

"We'd just gotten jacked by the CPD—"

"There were *cops* involved in this, too? *Christ*—"

"So, no, I didn't gum-flap."

The voices grew muffled until the Brother Zsadist said more loudly, "You consider what that would do to him? The Brotherhood is his life."

"You're the one who brought this to my attention. Use your head. A week off rotation and a little vacay is not going to be enough to fix this."

There was another silence. "Look, I need to go check on Bella. Just talk to Phury before you burn his house down. He'll listen to you. And give him this back."

When something heavy hit what was likely a desk, Cormia ducked into one of the guest rooms. A moment later she heard the Brother Zsadist's heavy footsteps as he went down to his room.

Danger to himself and others.

She couldn't picture the Primale brutalizing their enemy or putting himself in harm's way because he was careless. But why would the Brother Zsadist lie?

He wouldn't.

Suddenly exhausted, she sat on the corner of the bed and idly looked around. The room was done in the same shade of lavender as her favorite rose.

What a lovely color, she thought, letting herself fall back against the duvet.

Lovely, indeed, though it did nothing to soothe her agitated nerves.

The Caldwell Galleria was two stories of Hollister, H&M, Express, Banana Republic, and Ann Taylor, located in the exurbs of the city. With JCPenney, Lord and Taylor, and Macy's anchoring the ends of the floor plan's three spokes, it was solidly in the middle tier as malls went, and the crowd it drew was three parts teenage and one part restless soccer mom. Food court had McD's, KuikWok, California Smoothie, Auntie Anne's, Cinnabon. Kiosks down the center aisles sold knitted shit, bobble-head dolls, cell phones, and animal calendars.

The place smelled like stale air and plastic strawberries.

Holy shit, he was in the mall.

John Matthew couldn't fricking believe that he was in the mall. Talk about your trippy full circles.

The place had been given a surface upgrade since he'd last seen it, the shades of beige having been replaced with a pink and ocean green Jamaican theme. Everything from the floor tiles to the garbage cans to the fake potted plants and the fountains screamed, *We be jammin'.*

It was kind of like a Hawaiian shirt on a fifty-year-old man. Cheerfully and unattractively out of whack.

God, how things changed. The last time he'd been here, he'd been a scrawny orphan tagging along behind a bunch of other unwanted kids. Now here he was, with fangs in his mouth and size-fourteen shoes and a big body that people didn't want to get in the path of.

He was still an orphan, though.

And speaking of orphans, man, he could remember so clearly those field trips here to the mall. Every year, St. Francis had taken its charges to the Galleria before Christmas. Which had been kind of cruel, as none of the kids had had money to buy any of the shiny, pretty stuff that was for sale. John had always been afraid that they'd get kicked out or something, because no one carried any shopping bags to validate the group's use of the bathrooms.

But that wasn't going to be a problem tonight, he thought, as he patted his back pocket. In his wallet was four hundred dollars he'd earned working in the training center's office.

What a relief to have green to burn and to belong amid the strolling masses.

"You forget your wallet?" Blay asked.

John shook his head. *Got it.*

Up ahead by a number of feet, Qhuinn was in the lead and moving quickly. He'd been in a rush since they'd walked in, and as Blaylock paused in front of Brookstone, the guy looked at his watch with bracing impatience.

"Let's hustle it, Blay," he snapped. "We've only got an hour before closing time."

"What is your damage tonight?" Blay frowned. "You're tight as hell, and not in a good way."

"Whatever."

They walked faster, passing groups of tweens that hung together like schools of fish, each by species and sex: Girls and boys didn't mix; Goths and preps didn't mingle. The lines were very clear, and John remembered exactly how all that worked. He'd been on the outside of every group, so he'd been able to watch all of them.

Qhuinn stopped in front of Abercrombie and Fitch. "Urban Outfitters' too core for you. We're going to A-and-F your flow."

John shrugged and signed, *I still don't think I need a ton of new clothes.*

"You have two pairs of Levi's, four Hanes T-shirts, and a set of

Nikes. And that fleece." *Fleece* was pronounced with the same enthusiasm as *fresh roadkill.*

I also have workout sweats.

"Which will abso put you on the cover of *GQ*. My b." Qhuinn
headed into the store. "Let's do this."

John followed along with Blay. Inside, the music was loud and the
clothes were crowded in tight and the pictures of the models on the
walls showed lots of perfect people in black and white.

Qhuinn started flipping through rows of hanging shirts with
vague disgust, like the shit was something his grandmother would
wear. Which made sense. He was definitely an Urban Outfitters
man, with a thick chain swinging from the blue-black jeans and the
Affliction T-shirt with the skull and wings on it and the black boots
that were big as your head. His dark hair was spiked up, and he had
seven gunmetal studs in his left ear running from lobe to upper car-
tilage.

John wasn't entirely sure where else he was pierced. Some things
you just didn't need to know about your buddies.

Blay, who fit in at the store, branched out and went over to the
distressed-jeans section, which he seemed to approve of. John hung
back, less concerned with the clothes than the fact that people were
looking at them. As far as he was aware, humans couldn't sense vampires, but man, the three of them were getting a lot of attention for
some reason.

"Can I help you?"

They turned around. The girl who'd asked was tall as Xhex, but
the comp between the two females ended right there. Unlike the
female of John's fantasies, this one spiked way high on the feminine
scale and suffered from hair-related Tourette's, a condition that man-
ifested itself in incessant head jerks and an evidently irresistible urge
to fondle her brunette frizz bomb. But she had skills. Somehow, she
managed to handle all that hair play without tipping over into a
T-shirt display.

Frankly, it was kind of impressive. Although not necessarily in a good way.

Now Xhex would never—

Fuck. Why the hell was Xhex always the standard?

As Qhuinn smiled at the girl, plans of the on-all-fours variety flared in his eyes. "Perfect timing. We totally need help. My buddy here needs a vibe injection. Can you hook him?"

Oh. God. No.

When the girl glanced over at John, her hot stare made him feel like she'd grabbed him between the legs and sized up his cock with a squeeze.

He took cover behind a rack of brand-new, old-looking button-downs.

"I'm the manager," she said, her drawl all about the bump and grind. "So you're in good hands. All of you."

"Niiiice." Qhuinn's mismatched eyes traced down the girl's smooth legs. "Why don't you get to work on him? I'll watch."

Blay stepped up beside John. "Whatever you pick out, I check first, and I'll bring it to him in the dressing room."

John sagged with relief and signed a quick thank-you to Blay for coming to the rescue yet again. The boy's middle name was buffer. For real.

Unfortunately, the manager just smiled even more widely. "Two for one sounds good to me. Check it, I didn't know we were having a sale on man candy tonight."

Okay, this was going to be horrible.

An hour later, though, John was feeling better. Turned out Stephanie, the manager, had a good eye, and once she got into the clothes she chilled out on the come-ons. John got jacked into some sweet ragged jeans, a bunch of those deconstructed button-downs, and a couple of tight muscle shirts, which even he had to admit showed off his guns and his pecs like they were worth seeing. A couple of necklaces were pushed on him, and so was a black hoodie.

When it was done, John went up to the register with the shit draped over his arm. As he put the clothes down, he glanced at a bunch of bracelets in a basket. Within the tangle of leather and shells, there was a flash of lavender, and he weeded through the pile to get to it. Pulling out a woven bracelet with beads the color of Cormia's rose on it, he smiled and surreptitiously put the thing underneath one of the muscle shirts.

Stephanie rang him up.

The total was over six hundred bucks. Six. Hundred. Dollars.

John wigged. He only had about four—

"I've got it," Blay said, handing over a black card and glancing at him. "You can pay me the rest later."

Stephanie's eyes bugged at the sight of the plastic, then narrowed on Blay as if she were changing the price tag on him. "I've never seen a black AmEx before."

"It's no big." Blay started poking through a bunch of necklaces.

John squeezed his friend's arm, then knocked on the counter to get Stephanie's attention. He spread his money out, but Blay shook his head and started signing.

Pay me the rest later, okay? I know you're good for it, and let's face it, do you really want to come back here and pick up the shit you can't cover? I don't.

John frowned, finding it hard to argue with that logic. *But I'm giving the rest to you,* he signed after he handed his four over.

When you have it, Blay returned. *Just whenever you have it.*

Stephanie whipped the card through the machine, punched in the amount, and waited with her fingertips on the slip. Seconds later there was a chattering sound, and then she ripped the paper off and handed it over to Blay with a blue Bic pen.

"So . . . we're closing now."

"Are you." Qhuinn leaned a hip against the counter. "And exactly what does that mean?"

"It's just going to be me here. I'm a great boss. I'm letting the others go early."

"But then you'd be all alone."

"I would. It's true. All by myself."

Shit, John thought. If Blay was the buffer, Qhuinn was the king of complication.

The guy smiled. "You know, me and my boys wouldn't feel right about leaving you here on your lonesome."

Oh, yes—yes, they would, John thought. Your boys would feel just great about that.

Tragically, Stephanie's slow smile sealed the deal. They were going nowhere until Qhuinn got into her cash register.

At least he worked fast. Ten minutes later, the store was empty and the chain-link security curtain had been pulled into place in the front. And he was getting pulled by the jeans chain into a lip-lock.

John held on to his two big bags while Blay got busy looking at shirts he'd already looked at.

"Let's go into a dressing room," the manager said against Qhuinn's mouth.

"Perf."

"We don't have to go alone, by the way." The girl looked over her shoulder, her stare landing on John. And staying. "There's plenty of room."

No way, John thought. NFW.

Qhuinn's mismatched eyes sparkled with trouble, and behind the girl's back he signed, *Come with us, John. It's time you did this.*

Stephanie picked that moment to take Qhuinn's full lower lip between her white teeth and his thigh between her legs. A guy could just imagine the things she was going to do to him. Before he did her.

John shook his head. *I'm staying here.*

Come on. You can watch me first. I'll show you how it's done.

The fact that Qhuinn was issuing the invite was not a surprise. He regularly had sex in pairs. He'd just never asked John to join in yet.

Come on, John, come back with us.

No, thanks.

A dark look came into Qhuinn's eyes. *You can't always be on the sidelines, John.*

John looked away. It would have been easier to get pissed at the guy if the same thing didn't occur to him on a regular basis.

"Fine," Qhuinn said. "We'll be back in a while."

With a lazy smile, he slid his hands onto the girl's ass and picked her up. As he walked backward, her skirt rode up so she flashed pink panties and white cheeks.

When the pair was in a dressing room, John turned to Blay to sign something about what a man-slut Qhuinn was, only to stop his hands. Blay was staring off in the direction the two of them had gone with an odd expression on his face.

John whistled low to get his attention. *You can go back, you know. If you want to be with them. I'm cool here.*

Blay shook his head a little too quickly. "Nah. I'm hanging."

Except his eyes went back to that dressing room and held steady as a moan drifted out. Going by the tenor of the sound, it was hard to know who had made it, and Blay's expression got even tighter.

John whistled again. *You okay?*

"We might as well get comfortable." Blay went behind the locked cash registers and sat on a stool. "We're going to be here for a while."

Right, John thought. Whatever was bumming the guy was off-limits.

John hopped up on the counter and let his legs dangle. As another moan sounded out, he started to think of Xhex and got hard.

Great. Just fab.

He was pulling his shirt out of his waistband to cover up his little problem when Blay asked, "So who's the bracelet for?"

John signed quickly, *It's for me.*

"Yeah, right. That thing wouldn't fit your wrist." There was a pause. "You don't have to tell me if you don't want to."

Honestly, it's no big deal.

"Okay." After a minute, Blay said, "So, you want to go to Zero-Sum after this?"

John kept his head down while he nodded.

Blay laughed softly. "Thought you might. Just like I'll bet if we go tomorrow night, too, you'll be okay with it."

I can't tomorrow night, he signed without thinking.

"Why not?"

Shit. *Just can't. Have to stay home.*

Yet another moan came out from the back, and then a muffled, rhythmic pounding started.

When the sounds stopped, Blay took a deep breath, like he'd been running intervals and had just finished the workout. John didn't blame him. He'd just as soon leave the store, too. With the lights down low and no other people around, all the hanging clothes seemed sinister.

Plus, if they got to ZeroSum ASAP, he had a good couple of hours of Xhex sightings to look forward to, and that was . . .

Pathetic, really.

Minutes ticked by. Ten. Fifteen. Twenty.

"Shit," Blay muttered. "What the hell are they doing?"

John shrugged. With their friend's predilections, it was anyone's guess.

"Yo, Qhuinn?" Blay called out. When there was no answer, not even a grunt, he slid off the stool. "I'm going to see what's up."

Blay went up to the dressing room and knocked. After a moment, he put his head in through the door. In a rush, his eyes flared and his mouth opened and he blushed from the roots of his red hair all the way to his palms.

Riiiiight. The session was evidently not finished. And whatever was doing was worth seeing, because Blay didn't turn around right away. After a moment his head went back and forth slowly, as if he were answering a question Qhuinn had posed.

As Blay returned to the register, his head was down, his hands deep in his pockets. He stayed quiet as he eased back onto the stool, but his foot started going a mile a minute, tapping up and down.

It was obvious the guy didn't want to hang around anymore, and John could totally get that.

Hell, they could be at ZeroSum.

Where Xhex worked.

As that happy little obsessive thought hit him, John wanted to bang his head into the counter. Man . . . clearly, the word *pathetic* had a new spelling.

And it was J-O-H-N M-A-T-T-H-E-W.

EIGHT

Among the problems with shame was that it in fact did not make you shorter or quieter or less visible. You just felt like you were.

Phury stood in the mansion's courtyard and stared up at the looming facade of the Brotherhood's home. All dour gray, with a lot of dark, glowering windows, the place was like a giant that had been buried up to its neck and was not happy with the dirt submersion.

He was no more ready to go into the mansion than it seemed ready to welcome him.

As a breeze came up, he looked to the north. The night was typical August in upstate New York. All around it was still summer, with the fat, leafy trees and the fountain going and the potted urns on either side of the house's entrance. The air was different, though. Little drier. Little cooler.

The seasons, like time, were relentless, weren't they?

No, that was wrong. The seasons were but a measure of time, just like clocks and calendars.

I'm getting older, he thought.

As his mind started to head off in directions that seemed worse than the ass-kicking he was likely to find in the mansion, he went through the vestibule and into the foyer.

The queen's voice came out of the billiards room, accompanied by a quartet of pool balls clapping gently together and a couple of thunks. Both the curse and the laughter that followed had a Boston accent. Which meant that Butch, who could beat everyone else in the house, had just lost to Beth. Again, evidently.

Listening to them, Phury couldn't remember the last time he'd played a game of pool or just hung out with his brothers—although even if he had, he wouldn't have been completely at ease. He never was. For him, life was a coin that had disaster on one side and waiting for disaster on the other.

You need another blunt, mate, the wizard drawled. *Better yet, have a bale of the stuff. Won't change the fact that you're a right bastard fool, but it'll increase the chance of you lighting your bed on fire when you pass out in it.*

On that note, Phury decided to face the music and go upstairs. If he was lucky, Wrath's door would be shut—

It wasn't, and the king was at his desk.

Wrath's stare lifted from the magnifying glass he was holding over a document. Even through his wraparounds, it was straight obvi the guy was pissed. "I've been waiting for you."

In Phury's head, the wizard swooped up his black robes and parked it in a Barcalounger slipcovered in human skin. *My kingdom for some popcorn and Junior Mints. This is going to be specTAAAcular.*

Phury walked into the study, his eyes barely registering the French blue walls and the cream silk sofas and the white marble mantel. The lingering smell of *lesser* in the air told him that Zsadist had just been right where he was.

"Guess Z talked to you already," he said, because there was no reason not to call a spade a spade.

Wrath put the magnifier down and leaned back behind his Louis XIV desk. "Shut the door."

Phury closed them in together. "You want me to talk first?"

"No, you do enough of that." The king lifted up his massive shit-kickers and let them fall on the dainty desk. The pair landed like cannonballs. "You do plenty of that."

Phury waited for the list of failures to get rolling out of courtesy, not curiosity. He was well aware of where he was at: trying to get killed out in the field; assuming the mantle of the Chosen's Primale but not completing the ceremony; being overinvolved with Z and Bella's life; not paying enough attention to Cormia; smoking all the time. . . .

Phury focused hard on his king and waited for a voice other than the wizard's to run down his fuckups.

Except none of it came. Wrath said absolutely nothing.

Which seemed to suggest that the problems were so loud and obvious it was like pointing at a bomb exploding and saying, *Boy, that's really noisy—going to leave a crater in the pavement, too, huh?*

"On second thought," Wrath said, "tell me what I should do about you. Tell me what the fuck I should do."

When Phury didn't reply, Wrath murmured, "No comment? You mean you have no idea what to do, either?"

"I think we both know what the answer is."

"I'm not so sure about that. What do *you* think I need to do?"

"Take me off rotation for a little while."

"Ah."

More silence.

"So is that where we're at?" Phury asked. *Man, he so needed a blunt.*

Those shitkickers knocked together at the toes. "Dunno."

"That mean you want me to fight?" Which would be a better outcome than he could hope for. "I'd give you my word—"

"Fuck. You." Wrath stood up in a quick surge and came around the desk. "You told your twin you were coming back here, but dollars to shit piles you went to see Rehvenge. You promised Z you'd stop with the slayers and you didn't. You said you'd be the Primale and you aren't. Hell, you keep talking out your ass about how you're going back to your room to get some sleep, but we all know what you do in there. And you honestly expect me to take your word about anything?"

"So tell me what you want me to do."

From behind the sunglasses, the king's pale, unfocusable eyes were searching. "I'm not sure time off and a fuckload of therapy is going to help, because I don't think you'll do either."

Cold dread curled up like a wet, wounded dog in Phury's gut. "Are you going to kick me out?"

It had happened before in the history of the Brotherhood. Not often. But it had. Murhder came to mind . . . shit, yeah, he was probably the last one to get the boot.

"Not as simple as that, is it," Wrath said. "If you get curbed, where does that leave the Chosen? The Primale has always been a Brother, and not just because of bloodlines. Besides, Z wouldn't take to that well, even as pissed off at you as he is now."

Great. His safety nets were saving his twin from a head fuck and being the Chosen's man-whore.

The king walked over to the windows. Outside, the summer trees swayed in a gathering wind.

"Here's what I think." Wrath popped his sunglasses up off his nose and rubbed his eyes like his head ached. "You should . . ."

"I'm sorry," Phury said, because that was all he had to offer.

"So am I." Wrath let the glasses fall back into place and shook his head. As he returned to his desk and sat down, his jaw was set along with his shoulders. Popping open a drawer, he took out a black dagger.

Phury's. The one that had been left in the alley.

Z must have found the damn thing and carried it home.

The king turned the weapon over in his hand and cleared his throat. "Give me your other blade. You're off rotation permanently. Whether or not you see a shrink or how the shit shakes out with the Chosen is not my business. And I'm out of advice, because the truth is, you're going to do what you're going to do. Nothing I demand or ask of you is going to make a difference."

Phury's heart stopped for a moment. Of all the ways he'd thought this confrontation would play out, Wrath's washing his hands of the mess had never been in the cards.

"Am I still a Brother?"

The king just stared at the dagger—which gave Phury the three-word answer: *in name only.*

Some things didn't need to be said, did they.

"I'll talk to Z," the king murmured. "We'll say you're on administrative leave. No more fieldwork for you, and you don't come to the meetings anymore."

Phury felt a rush as if he were free-falling off a building and had just made eye contact with the pavement that had his name on it.

No nets anymore. No promises to break. As far as the king was concerned, he was on his own.

Nineteen thirty-two, he thought. He'd been in the Brotherhood for only seventy-six years.

Bringing his hand up to his chest, he palmed the grip of his remaining dagger, unsheathed the weapon in a single pull, and put it on the silly pale-blue desk.

He bowed to his king and left without another word.

Bravo, the wizard called out. *Such a shame your parents are already dead, mate. They'd be so delighted in this proud moment—wait, let's bring them back, shall we?*

He was slammed with two quick images: his father passed out in a room full of empty ale bottles, his mother lying in a bed with her face turned to the wall.

Phury went back to his room, took out his stash, rolled up a blunt, and lit it.

With everything that had happened tonight, and the wizard playing the role of the anti-Oprah, he either smoked or he screamed. So he smoked.

Across town, Xhex was not in her happy place as she escorted Rehvenge out of ZeroSum's back door and into his bulletproof Bentley. Rehv didn't look any better than she felt, her boss nothing but a grim dark shadow in a full-length sable coat as he slowly moved through the alley.

She opened the driver's-side door for him and waited as he eased himself into the bucket seat with the help of his cane. Even in the seventy-degree night, he cranked the heater and pulled his coat's lapels closer to his neck—a sign that his last hit of dopamine had yet to wear off. It would soon enough. He always went unmedicated. It wasn't safe otherwise.

Wasn't safe, period.

For twenty-five years, she had wanted to go with him to back his ass up for these visits with his blackmailer, but getting shut down every time she asked had made her cut her losses and keep her yap shut. The cost of her silence was a bad fucking mood, though.

"You staying at your safe house?" she said.

"Yeah."

She shut the door and watched him drive off. He didn't tell her where the meetings were, but she knew the rough vicinity. The GPS system in the car indicated he went upstate.

God, she hated what he had to do.

Thanks to her fuckup two and a half decades ago, Rehv had to whore himself out the first Tuesday of every month to protect them.

The *symphath* Princess he serviced was dangerous. And hungry for him.

At first, Xhex had waited for the bitch to turn him and Xhex in anonymously for deportation to the *symphath* colony. But she was smarter than that. If they got shipped, they'd be lucky to survive six months, even as strong as they were. Half-breeds were no match for the full-bloods, and besides, the Princess was mated to her own uncle.

Who was a power-driven, possessive despot if there ever was one.

Xhex cursed. She had no idea why Rehv didn't hate her, and she couldn't fathom how he could stand the fucking part of it. She had a feeling, though, these nights were why he took such good care of his girls. Unlike your average pimp, he knew exactly how the prostitutes felt, knew precisely what it was like to screw someone you didn't want because they had something you needed, be it cash or silence.

Xhex had yet to find them a way out, and what made the situation even more untenable was that Rehv had stopped looking to get free. What had once been a crisis situation had become the new reality. Two decades later, he was still fucking to protect them, and it was still Xhex's fault, and every first Tuesday of the month, he went and did the unthinkable with someone he hated . . . and that was life.

"Fuck," she said to the alleyway. "When is this going to change?"

The only reply she got was a gust that blew newspaper pages and plastic bags her way.

As she went back into the club, her eyes adjusted to the flaring lasers, her ears absorbed the trippy music, her skin registered a slight drop in temperature.

The VIP section seemed relatively quiet with just the usual regulars, but she made eye contact with both her bouncers anyway. After they nodded the all-clear, she looked over the girls who were working the banquettes. Watched the cocktail waitresses tray empties and deliver replacements. Measured the bottle levels behind the VIP bar.

When she got to the velvet rope, she looked over the crowd in the main part of the club. The great throng on the dance floor was moving like an unsettled ocean, surging and parting and coming together

again. Couples and trios on the fringes were gyrating while they hooked up, the lasers bouncing off shadowy faces and bodies that were melded together.

Tonight was relatively low traffic, as the weeks geared up slowly, attendance growing until traffic peaked on Saturday nights. For her as head of security, Fridays were usually the most intense, with idiots burning off the residue of a bad workweek by doing too many drugs and either OD'ing or breaking into brawls.

That being said, as dumb-asses with addictions were the club's bread and butter, shit could go south any moment of any night.

Good thing she rocked at her job. Rehv handled the sale of drugs, booze, and women, managed his fleet of sports bookies that ran lines to the mob in Vegas, and contracted for certain special projects involving "enforcement." She was in charge of keeping the club's environment in control so business could be conducted with as little interference from the human police and the idiot patrons as possible.

She was about to go check the mezzanine level when she saw what she referred to as the Boys come in the front door.

Stepping back into the shadows, she watched as the three young males came through the VIP section's velvet rope and headed for the back. They always went for the Brotherhood's table if the thing was empty, which meant they were either strategic, as it was next to an emergency exit and in a corner, or they'd been told to sit there and mind their manners by the powers that be.

"Powers" as in the king, Wrath.

Yeah, the Boys weren't your average little cock cabal, she thought as they parked it. For a whole host of reasons.

The one with the mismatched eyes was trouble looking for a landing pad, and true to form, after he ordered his Corona he got up and went out to the main part of the club to find some tail. The redhead stayed behind, which was also not a surprise. He was your essential Eagle Scout, straight up as a ruler. Which made her suspicious as to what was under that apple-pie image.

Of the three, though, the mute was the real issue. His name was Tehrror, a.k.a. John Matthew, and the king was his *whard*. Which meant the kid was a china plate in a bullpen, as far as Xhex was concerned. Anything happened to him? The club was flushed.

Man, the kid had changed over the last few months. She'd seen him pretransition, all scrawny and weak, totally crushable, but now she was looking at one fuck of a big male . . . and big males were problems if they got to throwing their meat around. Although John had up until now been a sit-back-and-watch type, the kid's eyes were way too old in his young face, which suggested he'd been through some bad shit. And bad shit tended to be the gas on the fire when people cracked.

Mismatched Eyes, a.k.a. Qhuinn, son of Lohstrong, came back with a pair of ready-and-willings, two blondes who'd evidently color-coordinated their outfits to match their cosmopolitans: Both were wearing not much pink.

The redhead, Blaylock, didn't have a lot of game, but that was no problem, because Qhuinn had plenty for both of them. Hell, the guy would have had plenty for John Matthew, too, except that one didn't play. At least, not that Xhex had ever seen.

After John's buddies disappeared into the back with the R&Ws, Xhex walked over to the kid for no good reason. He stiffened as he caught sight of her, but he always did that, just like he always watched her. When you were head of security, folks tended to want to know where you were.

"How you doing?" she asked.

He shrugged and fiddled with his Corona bottle. Bet he wished it had a label to pick off, she thought.

"Mind if I ask you something?"

His eyes popped a little, but he shrugged again.

"Why don't you ever go to the back with your boys?" It was, of course, none of her damned business, and what was more, she didn't know why she cared. But hell . . . maybe it was all the first-Tuesday-of-the-month shit. She was looking to get out of her own head.

"The girlies like you," she prompted. "I've seen them checking you out. And you look at them, but you always stay out here."

John Matthew flushed so deep she could see the red even in the dim light.

"You already tied up?" she murmured, even more curious. "The king pick you out a female?"

He shook his head.

Okay, she needed to leave him alone. The poor kid was a mute, so how did she expect him to answer her?

"I want my drink now!" The booming male voice cut through the music, and Xhex swiveled her head around. Two banquettes away, one of the big-daddy blowhard types was aggressing on a waitress, clearly on the express train to I'm-an-Ass-ville.

"Excuse me," Xhex said to John.

As the loudmouth reached out his bear claw and grabbed the waitress's skirt, the poor girl lost control of her tray and cocktails went flying. "I said, gimme my drink *now!*"

Xhex stepped up behind the waitress and steadied her. "Don't worry about it. He's leaving."

The man lumbered up out of his seat to a full height of about six-four. "Am I?"

Xhex stepped in close until they were breast-to-chest. She locked eyes on him, her *symphath* urges screaming to be let out, but she focused on the metal barbs she had clamped around her thighs. Taking strength from the pain she inflicted on herself, she fought off her nature.

"You will leave now," she said softly, "or I will drag you out of here by your hair."

The man had breath like a day-old tuna sandwich. "I hate dykes. You always think you're tougher than you really—"

Xhex grabbed the man's wrist, turned him in a little circle, and cranked his arm up to the middle of his back. Then she clipped her leg around his ankles and shoved him off balance. He landed like a side of beef, the wind getting knocked out of him on a curse, his body plowing into the short-napped carpet.

In a quick move, she bent down, buried one hand in his gelled-up hair, and locked the other on the collar of his suit jacket. As she dragged him face-first to the side exit, she was multitasking: creating a scene, committing both an assault and a battery, and running the risk of a brawl if his buddies in the Hall of Fucktards got involved. But you had to put on a show every once in a while. Every one of the entitled assholes in the VIP section was watching, as were her bouncers, who were edgy characters to start with, and the working girls, most of whom had totally understandable anger-management issues.

To keep the peace, you had to get your hands dirty every once in a while.

And, considering all the hair product this bigmouth used, she was so going to need to wash up after this was over.

When she got to the side exit by the Brotherhood's table, she paused to open the door, but John got there first. Like a total gentleman, he swung the thing wide and held it that way with his long arm.

"Thanks," she said.

Out in the alley, she flipped the bigmouth asshole over on his back and went through his pockets. As he lay there blinking like a fish in the bottom of a boat, the search was another infraction on her part. She had police powers on club property, but the alley was technically owned by the city of Caldwell. More to the point, though, the zip code of this hand job was irrelevant. The search would have been illegal, as she didn't have probable cause to believe he had drugs or concealed weapons.

According to the law, you couldn't frisk someone for just being a cocksucker.

Ah . . . but, see, this was where instinct paid off. In addition to his wallet, she found a nice load of coke on him, as well as three tabs of X. She dangled the cellophane bags in front of the man's eyes.

"I could have you arrested." She smiled as he started to stammer.

"Yeah, yeah, not yours. Don't know how they got there. You're innocent as a two-year-old. But look up over that door."

When the guy didn't respond quickly enough, she clamped a hand on his jowls and pushed his face around.

"See that little red blinking eye? That's a security camera. So this shit . . ." She jogged the packets at the camera, then flipped open the wallet. ". . . this two grams of cocaine and three hits of Ecstasy that came out of the breast pocket of your suit, Mr. . . . Robert Finlay . . . has been digitally recorded. Huh . . . check this out, you have two nice-looking kids. Bet they'd rather have breakfast with you tomorrow morning than eat with a babysitter because your wife is trying to spring you out of jail."

She put his wallet back in his suit and held on to the drugs. "The way I'd like to suggest we handle this is to go our separate ways. You don't ever come into my club again. And I don't send your dime-sized balls to jail. What do you say? Deal or no deal?"

As he pondered whether to take what the Banker offered or open another case, Xhex got to her feet and backed up a little so she had a clear kick shot if she needed it. She didn't think that shit was going to be necessary, though. People who were going to fight had tense bodies and sharp eyes. Bigmouth was loose as dishwater, clearly having run out of gas and ego.

"Go home," she said to him.

And he did.

As he lumbered off, Xhex put the drugs in her back pocket.

"You enjoy the show, John Matthew?" she said without turning around.

When she looked over her shoulder, her breath stopped in her throat. John's eyes were glowing in the darkness . . . as the kid stared at her with the kind of single-minded focus males got when they wanted sex. Hard-core sex.

Holy . . . shit. This was no little boy she was looking at.

Without being aware she was doing it, she reached into his mind with a lick of her *symphath* nature. He was thinking of . . . him on a bed in tangled sheets, his hand between his legs on a gigantic cock, his mind picturing her as he pumped himself off.

He'd done that a lot.

Xhex pivoted and walked over. When she came up to him, he didn't step back, and she wasn't surprised. In this raw instant, he was no awkward youngling to cut and run. He was all male animal, meeting her head-on.

Which was . . . oh, fuck her, it was not attractive. It. Really. Was. Not.

Shit.

As she looked up at him, she meant to tell him to go train those glowing blue marbles on the human women in the club and leave her out of it. She meant to say that she was beyond off-limits and to let his fantasy go. She meant to warn him off, as she had all others except for the hardened, half-dead Butch O'Neal before he'd become a Brother.

Instead, she said in a low tone, "Next time you think of me like that, say my name when you come. It'll get you off even better."

She let her shoulder brush across the front of his chest as she leaned to the side and opened the door to the club.

His harsh suck of breath lingered in her ear.

As she went back to work, she told herself her body was hot because of the effort she'd just expended dragging that dickhead out the door.

It had absolutely nothing to do with John Matthew.

As Xhex walked back into the club, John stood there like a frickin' idiot. Which made sense. Most of his blood had rushed from his brain to the arousal in his brand-new, old-looking A & F jeans. The rest of the shit was in his face.

Which meant his brain was running on empty.

How the *hell* did she know what he did when he thought of her?

One of the Moors who guarded Rehvenge's office came over. "You in or out of this door?"

John shuffled back to the banquette, downed his Corona in two swallows, and was glad when one of the waitresses came over with a freshie without his even asking.

Xhex had disappeared into the main part of the club, and he searched for her, trying to see through the waterfall that separated the VIPs from the others.

He didn't need his eyes to know where she was, though. He could sense her. In the midst of all the bodies in the club, he knew which one belonged to her. She was over by the bar.

God, the fact that she could manhandle a guy twice her size without breaking a sweat was hot as hell.

The fact that she didn't seem offended that John had fantasized about her was a relief.

The fact that she wanted him to say her name when he came was . . . making him want to come right now.

Guess this answered whether he liked sunshine or thunder better, didn't it. And told him exactly what he would be doing as soon as he got home.

NINE

Out past the sprawling patchwork of Caldwell's rural farms, farther north than the towns along the Hudson River's winding flanks, about three hours from the Canadian border, the Adirondack Mountains spring up from the earth. Majestic, carpeted in pines and cedars at their heads and shoulders, the ranges had been created by glaciers that had stretched down from the Alaskan frontier before it had been known as Alaska and before there were humans or vampires to call it a frontier.

When the last ice age retreated into history books that would be written much later, the great valley gouges that were left in the land filled with the melt-off from the icebergs. Over generations of humans, the vast geological pools were assigned names like Lake George and Lake Champlain and Saranac Lake and Blue Mountain Lake.

Humans, those bothersome, parasitic rabbits with their many, many children, settled in the Hudson River corridor, seeking the water, as many other animals did. Centuries passed and towns

sprouted up and "civilization" was established, with all its intrusions into the environment.

The mountains remained the masters, though. Even in the age of electricity and technology and automobiles and tourism, the Adirondacks dictated the landscape of this stretch of northern New York.

So there are a lot of lonesome stretches in the midst of all those forests.

Heading up I-87, a.k.a. the Northway, the exits get farther and farther apart until you can go five miles, ten miles, fifteen miles without having a way off the road. And even if you do put your blinker on and ease onto a ramp that takes you to the right, all you'll find is a couple of stores and a gas station and two or three houses.

People can hide in the Adirondacks.

Vampires can hide in the Adirondacks.

At the end of the night, as the sun readied itself for a big, splashy entrance stage right, a male walked through the dense woods of Saddleback Mountain alone, dragging his withered body over the ground as he would have a bag of garbage in his earlier life. His hunger was all that moved him, the primordial instinct for blood all that kept him on his feet and fighting through the branches.

Up ahead in a tangle of pine boughs, his prey was twitchy, nervous.

The deer knew it was being tracked, but it couldn't see what it was hunted by. Lifting its muzzle, it sniffed at the air, ears pricking forward and back.

The night was cold this far north and this high up on Saddleback. Given that the male didn't have much left on his back except rags, his teeth chattered and his nail beds were blue, but he wouldn't have put more clothes on if he'd had them. Feeding his blood hunger was the extent of his concessions to existence.

He would not take his own life. He'd heard long ago that if you committed suicide, you couldn't make it into the Fade, and that was where he had to end up. So he passed his days in a narrow bandwidth of suffering, waiting until he either starved to death from malnutrition or was grievously injured.

The process was taking too damn long. Then again, his escape from his old life months and months ago had brought him to these woods by erratum rather than engineering. He'd meant to send himself somewhere else, somewhere even more dangerous.

Couldn't remember anymore where that had been, though.

The fact that his enemies were not this far and this deep in the Adirondacks had first saved, but now frustrated him. He was too weak to dematerialize around trying to find slayers, and he wasn't strong enough for long walks, either.

He was stuck here in the mountains, waiting for death to find him.

During the day, he hid from the sunshine in a cave, an abscess in the mountain's granite his shelter. He didn't sleep much. Hunger and his memories kept him mercilessly alert and aware.

Up ahead, his prey took two steps away from him.

Taking a deep breath, he forced himself to gather his strength. If he didn't do this now, he was finished for the night, and not just because the sky was beginning to lighten to the east.

In a rush, he disappeared and took form around the deer's neck. Clamping onto its slender withers, he sank his fangs into the jugular that ran up from its flickering, panicked heart.

He didn't kill the lovely animal. Took only enough to see him through another black day and into another blacker night.

When he was done he opened his arms wide and let the thing bounce off in four-footed flight. Listening to it crash through the forest's skirt, he envied the animal's freedom.

There was little return of strength for the male. Lately, it was nearly a wash between the energy he expended to feed and what he got in return. Which meant the end had to be coming soon.

The male sat down on the forest's bed of decaying pine needles and looked up through the boughs. For a moment, he imagined that

the night sky was not dark, but white, and that the stars above were not cold planets reflecting light, but the souls of the dead.

He imagined he was looking up at the Fade.

He did this often, and among the great scattering of sparkles overhead, he found the two that he counted as his own, the two that had been taken from him: a pair of stars, one larger and glowing superbright, the other smaller and more tentative. They were close together, as if the little one were seeking the shelter of its m—

The male couldn't say that word. Even in his head. Just like he couldn't say the names he associated with the stars.

Didn't matter, though.

Those two were his.

And he would join them soon.

TEN

The clock next to Phury ticked over so that the digital readout formed a pattern of toothpicks: eleven eleven in the morning.

He checked his stash. It was getting a little low, and even as cooked as he was, he got a case of the cardio-shimmies. As he worked the math, he tried to smoke slower. He'd been dipping into the open Baggie of red smoke for about seven hours now . . . so if he did some extrapolating, he was going to run out around four in the afternoon.

Sun went down at seven thirty. He could be at ZeroSum no earlier than eight.

Four-hour dead zone. Or, more accurately, four hours that he might live a little too clearly.

If you'd like, the wizard said, *I could read you a bedtime story. It's the dog's bollocks. Male models self after alcoholic father. Ends up dead in an alley. Is mourned by no one. Classic, practically Shakespearian.*

Unless you've heard it before, mate?

Phury turned up *"Donna non vidi mai"* and inhaled hard.

As the tenor's voice soared according to Puccini's dictations, he thought of Z's singing. What a voice that brother had. Like a church organ, his range went from liquid highs to basses so deep they turned your marrow into an eardrum, and if he heard something once, he could replicate it perfectly. Then put his own spin on the melody or think of something entirely new. Everything was his forte: opera, blues, jazz, old-fashioned rock and roll. He was his own XM Radio.

And he always led the chants in the Brotherhood's temple.

Hard to fathom that Phury would never hear that voice in the sacred cave again.

Or around the house, come to think of it. It had been months since Z had sung anything, probably because worrying about Bella didn't put him in a Tony Bennett kind of way, and there was no telling whether his impromptu concerts would return or not.

Bella's destiny would be the decider on that.

Phury took another hit off the blunt. God, he wanted to go see her. Wanted to reassure himself that she was okay. Visual confirmation was so different from an abundance of no-news-is-good-news.

But he wasn't in visitation shape, and not just because he was toasted. Reaching up, he put his hands to his neck and prodded the residual injury from that chain being wrapped around his throat. He was a quick healer, but not that quick, and Bella's eyes were working just fine. No reason to upset her.

Plus Z would be with her, and going eyeball-to-eyeball with his twin was way too bullet-to-chamber, considering the way things had been left in that alley.

A rattling sound from over on the bureau brought his head up.

Across the room, the Primale medallion was vibrating, the ancient gold talisman acting like a beeper. He watched as it moved around on the wood, dancing in a little circle as if it were looking for a partner among the silver brush set he'd put it next to.

He was so not going over to the Other Side. No way. Getting bootlicked out of the Brotherhood was enough for one day.

Finishing his blunt, he got up and left his room. As he stepped into the hall, he looked to Cormia's door out of habit. It was slightly ajar, which was unusual, and he heard a flapping noise.

He walked over and knocked on the jamb. "Cormia? Are you okay?"

"Oh! Yes . . . yes, I am." Her voice was muffled.

When she said nothing further, he leaned in. "Your door's open." Well, wasn't he Einstein. "Do you want me to close it?"

"I didn't mean to leave it like that."

As he wondered how she'd gotten along with John Matthew, he said, "Mind if I come in?"

"Please."

He pushed the door wide—

Oh . . . wow. Cormia was sitting cross-legged on her bed, braiding her damp hair. There was a towel next to her, which explained the flapping, and her robe . . . her robe was open in a deep V, the soft swells of her breasts in danger of being fully exposed.

What color were her nipples?

He quickly looked elsewhere. Only to find a single lavender rose in a crystal vase on the bedside table.

As his chest grew tight for no good reason, he frowned. "So did you and John enjoy yourselves?"

"Yes, we did. He was quite lovely."

"Was he?"

Cormia nodded as she wrapped a white satin ribbon around the end of the braid. In the dim light of the lamp, the thick rope of her hair glowed as if it were gold, and he hated to see her wrap the long stretch in circles at the base of her neck. He wanted to stare at it some more, but had to take solace in the wisps that were already appearing around her face.

What a picture she made, he thought, wishing he had some paper and his quill.

Strange . . . she looked different, he thought. Then again, maybe it was because there was color in her cheeks. "What did you guys do?"

"I ran outside."

Phury felt his frown get deeper. "Because something frightened you?"

"No, because I was free to."

He had a quick vision of her racing over the grass in the backyard, her hair streaming behind her. "And what did John do?"

"He watched."

Did he.

Before Phury could say anything, she continued. "You're right, he's very kind. He's going to show me a movie this evening."

"He is?"

"He taught me to use the television. And look at what he gave me." She extended her wrist. On it was a bracelet made of lavender beads and silver links. "I've never had something like this before. I've always just had my Chosen pearl."

As she touched the iridescent teardrop at her throat, he narrowed his eyes. Her stare was guileless, as pure and lovely as the rosebud across the room.

John's attention to her made Phury see his neglect all the more clearly.

"I'm sorry," she said in a quiet voice. "I'll take the bracelet off—"

"No. It suits you. Beautifully."

"He said it was a gift," she murmured. "I should like to keep it."

"And so you shall." Phury took a deep breath and looked around the bedroom, catching sight of a complex structure made of toothpicks . . . and peas? "What is that?"

"Ah . . . yes." She went over quickly, as if she wanted to shelter whatever it was.

"What is it?"

"It's what is in my head." She turned to him. Turned away. "It's just something I've started doing."

Phury walked across the room and knelt down next to her. With care, he ran his finger down a couple of the links. "It's fantastic. It looks like the frame of a house."

"You like it?" She knelt down. "I really just made it up."

"I love architecture and art. And this . . . the lines are great."

Her head tilted as she considered the structure, and he smiled, thinking he did the same thing with his drawings.

On impulse, he said, "Would you like to go down to the hall of statues? I was just going to go for a wander. It's past the top of the stairs."

As her eyes lifted to his, there was a knowledge in them that took him aback.

Maybe it wasn't that she looked any different, he realized. It was that she was looking at him differently.

Shit, maybe she'd really liked John. As in *liked* John. What a wrench that would put into the mix.

"I would like to go with you," she said. "I should like to see the art."

"Good. That's . . . good. Let's go." He rose to his feet and extended his hand for no apparent reason.

After a moment, she slid her palm into his. As they tightened their grips on each other, he realized that the last time they'd had any physical contact had been that trippy morning in his bed . . . when he'd had that erotic dream and woke up with his hard body all over her.

"Shall we," he murmured. And led her to the door.

When they stepped out into the hall, Cormia couldn't believe her hand was in the Primale's. After she'd wanted some private time with him for so long, it was surreal that she finally had not only that, but actual physical contact.

As they headed for where she had already been, he dropped her hand but stayed close. His limp was barely noticeable, just a slight shadow in his elegant gait, and as usual he was lovelier to her than any piece of art she could possibly behold.

She worried for him, though, and not just because of what she'd overheard.

The clothes he had on were not the ones he wore to meals. The leathers and the black button-down were what he'd been fighting in, and they were marked with stains.

Blood, she thought. His and the race's enemies.

That wasn't the worst of it. There was a fading streak around his neck, as if some damage had been done to the skin there, and he had bruises, too, on the backs of his hands and the side of his face.

She thought of what his king had said about him. *Danger to himself and others.*

"My brother Darius was an art collector," the Primale said as they went by Wrath's study. "Like everything else in this house, these were all his. Now they're Beth and John's."

"John is the son of Darius, son of Marklon?"

"Yes."

"I read of Darius." And of Beth, the queen, being his daughter. But there had been nothing on John Matthew. Odd . . . as son of the warrior, he should have been listed on the front page with the Brother's other progeny.

"You read D's biography?"

"Yes." She'd gone looking for information on Vishous, the Brother she'd been originally promised to. Had she known who the Primale would turn out to be, however, she would have checked the rows of red leather volumes for the ones on Phury, son of Ahgony.

The Primale paused at the head of the hall of statues. "What do you do when a Brother dies?" he asked. "With his books?"

"One of the scribes marks any vacant pages with a black *chrih* symbol, and the date is noted on the front page of the first volume. There are ceremonies, as well. We performed them for Darius and we wait . . . with regard to Tohrment, son of Hharm."

He nodded once and walked forward, as if they had discussed nothing of particular import.

"Why for do you ask?" she said.

There was a pause. "These statues are all from the Greco-Roman period."

Cormia drew the lapels of her robing more closely to her neck. "Are they."

The Primale bypassed the first four statues, including the fully nude one, thank the Virgin Scribe, but paused by the one with the missing parts. "They're a little beaten up, but considering they're over two thousand years old, it's a miracle any part of them survived. Er . . . I hope the nudity doesn't offend you?"

"No." But she was glad he didn't know how she'd touched the naked one. "I think they're beautiful no matter whether they are covered or not. And I don't care if they are imperfect."

"They remind me of where I grew up."

She waited, acutely aware of how much she wanted him to finish the thought. "How so?"

"We had a statuary." He frowned. "It was covered in vines, though. The gardens all were. Vines everywhere."

The Primale resumed walking.

"Where did you grow up?" she asked.

"In the Old Country."

"Are your parents—"

"These statues were bought in the forties and fifties. Darius went through a three-dimensional stage, and as he'd always hated modern art, this was what he bought."

As they came to the end of the corridor, he stopped in front of the door into one of the bedrooms and stared at it. "I'm tired."

Bella was in that room, she thought. It was obvious from his expression. "Have you eaten?" she asked, thinking it would be lovely to head him in the opposite direction.

"I don't remember." He looked down at his feet, which were in heavy boots. "Good . . . God. I haven't changed, have I?" There was an odd hollowness to his voice, as if the realization had emptied him out. "I should have changed. Before we did this."

Reach out, she told herself. *Reach out and take his hand. Just as he reached out for yours.*

"I should change," the Primale said quietly. "I need to change."

Cormia took a deep breath, and, extending her arm, she clasped his hand. It was cold to the touch. Alarmingly so.

"Let us go back to your room," she told him. "Let us go back there."

He nodded but didn't move, and before she knew it, she was leading him. Or his body, at any rate. She sensed his mind had gone off somewhere else.

She took him into his room, to the marble confines of his bath, and when she stopped him, he stood where she left him, in front of the two sinks and the wide mirror. While she turned on the spray chamber they called a shower, he waited not so much patiently as with unawareness.

When the rush of water was warm enough under her hand, she turned back to him. "Your Grace, it is all set for you. You may wash."

His yellow eyes stared straight ahead into one of the mirrors, but there was no recognition of his reflection in his handsome face. It was as if a stranger confronted him in the glass, a stranger he didn't trust or approve of.

"Your Grace?" she said. The stillness in him was alarming, and had he not been upright, she would have checked the beating of his heart. "Your Grace, the shower."

You can do this, she told herself.

"May I disrobe you, Your Grace?"

After he nodded a little, she stepped in front of him and raised tentative hands to the buttons on his shirt. One by one she freed them, the black cloth gradually parting open to expose his broad chest. When she got down to his belly button, she tugged the tails free of his leathers and kept going. All the while, he stayed still and unresisting with his eyes locked on the mirror, even as she parted the two halves of the shirt and pushed them off his shoulders.

He was magnificent in the dim light of the bath, putting all the statues to shame. His chest was enormous, the width of his shoulders nearly three times that of her own. The star-shaped scar on his left pectoral looked as if it had been engraved on his otherwise smooth, hairless skin, and she wanted to touch that place, to trace the spokes that radiated out from the center of the marking.

She wanted to press her lips to him there, she thought, press them over his heart. Over the flesh badge of the Brotherhood.

Laying his shirt out on the edge of the deep-bellied bath, she waited for the Primale to take over the undressing. He did nothing of the sort.

"Shall I . . . remove your pants?"

His head nodded.

Her fingers trembled as she worked loose his belt's buckle, then freed the button of his leathers. His body eased back and forth under her tugging, but not by much, and she was struck by how solid he was.

Dearest Virgin Scribe, he smelled fantastic.

The copper zipper went down slowly, and she had to hold the two halves of the waistband together because of the angle she was working from. When she let go, the front burst open. Beneath the leathers, he wore a tight loin cover in black, which was a relief.

Of sorts.

The bulge of his sex in it made her swallow hard.

She was about to ask him if she should continue when she looked up and realized he was gone, for all intents and purposes. Either she kept at what she was doing, or he was going under the water partially dressed.

As she tugged the leather down his thighs to his knees, her eyes stuck to the male flesh that was cradled in soft cotton. She remembered what it had felt like when he had come up against her body in his sleep. What she was looking at now had seemed much larger then, and it had been stiff as it pressed into her hip.

That was the change of arousal, wasn't it. The previous Directrix's

stern lecture on the mating ritual had detailed all about what happened when males grew ready for sex.

Had detailed too the pain females bore from that hardened staff.

Forcing herself to stop thinking along those lines, she sank into a kneeling position to do away with the pants and realized she should have taken the boots from his feet first. Fighting her way through the folds of leather at his ankles, she managed to get one boot off by leaning into his legs and forcing him to shift his weight. She went to work on the other side . . . and found the foot that wasn't real.

She kept going, not pausing even a moment. His infirmity didn't matter to her, although she wished she knew how he had been injured so badly. It must have been in fighting. To sacrifice so much for the race . . .

The leathers came off the same way the boots did: with an awkward series of pulls that the Primale didn't seem to notice. He simply stood on whichever foot she let him have on the marble, as steady as an oak. When she finally glanced up again, there were but two adornments on his body: his loin cover, which had the words *Calvin Klein* around the waistband, and the metal rods and foot that filled the gap between his right knee and the floor.

She went over and opened the door to the spray chamber. "Your Grace, the falling bath is ready for you."

His head swiveled to her. "Thank you."

In a quick surge he swept the loin cover off and walked toward her, naked.

Cormia's breath stopped. His massive sex hung soft and long from its base, the blunt head swinging slightly.

"Will you stay while I shower?" he said.

"Wha . . . ah, is that what you wish?"

"Yes."

"Then I . . . Yes, I shall stay."

ELEVEN

The Primale disappeared behind the glass, and Cormia watched him back up to the spray, his magnificent hair flattening down as it grew wet. With a groan, he arched his back and lifted his hands to his head, his body forming an elegant, powerful curve as the water ran through his hair and over his chest.

Cormia bit her lower lip as he reached to the side and picked up a bottle. There was a sucking noise as he squeezed it over his palm once . . . twice. . . . He returned it to its resting place, then brought his hands to his hair to massage his locks. Foaming clumps ran down his forearms and dropped off his elbows onto the tile at his feet. The spicy scent wafting up reminded her of the outdoor air.

With her knees feeling unreliable, and her skin warm as the water he was in, Cormia sat down on the marble edge of the Jacuzzi.

The Primale took a bar of soap, worked it between his palms, and

washed his arms and his shoulders. The scent told her it was the same kind she used and it mingled beautifully with whatever he'd washed his hair with.

To her chagrin, she found the suds running down his torso and his hips and his heavy, smooth thighs were worthy of jealousy, and she wondered if he would have let her join him. There was no way of knowing for sure. Unlike some of her sisters, she couldn't read the thoughts of others.

But really, could she imagine standing before him with her hands on his skin under that warm spray . . . ?

Yes. Yes, she could.

The Primale went lower with the soap, down his chest and stomach. Then he cupped what was between his thighs, swiping his hands over and under his sex. As with the rest of his ministrations, he moved with disappointing economy.

It was a strange torture, a pleasurable pain to watch him in his private moment. She wanted this to last forever, but knew she would have to make do with her memories.

When he turned off the water and stepped out, she handed him a towel as quickly as she could to shield that heavy, dangling male flesh from her eyes.

As he dried off, his muscles flexed under his golden skin, tightening up hard, then stretching out lean. After he wrapped the towel around his hips, he reached for another and dried his hair off by rubbing the dense, wet waves back and forth. The flapping of the terry cloth seemed loud in the marble room.

Or maybe that was the pounding of her heart.

His hair was tangled when he was finished, but he didn't seem to notice as he looked over at her. "I should go to bed now. I have four hours to fill, and maybe I can start going through them now."

She didn't know what that meant, but nodded. "All right, but your hair . . ."

He touched it as if only just realizing now that it was attached to his head.

"Would you like me to brush it?" she asked.

An odd expression hit his face. "If you'd like to. Someone . . . someone once told me I'm too rough with it."

Bella, she thought. Bella had told him that.

She wasn't sure how she knew it, but she was dead certain—

Oh, who was she fooling? He had an ache in his voice. That was how she knew. The tone was the verbal equivalent to what was in his eyes when he sat across the dining room table from the female.

And although it seemed petty, Cormia wanted to brush his locks in order to replace Bella with herself. She wanted to imprint a memory of herself over the one he had of the other female.

The possessiveness was a problem, but she couldn't change the way she felt.

The Primale handed her a brush, and though she expected him to sit on the edge of the deep bath, he went out to the chaise by the bed and sat down. As he put his palms atop his knees, he bent his head and waited for her.

As she approached him, she thought of the hundreds of times she had brushed the hair of her sisters in the bath. In this moment, though, the thing in her hand with all the bristles was a tool she wasn't sure how to use.

"Tell me if I hurt you," she said.

"You won't." He reached over and picked up a remote unit. When he hit a button, that music he always played, the opera, swelled in the room.

"How lovely," she said, letting the sounds of the male tenor seep into her. "What is the language?"

"Italian. It's Puccini. A love song. This is about a man, a poet, who meets a woman whose eyes steal the only wealth he has. . . . One look into her eyes and his dreams and visions and castles in the

air are stolen by her and replaced by hope. He's telling her who he is now . . . and will ask who she is at the end of the solo."

"What is the song called?"

" '*Che Gelida Manina*.' "

"You play it often, do you not?"

"It is my favorite among all solos. Zsadist . . ."

"Zsadist what?"

"Nothing." He shook his head. "Nothing . . ."

As the tenor's voice soared, she fanned his locks out across his shoulders and started at the ends, taking the brush to the waves in careful, gentle sweeps. The rasping noise from the bristles joined the opera, and the Primale must have been comforted by both, because his rib cage expanded as he drew in a long, slow breath.

Even when all the tangles were gone, she kept on going, continuing to smooth the wake of the brush with her free hand. As his hair dried, the colors came out and its thickness returned, the waves reforming after each pass, the mane she knew as his emerging.

She couldn't keep this up forever. And what a pity. "I believe I am finished."

"You haven't done the front."

Actually, she mostly had. "All right."

She walked around to stand before him, and there was no ignoring the way he opened his thighs wide, as if he wanted her to come between them.

Cormia stepped into the space he made for her with his legs. His eyes were closed, his golden lashes down on his high cheekbones, his lips slightly open. His head lifted to her with the same kind of invitation offered by his mouth and his knees.

She took it.

Sweeping the brush back through his hair, she followed the loose center part that had formed. With each pull, his neck muscles corded to keep his head in place.

Cormia's fangs sprang out of the roof of her mouth.

The instant they did his eyes flashed open. Brilliant yellow met her stare.

"You're hungry," he said in a strangely guttural tone.

She let her hand with the brush fall to her side. Her voice gone, she simply nodded. In the Sanctuary, the Chosen didn't need to feed. Here on this side, however, her body demanded blood. Which was why she'd been struggling with lethargy.

"Why didn't you tell me before now?" His head tilted to the side. "Although if it's because you don't want me, that's okay. We can find someone else for you to use"

"Why . . . why wouldn't I want you?"

He tapped the artificial leg. "I am not whole."

True, she thought sadly. He was not whole, although it had nothing to do with him missing part of a limb.

"I didn't want to impose," she said. "That is the only why of it. You are comely to me with or without your lower leg."

Surprise flickered over his features, and then an odd pumping sound came out of him . . . a purr. "It's no imposition. If you want to take my vein, I'll give it you."

She stood motionless, held still by the look in his eyes and the way the features of his face changed as something came into his expression that she'd never seen on anyone's face before.

She wanted him, she thought. Badly.

"Kneel," he said in a dark voice.

As Cormia sank down onto her knees, the brush fell out of her hand. Without a word, the Primale leaned into her, his huge arms going around her. He didn't draw her to him. He undid her hair, all of it, the chignon and then the braid.

He growled as he fanned her hair out around her shoulders, and she became aware that his body was trembling. Without warning, he grabbed the back of her neck and pulled her into his throat.

"Take from me," he demanded.

Cormia let out a hiss that sounded like a cobra, and before she

knew what she was doing, she nailed her fangs into his jugular. As she struck, he barked out a curse and his body jumped.

Holy mother of Words . . . His blood was a fire, first in her mouth then down in her gut, an all-powerful wave that filled her out from the inside, giving her a strength she'd never known before.

"Harder," he bit out. "Suck me. . . ."

She ran her arms under his and sank her nails into his back and took great pulls from his vein. She grew dizzy—no, wait, he was pushing her backward, taking her down onto the floor. She didn't care what he did to her or where they ended up, because his taste was all-consuming as she consumed him. All she knew was the fountain of his life at her lips and down her throat and in her belly, and that was all she needed to know.

Robes . . . her robes were being pushed up to her hips. Thighs . . . hers parting, this time hers parting by his hands . . .

Yes.

Phury's brain was up on a shelf somewhere, way out of the reach of his body, way out of sight. He was all instinct with his female's feeding, his cock on the verge of coming, his sole focus on getting inside of her before it did.

Everything about her, about him, was suddenly different. And urgent.

He needed himself in her in as many ways as possible, and not just the temporary kind of *in* that sex provided. He needed to leave himself behind, mark her up good, get his blood and his come in her, and then repeat the process again tomorrow and the day after and the day after that. He had to be all over her so that every fucking asshole on the planet knew that if they got near her they were going to tangle with him until they spit their teeth out and needed splints for their arms and legs.

Mine.

Phury yanked the robing out of the way of her sex and— Oh, yeah, there it was. He could feel the heat come up and—

"*Fuck*," he groaned. She was wet, welling up, overflowing.

If there had been any way to keep her at his vein while he went down on her, he would have shifted around in a heartbeat. The best he could do was whip his hand up and shove it into his mouth and suck. . . .

Phury shuddered at the taste, licking and drawing at his fingers as his hips pushed forward and the head of his cock nudged at the entrance of her core.

Just as he pressed in and felt her flesh give way to his . . . that goddamn, motherfucking Primale medallion went off on the bureau right next to them. Loud as a fire alarm.

Ignore it, ignore it, ignore—

Cormia's mouth broke its seal on his throat, and her eyes, wide, fuzzy with bloodlust and sex, lifted to the sound of the rattling. "What is that?"

"Nothing."

The thing shook even harder, as if it were protesting. Either that or celebrating the fact that it had ruined the moment.

Maybe it was in with the wizard.

Ya welcome, the wizard sang out.

Phury rolled off Cormia, covering her up as he did. With a nasty, vicious stream of curses, he pushed himself back until he was leaning against his bed and cradling his head in his hands.

Both of them panted while that slug of gold banged around the brush set.

The sound of the thing reminded him that there was no privacy between him and Cormia. The mantle of tradition and circumstance was all around them, and anything they did had huge repercussions that were greater than just feeding and sex between a male and a female.

Cormia got to her feet as if she knew exactly what he was thinking. "Thank you for the gift of your vein."

There was nothing he could say in response. His throat was too full of frustration and curses.

As the door shut behind her, he knew precisely why he'd stopped, and it had nothing to do with the interruption. Had he wanted to, he could have kept going.

But thing was, if he slept with her, he had to sleep with them all.

He reached up to the bedside table, got a blunt, and lit it.

If he slept with Cormia, there was no going back. He had to create forty Bellas . . . impregnate forty Chosen and leave them at the mercy of the birthing bed.

He had to be a lover to all of them and a father to all their children and a leader for all their traditions, when he felt as though he could barely get through the days and nights with only himself to worry about.

Phury stared at the glowing tip of the hand-rolled. It was a shock to realize that he would have taken Cormia if it had just been about them. He wanted her that much.

He frowned. Jesus . . . he'd wanted her all along, hadn't he.

But it was more than that. Wasn't it.

He thought of her brushing out his hair, and realized with a shock that she had actually managed to calm him in those moments—and not just through the strokes of the brush, either. Her very presence eased him, from her jasmine scent, to the way she moved so fluidly, to the soft sound of her voice.

No one, not even Bella, could ease him down. Make the cage of his ribs loosen. Allow him to take a deep breath.

Cormia could.

Cormia did.

Which meant that at this point he craved her on pretty much every godforsaken level he had.

And doesn't that make her a lucky girl, the wizard drawled. *Hey, why don't you tell her that you want to turn her into your new drug of choice. She'll be thrilled to know that she can be your next addiction, used to try and get you out of your fucked-up head.*

She'll be thrilled, mate, because that's every lass's dream—and besides, we all know how you're the king of healthy relationships. A real golden-boy winner in that department.

Phury let his head fall back, inhaled hard, and held the smoke until his lungs burned like a brush fire.

TWELVE

That evening, as night fell across Caldwell and did absolutely nothing to improve the humidity, Mr. D stood in the hot upstairs bathroom of the farmhouse and peeled off a bandage he'd applied hours and hours earlier to his gut. The gauze was stained black. The patch of skin underneath was much improved.

At least one thing was workin' for him, although it was only the one. Less than twenty-four hours as the *Fore-lesser* and he felt like someone had pissed in his truck's gas tank, fed his dog rotten meat, and lit his barn on fire.

He should have stayed just a soldier.

Although it wasn't as if he'd had the choice.

He tossed the dirty bandage into the drywall bucket the dead people evidently used as a wastepaper basket and decided not to replace it. The internal damage had been real big, going by how bad it had hurt and how far that black dagger had gone in. But for *lessers*, the intestinal tract was made up of useless meat. That his guts were a sure-fire tangled mess didn't matter none, long as the bleeding was stemmed.

Boy, last night he'd barely got out of that alley alive. If the Brother with the sissy locks hadn't been reined in, Mr. D was darned certain he'd have been deboned like a catfish.

A knocking from downstairs brought his head up. Ten o'clock sharp.

At least they were on time.

He strapped on his heat, picked up his Stetson, and hit the stairs. Outside, there were three trucks and a beater in the dirt drive and two squadrons of *lessers* on the front stoop. As he let the boys in, the fuckers topped him by at least a foot, and he could tell they weren't impressed none too good about his promotion.

"In the living room," he told them.

As the eight of them filed past, he flipped free the holster strap on his gun, palmed the Magnum .357, and leveled it at the last one in the house.

He pulled the trigger once. Twice. Three times.

The sound was like thunder; none of that subtle popping like you got with nines. The slugs went into the small of the *lesser*'s back, obliterating his spine and blowing a hole through the front of his torso. The guy hit the ratty rug with a thump, a little cloud of dust wafting up.

As Mr. D reholstered his weapon, he wondered when the place had last been vacuumed. Probably back when it had been built.

"I'm 'fraid I have to get m' spurs on," he said as he stepped around the writhing slayer.

While oily black blood oozed out on the brown rug, Mr. D put his foot on the slayer's head and pulled out the wallpaper section the Omega had burned the target's image onto.

"I want to make sure I got y'all's attention last night," he said as he held the thing up. "You find this male. Or I'ma pick you off one by one and start with a new crew."

The slayers stared at him in collective silence, like they had one brain and it was spinning to come to terms with a new world order.

"Y'all stop looking at me and look at this right chere, now." He jogged the picture. "Bring him to me. Alive. Or I swear to my Lord and savior that I will find me some new hound dogs and feed strips of you to 'em. We all on the same page here?"

One by one, they nodded as the downed man moaned.

"Good." Mr. D pointed the Magnum's muzzle at the *lesser*'s head and blew that fucker to smithereens. "Now let's get movin'."

About fifteen miles to the east, in the underground training center's locker room, John Matthew fell in love. Which was not something he expected to happen in that particular place.

"Kicks from Ed Hardy," Qhuinn said, as he held out a pair of sneakers. "For you."

John reached out and took them. Okay, they were hot. Black. White soled. Skull on each one with Hardy's siggy in rainbow colors.

"Whoa," one of the other trainees said on his way out of the locker room. "Where'd you get those?"

Qhuinn jogged his eyebrows at the guy. "Spank, huh?"

They were Qhuinn's, John thought. Probably something he was really dying to wear and had saved up for.

"Try 'em on, John."

They're awesome, but really, I can't.

As the last of their classmates filed out, the door eased shut and Qhuinn's bravado eased off. He grabbed the sneakers, put them at John's feet, and looked up.

"I'm sorry for busting on you last night. You know, at A and F, with that girl . . . I was a prick."

It's cool.

"No, it isn't. I was in a bad mood and I took it out on you, and that is *not* cool."

See, this was the thing with Qhuinn. He could be out there and he could let his edge get away from him, but he always came back and made you feel like you were the single most important person in the world to him and that he was truly sorry for hurting your feelings.

You're a freak. But I really can't accept these—

"Were you raised in a barn? Don't be ruuuuuuuuuuuuude, my boy. They're a gift."

Blay shook his head. "Take them, John. You're just going to lose this argument, and it will save us from the theatrics."

"Theatrics?" Qhuinn leaped up and assumed a Roman oratory pose. "Whither thou knowest thy ass from thy elbow, young scribe?"

Blay blushed. "Come on—"

Qhuinn threw himself at Blay, grasping onto the guy's shoulders and hanging his full weight off him. "Hold me. Your insult has left me breathless. I'm agasp."

Blay grunted and scrambled to keep Qhuinn up off the floor. "That's agape."

"Agasp sounds better."

Blay was trying not to smile, trying not to be delighted, but his eyes were sparkling like sapphires and his cheeks were getting red.

With a silent laugh, John sat on one of the locker room benches, shook out his pair of white socks, and pulled them on under his new old jeans.

You sure, Qhuinn? 'Cuz I have a feeling they're going to fit and you might change your mind.

Qhuinn abruptly lifted himself off Blay and straightened his clothes with a sharp tug. "And now you offend my honor." Facing off at John, he flipped into a fencing stance. "Touché."

Blay laughed. "That's *en garde*, you damn fool."

Qhuinn shot a look over his shoulder. "*Ça va*, Brutus?"

"*Et tu!*"

"That would be *tutu*, I believe, and you can keep the cross-

dressing to yourself, ya perv." Qhuinn flashed a brilliant smile, all twelve kinds of proud for being such an ass. "Now, put the fuckers on, John, and let's be done with this. Before we have to put Blay in an iron lung."

"Try sanitarium!"

"No, thanks, I had a big lunch."

The sneakers fit perfectly and somehow made John feel taller, even though he had yet to stand up in them.

Qhuinn nodded and made like he was sizing up a masterpiece. "They look tight. You know, maybe we should rough your threads up a little. Get you wearing some chains. Hey, pierce your shit like mine and add more black—"

"You know why Qhuinn likes black?"

They all whipped their heads around and looked to the shower. Lash was coming out of it, white towel held in front of his privates, water dripping off his heavy shoulders.

"It's because Qhuinn's color-blind, isn't that right, cuz." Lash sauntered over to his locker and flipped the thing open so it slapped against its neighbor. "He only knows he's got mismatched eyes because people tell him so."

John stood up, noting absently that the sneaks had awesome traction. Which, considering the way Qhuinn was glaring at Lash's bare ass, might be a useful thing in about a second and a half.

"Yeah, Qhuinn's *special*, aren't you." Lash pulled on a pair of camo pants and a muscle shirt, then made a show of sliding a gold signet ring onto his left forefinger. "Some people don't fit in and never will. It's sad as fuck that they keep trying to."

Blay whispered, "Let's go, Qhuinn."

Qhuinn gritted his teeth. "You need to shut your hole, Lash. For real."

John stepped into his buddy's grille and signed, *Let's just go to Blay's and chill, okay?*

"Hey, John, a question just occurred to me. When you were raped in the stairwell by that human guy, did you scream with your hands? Or just breathe really hard?"

John went devastation-still. As did his two friends.

No one moved. No one breathed.

The locker room became so quiet that the dripping from the communal shower sounded like a snare drum.

Lash shut his locker door with a smile and looked at the two others. "I read his medical file. It's all in there. He was sent to Havers's for therapy because he was exhibiting symptoms of"—Lash did air quotations—"'post-traumatic stress.' So come on, John, when the guy fucked you, did you try to scream? Did you, John?"

Surely. This. Was. A. Nightmare, John thought as his balls shriveled up.

Lash laughed and shoved his feet into combat boots. "Look at you. All three of you struck stupid. It's the cocksucking Retarda-teers."

Qhuinn's voice took a tone it never had before. There was no bravado, no heated anger. It was stone-cold nasty. "You better pray this doesn't get out. To anyone."

"Or what? Come on, Qhuinn, I'm a firstborn son. My father is your father's eldest brother. Do you really think you can touch me? Hmm . . . nah, not so much, my boy. Not so much."

"Not one word, Lash."

"Whatever. If you'll excuse me, I'm going to get ghost. The bunch of you are sucking the will to live right out of me." Lash shut his locker and walked over to the door. Naturally, he paused and looked over his shoulder, smoothing his blond hair. "Bet you didn't scream, John. Bet you asked for more. Bet you begged the—"

John dematerialized.

For the first time in his life, he moved from one spot to another right through the air. Taking form in front of Lash and planting his body against the door to block the guy's exit, he looked back at his friends and bared his fangs. Lash was his and his alone.

When they both nodded, the beat-down began.

Lash was ready for the first punch, all braced with his hands up and his weight on his thighs. So instead of throwing a fist, John ducked, lunged forward, and bear-hugged the bastard's waist, crashing him back into a wall of lockers.

Lash wasn't fazed in the slightest and recovered with a knee crack that nearly broke John's face. Recoiling from the smash, John stumbled back, then reengaged, grabbing Lash's throat, jamming his thumbs up under the guy's chin, and locking in tight. He head-butted Lash's nose, busting that fucker open like a geyser, but Lash didn't give a shit. He smiled through the blood that ran down into his mouth and threw a low rightie gut punch that kicked John's liver up into his lungs.

Fists were traded back and forth, back and forth, as the two of them plowed into banks of lockers and benches and trash bins. At some point, a couple of trainees tried to come in, but Blay and Quinn forced them out and locked the door.

John grabbed onto Lash's hair, reared back, and bit him on top of the shoulder. As he pulled away, flesh tore free, and the two of them spun around while Lash welded his palms together and swung a two-hander square into John's temple. The impact sent him tap-dancing into the shower, but he caught himself before he fell. Unfortunately, his reflexes weren't fast enough to keep him from getting cracked in the jaw.

It was like getting hit with a baseball bat, and he realized Lash had somehow slipped on a pair of old-fashioned brass knuckles—probably because he needed the advantage, given that John was bigger. Another hit landed somewhere on John's face, and suddenly it was the Fourth of July in his head, fireworks everywhere. Before he could blink clear his vision, he got slammed face-first into the tiled wall in the shower and held in place.

Lash reached around to the front of John's pants.

"How about a replay, John-boy?" the guy rasped. "Or do you only like humans in your ass?"

The feel of a big body pressing into his from behind froze John solid.

It should have energized him. It should have sent him wild. Instead, he became the frail boy he'd been, helpless and terrified and at the mercy of someone much, much bigger. He was instantly where he'd been in that decrepit stairwell, pushed against the wall, trapped, overpowered.

Tears sprang to his eyes. No, not this . . . not this again—

From out of nowhere, a war cry came, and the weight was lifted from him.

John fell to his knees and threw up on the wet tile floor.

When his retching receded, he let himself fall onto his side and twisted into a fetal position, shaking like the nancy he was—

Lash was down on the tile right next to him . . . and his throat was cut wide-open.

The guy was trying to breathe, trying to hold his blood in, and it wasn't working.

John looked up in horror.

Qhuinn stood above them both, panting. In his right hand was a bloody hunting knife.

"Oh, Jesus . . ." Blay said. "What the fuck did you do, Qhuinn?"

This was bad. This was life-altering bad. For all of them. What had started as a brawl . . . had likely ended up as a murder.

John opened his mouth to holler for help. Naturally, nothing came out.

"I'll get someone," Blay said, and ran out.

John sat up, whipped off his shirt, and leaned over Lash. Taking the guy's hands away, he pressed what had been on his back to the open wound and prayed the blood would stop. Lash met his eyes, then brought his own hands up as if to help.

Lie still, John mouthed. *Just lie still. I can hear people coming.*

Lash coughed and blood came out of his mouth, spattering over his lower lip and running down his chin. Shit, the red stuff was everywhere.

But they had done this before, John told himself. The two of them had fought right here in this shower, and the drain had run red then, too, and it had been okay.

Not this time, a voice inside of him warned. *Not this time . . .*

A roar of panic flared, and he started to pray for Lash to live. Then he prayed for time to go backward. Then he wished for this to be a dream. . . .

Someone was standing over him and saying his name.

"John?" He looked up. It was Doc Jane, the Brotherhood's private physician, and Vishous's *shellan*. Her translucent, ghostly face was calm, her voice even and soothing. As she knelt down, she became as solid as he was. "John, I need you to step back so I can get a look at him, okay? I want you to let go and step back. You've done a good job, but I need to take care of him now."

He nodded. But even still, she had to touch his hands to get him to release his hold on his shirt.

Someone picked him up off his knees. Blay. Yeah, it was Blay. He could tell by the guy's aftershave. Jump by Joop!

There were a lot of other people in the locker room. Rhage was just inside the shower, and next to him was V. Butch was there.

Qhuinn . . . where was Qhuinn?

John looked around and found him across the way. The bloody knife was gone from his hand, and Zsadist was next to the guy, looming.

Qhuinn was paler than the white tile, his mismatched eyes unblinking as he stared at Lash.

"You're under house arrest at your parents'," Zsadist said to Qhuinn. "If he dies, you're up for murder."

Rhage went over to Qhuinn, as if thinking that Z's hard tone wasn't helping the sitch. "Come on, son, let's get your stuff from your locker."

Rhage was the one who led Qhuinn out of the locker room, and Blay followed them.

John stayed right where he was. Please let Lash live, he thought. Please . . .

Man, he didn't like the way Doc Jane kept shaking her head as she worked on the guy, her doctor's bag cracked open, instruments flying as she tried to stitch up Lash's neck.

"Tell me."

John jumped and turned his head. It was Z.

"Tell me how it happened, John."

John looked back down at Lash and replayed the scene. Oh, Jesus . . . he didn't want to go into the whys. Even though Zsadist knew about his past, he couldn't bring himself to tell the Brother the reason Qhuinn had hard-cored it.

Maybe it was because he still couldn't believe his past had come out like that. Maybe it was because the old nightmare had just been renewed.

Maybe it was because he was a pussy who couldn't man up for his friends.

Z's deformed lip tightened. "Listen, John, Qhuinn's in deep shit. Legally he's still a minor, but that's assault with a deadly against a first son. The family is going to come gunning for him even if Lash survives, and we're going to need to know what happened here."

Doc Jane stood up. "He's closed, but he's at risk for stroke. I want him to go to Havers's. *Stat.*"

Z nodded and called forward two *doggen*, who had a gurney between them. "Fritz is ready with the car, and I'll be going with them."

As Lash was lifted up off the tile, the Brother pegged John with grim eyes. "You want to save your friend, you're going to need to tell us what went down."

John watched the group roll Lash out of the locker room.

As the door eased shut, his knees wobbled, and he looked at the pool of blood in the center of the shower.

Over in the corner of the locker room, there was a hose that was used for the daily cleaning of the facilities. John forced his feet to go across to where the thing was mounted on the wall. Uncoiling it, he turned the water on, pulled the head over into the shower, then twisted the nozzle open. He swept the spray back and forth, back and forth, moving inch by inch, chasing the blood away toward the drain, where it was swallowed with a gurgle.

Back and forth. Back and forth.

The tile went from red to pink to white. But it didn't clean up the mess. Not in the fucking slightest.

THIRTEEN

Phury felt hands on his skin, small, light-fingered hands, and they were traveling down his belly. They were headed for the juncture of his thighs, and thank God for that. His arousal was swollen and hot and hungry for release, and the closer the hands got to it, the more his hips pushed up and retreated back, his ass clenching and releasing as it gave in to the thrusting he was dying to do.

His cock wept—he could feel the wetness on his stomach. Or maybe he'd already come once?

Oh, those hands, just tickling across his skin. That special feathery touch made his arousal strain even harder, as if it could reach out and get in the way if it tried hard enough.

Small hands, heading for his—

Phury woke up on a body jerk that sent his pillow popping off the bed.

"*Shit.*"

Underneath the roll of blankets, his cock throbbed, and not with the usual ambient need that was a male's evening wake-up call. No . . . this was specific. His body wanted something very specific from one particular female.

Cormia.

She's right next door, he pointed out to himself.

And what a prize you are, the wizard shot back. *Why don't you go to her, mate. I'm sure she'll be just thrilled to see you after the way you let her leave last night. Not a word to her. Not even an acknowledgment of her gratitude to you.*

Not able to argue with that, Phury looked to the chaise.

It was the first time he had ever fed a female.

As he felt for her bite mark on his neck, he noted that it was gone, healed away.

One of life's great milestones had been met . . . and it saddened him. Not that he regretted it was with her. Not at all. But he wished he had told her that she was his first at the time.

Pushing his hair out of his eyes, he looked at the clock. Midnight. *Midnight?* Man, he'd been asleep for about eight hours, clearly because of the feeding. He didn't feel refreshed, though. His stomach was rolling and his head was pounding.

As he reached for the wake-up blunt he'd prepared before he'd crashed, he stopped short. His hand was shaking so badly, he doubted he could pick the thing up, and he stared at his palm, willing it to still, making no impression whatsoever.

It took him three tries to get the hand-rolled off the bedside table, and he watched his fumbles from a distance, as if it were someone else's hand, someone else's blunt. Once the twist of leaves and paper was between his lips, he struggled to get his lighter in position and work the flint wheel.

Two tokes in and the shaking stopped. The headache evaporated. His stomach calmed.

Unfortunately, another rattling went off across the room and all three came back: The Primale medallion went into its dance routine on the bureau again.

He left the thing where it was and worked his way through the blunt, thinking about Cormia. He doubted she would have told him she needed to feed. What had happened during the daylight hours in this room had been a spur-of-the-moment combustion generated by her bloodlust, and he couldn't take it as evidence that she wanted him sexually. She hadn't turned away from the sex last night, true, but that was very different from her wanting him, wasn't it. Need was not the same as choice. She'd needed his blood. He'd needed her body.

The Chosen needed both of them to get with the program.

Stabbing out what little was left of the hand-rolled, he stared across his bedroom at the bureau. The medallion had finally stalled out.

It took him less than ten minutes to shower, dress in white silks, and put the Primale medallion's leather thong over his head. As the slab of gold settled between his pecs, its weight was warm, probably because of its workout.

He traveled directly to the Other Side, having special dispensation as Primale to skip being routed through the Scribe Virgin's courtyard. Taking form in front of the Sanctuary's amphitheater, where the whole thing had started five months ago, he found it hard to believe he really had taken Vishous's place as Primale.

It was kind of like looking at his shaky hand: This just wasn't him.

Yeah, except it totally was.

Up ahead, the white stage with its heavy white curtain glowed in the odd, relentless light of the Other Side. Here there were no shadows, as there was no sun in the pale sky, and yet there was plenty of illumination, as if everything were its own light source. The temperature was seventy degrees, neither too hot nor too cold, and there was no breeze to brush over your skin or ruffle your clothes. Everything was a soft, eye-soothing white.

The place was the landscape equivalent of Muzak.

Walking over cropped white grass, he headed around the back of the Greco-Roman theater toward the various temples and living quarters. On the fringes, all around, there was a white forest bracketing the compound that cut off any long vistas. He wondered what was on the far side of it. Probably nothing. The Sanctuary had the feel of an architect's model or a train set, as if, were you to walk to the edge, all you would find was a steep drop-off to some giant's wall-to-wall-carpeted floor.

As he went along, he wasn't sure how to get the Directrix's attention, but he wasn't in a big hurry to make that happen. To delay, he went to the Primale's temple and used his gold medallion to unlock the double doors. After stepping through the white marble foyer, he went into the temple's single, lofty room and stared at the bedding platform with its white satin sheets.

He remembered what Cormia had looked like tied down naked, a white sheet falling from above and pooling at her throat to mask her face. He had torn the thing down and been horrified to meet her tear-filled, terrified eyes.

She'd been gagged.

He looked up to the ceiling, where the draping that had covered her face had been hung. There were two tiny gold hooks embedded in the marble. He wanted to take them out with a fucking jackhammer.

As he stared upward, he randomly thought back to a conversation he'd had with Vishous right before all the shit had gone down with this Primale business. The two of them had been in the dining room at the mansion, and V had said something about having had a vision of Phury.

Phury hadn't wanted deets, but they'd come out anyway, and the words the Brother had spoken were oddly clear to him now, like a recording replayed: *I saw you standing at a crossroads in a field of white. It was a stormy day . . . yeah, lots of storms. But when you took a cloud from the sky and wrapped it around the well, the rain stopped falling.*

Phury narrowed his eyes on those two hooks. He'd torn the sheet down from there and wrapped Cormia in it. And she had stopped crying.

She was the well . . . the well that he was supposed to fill. She was the future of the race, the source of new Brothers and new Chosen. The fountainhead.

As were all of her sisters.

"Your Grace."

He turned around. The Directrix was standing in the doorway of the temple, her long white robe brushing the floor, her dark hair coiled up high on her head. With her calm smile and the peace that radiated from her eyes, she had the beatific expression of the spiritually enlightened.

He envied all that serene conviction.

Amalya bowed to him, her body lean and elegant in its Chosen dress code. "I am pleased to see you."

He bowed back to her. "And I you."

"Thank you for this audience." She straightened and there was a pause.

He didn't fill it.

When she finally did, she seemed to be choosing her words carefully. "I thought perhaps you might wish to meet some of the other Chosen?"

What kind of meeting did she have in mind, he wondered.

Oh, just a bit of high tea, the wizard chimed in. *With cunnilingus sandwiches and sixty-nine scones and handfuls of your nuts.*

"Cormia's doing well," he said, deflecting the meet-and-greet offer.

"I saw her yesterday." The Directrix's tone was kind but neutral, as if she didn't agree with him.

"You did?"

She bowed low again. "Forgive me, Your Grace. It was the anniversary of her birthing, and I was required by custom to give her a

scroll. When I didn't hear from you, I appeared to her. I tried to reach you again during the day."

Good Lord, Cormia's birthday had come and gone and she'd said nothing about it?

She had told John, though, hadn't she. That was what the bracelet had been for.

Phury wanted to curse. He should have gotten her something.

He cleared his throat. "I'm sorry I didn't respond."

Amalya righted herself. "It is your purview. Please, worry not."

In the long silence that followed, he read the question in the Directrix's kind eyes. "No, it's not done yet."

The female's shoulders sagged. "Has she denied you?"

He thought back to the floor in front of his chaise. He'd been the one who had stopped. "No. It's me."

"No fault could ever be yours."

"Untrue. And trust me on that one."

The Directrix walked around, her hands worrying the medallion around her neck. The thing was an exact copy of what he had on, only hers was suspended from a white satin ribbon, and the chain to his ball was black.

She paused by the bed, her fingers lightly brushing a pillow. "I thought perhaps you would like to meet some of the others."

Oh, hell, no. He wasn't passing over Cormia for a different First Mate. "I can guess where you're going with this, but it's not that I don't want her."

"Perhaps, though, you should like to meet another."

This was clearly as close as the Directrix was going to get to putting her foot down and making a demand that he either have sex with Cormia or get another First Mate. He couldn't say he was surprised. It had been five long months.

God, maybe it would solve some problems. Trouble was, taking another First Mate would be tantamount to laying a curse on

Cormia. The Chosen would see her as having failed, and she would feel the same way, even though that wouldn't be the case at all.

"Like I said, I'm good with Cormia."

"Indeed . . . except might you perhaps be more likely to engage if it were a different one among us? Layla, for instance, is quite fair of visage and limb, and she is trained as an *ehros*."

"Not going to do that to Cormia. It would kill her."

"Your Grace . . . she suffers now. I saw it within her eyes." The Directrix drifted over to him. "And moreover, the rest of us are trapped within our tradition. We had such great hopes that our functions would return to where they have always been. If you take another as First Mate and complete the ritual, you release all of us from this burden of futility, and that includes Cormia. She is not happy, Your Grace. Any more than you are."

He thought of her again on that bed, tied down. . . . She hadn't wanted this from the very beginning, had she?

He thought of her so quiet in the mansion. He thought of her not feeling comfortable enough to tell him that she had to feed. He thought of her saying nothing about her birthday. Nothing about her wanting to go outside. Nothing about those constructions in her bedroom.

One stroll down a hallway didn't make up for all he'd abandoned her to.

"We are trapped, Your Grace," the Directrix said. "As it stands now, we are all trapped."

What if he was holding on to Cormia because, if she was his First Mate, he didn't have to worry about the whole sex thing? Sure, he wanted to protect her and do right by her, and those were honorable truths, but the ramifications protected him as well.

There were Chosen who wanted it, wanted him. He'd felt their stares when he'd been sworn in.

He had given his word. And he was getting damn tired of breaking oaths that he'd made.

"Your Grace, may I ask you to come with me? I wish to show you a place here in the Sanctuary."

He followed Amalya out of the Primale Temple, and the two of them were silent as they walked down the hill toward a thicket of four-story white structures with columns.

"These are the Chosen's living quarters," she murmured, "but you and I are not bound for them."

Good thing, he thought, glancing over.

As he passed by, he noted that none of the windows was glassed in, and he imagined there was no reason for the bother. There were no bugs or animals . . . no rain, either, he guessed. And what the lack of panes meant, of course, was that there were no barriers between him and the Chosen who stared back at him from their quarters.

There was one female in every window of every room in each of the buildings.

Oh, Jesus.

"Here we are." The Directrix stopped in front of a one-story structure and unlocked a pair of double doors. As she opened them wide, his heart fell.

Cribs. Rows and rows of empty white cribs.

As he tried to keep breathing, the Directrix's voice grew wistful. "This used to be such a place of joy, filled with life, teeming with the future. If you would only take another— Are you unwell, Your Grace?"

Phury backed away. He couldn't breathe. He couldn't . . . breathe.

"Your Grace?" She reached out.

He jerked away from her. "I'm fine."

Breathe, damn it. Breathe.

This was what you agreed to. Man up.

In his mind, the wizard served up example after example of him letting people down, starting in the present with Z and Wrath and that shit about the *lessers,* then going all the way back into the past to his failures with his parents.

He was deficient everywhere in his life, trapped everywhere, too. At least Cormia could be free of this. Free of him.

The Directrix's voice grew tight with alarm. "Your Grace, perhaps you might have a lie-down—"

"I'll take another."

"You'll—"

"I'll take another First Mate."

The Directrix seemed stunned, but then bowed deeply. "Your Grace, thank you . . . thank you. . . . Verily you are the strength of the race and leader to us all. . . ."

He let her go on and on singing empty praises while his head spun and he felt like a load of dry ice had been dumped in his gut.

The Directrix clasped her medallion, joy suffusing her serene face. "Your Grace, what do you favor in a mate? I have a couple in mind."

He pegged Amalya with hard eyes. "They have to want this. No coercion. No binds. They have to want it. Cormia didn't, and that wasn't fair to her. I volunteered for this, she didn't have a choice."

The Directrix put her hand on his arm. "I understand, and moreover, I agree. Cormia was never suited for her role, had in fact been anointed as First Mate specifically for that cause by the previous Directrix. I shall never be so cruel."

"And Cormia will be okay. I mean, she's not kicked out of here, correct?"

"She shall be welcomed back herein. She is a fine female. Just not . . . as well suited to this life as some of us are."

In the quiet heartbeats that followed, he had an image of her undressing him for the shower, her guileless, innocent green eyes looking up at him as she fumbled with his belt and his leathers.

She only wanted to do what was right. Back when this whole mess had gotten started, even though she'd been terrified, she would have done the right thing by her tradition and taken him in her. Which made her stronger than him, didn't it. She wasn't running. He was the one with the track shoes on.

"You tell the others I was not worthy of her." As the Directrix's mouth fell open, he pointed his finger at her. "That's a goddamned order. You tell them . . . she is too good for me. I want her elevated to a special rank. . . . I want her fucking enshrined, do you understand me? You do right by her or I'll bust this place into ruins."

While the Directrix's mind clearly scrambled, he helped her sort shit out by reminding her, "This is my world here. I call the shots, do I not. I'm the strength of the goddamn race, so you do what I tell you. Now nod."

When she did, his chest eased up. "Good. Glad we agree. Now, do we need to do another ceremony?"

"Ah . . . ah, when you said the words t-to Cormia, you bound yourself to all of us." She put her hand on her medallion again but this time he had a feeling it wasn't with joy. More like she needed a little reassurance. "When will you . . . be coming here to stay?"

He thought of Bella's pregnancy. He couldn't miss the birth, and with the way things stood between him and Z, he might not even be told. "Not for a while. Could be up to a year."

"Then I shall send the first of them to you on the far side, shall I?"

"Yeah." He turned away from the nursery, feeling like he still needed more air. "Listen, I'm going to walk around a bit."

"I'll tell the others to leave you to your privacy."

"Thanks, and I'm sorry for being such a hard-ass." He paused. "One last thing . . . I want to talk to Cormia. I'm going to tell her."

"As you wish." The Directrix bowed low. "I shall need a couple of days to ritually prepare—"

"Just let me know when you're sending one of them over."

"Yes, Your Grace."

When she left, he stared out over the white landscape, and after a moment, the expanse changed before his eyes, shifting into another view entirely. Gone were the well-ordered, colorless trees and the grass that looked as if it were covered in fine snow. Instead, he saw the choked gardens of his family's home back in the Old Country.

Out behind the vast stone house he'd grown up in, there had been a walled-off garden about two acres in size. Split into quadrants by pebbled walkways, it had been intended to showcase specimen plantings and offer a place of natural beauty to calm the mind. The masonry wall that corralled the landscape had been marked by four statues at its corners, the figures reflecting the stages of life, from an infant in his father's arms, to a strapping young male standing on his own, to that male holding a young in his own arms, to him seated in his aged wisdom with his grown son standing behind him.

When the garden had first been constructed, it must have been truly elegant, a real showplace, and Phury could imagine the joy of his parents as they had looked over its splendor as newly mateds.

He had known none of the perfections promised in the fine bones of the layout. What he had seen of the garden had been only the chaos of neglect. By the time he was old enough to be aware of his surroundings, the beds were overgrown with weeds, the reflection benches were wading in algae water, and grass had overtaken the walkways. Saddest to him were the statues. Ivy tangled around them, consuming them more thickly each year, the leaves obscuring more and more of what the sculptor's hand had wanted to show.

The garden was the visual representation of his family's ruination.

And he had wanted to fix it. All of it.

After his transition, which had nearly killed him, he had walked away from the shambles of the family home, and he could remember the leaving as clearly as he saw in his mind that wretched garden. The night of his departure had been marked by an October full moon, and he had packed some of his father's old, fine clothes by its brilliant light.

Phury had had only a loose plan: to pick up on the trail his father had let grow cold. On the night of Zsadist's abduction, it had been clear which nursery maid had taken the young, and Ahgony, as any father would, had gone after her with a vengeance. She had been smart, however, and he had found nothing concrete until about two

years thereafter. Following tips and leads and the ramblings of gossips, the Brother had scoured the Old Country and eventually located Zsadist's baby blanket in the things of the female—who had died only a week prior.

The near miss was just another page in the tragedy.

It was at that point that Ahgony had been informed that his young had been picked up by a neighbor and sold into the slavery market. The neighbor had taken the money and run, and though Ahgony had gone to the nearest slave dealer, there were too many parentless infants being bought and traded to track Zsadist down.

Ahgony had given up and gone home and started to drink.

As Phury prepared to take up his father's search, it seemed appropriate to wear the suits and silks of his elder. Important, too. Appearing the penniless gentleman would make it easier to infiltrate the great houses, which were where slaves were held. In his father's old wardrobe, Phury could be just another well-mannered vagrant, looking to pay for his keep with his wit and his charm.

Dressed in twenty-five-year-old fashion, and with a battered leather clothing case in his hand, he'd gone to both of his parents to tell them what he was doing.

He knew his mother was in her bed in the basement of the house, because that was where she lived. He also knew she wouldn't look at him as he entered. She never did, and he hadn't blamed her for that. He was the exact replica of the one that had been stolen, the walking, talking, breathing reminder of the tragedy. That he was an individual and separate from Zsadist, that he mourned the loss as she did because he'd been missing half of himself ever since his twin had been taken, that he needed nurturing and caring, was beyond her because of her own pain.

His mother had never touched him. Not once, even to bathe him when he had been young.

After knocking on her door, Phury had been careful to tell her who it was before he entered so she could brace herself accordingly.

When she didn't answer, he opened the door and stood in her doorway, filling the jamb with his newly transitioned body. As he'd told her about what he was going to do, he wasn't sure what exactly he expected from her, but he got nothing. Not a single word. She didn't even lift her head from her tattered pillow.

He'd closed the door and gone across the way to his father's quarters.

The male had been out cold, dead drunk among the bottles of cheap ale that kept him, if not sane, then at least non compos mentis enough not to think too much. After trying to rouse him, Phury had scribbled a note, left it on his father's chest, then gone upstairs and out of the house.

Standing on the pitted, leaf-strewn terrace of the family's once-grand house, he had listened to the night. He knew there was a good possibility he would never see his parents again, and he was worried that the one *doggen* who remained would either die or get injured. And then what would they do?

Staring out over the majesty that had once been, he sensed his twin was somewhere in the night, waiting to be found.

As a streak of milky clouds drifted free of the moon's face, Phury had searched deep in himself for some kind of strength.

Verily, a low voice had said inside of his skull, *you could search until a thousand morns arrive, and even find the breathing body of your twin, yet it is certain you shall not save what cannot be rescued. You are not up to this task, and moreover, your destiny decrees that you shall fail no matter the goal, as you bring with you the curse of the* exhile dhoble.

It was the wizard speaking for the first time.

And as the words sunk into him, with him feeling far too weak for the journey ahead, he took his vow of celibacy. Looking up to the great shining disk in the blue-black sky, he'd sworn to the Scribe Virgin that he would keep himself apart from all distractions. He would be the clean and focused savior. He would be the hero who brought his twin back. He would be the healer who resurrected the sad, tan-

gled mess of his family and returned them to their former state of health and beauty.

He would be the gardener.

Phury came back to the present as the wizard spoke up. *But I was right, was I not? Your parents both died early and in misery, your twin was used like a whore, and you're a head case.*

I was right, wasn't I, mate.

Phury refocused on the eerie white expanse of the Other Side. It was so perfect, everything in order, nothing out of bounds. The white tulips with their white stems stayed within their beds around the buildings. The trees didn't breach the forest's edge. There wasn't a weed to be seen.

He wondered who mowed their lawn, and had a feeling the grass, like all the rest of it, just grew that way.

Must be nice.

FOURTEEN

Back at the Brotherhood's mansion, Cormia checked the clock on her bureau again. John Matthew had been due to come for her an hour ago to watch a movie, and she hoped nothing had gone wrong.

Pacing around a little more, she found that her room seemed way too small tonight, way too crowded, even though it had no new furniture and she was all alone.

Dearest Virgin Scribe, she had too much energy.

It was the Primale's blood.

That and a crushing, unsatisfied urgency.

She stopped by the window, put her fingertips to her lips, and remembered the taste of him, the feel of him. What a mad rush, what a glorious ecstasy. But why had he stopped? That question had been swirling in her head. Why had he gone no further? Yes, the medallion had summoned him, but as Primale everything was on his

terms. He was the strength of the race, the ruler of the Chosen, free to ignore any and all at his will.

The only answer she had made her sick to her stomach. Had it been his feelings for Bella? Had he believed that he was betraying the one he loved?

It was hard to know what was worse: him being with her and all her sisters, or him being with none of them because his heart was held by another.

Looking out at the night, she was sure she was going to go crazy if she stayed in her room, and the pool with its undulating surface caught her eye. The gentle waving motion reminded her of the deep baths on the other side, promising a peaceful respite from all that was on her mind.

Cormia was at her door and out in the hall before she knew she'd left her bedroom. Moving quickly and silently in her bare feet, she took the grand staircase down to the foyer and crossed the mosaic floor. In the billiards room, she used the door John had let them out of the night before and stepped free of the house.

Standing on the cool stones of the terrace, she let her senses reach into the darkness and ran her eyes down what she could see of the massive wall at the edge of the property. There seemed to be no danger. Nothing moved among the flowers and trees of the garden except the thick night air.

She glanced back up at the massive house. Lights glowed in leaded windows, and she could see *doggen* moving around. There were plenty of folks close by should she need help.

She closed the door most of the way, picked up the skirting of her robes, and jogged across the terrace to the water.

The pool was rectangular and ringed with the same flat black stones that covered the terrace. Long chairs made up of woven strips and tables with glass tops. Off to one side, there was a black contraption with a white tank. Flowers in pots added color.

Kneeling down, she measured the water, its surface appearing oily in the moonlight, probably because the pool's belly was lined in more of the black stone. The way it was set up was not like the baths at home; there was no gradual wading in, and she suspected the depths were substantial. You would not get trapped, however. At regular intervals on the sides, there were curving handles that you could use to help yourself free of the water.

Her toe went in first and then her whole foot, the pool's surface rippling out from the penetration, as if the water were clapping in encouragement.

There were stairs over to the left, shallow steps that were clearly the way you went in. She went to them, took off her robe, and walked naked into the pool.

Her heart was pounding, but oh, the luxury of the water's soft buffer. She kept going forward until she was clothed in a gentle, moving embrace from breast to heel.

How lovely it was.

Instinct told her to push off with her feet, and she did, her body slipping forward in a weightless slice. Sending her arms up and out and then drawing them back in, she discovered she could make her way around, going wherever she chose—first to the right, then to the left, then down, down, down to the end, where a thin board over-hung the water.

Finished with exploring, Cormia rolled onto her back and floated along and looked at the sky. The twinkling lights above made her think of her place in the Chosen and of her duty to be one among many, a molecule that was part of a whole. She and her sisters were indistinguish-able within the grand tradition they served: just like this water, seamless and fluid, with no boundaries; just like the stars above, all the same.

Looking up at earth's heaven, she had another one of those ran-dom, heretical thoughts, only this one wasn't about house design or what someone wore or whether she liked a bit of food or didn't.

This one went straight to the core of her and marked her as a sinner and a heretic:

She did not want to be one of many.

Not with the Primale. Not to him.

And not to herself.

Across town, Qhuinn sat on his bed and stared down at the cell phone in his palm. He'd typed out a text that was addressed to both Blay and John, and was just waiting to send the fucker.

He'd been sitting here for what seemed like hours, but had probably just been one at the most. After he'd taken a shower to wash Lash's blood off, he'd planted his ass down and braced himself for what was coming.

For some reason, he kept thinking about the one nice thing he could remember his parents ever doing for him. It had been back about three years ago. He'd been bugging them to be allowed to go to his cousin Sax's in Connecticut for, like, months. Saxton had already gone through his transition and was a little wild, so naturally he was Qhuinn's hero. And naturally, the 'rents didn't approve of Sax or his parents—who were not all that interested in the *glymera*'s self-imposed social wedgies.

Qhuinn had begged and pleaded and whined and gotten a whole lot of nothing for his efforts. And then out of the blue his father had informed him that he was getting his way and going south for the weekend.

Joy. Total fucking joy. He'd packed up three days early, and when he'd gotten in the back of the car after dark and been driven over the border into Connecticut, he'd felt like he was king of the world.

Yeah, it had been nice of his parents.

Course, then he'd learned why they'd done it.

The adventure at Sax's hadn't worked out all that well. He'd ended up drinking up a storm with his cuz during Saturday's daylight hours and had gotten so sick off a lethal combo of Jägermeister and vodka Jell-O shots that Sax's parents had insisted he head home to recover.

Being driven back by one of their *doggen* had been such the ride of shame, and what was worse, he kept having to ask the chauffeur to stop so he could throw up some more. The only saving grace was that Sax's folks had agreed not to tell his parents—on the condition that he make a full confession when he was dropped at his front door. Clearly, they didn't want to deal with his mother and father, either.

As the *doggen* had pulled up in front of the house, Qhuinn had figured he was just going to say he felt ill, which was true, and that he'd asked to come back home, which was not true and never would be true.

Except things didn't go down like that.

Every light in the place had been on, and music had been streaming in the air, coming from a tent set up out back. Candles were lit in every window; people were moving around in every room.

"'Tis a good thing we got you back in time," the *doggen* at the wheel had said in his happy *doggen* voice. "Would be a shame for you to miss this."

Qhuinn had gotten out of the car with his bag and not noticed as the servant drove off.

Of course, he'd thought. His father was stepping down as *leahdyre* of the *glymera* after a distinguished term of service heading the Princeps Council. This was the party to celebrate his work and to mark the passing of the position to Lash's father.

And this was what the staff had been bustling around about for the last couple weeks. He'd just figured his mother was going through another one of her anal, clean-everything periods, but no. All the spic-n-span had been in anticipation of this night.

Qhuinn had headed around to the back of the house, sticking to the shadows thrown by the hedges, his backpack dragging on the ground. It had been so lovely in the tent. Twinkling lights hung from chandeliers and flickered on tables with arrangements of beautiful flowers and candles. Each and every chair had been trimmed out in satin bows, and there were runners down the aisles between the seat-

ing arrangements. He'd imagined the color scheme of everything was turquoise and yellow, reflecting his family's two sides.

He stared at the faces of the partygoers, recognizing each and every one of them. The whole of his bloodline was there, along with the leading families of the *glymera,* and all of the guests were dressed formally, the females in gowns, the males in tuxedoes with tails. There were young darting between the grown-ups like fireflies and the advanced aged sitting on the sidelines smiling.

He had stood there in the darkness and felt like part of the clutter in the house that had gotten shut away before company had come, another useless, ugly object to be stashed in a cupboard so no one saw. And not for the first time had he wanted to take his fingers and press them into his eye sockets and ruin what had ruined him.

Abruptly, the band had gone quiet, and his father had stepped up to the microphone at the head of the parquet dance floor. As all the guests assembled, Qhuinn's mother and brother and sister came up to stand behind his father, the four of them glowing in a way that had nothing to do with all the twinkling lights.

"If I may have your attention," his father had said in the Old Language. "I'd like to take a moment to acknowledge the founding families who are here tonight." Round of applause. "The other members of the Council." Round of applause. "And the rest of you who form the core of the *glymera,* as well as fill out mine bloodline." Round of applause. "These past ten years as *leahdyre* have been challenging, but we've made good progress, and I know that my successor will take the reins with a firm hand. With the king's recent ascension, it is even more paramount that our concerns be marshaled and brought forward with appropriate care. Through the Council's continuing work, we shall see our vision carried outward to the race . . . without regard to meritless dissention from those who do not understand the issues as fully as we do. . . ."

There was resounding approval at this point, followed by a toast to Lash's father. Then Qhuinn's dad had cleared his throat and glanced at the three people behind him. In a slightly hoarse voice, he'd said, "It has been an honor to serve the *glymera* . . . and though I will miss my station, I would be remiss if I didn't admit that having more time for my family pleases me to no end. Verily, they are the seat of my life, and I must needs thank them for the lightness and warmth they bring unto my heart each day."

Qhuinn's mother had blown a kiss and blinked rapidly. His brother had gone all robin-breasted-proud, with hero worship filling his eyes. His sister had clapped and jumped up and down, her ringlets bouncing with joy.

In that moment, the rejection of him as a son and a brother and a family member had been so complete that no words spoken to him or about him could have added to his cringing sadness.

Qhuinn came out of the memories when his father's knock landed sharply on his door, the rap of the knuckles breaking the past's hold, snapping the scene free from his mind.

He hit *send* on the text, put the phone in the pocket of his shirt, and said, "Come in."

It wasn't his father who opened the door.

It was a *doggen*, the same butler who had told him he wasn't to go to the *glymera*'s ball this year.

When the servant bowed, it wasn't intended as a gesture of specific respect, and Qhuinn didn't take it that way. *Doggen* bowed to everyone. Hell, if they interrupted a raccoon raiding the garbage, their first move before getting into all the shooing would be the old bend-at-the-waist routine.

"Guess I'm leaving," Qhuinn said as the butler quickly ran through the hand motions to ward off the evil eye.

"With all due respect," the *doggen* said, with his forehead still pointed to his feet, "your father has requested your departure from the premises."

"Cool." Qhuinn stood up with the duffel bag into which he'd packed his collection of T-shirts and his four pairs of jeans.

As he slung the strap on his shoulder, he wondered how long his cell phone service would be paid for. He'd been waiting for it to get cut off for the past couple months—ever since his allowance had suddenly disappeared.

He had a feeling T-Mobile, like him, was SOL.

"Your father asked that I should give you this." The *doggen* didn't straighten as he extended his hand and held out a thick, business-sized envelope.

The urge to tell the servant to take the damn thing and airmail it up his father's ass was close to irresistible.

Qhuinn took the envelope and opened it. After looking at the papers, he calmly folded them up and put them back inside. Stuffing the thing into the back of his waistband, he said, "I'll just go wait for my ride."

The *doggen* lifted himself up. "At the end of the drive, if you would."

"Yeah. Sure. Fine." Whatever. "You need blood from me, don't you."

"If you would be so kind." The *doggen* held out a brass goblet, the belly of which was lined in black glass.

Qhuinn used his Swiss Army knife, because his hunting one had been confiscated. Streaking the blade across his palm, he made a fist to squeeze some red drops out into the cup.

They were going to burn the stuff when he was out of the house as part of a cleansing ritual.

They weren't just jettisoning the defective; they were getting rid of the evil.

Qhuinn left his room without looking back and headed down the hall. He didn't say good-bye to his sister, even though he heard her practicing her flute, and he left his brother alone to continue reciting Latin verses. He didn't stop by his mother's drawing room when he heard her talking on the phone, either. And he sure as fuck kept going right by his father's study.

They were all in on his evac. The proof was in the envelope.

Down on the first floor, he didn't shut the grand front door loudly. No reason to make a show. They all knew he was leaving, which was why they were all so studiously busy instead of having tea in the family room.

He bet they convened as soon as the *doggen* told them he was out of the house. Bet they had some Earl Grey and sucked back a couple of scones. Bet they breathed a deep, deep sigh of relief, then lamented about how hard it was going to be to hold up their heads after what he'd done to Lash.

Qhuinn wandered down the long, winding drive. When he got to the big iron gates, they were open. After he walked through them, they closed with a clang like they'd booted him in the ass.

The summer night was hot and humid, and lightning flashed off to the north.

The storms always came from the north, he thought, and this was true in both summer and winter. In the cold months, Nor'easters could bury you with so much snow you felt like a—

Wow. He was so rattled, he was talking about the weather with himself.

He put his duffel down on the pavement at the curb.

He supposed he should text Blay now to see if he could, in fact, get picked up. Dematerializing with the weight of his duffel could be tricky and he'd never been given a car, so there you had it. He was going nowhere fast.

Just as he reached for his phone, the thing went off. It was a text from Blay: *U gotta come stay w us. Let me pick u up.*

He started to text his boy back, but then thought about the envelope and stopped. Putting the phone in his duffel, he slung the bag full of his shit back on his shoulder and started walking along the side of the road. He headed east, because with the way the road went, the random choice to go left took him in that direction.

Man . . . now he really was an orphan. It was like his inner suspicions had come true. He'd always thought he was adopted or some

shit, because he'd never fit in with his family—and not just because of the whole mismatched-eyeball thing. He was cut from different cloth. Always had been.

Part of him wanted to get all fired up angry at getting kicked out of the house, but what did he expect? He'd never been one of them, and taking down his first cousin with a hunting knife, even if he'd been totally justified, was unforgivable.

It was also going to cost his pops big green.

In cases of assault—or murder, if Lash died—if the victim was a member of the *glymera*, they or their bloodline were due a sum, depending on the relative worth of the injured or dead. A young, post-transition male who was the first son of one of the founding families? Only the death of a Brother or a pregnant noble female would be more expensive. And his parents were the payors, not Qhuinn, as legally you weren't considered an adult until one full year after your transition.

The good thing, he supposed, was that as he was still technically a minor, he wouldn't be sentenced to death. But even so, he was definitely going to be charged, and life as he knew it was now officially gone.

Talk about your makeovers. He was out of the *glymera*. Out of his family. Out of the training program.

Short of getting a botched sex change, it was hard to imagine what more could be done to shit on his identity.

As it stood now, he had until dawn to decide where he would go to wait to hear what was going to happen to him. Blay's would be the obvious choice, except for one big, fat, hairy problem: Sheltering an outcast from the *glymera* would totally H-bomb that family's social status, so that was a no-go. And John couldn't take him in either. The guy lived with the Brothers, and that meant his residence was so top-secret he couldn't have visitors, much less semipermanent overnight guests.

Who'd slaughtered a fellow trainee. And were waiting for their orange jumpsuit.

God . . . John. That shit that Lash had said.

He hoped it wasn't true, but feared it was.

He'd always assumed John hung back from the females because he was even more socially awkward than Blay was. Now? Obviously the guy had serious issues . . . and Qhuinn felt like an asshole of nightmarish proportions for riding his buddy about sex like he had.

No wonder John had never wanted to take a female to the back when they were hanging at ZeroSum.

Fucking Lash.

Man, no matter what happened as a result of what he'd done with that knife, he wouldn't change a thing. Lash had always been a bastard, and Qhuinn had spent years wanting to pop the fucker in the piehole. But for jumping on John like that? He really hoped the kid died.

And not just because one less cruel bastard in the world was a good thing.

The reality was, Lash had a big mouth, and as long as he was breathing that information about John was not secure. And that was dangerous. There were those in the *glymera* who would regard shit like that as totally emasculating. If John ever hoped to become a full Brother and be respected in the aristocracy, if he ever hoped to get mated and have a family, no one could know that he'd been violated by any male, much less a *human* male.

Shit, the fact that it had been a human made it all astronomically worse. In the *glymera's* eyes, humans were rats that walked upright. To be overpowered by one of them? Untenable.

No, Qhuinn thought as he walked alone, he wouldn't change a thing about what he'd done.

FIFTEEN

After John cleaned up the locker room's shower area, he went into the office, sat at the desk, and spent God only knew how long staring at papers he should have been shuffling. In the silence, his fat lip throbbed and so did his knuckles, but those were just minor aches in the midst of the dull roar in his head.

Life was just too fucking weird.

The vast majority of it passed at a predictable rate, events flowing by you at or just below the speed limit. Every once in a while, though, things happened in a flash, kind of like a Porsche sucking your doors off on the highway. Shit just came from out of nowhere and changed everything in a heartbeat.

Wellsie's death had been like that. Tohr's disappearance had been like that.

Qhuinn's move on Lash had been like that.

And the horrible thing that had happened to John on the stairwell . . . yeah, that, too.

It was fate's version of a lead foot.

Clearly Lash's throat had been destined to be cut at that moment by Qhuinn, and time had sped up so that there could be no interference by anyone or anything else.

Giving up on the paperwork, John left the desk and headed through the back of the closet. As he stepped into the underground tunnel that would take him back to the mansion, he hated himself for hoping that Lash didn't survive. He didn't like thinking he was that cruel, and besides, if Lash died, things would be harder on Qhuinn.

He didn't want his secret to get loose, though.

As he stepped out into the foyer, his phone went off with a beep. It was Qhuinn: *Hav left home. Dont kno hw long fone will work. Will turn self in2 Wrath wheneva he wants.*

Shit. John quickly hit his friend back: *Blay's ready 2 cum & pick u up.* No reply.

He tried again: *Q? W8 4 Blay, don't leave w/o him. U can stay thur.*

John stopped at the base of the stairs and waited for an answer. What he got a minute later was from Blay: *Dont worry, im on Q. Will let u kno wen i hear bck frm him. Worst case? I pick him up.*

Thank fuck.

Ordinarily, John would have gone over and met his boys at Blay's, but he couldn't face them just yet. How could they not be thinking about him differently? Plus, what had happened to him was going to be tight on their minds, just as it had been for him in the beginning.

After the attack had first occurred, he'd thought nonstop about what had been done to him. Then it had been most of the time during the day and all the time during the night. And then it was sometimes during the day, then every other day; then a whole week might pass without him giving it a thought. The nights had taken much, much longer, but eventually even the dreams had dried up, too.

Yeah, he had zero interest in looking into his friends' eyes right now and knowing what they were thinking. Picturing. Wondering about.

Nah, he couldn't be with them yet.

And besides, he couldn't shake the feeling that the whole thing with Lash was his fault. If he wasn't carrying that baggage around with him, the guy wouldn't have trotted it out in front of his friends and the fight wouldn't have happened and Qhuinn wouldn't have Rambo'd his first cousin.

Once again, that fucked-up shit from that stairwell was causing problems. It was like the aftershocks from what had happened to him were never, ever going to end.

As John passed by the library to go upstairs, he went in on a whim and scanned the stacks until he got to the legal section . . . which was about twenty feet in length. God, there must have been about seventy volumes on law in the Old Language. Evidently vampires were as litigious as humans.

He flipped through some of the tomes and got a picture from the penal code of what might happen. If Lash died, Qhuinn would go up in front of Wrath for murder, and things didn't look good, as Qhuinn hadn't been the one being attacked, so he couldn't argue self-defense. His best shot was to raise justifiable honor homicide, but even that carried jail time, in addition to a high fine that had to be paid to Lash's parents. On the other hand, if Lash lived, it was an issue of assault and battery with a deadly weapon, which would still lead to time behind bars and a fine.

Both outcomes raised the same problem: According to what John knew, the race had no jails, as the penile system for vampires had degraded over the four hundred years prior to Wrath's ascension. Qhuinn would therefore be held on house arrest somewhere until a prison was built.

It was hard to imagine Blay's parents being okay with keeping a felon under their roof indefinitely. So where would the guy go?

With a curse, John shoved the leather-bound volumes back into the stacks. As he turned away, he caught a vision in the moonlight and forgot about what he had just been reading.

On the other side of the library's French doors, Cormia was getting out of the pool, her naked body dripping with crystals of water, her skin so smooth it looked polished, her long, elegant arms and legs graceful as a summer breeze.

Oh . . . whoa.

How in the hell had Phury stayed away from her?

As she put her robe on, she pivoted toward the house and froze as she saw him. He felt like a total Peeping Tom while he raised a hand up for an awkward wave. She hesitated, as if she wasn't sure whether she'd been caught doing something bad, then returned the greeting.

Opening the door, he signed without thinking, *I'm really sorry I'm late.*

Oh, that was brilliant. She didn't know ASL—

"You're sorry you saw me or that you're late? I'm guessing either one of those is what you said." When he tapped his watch, she blushed a little. "Ah, the late part."

As he nodded, she came over, her feet making no noise as they left wet prints on the flagstone. "I waited for you— Oh, dearest Virgin Scribe. You're hurt."

He put his hand up to the bruise on his mouth, wishing her eyes weren't so good in the dark. He started to sign something to divert her attention, got frustrated with the communication barrier, and had a flash of inspiration.

Taking his phone out, he typed in a text: *I'd still like to watch a movie, if you're up to it?*

It had been a hellacious night so far, and he knew that when the Brothers returned from the clinic and Lash's outcome was made clear, things were going to get even harder. As he could barely stand to be in his own skin, much less his own head, the idea of sitting in the dark with her and zoning out was all he could handle at this point.

She measured him for a time, eyes narrowing. "Are you all right?"

Yeah, just fine, he typed. *Sorry I was late. Would really like to watch a movie.*

"Then it would be my pleasure," she said with a bow. "I should like to rinse and change, however."

The two of them went back in through the library and up the grand staircase, and he was impressed. She wasn't overly awkward, considering all he'd seen, and that was attractive, it truly was.

At the top, he waited for her as she went into her room and expected to be there for a while, but she was back in a flash. And her hair was down.

Oh, sweet Jesus, what a sight. The blond ringlets fell down to her hips, the color darker than its usual pale wheat because of its dampness.

"My hair is wet." With a flush, she held out a handful of gold clips. "I shall put it up as soon as it is dry."

Not on my account, John thought as he stared at her.

"Your Grace?"

John snapped to it and led the way down the hall of statues to the pair of flapping doors that marked the entrance to the staff quarters. He held them open for Cormia and then went to the right, over to a leather-padded door that pulled wide to reveal carpeted steps inset with strips of glowing lights.

Cormia picked up her white robes and ascended, and as he followed her, he tried not to watch the curling ends of her hair brush the small of her back.

The movie theater on the third floor had a real 1940s Metro-Goldwyn-Mayer vibe, its black and silver walls done up with art deco lotus reliefs and ornate gold-and-silver light sconces. The stadium seating in the place was the quality of what you'd find in a Mercedes, not a ballpark: Twenty-one leather chairs were set back in three sections, the aisles marked with more little lights. Each of the superpadded ass-palaces was the size of a twin bed, and collectively they had more drink cup holders than on a Boeing 747.

All down the back wall of the theater were thousands of DVDs, and there were eats, too. Along with a popcorn machine, which hadn't been turned on, as they hadn't told Fritz they were coming, there was a Coke fountain and a real candy counter.

He stopped and looked over the Milk Duds, Raisinets, Swedish Fish, M&M's, and Twizzlers. He was both hungry and nauseated, and had to vote with the greasy feeling in his stomach, but he thought maybe Cormia would like some. As she was busy looking around with wide eyes, he took out M&M's, because they were a staple, and a bag of the Swedish Fish in case she wasn't into chocolate. He popped two Coke cups free, stocked them with a ton of ice, and fired up two dark and lovelies.

Whistling softly to get her attention, he nodded down toward the front. Cormia followed, seemingly fascinated by the inset lights that went down the low stairs. Once he got her situated in one of the loungers, he jogged up the stairs and tried to figure out what the hell to put on.

Okay, straight horror was out, both because of her delicate sensibilities and because of the real-life nightmare he'd been in earlier. Of course . . . that eliminated about fifty percent of the collection, because Rhage was usually the one who put in movie requests to Fritz.

John bypassed the Godzilla section because it reminded him of Tohr. Raunchy comedies like *American Pie* and *Wedding Crashers* weren't classy enough for her. Mary's collection of deep, meaningful foreign films was . . . yeah, way too valid for John to sit through even on a good night. He was looking for escapism, not a different kind of grinding torture. Action flicks? Somehow he didn't think Cormia would grasp the subtleties of Bruce Willis, Sly Stallone, or Ahnold.

That left chick flicks. But which one? There were the John Hughes classics: *Sixteen Candles, Pretty in Pink, The Breakfast Club*. The Julia Roberts section with *Mystic Pizza, Pretty Woman, Steel Magnolias, My Best Friend's Wedding* . . . Jennifer Aniston's layer upon layer of forgettable. All the Meg Ryans from the nineties . . .

He slid a case free.

As he turned the thing over in his hand, he thought of Cormia dancing over the grass. *Bingo.*

John was just turning around when his phone went off. The group text was from Zsadist, who was evidently still at Havers's clinic: *Lash doesn't luk gud. Treatment ongoing. Will keep all posted.*

The message was a blast to everyone in the house, and as John reread it, he wondered if he should forward it to Blay and Qhuinn. In the end, he put the phone back in his pocket, figuring the two of them had enough to deal with without flip-flopping reports about Lash's condition. If the guy died, then John would get in touch with his friends.

He paused and looked around. It was utterly surreal to be doing something as normal as copping a movie, and it felt vaguely inappropriate. But right now was all about waiting. He and everyone else involved were in neutral.

As he went over to the DVD player and put the disk on the machine's black tongue, all he could see was Lash down on that tile, fear in his eyes, blood running out of his neck.

He started to pray that Lash would make it.

Even if it meant he had to live in fear of his secret being exposed, better that than having Qhuinn condemned as a murderer, and a death on John's conscience.

Please, God, let Lash live.

SIXTEEN

Downtown at ZeroSum, Rehv was having a bad fucking night, and his chief of security was making it worse. Xhex was standing in front of his desk with her arms crossed, looking down her nose at him like he was dog shit on a hot night.

He rubbed his eyes, then glared back at her. "And why are you telling me to stay in here?"

"Because you're toxic and the staff are scared of you."

Which proved they had half a brain, he thought.

"What happened last night?" she asked softly.

"Did I tell you I bought that lot four blocks down?"

"Yes. Yesterday. What happened with the Princess."

"This town needs a Goth club. I think I'll call it the Iron Mask." He leaned in toward the glowing screen of his laptop. "Cash flow here is more than strong enough for me to cover a construction loan. Or I could just cut a check, although that would get us audited

again. Dirty money is so fucking complicated, and if you ask me about last night one more time, I'm going to kick you the fuck out of here."

"Well, aren't we feeling precious."

His upper lip twitched as his fangs shot out into his mouth. "Don't push me, Xhex. I'm so not in the mood."

"Look, you can keep your yap shut, that's fine, but don't take your head fuck out on the staff. I'm not interested in cleaning up the interpersonal debris— Why are you rubbing your eyes again?"

Wincing, he gave his watch a look-see. In the midst of his vision's flat plane of red, he realized that it had been only three hours since his last hit of dopamine.

"Do you need another dose already?" Xhex asked.

He didn't bother nodding, just opened his drawer and took out a glass vial and a syringe. Peeling his suit jacket off, he rolled up his sleeve, tourniqueted his upper arm, and then tried to push the needle's fine head through the red seal on the drug's container.

He couldn't quite manage to hit the bull's-eye. With no depth perception, he was fishing through empty space, trying to match the point of the needle with the top of the little bottle and getting a whole lot of skipping misses.

Symphaths saw only shades of red, and in two dimensions. When his drug didn't work, either because he was stressed or had missed a dosage, his vision change was the first sign of trouble.

"Here, let me."

As a wave of ill swept through him, he found he couldn't speak, so he just shook his head at her and kept at it with the syringe. In the meantime, his body started to wake up from its deep freeze, sensation flooding into his arms and his legs on a fleet of tingles.

"Okay, enough with your ego." Xhex came around the desk in all-purpose mode. "Just let me—"

He tried to get his shirtsleeve down in time. Didn't make it.

"Jesus *Christ*," she hissed.

He shuffled his forearm away from her, but it was too late. Way too late.

"Let me do it," Xhex said, putting her hand on his shoulder. "Just ease up, boss . . . and let me take care of you."

With surprisingly gentle hands, she took the syringe and vial, then extended his wretched black-and-blue forearm straight out on the desk. He'd been shooting up so much lately that even with how fast he healed, his veins were decimated, all swollen and full of holes, pitted like roads too heavily traveled.

"We're going to use your other arm."

As he stretched out his right one, Xhex managed the whole needle-in-the-lid thing with no problem, drawing out what should have been his normal dose. He shook his head and held up two fingers so she'd double it.

"That's way too much," she said.

He lurched for the syringe, but she moved it out of reach.

He slammed his fist into the desk, and his eyes shot to hers, all stark demand.

With a couple of choice words, she drew more of the drug out of the vial, and he watched as she hunted around his drawer for an alcohol towelette, tore the thing open, and scrubbed a patch on the crook of his elbow. After she shot him up, she snapped free the tourney, and put his hit kit back in the desk.

Easing into his chair, he shut his eyes. The red persisted even with his lids down.

"How long's this been going on?" she asked quietly. "The double dosing? The shooting up without disinfecting the injection site? How many times are you doing this every day?"

He just shook his head.

Moments later, he heard her open the door and tell Trez to bring the Bentley around. Right as he was getting ready to no-fucking-way her, she took one of his sable dusters out of the closet.

"We're going to Havers's," she said. "And if you argue with me,

I'm going to call the boys in here and they're going to carry you out of this office like a rug roll."

Rehv glared at her. "You are not . . . the boss around here."

"True. But do you think if I tell your boys how infected your arm is, they would take even a breath before manhandling you? If you were nice, you might end up in the backseat instead of the trunk. If you were a prick, you'd be the hood ornament."

"Fuck you."

"We tried that, remember? And neither of us liked it."

Shit, *there* was something he needed reminding of right now.

"Be smart, Rehv. You're not winning this one, so why bother with the argue? Sooner you go, sooner you'll be back." They glowered at each other until she said, "Fine, leave out the double-dipping. Just let Havers look at your arm. One word: sepsis."

As if the doc wouldn't figure out what was doing when he saw the thing?

Rehv palmed his cane and slowly pushed up off his chair. "I'm too hot . . . for the coat."

"And I'm bringing it so that when the dopamine kicks in and you cool off you won't get a chill."

Xhex offered him her arm without looking at him because she knew he was too much of a pride-filled dickhead to lean on her otherwise. And he needed to lean on her. He was weak as shit.

"I hate when you're right," he said.

"Which explains why you're usually so short-tempered."

Together they walked slowly out of the office and into the alley.

The Bentley was there waiting, with Trez behind the wheel. The Moor asked no questions and made no comments, as was his way.

And, of course, all the crushing quiet always made you feel worse when you were being an ass.

Rehv ignored the fact that Xhex settled him into the backseat and slid in next to him as if she were worried he would get carsick or some shit.

The Bentley took off with the smoothness of a magic carpet ride, and that was so fucking apropos, because he felt as if he were on one. With his *symphath* nature battling his vampire blood, he was doing the seesaw between his bad side and his halfway decent one, and the shifts in moral gravity were making him nauseous as fuck.

Maybe Xhex was right to be concerned about the throwing-up thing.

They hung a left on Trade, hooked up with Tenth Avenue, and shot down toward the river, where they got on the highway. Four exits up, they turned off and glided through a high-rent district, where big houses on parklike lots were set back from the road, kings waiting to be knelt before.

With his red, two-dimensional vision Rehv didn't see much with his eyes. With his *symphath* side, he knew too much. He could sense the humans in the mansions, knew the inhabitants by the emotional footprint they emitted, thanks to the energy their feelings released. Whereas his sight was flat as a TV screen, his sense of the people was in three dimensions: They registered as psychic grid patterns, their interplay of joy and sadness, guilt and lust, anger and hurt creating structures that to him were as solid as their houses.

Though his stare couldn't penetrate the retaining walls and well-planted trees, couldn't breach the stone-and-mortar of the manses, his evil nature saw the men and women inside as clearly as if they stood before him naked, and his instincts came alive. He focused on the weaknesses percolating in those emotional grids, finding the loose parts in the people's boxes and wanting to rattle them even more. He was the canny cat to their meek mouse, the clawed stalker who wanted to toy with them until their little heads bled with their dirty secrets and their dark lies and their shameful worries.

His evil side hated them with calm detachment. To his *symphath* nature, the weak were not to inherit the earth. They were to eat it until they choked to death. And then you were to grind their car-casses in the mud of their blood to get to your next victim.

"I hate the voices in my head," he said.

Xhex glanced over. In the glow of the backseat, her hard, smart face was curiously beautiful to him, probably because she was the only one who truly understood the demons he fought, and that connection made her lovely.

"Better to despise that part of you," she said. "The hate keeps you safe."

"Fighting it's a bore."

"I know. But would you have it any other way?"

"Sometimes, I'm not so sure."

Ten minutes later, Trez pulled them through the gates of Havers's property, and by then the numbness in Rehv's hands and feet was returning, and his core temperature had dropped. As the Bentley went around back and stopped at the clinic's entrance, the sable duster was a godsend, and he huddled into it for warmth. When he got out of the car, he noted that the red vision receded as well, the world's full palette of colors returning to his sight, his depth perception putting objects in the spatial orientation he was used to.

"I'm staying out here," Xhex said from the backseat.

She never went into the clinic. But then, considering what had been done to her, he could understand why.

He palmed his cane and leaned into it. "I won't be long."

"You'll be as long as it takes. And Trez and I'll be waiting."

Phury returned from the Other Side and poofed his ass right to ZeroSum. He made his buy from iAm as Rehv was out and the Moor had been left in charge, and then he went back home and jogged up to his bedroom.

He was going to have a blunt to take the edge off before he knocked on Cormia's door and told her she was free to return to the Sanctuary. And when he talked to her, he was going to give her his vow that he would never call on her as Primale, and tell her that he would protect her from comment or criticism.

He was also going to make it clear that he was sorry for shutting her out on this side.

As he sat on his bed and picked up his rolling papers, he tried to practice what he would say to her . . . and ended up thinking of her undressing him the night before, her pale, elegant hands tugging at his belt before taking on the waistband of his leathers. In a rush, a shot of red-hot rabid-erotic nailed into the head of his cock, and though he did his best not to dwell on it, pretending he was calm and cool was like being in the kitchen of a house that was on fire.

You tended to notice the heat and all the smoke alarms that were going off.

Ah . . . but it didn't last. The fire engine and its crew of masked and gloved arrived in the form of an image of all those empty cribs. The memory of them was like a loaded gun to his head, and sure as shit put the douse on his flames.

The wizard appeared in his mind, standing in his field of skulls, silhouetted against the gray sky. *When you were growing up, your father was drunk night and day. Do you remember what that made you feel like? Tell me, mate, what kind of papa are you going to be to all of these young of your loins, considering you're smoked out twenty-four/seven?*

Phury stopped what he was doing and thought of the number of times he had picked his father up out of the weeds of the garden and dragged him back into the house right as the sun was rising. He'd been five when he'd first done it . . . and terrified that he wouldn't be able to get his father's tremendous weight to shelter soon enough. What a horror. That messy garden had seemed big as a jungle, and his little hands had kept losing their grip on his father's belt. Tears of panic had streamed down his face as he'd checked the sun's progress over and over and over again.

When he'd finally gotten his father into the house, Ahgony's eyes had opened, and he'd slapped Phury across the face with a hand as big as a frying pan.

I'd meant to die there, you idiot. There had been a beat of silence; then his father had burst into tears and grabbed him and held him and promised never to try and kill himself again.

Except there had been a next time. And a next time. And a next time. Always with the same exchange at the end.

Phury had done the saving, because he'd been determined that Zsadist would come home to a father.

The wizard smiled. *And yet that wasn't what happened, was it, mate. Your father died anyway, and Zsadist never knew him.*

Good thing you took up smoking so that Z got to experience the family legacy firsthand after all.

Phury frowned and looked through the double doors of the bathroom to the toilet. Closing his fist around the bag of red smoke, he started to get up, ready to do some serious flushing.

The wizard laughed. *You won't be able to do it. There's no bloody way you can quit. You can't even make it for four hours in the afternoon without getting panicked. Can you honestly imagine never having another smoke for the next seven hundred years of your life? Come on, mate, be sensible.*

Phury sat back down on the bed.

Oh, look, he has a brain. What a shock.

His heart was killing him as he finished the lick and twist on the blunt in his hand and put the thing between his lips. Just as he got his lighter out, his phone went off across the room.

Intuition told him who it was, and when he fished the cell from his leathers, he was right. Zsadist. And the Brother had called three times.

As he answered, he wished his blunt were already lit. "Yeah?"

"Where are you?"

"I've just come back from the Other Side."

"Okay, well, get your ass down here to the clinic. There was a fight in the locker room. John Matthew started it, we think, but Qhuinn finished it off by knifing Lash in the neck, and the kid's already gone into cardiac arrest once. They say they've stabilized him, but no one knows what's going to happen. I've just tried to call his parents again, but I'm getting voice mail, probably because of that gala. I want you here when they arrive."

Wrath must not have told Z about the big boot that had been fired up Phury's ass.

"Hello?" Zsadist snapped. "Phury? You got a problem with me?"

"No." A quick flip of his lighter top and a stroke of his thumb and he had a flame. As he put the hand-rolled back to his mouth and leaned in, he braced himself. "I can't come, though."

"What do you mean, you can't? My fucking *shellan* is pregnant and bed-bound, and I managed to get here. I need you as a rep for the training program and a member of the Brotherhood—"

"I can't."

"*Jesus Christ*, I can hear you smoking up! Put down the fucking blunts and do your goddamned job!"

"I'm not a Brother anymore."

Pure silence on the phone. Then his twin's voice, low and almost inaudible. "What."

It wasn't a question. More like Z knew the answer, but was hoping for a miracle anyway.

Phury couldn't give that to his twin. "Look . . . Wrath removed me from the Brotherhood. Last night. I assumed he'd told you." Phury inhaled hard and let the smoke roll out from between his lips slow as molasses. He could just imagine what his twin looked like at the moment, RAZR clenched in a fist, eyes black from anger, distorted upper lip curled back.

The snarl that shot into his ear was so not a surprise. "Great. Well fucking done."

The phone went dead.

Phury dialed Z back and got dumped into voice mail. Also not a surprise.

Shit.

He didn't just want to smooth things over with Zsadist; he wanted to know what the hell had happened down in the training center. Was John all right? Was Qhuinn? Both of those boys were hot tempered, as all newly transitioned males were, but they had good hearts.

Lash must have done something awful.

Phury smoked his way through the blunt in record time. As he rolled another and lit up, he decided Rhage would hook him up with details. Hollywood was always the source—

The wizard shook his head. *You do realize, mate, that Wrath wouldn't appreciate you getting all into the Brotherhood's business. You're just a houseguest here, you sodding bastard. Not family anymore.*

Upstairs in the movie theater, Cormia settled back in a seat that was so comfortable it was as the water in the pool had been, all-encompassing, the palm of a gentle giant.

The lights dimmed and John came down to the front.

He typed something into his phone, then flashed her the screen: *You ready?*

When she nodded, the dim room was lit up by a massive picture and sound came from everywhere.

"Dearest Virgin!"

John reached over and put his hand on top of hers. After a moment, she calmed and focused properly on the screen, which was suffused in shades of blue. Images of humans appeared and disappeared, the males and females dancing together, their bodies pressing close, their hips gyrating to music.

English writing appeared in a pink color at intervals.

"This is the same as the television?" she said. "It works the same way?"

John nodded just as the English words *Dirty Dancing* appeared in pink.

Abruptly, there was a machine called a car going down a road through green hills. There were people in the car. A family of humans with a father, a mother, and two daughters.

A female voice came from all around the room: "It was the summer of 1963. . . ."

When John pressed something into her hand, she could barely stand to look away from the screen long enough to see what it was. The thing turned out to be a bag, a small, dark brown bag that was open at the top. He made a motion to take something from it and put it in her mouth, so she dipped her hand in. Little multicolored rounds came out and she hesitated.

They were definitely not white. And even on this side she had eaten only white food, as was traditional.

But honestly, what was the harm?

She glanced around, even though she knew there was no one else in with them, and then, feeling as if she were breaking the law, she popped a few into her—

Dearest . . . Virgin . . . Scribe!

The taste made her tongue come alive in a way that made her think of blood. What *was* this food? Cormia looked at the bag. There were a pair of cartoon characters on the front that looked like the candy. *M&M's*, the package read.

She needed to eat the whole bag. Right now. It didn't matter that what was inside was not white.

As she had more and moaned, John laughed and handed her a tall drink that said *Coke* on the red container. Ice rattled inside, and there was a stick punched through the lid. He lifted his own and took a draw on the stick. She did the same and then went back to her bag of magic and the screen.

A bunch of people were now lined up at the edge of a lake, trying to follow the lead of a pretty blond female as she moved to the right, then the left. The young female, Baby, the one who'd been

doing the talking, struggled to get her body going where everyone else's was.

Cormia turned to ask John a question and saw that he was looking at his phone and frowning as if disappointed.

Something had happened earlier in the evening. Something bad. John was far more grim then she'd ever seen him, but he was also incredibly reserved. Though she wanted to help in any way possible, she wasn't going to press him.

As someone who kept many things to herself, she understood the importance of privacy.

Leaving him be, she settled into her chair and allowed herself to get swept away by the movie. Johnny was handsome, though not as much as the Primale was, and oh, how he moved when the music played. And the best part was seeing Baby get better at the dancing. Watching her fumble and practice and stumble and finally do the moves well made your heart cheer for her.

"I love this," Cormia said to John. "I feel like I'm living this."

John's phone appeared. *We've got more movies. Tons of them.*

"I want to see them." She took a pull from her cold drink. "I want to see all of them—"

Suddenly, Baby and Johnny were alone in his private space.

Cormia was transfixed as the two of them came together and started to dance in private. Their bodies were so different, Johnny's so much bigger than Baby's, so much more muscular, and yet he touched her with reverence and care. And he wasn't the only one doing the stroking. She returned his caresses, running her hands over his skin, looking as if she loved what she was feeling.

Cormia's mouth parted and she sat up, getting closer to the screen. In her mind, the Primale took the place of Johnny and she became Baby. Together they were moving against each other, hips rubbing, clothes disappearing. The two of them were alone in the dark, in a safe place where no one could see them or interrupt them.

It was what had happened in the Primale's bedroom, only there was no stopping and there were no other implications, no weighty traditions, no fear of failing, and her thirty-nine sisters were out of the picture.

So simple. So real, though it was only in her head.

This was what she wanted with the Primale, she thought, staring at the movie. This was it.

SEVENTEEN

As John sat next to Cormia, he checked his phone again for two reasons. The sex scene was making him feel awkward, and he was twitching for word about Qhuinn and Lash.

Damn it.

He texted Blay again, who hit right back and said he hadn't heard from the guy either and was thinking it was time to get out the car keys.

John let the phone rest on his thigh. Qhuinn couldn't possibly have done something really stupid. Like hang-himself-in-the-bathroom stupid. Nah. No way.

That father of his, though, was capable of anything. John had never met the male, but he'd heard the stories from Blay—and seen the evidence in that black eye Qhuinn had sported the night after his transition.

John felt his foot tapping and stopped it by putting his palm on his knee. Superstitious son of a bitch that he was, he kept thinking about that old wives' tale that said bad news always came in threes. If Lash died, there would be two to follow.

He thought of the Brothers out on the streets with *lessers*. And Qhuinn in the night somewhere, alone. And Bella with her pregnancy.

He checked his phone again and mouthed a curse.

"If you need to go," Cormia said, "I'm happy to be here on my own."

He started to shake his head, and she stopped him by lightly touching his forearm. "Take care of whatever it is. It's obvious you've had a difficult evening. I would ask you to talk about it, but I don't think you would."

Just because it was on his mind, he typed out: *I wish I could go back and not put the shoes on.*

"I'm sorry?"

Well, shit, now he had to explain or he looked like an idiot. *Something bad happened tonight. Right before it went down, my friend gave me this pair of sneakers I'm wearing. If I hadn't changed into them, the three of us would have been gone before . . .* He hesitated, thinking that he and his buddies would have been gone before Lash got out of the shower. . . . *what happened went down.*

Cormia looked at him for a moment. "Would you like to know what I believe?"

When he nodded, she said, "If it hadn't been the shoes, you would have dallied wherever you were for another reason. It would have been someone else putting something on. Or a conversation. Or a door that wouldn't open. As much as we have free choice, absolute destiny is immutable. What is meant to happen does, through one measure or another."

God, he'd been thinking along those lines back in the training center's office. Except . . .

It's my fault, though. It was about me. The whole thing happened because of me.

"Did you wrong another?" When John shook his head, she asked, "So how is it your fault?"

He couldn't go into the details. No way. *Just was. My friend did something horrible to save my reputation.*

"But that was his choice as a male of worth." Cormia squeezed his forearm. "Do not mourn his free will. Instead, ask yourself what you may do to help him now."

I feel so damn powerless.

"That's your perception. Not reality," she said quietly. "Go and think. The path will come to you. I know it."

Her quiet faith in him was all the more powerful because it was in her face, not just her words. And it was exactly what he needed.

You are really cool, he typed.

Cormia glowed with pleasure. "Thank you, sire."

Just John, please.

He handed her the remote and made sure she knew how to work the thing. When she caught on quickly, he wasn't surprised. She was just like him. Her silences didn't mean she wasn't smart.

He bowed to her, which felt a little weird but seemed like the thing to do, and then he beat feet out of there. On his way down the stairs to the second floor, he texted Blay. It had been about two hours at this point since they'd last heard from Qhuinn, and it was definitely time to go looking. As he was likely to have stuff with him, dematerializing wouldn't be an option, so he couldn't have gone far because he didn't have a car. Unless he'd used one of the household's *doggen* to take him somewhere?

John punched through the double doors that opened to the hall of statues and thought Cormia was so right: Sitting on his ass wasn't going to help Qhuinn as he grappled with having been kicked out of his family, and it wasn't going to change whether Lash lived or died.

And however awkward he felt about what his buddies had heard, the two of them were more important than those words that had been thrown out with cruelty in that locker room.

Just as he hit the stairs, his phone went off with a text. It was from Zsadist: *Lash has flatlined. Doesn't look good.*

Qhuinn walked along the side of the road, his duffel slapping his ass as he put one foot in front of the other. Up ahead, a stripe of lightning snaked down out of the sky and illuminated the oak trees, turning their trunks into what looked like a line of thick-shouldered thugs. The thunder that followed was not so far off in the distance and there was ozone in the air. He had a feeling he was about to get drenched.

And he was. At first, the storm's raindrops were fat and far between, but then they grew smaller and greater in number, kind of like the grown-up ones had jumped out of the clouds first and the young guys had followed only after it was safe.

The water hitting his nylon duffel made a popping sound, and the hair on the top of his head started to flatten out. He took no measures to shield himself, because the rain was going to win. He didn't have an umbrella and wasn't about to stand under an oak tree for shelter.

Extra-crispy was so not a look.

It was about ten minutes after the rain started that the car pulled up behind him. Its headlights hit his back and cast his shadow on the pavement ahead, the glow growing brighter as the engine's whine dropped on the approach.

Blay'd come after him.

He stopped and turned around, shielding his eyes with his forearm. The rain showed up as a fine white pattern in the lights, and mist drifted across the beams, reminding him of episodes of *Scooby-Doo.*

"Blay, could you dim the highs? I'm going blind here."

The night went dark and four car doors opened, with no interior light coming on.

Qhuinn slowly dropped his duffel to the ground. These were

males of his species, not *lessers*. Which, considering he was unarmed, was only moderately reassuring.

The doors shut in a round-robin series of *thunch*. As another bolt of lightning shot through the sky, he got a gander at what he was facing: The four were dressed in black and had hoods covering their facial features.

Ah, yes. The traditional honor guard.

Qhuinn didn't run as one by one they took out black clubs; he fell into his fighting stance. He was going to lose this one and lose it big, but damn it, he was going down with two sets of bloody knuckles and the teeth of these boys on the road.

The honor guard surrounded him in classic group-pound fashion, and he circled in place, waiting for the first strike. These were big guys, all his size, and their purpose was to exact physical reparation out of his body for what he'd done to Lash. As this was not a *rythe*, but repayment, he was allowed to fight back.

So Lash must have lived—

One of the clubs nailed him in the back of the knee, and it was like getting Tasered. He fought to keep his balance, knowing that if he got grounded he was fucked, but someone else took out his other leg with a ripping crack to the thigh muscle. As he landed on his hands and knees, clubs pummeled his shoulders and back, but he lunged and caught one of the guards by both ankles. The guy tried to step forward, but Qhuinn kept his prize, causing a mad shift in the male's center of gravity. Fortunately, while the bastard went down like an anvil, he was kind enough to take one of his buddies with him.

Qhuinn needed a club. That was his only shot.

In an awesome surge, he made a grab for the weapon of the one he'd throw-rugged, but another club caught him square on the wrist. The pain was like a neon sign reading, *Fuckin' A*, and his hand was instantly incapacitated, hanging limp and useless off his arm. Good thing he was an ambidextrous motherfucker. He grabbed the club with his leftie and nailed the one in front of him right in the knee.

Things got fun after that. Standing up was a no-go, so he was lethal quick on the ground, going after their legs and their 'nads. It was like being surrounded by snapping dogs as they rushed up and fell back, depending on where his swing was at.

He was actually thinking he could hold them off when one of them picked up a fist-sized rock and threw it at his head. He ducked just fine but caught the bitch on the rebound from the pavement—right in his temple. He went still for a heartbeat, and that was all it took. They crowded around him, the true beating getting started. Tucking into a ball, he put his arms over his head and protected his vital organs and his brain as best he could while he got good and pounded.

They weren't supposed to kill him.

They really weren't.

But one of them kicked him in the small of his back, nailing him directly in the kidneys. As he arched, because he couldn't help it, he opened up a clean shot to the underside of his chin. Which was where the second kick nailed him.

His jaw wasn't a good shock absorber—in fact, it was an amplifier, as his lower teeth banged into his upper ones and his skull sucked up the brunt of the impact. Stunned, he went limp, his arms loosening their hold, his defensive position weakening.

They weren't supposed to kill him, because Lash was still alive if they were doing this. If the guy had died, he would have been taken in front of the king by his cousin's parents, and they would have argued that he should be put to death even though he was technically a minor. No, this beat-down was just an eye for an eye for a bodily injury. Or at least, that was the way it was meant to be.

Trouble was, they kicked him over onto his back, and then one of them took a running start and planted both his combat boots in the center of Qhuinn's chest.

His breath shot out of him. His heart stopped pumping. Everything came to a halt.

And that was when he heard his brother's voice. "Don't do that again. It's against the rules."

His brother . . . *his brother* . . . ?

This wasn't for Lash's injury, then.

This was from his own family, to recoup the injury to their name.

Qhuinn gasped for air and got nowhere with the inhales as the four argued with one another. His brother's voice was the loudest.

"That's enough!"

"Fucking mutant bastard, he deserves to die!"

Qhuinn lost interest in the drama as it dawned on him that his heart still hadn't started up again—and not even the panic he suddenly felt at the realization kick-started the damn thing. His eyesight went checkerboard and his hands and feet started to numb out.

That was when he saw the bright light.

Shit, the Fade was coming for him.

"Christ! Let's go!"

Someone leaned down to him. "We'll be back for you, asshole. Without your fucking brother next time."

There was a scramble of boots, a lot of doors opening and closing, and then a screech as the car took off. When another approached close on its heels, he realized the lights on him were not the afterlife, but someone else driving down the road.

Lying in the heap he'd been left in, he had some passing thought that maybe he could pound on his own chest. Like pull a *Casino Royale* and do self-CPR.

He closed his eyes. Yeah, if only he could 007 it . . . Not a chance, though. He couldn't get his lungs to work in more than shallow draws and his heart was still nothing but a loose knot of muscle in his chest. The fact that he had no pain anymore was even more worrisome.

The next white light that came to him was like the mist that hung over the road, a gentle and soft fog that bathed him, eased him. As he was illuminated, he went from being terrified to utterly unafraid. This, he knew, was not a car. This now was the Fade.

He felt himself levitate off the pavement and he soared, weightless, until he was at the head of a white corridor. Down at the far end, there was a door he felt compelled to go and open. He walked toward it with growing urgency, and the moment he reached it, he went for the knob. As his hand wrapped around the warm brass, he had some vague thought that once he walked through, that was it. He was in between as long as he didn't open the door and step into what was on its other side.

Once he was in, there was no going back.

Just as he was about to twist his palm, he saw an image on the panels of the door. It was hazy and he paused, trying to figure out what it was.

Oh . . . God . . . he thought, when he realized what he was looking at.

Holy . . . shit.

EIGHTEEN

ormia was not in her bedroom or her bath.

As Phury went downstairs to the foyer to look for her, he came to a decision. If he ran into Rhage, he wasn't going to ask the questions that were on his mind. The shit with the trainees and the *lessers* and the war was no longer his territory, and he'd better get used to it.

The answers about the Brothers and the trainees were not due to him anymore.

Cormia was his business. She and the Chosen. And it was about damn time he manned up.

Phury stopped short as he got to the dining room's arch. "Bella?"

His twin's *shellan* was sitting down on one of the chairs next to the sideboard, her head bent, her hand on her pregnant belly. She was breathing in little puffs.

She lifted her eyes to him and smiled weakly. "Hi."

Oh, God. "Hi. Whatcha doing?"

"I'm fine. And before you say . . . I should be in bed . . . I'm headed there now. . . ." Her eyes shifted over to the grand staircase. "It just seems a little far away at the moment."

For propriety's sake, Phury had always been careful not to seek Bella's company outside of communal meals, even before Cormia had come into the house.

Now was not the time for distance, though.

"Why don't I carry you?"

There was a pause, and he geared himself up for her arguments. Maybe she'd at least let him take her arm—

"Yes. Please."

Oh . . . shit. "Look at you, being all reasonable."

He smiled, as if he weren't completely freaking out, and went over to her. She seemed light as air as he picked her up with one arm under her legs and the other around her back. She smelled of night-blooming roses and something else. Something . . . not quite right, as if her pregnancy hormones were out of whack.

Maybe she was bleeding.

"So how are you feeling?" he asked in an amazingly calm voice while he took her to the stairs.

"The same. Tired. But the young is kicking a lot, which is good."

"That is good." He got to the second floor and strode down the hall of statues. As Bella laid her head on his shoulder, she shuddered a little and made him want to start running.

Just as he came up to her bedroom, the doors at the end of the corridor opened. Cormia came through them and faltered, her eyes going wide.

"Could you get this door," he said to her.

She sprang forward and opened the way so that he could step through into the room. He headed straight for the bed and laid Bella out in the wedge created by the sheets and blankets that were folded back.

"Would you like some food?" he asked, trying to ease into the whole let's-get-Doc-Jane thing.

Some of the old sparkle came back into her eyes. "I think that's the problem—I just ate too much. I kicked two pints of Ben and Jerry's Mint Chocolate Chip."

"Good choice, if you're going to spoon up." He tried to sound casual as he murmured, "So how about I call Z?"

"For what? I'm only tired. And before you ask, no, I wasn't up for more than the hour I've been allotted. Don't bother him, I'm fine."

Maybe so, but he was still calling his twin. Just not in front of her.

He glanced over his shoulder. Cormia was standing just outside of the room, a silent, robed figure with worry on her lovely face. He turned back to Bella. "Hey, how would you like some company?"

"I would love some." She smiled at Cormia. "I TiVo'd a *Project Runway* marathon and was about to watch it. You want to join me?"

Cormia's eyes shot to his, and his pleading must have come through in what she saw. "I'm not sure what that is, but . . . yes, I would like to join you."

As she came in, he took her arm and whispered, "I'm getting Z. If she shows any signs of distress, dial star-Z on the phone, okay? That's him."

Cormia nodded and said softly, "I'll take care of her."

Giving her arm a little squeeze, he murmured, "Thank you."

After saying good-bye, he shut the door and went down the hall a number of yards before he dialed Z on his cell. *Pick up, pick up. . . .*

Voice mail.

Shit.

"That ain't him. *That ain't him!*"

Standing in the rain at the ass end of the alley next to McGrider's, Mr. D wanted to take the slayer in front of him and use the guy as a speed bump out in the middle of Trade Street.

"What the fuck is your problem?" the *lesser* shot back while pointing to the civilian vampire at their feet. "This is the third male we got tonight. More than we've bagged in a year—"

Mr. D whipped out his switchblade. "And they're not the one we need. So you saddle on up again and hit that there pavement or your Rocky Mountain oysters are on my plate."

As the slayer took a step back, Mr. D bent down and sliced open the jacket of the civilian. The male was out cold and worse for the wear, looking like a limp suit in desperate need of dry cleaning. There was red blood all over his clothes, and his face was like a Rorschach test, nothing but blotches.

Fishing around for a wallet, Mr. D agreed with his subordinate up to a point, but he kept that to himself. It was hard to believe that they'd got three snatch and grabs in one night—and he was still shitting in his pants like he'd been sucking on prunes for days.

Thing was, there was no good news to share with the Omega, and he was the one whose Levi's were on the line.

"Take this thing back to the Lowell Street house," he said as a pale blue minivan full of backup eased down the alley. "When it comes around, let me know. I'll see if it can tell us anything about the one we're looking for."

"Whatever you say, boss." *Boss* was pronounced like *asshole*.

Mr. D considered taking his switchblade and skinning the son of a bitch where he stood. But after already offing one slayer tonight, he forced himself to sheathe the blade and put the weapon back in his coat. Thinning the herd was not a great idea right now.

"I would watch your manners, boy," he murmured as two *lessers* got out of the minivan and came over to pick up the civilian.

"Why? This isn't Texas."

"True enough." Mr. D froze the large muscle groups of the slayer, grabbed the fucker by the balls, and twisted those family jewels like taffy. The slayer screamed, proving that even if you were impotent, a man's soft spot was still the best way to get his attention.

"There still ain't no reason to be rude," Mr. D whispered as he looked up into the guy's scrunched face. "Din't your mama teach you nothing?"

The reply that came back could have been anything from the Twenty-third Psalm to a blonde joke to a grocery list, for all the sense it made.

Just as Mr. D was releasing his hand, every square inch of his skin started to itch.

Great. The night just kept getting better.

"Cage that there male," Mr. D said, "then get back out here. We ain't done for the night."

By the time the minivan took off, he was ready to take a sheet of sandpaper to himself. The incredible tickling itch meant the Omega wanted to see him, but where the hell could he go for an audience? He was downtown, and the closest piece of property the Lessening Society had was a good ten-minute drive away—and considering he had no news to share, he didn't think any kind of delay was a good call.

Mr. D jogged up Trade and checked out the blocks of abandoned buildings. In the end, he decided he couldn't run the risk of taking an audience with the Omega in any of them. The human homeless were into everything downtown, and on a night like tonight, no doubt they'd be a-lookin' to get out from under the storms. The last thing Mr. D needed was a human witness, even a drugged-out or drunk one, especially considering he was going to get a whuppin'.

Couple blocks farther and he came up to a construction site with a ten-foot fence all around it. He'd been watching the building go up since this past spring, with first the exoskeleton rising from the dirt, then the skin of glass wrapping the girders up, then the nervous system of wires and piping getting roughed in. The crews had stopped working at night, which meant he was pig-in-shit for what he needed.

Mr. D took a running jump, two-handed the upper lip of the fence, and vaulted his ass over the top. He hit the ground in a crouch and stayed put.

No one came at him and no dogs rushed his way, so he willed a couple of the caged lights off and scooted through the shadows toward a door that was—score—unlocked.

The building had the dry smell of Sheetrock and plaster, and he went deep into the center, his footsteps echoing around. The place was standard-issue office space, a big, open stretch that would some-day soon be filled with cubes. Poor bastards. He never could have handled a desk job. For one, he weren't book smart, and for two, if he couldn't see the sky he felt like he was going to scream.

When he was thick in the middle of the building, he got down on his knees, took off his cowboy hat, and settled in for one hell of a tongue-lashin'.

Just as he opened himself to the master, the newest storm got serious about coming in, its thunder rolling into downtown, then echoing as it bounced off the tall buildings. Perfect timing. The Omega's arrival sounded like just another thunderclap as the master broke through into Caldwell's version of reality, busting out of thin air as if he were leaping out of a lake. When he'd fully arrived, the background of the construction site wobbled like it was rubber snap-ping back into shape.

White robes settled around the Omega's ghostly black form, and Mr. D got ready to pull the trigger on a whole lot of we're-doin-the-best-we-can.

But the Omega spoke first. "I have found what belongs to me. His death was the way. You shall give me four men and you shall procure necessaries and you shall go to the farmhouse to ready it for an induction."

Okay, that was not what he'd expected to come out of the master's mouth.

Mr. D got up and took out his phone. "There's a squadron on Third Street. I'll tell them to come here."

"No, I shall pick them up there and they shall travel with me. When I return to the farmhouse, you shall assist me in what tran-spires, and then you shall provide a service."

"Yes, master."

The Omega extended his arms, his white robe unfurling like a

pair of wings. "Rejoice, for we are strengthened tenfold. My son is coming home."

With that, the Omega up and disappeared, a rolled scroll falling to the concrete floor in the wake of his departure.

"Son?" Mr. D wondered if he'd heard that right. *"Son?"*

He bent down and picked up the scroll. The list was long and kind of gruesome, but not exotic.

Cheap and easy. Cheap and easy. Which was good because his wallet was darned slim.

He put the list in his jacket and his cowboy hat back on.

Son?

Across town in Havers's underground clinic, Rehv waited in an examination room with no patience whatsoever. Checking his watch for the eight hundred and fiftieth time, he felt like a race car driver whose pit crew was made up of ninety-year-olds.

What the hell was he doing here anyway? The dopamine had kicked in and the panic had faded, and now he felt ridiculous with his Bally loafers dangling off the end of a doctor's table. All was normal and under control, and for chrissakes, his forearm would heal up eventually. The fact that it was slow probably meant he just needed to feed. A quick session with Xhex and he'd be good to go.

So really, he should just take off.

Yeah, the only problem with that was the fact that Xhex and Trez were waiting for him in the parking lot. If he didn't come out of here with some mummy wrapping over his needle marks, they were going to scramble his ass like eggs.

The door opened and a nurse came in. The female was dressed in a white shirtwaist dress, white hose, and white soft-soled shoes, a right-out-of-central-casting routine that was all about Havers's old-fashioned ways and standards. As she shut the door, she had her head buried in his medical chart, and though he didn't doubt she was checking on whatever was written there, he was well aware that the added bene was that she didn't have to meet his eyes.

All the nurses did that when they were with him.

"Good evening," she said stiffly while flipping through pages. "I'm going to take a blood sample, if you don't mind."

"Sounds good." At least something was happening.

While he took off one side of his sable coat and shrugged out of his jacket, she bustled around washing her hands and snapping on gloves.

None of the nurses liked dealing with him. It was female intuition. Even though there was no mention in his chart that he was a half-breed *symphath*, they could sense the evil in him. His sister, Bella, and his former flame, Marissa, were the only notable exceptions, because they both brought out his good side: He cared for them and they sensed it. As for the rest of the race, though? Anonymous folks meant absolutely nothing to him, and somehow the fairer sex always picked up on that.

The nurse came at him with a little tray of vials and a rubber tourniquet, and he rolled up his sleeve. She worked fast and didn't say a word as she drew the blood then hit the door as quickly as she could.

"How much longer is it going to be?" he asked before she could get away.

"An emergency's come in. It's going to be a while."

The door clapped shut.

Shit. He didn't want to leave his club alone all night. With both Trez and Xhex off-site . . . yeah, that was no good. iAm was a hardass, for sure, but even ruff-tuffs needed solid backup when they were facing a crowd of four hundred fucked-up humans.

Rehv popped open his phone, dialed Xhex, and fought with her for about ten minutes. Which wasn't fun but helped kill some time. She wouldn't budge on him pulling out, but at least he got her to agree to go back to the club with Trez.

Of course, that was only after he direct-ordered the both of them.

"Fine," she snapped.

"Fine," he bit out, ending the call.

He shoved his phone in his pocket. Cursed a couple of times. Took the fucking thing back out and texted: *I'm sorry I'm such a shit. Forgive me?*

Just as he hit send, a text came through from her: *U can be such a shit abt this. I only ride u cuz I care.*

He had to laugh, especially when she texted again: *UR 4given but ur still a shit. TTYL*

Rehv put his phone back in his pocket and looked around, cataloging the tongue depressors in their glass jar by the sink and the blood-pressure cuff hanging off the wall and the desk and computer setup in the corner. He'd been in this room before. He'd been in all the examination rooms before.

He and Havers had been doing the doctor/patient thing for quite a while, and it was tricky shit. If anyone had evidence that there was a *symphath* around, even a half-breed, by law they had to report the individual so they could be removed from the general population and dumped off at the colony up north. Which would ruin everything. So each time Rehv came for one of these visits, he burrowed into the good doctor's brain and opened what he liked to think of as his own personal trunk in Havers's attic.

The trick wasn't dissimilar to what vampires could do to erase the short-term memories of humans, just more in-depth. After putting the doc in a trance, Rehv sprang the information about himself and his "condition," and Havers was able to treat him accurately—and without all the unpleasant social ramifications. When the appointment was over, Rehv packed up his "belongings" in the guy's brain and secured them again, locking them down tight in the doctor's cerebral cortex until the next time.

Was it sneaky? Yes. Was there another option? No. He needed

treatment—he wasn't like Xhex, who managed to quell her urges on her own. Although God only knew how she did—

Rehv straightened, his spine tingling in a rush, his instincts pulling a ring-a-ding-ding.

His palm found his cane and he slid off the table, landing on two feet he couldn't feel. The trip to the door was three steps, and then his hand grabbed onto the handle and twisted. Outside, the corridor was empty in both directions. Down far to the left, the nursing station and the waiting room seemed all business as usual. To the right, there were more patient rooms and beyond them, the double doors that led to the morgue.

No drama.

Yeah . . . nothing appeared out of place. Medical staff walked with purpose. Someone coughed in the examination room next door. The hum of the HVAC system was a constant slow boil of white noise.

He squinted and was tempted to reach out with his *symphath* side, but it was too risky. He'd just gotten himself restabilized. Pandora and her box needed to stay closed.

Ducking back into the exam room, he got out his phone and started to dial Xhex to call her back to the clinic, but the door opened before the call went through.

His brother-in-law, Zsadist, put his head through the door. "Heard you were in."

"Hey." Rehv put the phone away and chalked up the surge of anxiety to the paranoia that seemed to come with double-dosing. Ah, the joy of side effects.

Shit. "Tell me you're not here because of Bella."

"Nah. She's good." Z shut the door and leaned back against it, effectively locking them in together.

The Brother's eyes were black. Which meant he was pissed off.

Rehvenge brought his cane up and let it dangle between his legs

just in case he needed it. He and Z had been cool following some dick tossing when the Brother and Bella had started off, but things could change. And given the way that stare was dark as the inside of a crypt, evidently they had.

"You got something on your mind there, big man?" Rehv asked.

"I want you to do me a personal favor."

The term *favor* was likely a misnomer. "Talk."

"I don't want you dealing to my twin anymore. You're going to cut off his supply." Z leaned forward on his hips. "And if you don't, I will make it impossible for you to sell so much as a fucking cocktail straw in that pit of yours."

Rehv tapped the tip of his cane against the exam table and wondered if the Brother would change his tune if he knew the profit from the club kept his *shellan*'s brother out of a *symphath* colony. Z knew about the half-breed thing; he didn't know about the Princess and her games.

"How is my sister?" Rehv drawled. "Doing well? Keeping calm? That would be important for her, wouldn't it. Not getting unnecessarily upset."

Zsadist's eyes narrowed to slits, his scarred face the kind of thing folks saw in nightmares. "I really don't think you want to go there, do you?"

"You fuck with my business and the repercussions will hurt her as well. Trust me." Rehv positioned his cane so it stood upright in his palm. "Your twin is an adult male. If you have problems with his usage maybe you need to talk with him, huh."

"Oh, I'm going to deal with Phury. But I want your word. You don't sell to him anymore."

Rehv stared at his cane as it stood up in the air, perfectly balanced. He'd long ago made peace with his business, no doubt with help from his *symphath* side, which made seizing opportunity from the weaknesses of others a kind of moral imperative.

The way he justified his dealing was that his customers' choices had nothing to do with him. If they fucked up their lives because of what he sold them, that was their prerogative—and no different from the more socially acceptable ways people destroyed themselves, like eating their way into cardiac disease because of what McDonald's peddled, or drinking themselves into liver failure thanks to the good folks at Anheuser-Busch, or gambling on reservations until they lost their houses.

Drugs were a commodity and he was a businessman, and users would just find their devastation somewhere else if his doors closed. The best he could do was make sure that if they bought from him, their shit was uncontaminated with dangerous fillers, and the purity was consistent so that they could tailor their doses reliably.

"Your word, vampire," Zsadist growled.

Rehv looked down at the sleeve covering his left forearm and thought of Xhex's expression when she'd seen what he'd done to himself. Odd, the parallels. Just because his drug of choice was prescribed didn't mean he was immune from abusing the shit.

Rehv lifted his eyes, then closed his lids and stopped breathing. He reached out through the air between him and the Brother and entered the male's mind. Yeah . . . underneath his anger was rank terror.

And memories . . . of Phury. A scene a while ago . . . seventy years or so earlier . . . a deathbed. Phury's.

Z was wrapping his twin in blankets and moving him closer to a coal-burning fire. He was worried . . . For the first time since he'd lost his soul to slavery, he was looking on someone with concern and compassion. In the scene, he blotted Phury's fever-soaked brow and then strapped on weapons and left.

"Vampire . . ." Rehv murmured. "Look at you go with the nursing care."

"Get out of my fucking past."

"You saved him, didn't you." Rehv flipped his eyes open. "Phury was sick. You went and got Wrath because you had nowhere else to go. The savage as savior."

"FYI, I'm in a bad mood, and you're making me lethal."

"That's how you both ended up in the Brotherhood. Interesting."

"I want your word, sin-eater. Not a narrative that bores me."

Moved by something Rehv didn't want to name, he placed his hand over his heart. In the Old Language, he said clearly, *"I hereby proffer my vow unto you. Never again shall your blooded twin leave my premises with drugs upon him."*

Surprise flared in Z's scarred face. Then he nodded. "They say never to trust a *symphath*. So I'm going to bank on the half of you that's my Bella's brother, feel me?"

"Good plan," Rehv murmured as he dropped his hand. " 'Cuz that's the side I pledged with. But tell me something. How're you going to make sure he doesn't buy from someone else?"

"To be honest, I have no idea."

"Well, best of luck with him."

"We're going to need it." Zsadist headed for the door.

"Yo, Z?"

The Brother looked over his shoulder. "What."

Rehv rubbed his left pec. "Have you . . . ah, have you picked up a bad vibe tonight?"

Z frowned. "Yeah, but how's that any different? Haven't had a good one in God only knows how long."

The door eased shut, and Rehv put his hand back over his heart. The damn thing was racing for no evident reason. Shit, it was probably best that he see the doc. No matter how long it took—

The explosion ripped through the clinic with a roar like thunder.

NINETEEN

Phury took form in the pines behind the garages of Havers's clinic—just as the security alarms in the place started going off. The shrill electronic screams made the neighborhood's dogs bark, but there was no danger of the police being called. The warning sounds were calibrated so that they were too high for humans to hear.

Fuck . . . he was unarmed.

He bolted toward the clinic entrance anyway, ready to fight with his bare hands if he had to.

It was a beyond-worst-case scenario. The steel door was hanging open like a split lip, and inside the vestibule the elevator doors were pushed wide, the shaft with its veins and arteries of cables and wires exposed. Down below, the roof of the elevator car had a blast hole in it, the equivalent of a bullet wound in a male's chest.

Plumes of smoke and the scent of baby powder boiled up, riding a draft from the underground clinic. The sweet-and-sour combo,

along with the sounds of fighting below, unsheathed Phury's fangs and curled his fists.

He didn't waste time wondering how the *lessers* had known where the clinic was, and he didn't bother with the ladder mounted on the shaft's concrete wall, either. He leaped down and landed on the part of the elevator's roof that was still solid. Another jump through the blown part and he was facing total chaos.

In the clinic's waiting area, a trio of granny-haired slayers were doing the thumpty dance with Zsadist and Rehvenge, the fight busting apart the land of plastic chairs and dull magazines and cheerless potted plants. The paled-out bastards were obviously well-trained long-timers, given how strong and sure they were, but Z and Rehv were taking no shit.

With the fight moving so fast, it was a jump-in-and-swim sitch. Phury grabbed a metal chair from the registration desk and swung it like a bat at the nearest slayer. As the *lesser* went down, he lifted the chair up and stabbed one of its spindly legs right into the fucker's chest.

Just as the pop and flash rang out, screams rippled down the clinic's hallway from the blocks of patient rooms.

"Go!" Z barked as he threw out a kick and caught one of the *lessers* in the head. "We'll hold them here!"

Phury exploded through the double flap doors.

There were bodies in the hall. A lot of them. Lying in pools of red blood on the pale green linoleum.

Though it killed him not to stop and check on those he was passing, his focus had to be on the medical staff and patients who were very definitely alive. A group of them was fleeing toward him in a panic, their white coats and hospital johnnies flapping like a load of wash hung out to dry in the wind.

He caught them by grabbing arms and shoulders. "Get in the patient rooms! Lock yourselves in! Lock those damn doors!"

"No locks!" someone hollered. "And they're taking patients!"

"Damn it." He looked around and saw a sign. "This medicine closet have a lock?"

A nurse nodded while she unclipped something from her waist. With a shaking hand she held a key out to him. "Only from the outside, though. You'll have . . . to lock us in."

He nodded over to the door that read, STAFF ONLY. "Move it."

The loose group shuffled over and filed into the ten-by-ten room with its floor-to-ceiling shelves of medications and supplies. As he shut the door, he knew he would never forget the way they looked, huddled under the low ceiling's fluorescent lights: seven panicked faces, fourteen pleading eyes, seventy fingers finding and linking together until their separate bodies were one solid unit of fear.

These were people he knew: people who had taken care of him with his prosthesis issues. People who were vampires like him. People who wanted this war to stop. And they were being forced to trust him because at the moment he had more power than they did.

So this was what being God was like, he thought, not wanting the job.

"I will not forget you." He shut the door on them, locked it, and paused for a second. Sounds of fighting were still coming from the registration area, but everything else was quiet.

No more staff. No more patients. Those seven were the only survivors.

Turning from the supply closet, he headed away from where Z and Rehv were in battle, tracking a pervasive sweet scent that led in the opposite direction. He ran down past Havers's lab, down farther by the hidden quarantine room Butch had been in months ago. All along the way, smudged prints left by black-soled combat boots mingled with the red blood of vampires.

Christ, how many slayers had gotten in here?

Whatever the answer to that was, he had an idea where the *lessers* were headed: the evac tunnels, likely with abductions. Question was, how did they know to go this way?

Phury busted through another set of double doors and stuck his head into the morgue. The banks of refrigerated units and the stainless-steel tables and the hanging scales were untouched. Logical. They wanted only what lived.

He went farther down the hall and found the exit the slayers had used to get out with the abductees. There was nothing left of the steel panel into the tunnel, the thing blown apart just like the back entrance and the elevator roof had been.

Shit. Totally clean op. In and out. And he was willing to bet this was just the first offensive. Others would be coming to loot, because the Lessening Society was medieval like that.

Phury hotfooted it back toward the fighting out in the registration area in case Z and Rehv hadn't already taken care of business. On the way, he put his phone up to his ear, but before V answered the call, Havers stuck his head out of his private office.

Phury hung up so he could deal with the doctor, and prayed that V's security system had been notified when the alarms had been triggered. He thought it likely had been, as the systems were supposed to be linked.

"How many ambulances do you have?" he demanded as he came up to Havers.

The physician blinked behind his glasses and held out his hand. In his rattling grip was a nine-millimeter. "I have a gun."

"Which you're going to tuck into your belt and not use." Last thing they needed was an amateur's finger on the trigger. "Go on, put it away and focus for me. We have to get the living out of here. How many ambulances do you have?"

Havers fumbled to get the Beretta's muzzle into his pocket, making Phury worry he was going to shoot himself in the ass. "F-f-four—"

"Give me that." Phury took the gun, checked that the safety was in place, and shoved it into the doctor's waistband. "Four ambulances. Good. We're going to need drivers—"

The electricity cut out, everything going to pitch-black. The abrupt darkness made him wonder if the second shift of slayers hadn't come down the shaft.

As the backup generator got rolling and dim security lights flared, he grabbed the doctor's arm and gave the male a shake. "Can we get to the ambulances through the house?"

"Yes . . . the house, my house . . . tunnels . . ." Three nurses made an appearance behind him. They were scared shitless, white as the overhead emergency lights.

"Oh, dearest Virgin," Havers said, "the *doggen* at the house. Karolyn—"

"I'll get them," Phury said. "I'll find them and get them out. Where are the keys to the ambulances?"

The doctor reached behind the door. "Here."

Thank. Fuck. "The *lessers* have found the southern tunnel, so we're going to have to get everyone out through the house."

"O-okay."

"We'll start the evac as soon as we have this facility temporarily secured," Phury said. "You four stay locked in here until you hear from one of us. You're going to be our drivers."

"H-how did they find us?"

"No clue." Phury shoved Havers back into the office, shut the door, and hollered for the guy to lock up.

By the time he got back to the reception area, the fighting was over, the last *lesser* being stabbed into oblivion by Rehv's red sword.

Z wiped his forehead with a hand that left a black smudge behind. Looking over, he demanded of Phury, "Status?"

"At least nine staff and patients killed, unknown number of abductions, area is not secured." Because God only knew how many *lessers* were still within the clinic's maze of corridors and rooms. "Suggest stabilize entrance and south tunnel as well as exit to house. Evac will require use of the back stairwell into the house, and then rapid departure with ambulances and private vehicles.

Medical staff will drive. Destination is backup clinical location on Cedar Street."

Zsadist blinked for a minute, as if he were surprised at the clean logic. "Good deal."

The cavalry arrived a second later, Rhage, Butch, and Vishous landing one, two, three in the elevator. The trio were armed like tanks and pissed off.

Phury glanced down at his watch. "I'm going to get the civilians and the staff out of here. You take care of finding any loose *lessers* in the facility and playing welcome wagon to the next wave."

"Phury," Zsadist called out as he turned around.

When Phury looked over his shoulder, his twin tossed across one of the pair of SIGs he always wore.

"Watch your ass," Z said.

Phury took the gun with a nod and jogged down the corridor. After doing a quick scope of the distances between the medical supply closet, Havers's office, and the stairwell, he felt like the three points were separated by miles, not yards.

He opened the door to the stairwell. Security lights glowed red, and the silence was golden. Moving quickly, he went up the steps, entered the code for the door lock into the house, and stuck his head out into a wood-paneled hallway. The scent of lemon polish was from the glossy floor. The perfume of roses came from a bouquet on a marble stand. The lamb-and-rosemary combo was from the kitchen.

No baby powder.

Karolyn, Havers's maid, leaned around the corner. "Sire?"

"Gather the servants—"

"We're all together. Right here. We heard the alarms." She nodded over her shoulder. "There are twelve of us."

"Is the house secure?"

"None of our security systems have gone off."

"Excellent." He tossed her the keys Havers had given him. "Take the tunnels out to the garages and lock yourselves in them. Start every ambulance and car you have, but do *not* pull out, and leave one person by the door so I can get in with the others. I will knock and identify myself. Do not open up for anyone else but me or a Brother. Got it?"

It was painful to watch the *doggen* swallow her fear and nod. "Is our master . . ."

"Havers is fine. I'm going to bring him to you." Phury reached out and squeezed her hand. "Go. Now. And be quick. We have no time here."

He was back down in the clinic in the blink of an eye. He could hear his brothers moving around, knew them by the sounds of their boots and their scents and their patter of talk. No more slayers yet, evidently.

He went to Havers's office and sprang the four who were in there first, because he didn't trust Havers to keep tight and stay put. Fortunately, the doctor manned up and did as he was told, moving quickly up the stairs to the main house with the nurses. Phury escorted them into the tunnels that led out to the garages, and jogged along with them through the cramped underground escape route that ran under the parking lot behind the mansion.

"Which one of the tunnels leads directly to the ambulances?" he asked when they got to a four-pronged split.

"Second from left, but the garages are all interconnected."

"I want you and the nurses in the ambulances with the patients. So that's where we're going."

They trucked it as fast as they could go. When they got to a steel door, Phury pounded on the thing and barked his name. The lock disengaged and he let his troop in.

"I'll be back with more," he said, as everyone embraced.

He went back down into the clinic and ran into Z. "Any more slayers?"

"None. I've got V and Rhage guarding the front, and Rehv and I are going to stake out the south tunnel."

"I could use some cover for the vehicles."

"Roger that. I'll send Rhage. You're going out the back, right?"

"Yup."

He and his twin parted, and Phury headed for the supply closet. His hand was rock-steady as he took the nurse's key out of his pocket and knocked on the door.

"It's me." He put the key in and turned the handle.

He met their faces once more and caught the flashes of relief. Which didn't last as they saw the gun in his hand.

"I'm taking you out through the house," he said. "Do we have any mobility issues?"

The little group parted to reveal an older male on the ground. He had an IV in his arm, which one of the nurses was holding above his head.

Shit. Phury glanced back at the hall. His brothers were nowhere around.

"You," he said, pointing to a male lab tech. "Carry him. You." He nodded to the female holding the bag. "Stay with them."

As the tech got the patient off the floor and the blond nurse kept the IV bag up high, Phury paired the remaining staff up, one to a patient.

"Move as fast as you can. You're going to use the stairwell to the house and proceed directly to the garage tunnels. It'll be your first right after you're inside the mansion. I'll be behind you. Go. Now."

Even though they did the best they could, it took years.

Years.

He was ready to jump out of his skin as they finally hit the red-lit stairway, and locking the steel door behind them gave him scant relief considering the *lessers* had explosives. The patients were slow, with two just a day or so out of surgery. He wanted to carry either or both of that pair but couldn't risk not having a gun at the ready.

On the landing, one patient, a female with a bandage around her head, had to stop.

Without being asked, the blond nurse quickly gave the IV bag to the male tech. "Just until we're in the tunnel." Then she scooped the sagging female up into her arms. "Let's go."

Phury shot her a nod and let her have at the stairs.

The group trickled out into the mansion to the sounds of shuffling feet and a couple of coughs. The total absence of alarms was spectacular as he locked the door to the clinic behind them and took them over to the tunnel entrance.

As the group hobbled in, the blond nurse with the female in her arms paused. "You have any other weapons? Because I can shoot."

Phury's brows shot up. "I don't have another—"

His eyes caught the shine of two ornamental swords on the wall above one of the doorways. "Take my gun. I'm good with sharp things."

The nurse offered him her hip, and he shoved Z's SIG in the pocket of her white coat. Then she turned away and marched into the tunnel as he popped both swords off their brass hooks, then jogged to catch up.

When they came up to the door to the garage with the ambulances, he pounded with his fist, shouted his name, and the thing sprang open. Instead of going through it, every single one of those vampires he'd led out looked at him.

Seven faces. Fourteen eyes. Seventy fingers still clenching.

But it was different now.

Their gratitude was the other half of the God job, and he was overwhelmed by their devotion and relief. Their collective realization that their faith in their savior had been well placed and the reward was their lives was a palpable force.

"We're not out of it yet," he told them.

When Phury looked at his watch again, it was thirty-three minutes later.

Twenty-three civilians, medical staff, and household *doggen* had

been evac'd from the garages. The ambulances and cars had taken off not from the regular doors that faced the back of the house, but from retractable rear panels that allowed the vehicles to shoot out into the shallow woods behind the mansion. One by one, they'd driven off without lights on and without brakes being used. And one by one, they'd made it free and ghosted away into the night.

The op was a total success, and yet he had a bad feeling about it all.

The *lessers* had never come back.

Wasn't like them. Under normal circumstances, once they infiltrated, they swarmed. It was their SOP to take as many civilians as possible for interrogation and then strip whatever premises they'd gotten into of anything of value. Why hadn't they sent more men? Especially given the assets in Havers's clinic and house, and the fact that the slayers had to know the Brothers would be all over the place, ready to fight.

Back in the clinic, Phury walked down the hall, double-checking that all the patient rooms were empty of the living. It was a pitiful review. Bodies. Lots of bodies. And the whole facility was totally trashed, as mortally wounded as any of the dead who lay strewn about. Bedsheets were on the floor, pillows scattered, heart monitors and IV poles knocked around. In the corridors, supplies were dropped randomly here and there, and there were all those horrid smudges of black-soled boots and red, shiny blood.

Rapid evacs were not a Martha Stewart kind of thing. Neither was fighting.

As he headed for the registration area, it seemed eerie that there was no more hustle and bustle in the place, just the HVAC system and the computers humming. Occasionally a phone rang, but it wasn't picked up.

The clinic truly had flatlined, with just remnants of brain activity left.

Neither it nor Havers's beautiful mansion would ever be used again. The tunnels as well as all intact exterior and interior retaining doors would be locked and the security systems and shuttering of the house engaged. Those entrances that had been blown open as well as the elevator doors would have sheets of steel welded in place. Eventually, an armed escort would be permitted to go in and remove the furniture and personal effects through the tunnels that had not been compromised, but that would be a while. And was dependent upon whether or not the *lessers* finally came back with their shopping carts.

Fortunately, Havers had a safe house, so he and his servants had somewhere to land, and the patients were already being settled at the temporary clinic. Medical records and lab results were stored on an off-site server, so they were still accessible, but the nurses were going to have to quickly stock up on more supplies at the new site.

The real issue was going to be kitting out another full-service, permanent clinic, but that was going to take months and millions of dollars.

As Phury came out to the registration desk, a phone that was still in its cradle went off. The ringing stopped as the call dumped into voice mail, the greetings of which had just been changed to, "This number is no longer in service. Please refer to the following general information number."

Vishous had set up the second number as a place where people could leave their contact information and their message. Once their identity and inquiry were verified, the staff at the new clinic would call them back. With V routing it all through his Four Toys back at the Pit, he'd be able to capture the numbers of anyone who phoned in, so if the *lessers* sneaked a peek, the Brothers could try to trace their lines.

Phury paused and listened hard, his grip tightening on the SIG. Havers had had the smarts to stash a gun under each of the driver's seats in the ambulances, so Z's nine was back in the family, so to speak.

Relative silence. Nothing out of order. V and Rhage were at the

new clinic in case the caravan had been trailed by the enemy. Zsadist was doing a welding job on the south tunnel's busted entrance. Rehvenge might even have left already.

Even though the clinic was fairly secure, he was prepared to shoot to kill. Ops like this one always made him twitchy—

Shit. This was probably his last op, wasn't it. And he'd been a part of this one only because he'd come for Zsadist, not because he'd been called in as a member of the Brotherhood.

Trying not to get all up in his head, Phury walked down another hallway, this one taking him to the emergency services part of the clinic. He was passing a supply room when he heard the sound of glass on glass.

He pulled Z's gun up tight to his face as he braced himself at the doorjamb. A quick lean in and he saw what was doing: Rehvenge was standing in front of a locked cabinet that had a fist hole through its door, and he was transferring vials from the shelves into the pockets of his sable coat.

"Relax, vampire," the male said without turning around. "This is just dopamine. I'm not black-marketing OxyContin or some shit."

Phury dropped the gun back to his side. "Why are you taking—"

"Because I need it."

When the last vial had been lifted, Rehv turned away from the cabinet. His amethyst eyes were characteristically shrewd, like those of a viper. Man, he always looked as if he were measuring his striking distance, even when he was among the Brothers.

"So how do you think they found this place?" Rehv asked.

"Don't know." Phury nodded to the door. "Come on, we're pulling out. This place is not secure."

The smile that flashed revealed fangs that were still elongated. "I'm quite confident I can handle myself."

"No doubt. But it's probably a good idea that you take off."

Rehv crossed the supply room with care, navigating around the fallen boxes of bandages and latex gloves and thermometer covers.

He leaned heavily on his cane, but only a fool would have mistaken him for having a disability.

His tone was as kind as it ever got as he said softly, "Where are your black daggers, celibate?"

"None of your biz, sin-eater."

"Indeed." Rehv nudged a spray of tongue depressors with his cane as if he were trying to get them back in their box. "I think you should know your twin talked to me."

"Did he."

"Time to go."

Both of them looked out into the hall. Zsadist was standing behind them, his brows down over eyes that were black.

"Like as in now," Z said.

Rehv smiled calmly as his phone went off. "And what do you know. My ride is here. Pleasure doing business with you, gentlemen. Laters."

The guy stepped around Phury, nodded at Z, and cocked his cell to his ear as he walked off with that cane of his.

The sound of him dimmed, and then there was a whole lot of silence.

Phury answered the question before his twin could ask it: "I came because you wouldn't answer my calls."

He held out the SIG, offering the weapon butt-first to Z.

Zsadist accepted the nine, checked the chamber, holstered it. "I was too pissed off to talk to you."

"I wasn't calling about us. I found Bella in the dining room looking weak and I carried her upstairs. I think Jane would be a good visitor, but that's your call."

Zsadist's face drained of color. "Did Bella say anything was wrong?"

"She was fine when she settled in bed. Said she'd had too much to eat and that was the problem. But . . ." Maybe he'd been wrong about her bleeding? "I really think Jane should visit her—"

Zsadist took off at a dead run, his shitkickers pounding down the empty hall, the thunderous sound reverberating throughout the empty clinic.

Phury followed at a walk. As he thought about his role as Primale, he pictured himself racing off to check on Cormia with the same concern and urgency and desperation. God, he could picture it with such clarity . . . her with his young inside of her, him on all-shift anxiety, just like Z.

He stopped and peered into a patient room.

How had his father felt while standing at his mother's birthing side when two healthy sons had been born to him? He'd probably been overjoyed beyond measure . . . until Phury had come out and been the excess of blessing.

Births were a total gamble on so many levels.

As Phury kept going down the hall toward the busted elevator, he thought, yeah, his parents had probably known right from the beginning that two healthy sons would lead to a lifetime of misery. They'd been strict religious adherents to the Scribe Virgin's value system of balance. On some level, they must not have been surprised at Z's abduction, because it had reset the family's equilibrium.

Maybe that was why his father had abandoned the search for Zsadist after he'd learned that the nursemaid had died and the son that had been lost had been sold into slavery. Maybe Aghony had figured his quest would merely doom Zsadist even further—that in seeking the return of the one who had been taken, he had caused the death of the nursemaid and triggered not just bad circumstances, but totally untenable ones.

Maybe he blamed himself for Z ending up in slavery.

Phury could so relate to that.

He paused and looked at the waiting room, which was as scrambled and out of order as a bar after a free-for-all.

He thought of Bella hanging in the balance with that pregnancy, and worried about whether the curse was through working its hell yet.

At least he'd gotten Cormia free of his legacy.

The wizard nodded. *Good work, mate. You've saved her. It's the first worthwhile thing you've ever done.*

She will be much, much better without you.

TWENTY

r. D pulled up behind the farmhouse and turned off the Focus. The bags from Target were in the passenger seat, and he grabbed them as he got out. The receipt in his wallet read $147.73.

His credit card had been rejected, so he'd written a check that he wasn't sure was going to clear, and wasn't that just like old times? His daddy'd been a master at bouncing, and not because he played basketball in high school.

As Mr. D kicked shut the driver's-side door, he wondered if the reason *lessers* drove shit boxes wasn't because the Society was just keeping a low profile, but because it was out of money. Used to be you never worried if your credit card worked or whether you could get new weapons ASAP. Dang it, under that there Mr. R as *Fore-lesser*? Back in the eighties? The company ran good-like.

Not so much anymore. And now that was his problem. He should probably find out where all the accounts were, but he didn't have no idea where to start. There had been so much turnover in *Fore-lessers*. When had the last one with any organiz—

Mr. X.

Mr. X had been good in the saddle, and he'd had that cabin in the woods—Mr. D had gone there once or twice. Chances were good that if there was account information around, it would be there in some form or another.

Thing was, if his credit cards were failing, others' were. Which meant slayers were probably foraging on their own for cash, stealing from humans or keeping stuff they'd looted.

Maybe when he got there, he'd luck out and find that the piggy bank was fulled up, just lost in the shuffle. But he had a feeling that weren't going to be the case.

As rain started falling again, he propped open the farmhouse's back screen door with his hip, unlocked the place, and went into the kitchen. He held his breath at the stench of the two bodies. The man and the woman, as they turned out to be, were still doing their best impression of gruesome throw rugs, but one good thing about being a *lesser* was you came with your own air freshener. Within moments he didn't smell them at all.

As he put the bull's-eye bags down on the counter, there was the oddest sound drifting around the house, a humming . . . like a lullaby.

"Master?" Either that or someone was playing Radio Disney.

He came around into the dining room and stopped dead.

The Omega was standing beside the ratty table, leaning over the naked body of a blond male vampire that was stretched out flat. The vampire had had its throat slashed right up close to the chin, but the injury had been stitched up, and not in an autopsy way. That was some pretty little threading right chere.

Was the thing alive or dead? He couldn't tell—no, wait, that big chest was going up and down a little.

"He is so beautiful, is he not." The Omega's black translucent

hand drifted over the male's facial planes. "Blond as well. The mother was a blond. Hah! I was told I could not create. Not like *her*. But our father was wrong. Look at my son. Flesh of my flesh."

Mr. D felt like he had to say something, kind of like he'd been presented with a baby for the praising. "He's a good-looking one, yes, suh."

"Do you have what I asked for?"

"Yes, suh."

"Bring me the knives."

When Mr. D came back in with the Target bags, the Omega put one hand over the male's nose and another over its mouth. The vampire's eyes popped open, but the thing was too weak to do more than paw at the Omega's white robes.

"My son, do not fight," the evil breathed with satisfaction. "The time for your second birth has arrived."

The jerky struggling crescendoed until the vampire's heels were banging on the table and its palms squeaked on the wood. It flopped about like a puppet, all flailing, uncoordinated limbs and useless panic. And then it was done and the male stared upward with blank eyes and a lax mouth.

As rain lashed the windows, the Omega swooped the white hood off his head and unclasped his robe. With an elegant toss, he cast the vestment from himself, sending the satin weight sailing across the room. The thing settled upright in the corner, as if draped over a mannequin.

The Omega stretched up, growing long and thin, rubber-man-ing it toward the cheapie chandelier that hung above the table. He grasped its chain at the point where it entered the ceiling, and with a quick yank pulled the fixture free and pitched it into the corner. Unlike the robe, it did not land neatly, but ended its useful life, if it hadn't already, in a tangled heap of broken bulbs and twisted brass arms.

In its place, exposed wires hung like swamp vines from the stained ceiling, dangling over the vampire's body.

"Knife, please," the Omega said.

"Which one?"

"The short bladed."

Mr. D rummaged through the bags, found the right knife, then struggled to bust through a consumer-proof plastic wrapping that was so strong it made him want to stab himself in frustration.

"Enough," the Omega snapped, and held out his hand.

"I can get me some scissors—"

"Give it to me."

The instant the packaging hit the master's shadowy palm, the plastic burned away, curling free of the blade and dropping to the floor in a twisted brown snakeskin.

As the Omega turned to the vampire, he tested the sharpness on his own shadowy forearm, smiling as black oil rose out of the slice he made.

It was like gutting a pig, and it happened just as fast. While thunder prowled around the house as if it were searching for a way to get in, the Omega drew the blade down the center of the male's body from the wound at the guy's throat to his belly button. The smell of blood and meat rose up, winning out over the baby-fresh scent of the master.

"Bring me the capped vase." The Omega pronounced the word *vahz*, not *vase*.

Mr. D brought over a blue ceramic jar what he'd found in the housewares section. As it changed hands, he was tempted to point out to the master that it was too soon to remove the heart, because the Omega's blood had to be circulated through the body first. 'Cept then he remembered the male was dead anyway, so what did it matter?

Clearly this was not your everyday induction to the Society.

The Omega took his fingertip and burned open the vampire's sternum, the smell of bone on fire sending Mr. D's nose to wrinkles. The ribs were then split open by unseen hands at the will of the master and the still heart exposed.

The Omega's translucent palm went in and penetrated the sac around the heart, forming a new nest for the organ. With an expression of annoyance, he plucked the knot of muscle free from its chains of arteries and veins, red blood falling in a stream onto the pale skin of the male's chest.

Mr. D got the vase ready, uncapping it and holding it under the Omega's hand. Flames burst up from the heart, and a stream of ash fell into the vessel.

"Get the buckets," the Omega said.

Mr. D capped the vase and put it in the corner, then went into a bag and pulled out four red Rubbermaid buckets, the kind his mama had called sloppers. He positioned one under each of the vampire's arms and legs as the Omega went around and opened cuts in the wrists and ankles to drain the body of blood. It was amazing how fast the vampire's skin lost its color, moving through the spectrum past white into a bluish gray.

"The serrated knife now."

Mr. D didn't waste his effort on the blade's plastic lockdown. The Omega burned right through the thing, then took the knife and put his free hand down on the table. Curling his fingers into a fist, the master sawed through his own wrist, the sound as sharp as if he were working through aged hardwood. When he was finished, he passed the knife back, picked up his hand, and placed it inside the empty chest.

"Be of good cheer, my son," the Omega whispered as another hand appeared at the blunt end of his forearm. "You shall feel mine blood course through you in but a moment."

With that, the Omega streaked the other knife across his newly formed wrist and held the wound over the black fist.

Mr. D remembered this part from his own induction. He'd screamed in what had been more than physical pain. He'd been duped. So duped. What he'd been promised weren't like what he'd received, and the agony and terror had made him pass out. When he'd done woke up, he'd been something else entirely, a member of the living dead, an impotent, roaming body doing evil work.

He'd thought it was just a gang. He'd thought what would happen to him was just going to be some hazing and maybe a branding to mark that he was in with them.

Didn't know that he were never getting out. Or that he wouldn't be human no more.

Whole thing reminded him of something his mama used to say: *If you make a deal with a copperhead, you can't be surprised you get bit.*

All at once, the electricity went out.

The Omega stepped back and a hum started. This time it weren't no Disney crib musical, but the calling of a great gathering of energy, an impending reaping of some unseen potential. As the vibrations grew louder, the house started to shake, dust falling from cracks in the ceiling, the buckets vibrating on the floor until they were doing the do-si-do. Mr. D thought of the bodies in the kitchen and wondered if they was dancing, too.

As he put his hands to ears and ducked his head, he got back just in time.

A blast of lightning hit the farmhouse's roof in what had to be a direct line of contact. With the noise it made, it couldn't have been a ricochet or the feathering off of a larger piece.

Yup, this weren't no chip of a stone that got in your eye; this was the whole boulder landing smack down on your head.

The sound registered as pain in the ears, at least to Mr. D, and the shattering force of the impact made him wonder whether the house was going to crash in on them. The Omega didn't have that worry, 'parently. He just looked up with Sunday-preacher zeal, all rapt and orgasmic, like he was a true believer and someone had just brought out the rattlers and the strychnine.

The lightning funneled through the house's electrical highways, or in this case its back roads and beaten paths, and came out in a liquid shaft of brilliant yellow energy right over the body. The chan-

delier's hanging wires gave it its guidance, and the vampire's open chest with its oiled heart was the basin.

The body exploded off the table, arms and legs flapping, chest inflating. In a flash, the master blanketed the male, as if forming a second skin so that the four quadrants of flesh didn't fly apart like blown tires.

As the lightning receded, the male hung suspended in midair with his Omega blanket shimmering in the darkness.

Time . . . stopped.

Mr. D could tell because the cheapie cuckoo clock on the wall halted. For a span, there was no longer any moment-to-moment, just an infinite now as what had been without breath found its way back to the life it had lost.

Or rather, had been robbed of.

The male floated gently back down to the table, and the Omega removed itself from it, taking form once more. Gasping noises came from the vampire's gray lips, and a whistle let off on every inhale as air passed into its lungs. The heart flickered in the open chest cavity, then got its act organized and started pumping in earnest.

Mr. D focused on the face.

The death pallor was slowly replaced by a freaky rosy glow, the kind of thing you saw in a kid's face after they'd been running around in the wind. But that weren't no health. Nope. That was reanimation.

"Come to me, my son." The Omega passed his hand over the chest, and the bones and flesh cleaved together and soldered shut from navel to the stitched-up throat wound. "Live for me."

The male vampire bared its fangs. Opened its eyes. And roared.

Qhuinn didn't float back down into his body. Nope. As he stepped back from the white door in front of him and then ran like a bastard, life on Earth returned to him in a rush, his spirit landing in his skin like he'd been bootlicked in the ass with the Fade's All-mighty Converse All Star.

Someone's lips were crushed against his mouth, and air was being pushed into his lungs. Then there was a pounding on his chest, with someone counting along with the push and shove. There was a little pause, followed by more breathing.

It was a nice alteration of things. Breathing. Pounding. Breathing. Breathing. Pounding—

Qhuinn's body gave a sudden heave-ho, as if it were bored with having training wheels on its respiration. Riding the jerky spasm, he broke contact with the other mouth and sucked in a breath of his own.

"Thank you, God," Blay said in a strangled voice.

Qhuinn caught a brief impression of his friend's wide, teary eyes, then he curled onto his side and cramped up into a ball. Sucking air down his throat in shallow huffs, he felt his heart pick up the ball and run with it, fisting and releasing on its own. He had a moment of the oh-goody-I'm-alives, but then the pain hit him, washing over him, making him want to go back to being out of it. His lower back felt as if it had been dug out with a hammer claw.

"Let's get him into the car," Blay barked. "He needs to go to the clinic."

Qhuinn cracked an eye open and looked down his body. John was at his feet, nodding like a bobble-head.

Except, hell, no . . . they couldn't take him there. That Honor Guard wasn't finished with him. . . . Shit, his own brother . . .

"No . . . clinic," Qhuinn wheezed.

Fuck that, John signed.

"No. Clinic." He might not have much to live for, but that didn't mean he was in a big hurry to eat a Death Whopper with fries.

Blay leaned down, getting eyeball to eyeball with him. "You were in a hit-and-run with a fucking car—"

"Not . . . car."

Blay got silent. "What was it?" Qhuinn just held the guy's eyes and waited for him to figure it out. "Wait . . . it was an honor guard? Lash's family sent an honor guard after you?"

"Not . . . Lash's . . ."

"*Yours?*"

Qhuinn nodded, because the energy it took to move his swollen lips was too much like work.

"They aren't supposed to kill you. . . ."

"Duh."

Blay looked at John. "We can't take him to Havers's."

Doc Jane, John signed. *Then we need Doc Jane.*

As John took out his phone, Qhuinn was about to shoot down that idea when he felt something flutter against his arm. Blay's hand was shaking so badly, the guy couldn't even grab on to anything. Shit, the guy's whole body was shaking.

Qhuinn closed his eyes and reached out for that palm. As he listened to the soft clicking noise of John texting, he squeezed Blay's hand to comfort his friend. And himself.

A minute and a half later there was a beep announcing the text had been replied to.

"What is it?" John must have signed something, because Blay breathed out, "Oh . . . my . . . God. But she's coming, right? Good. My house? Right. Okay. Let's move him."

Two sets of hands lifted him up off the road shoulder, and he grunted from the agony . . . which he supposed was good, because it meant that the whole back-from-the-dead thing was probably for real. After he was settled in the backseat of Blay's car and his buddies were in with him, he felt the subtle vibrations of the BMW accelerating.

When he opened his eyes again, it was to meet John's stare. The guy was in the front seat, but he was cranked all the way around so he could keep a look-see on Qhuinn.

The guy's stare was worried and wary. Like he was not sure Qhuinn was going to make it . . . and he was thinking about what had gone down four hours and ten million years ago back in the locker room.

Qhuinn lifted his busted hands and signed in a messy way, *You are still the same to me. Nothing has changed.*

John's eyes shot to the left and he stared out one of the windows.

Headlights from a car behind them splashed against the guy's face, pulling it free of the darkness. Doubt was written clear as day in those proud, handsome features.

Qhuinn closed his eyes.

What a horrible night this was.

TWENTY-ONE

"Oh. My. God. That dress is a train wreck."

Cormia laughed and looked up at Bella and Zsadist's television. *Project Runway* was a fascinating "show," as it turned out. "What is that hanging down off the back?"

Bella shook her head. "Bad taste made manifest by satin. I think it started as a bow, though."

The two of them were stretched out on the mated couple's bed, leaning back against the headboard. The household's black cat was between them, enjoying the fruits of some two-handed petting, and Boo didn't seem to like the gown any more than Bella did. His green eyes regarded the TV with distaste.

Cormia shifted her hand from the cat's back to his flank. "The color is kind of nice."

"That doesn't make up for the fact that it's like shrink-wrap for a boat. And has a grappling rope tacked on the butt."

"I don't even know what a boat is. Much less shrink-wrap."

Bella pointed at the flat screen across the room. "You're looking at it. Just picture something that looks like a floating car under that nightmare and voilà."

Cormia smiled and thought that her time with the female had been both revelatory and strangely disorienting. She *liked* Bella. She honestly did. The female was funny and warm and thoughtful, as beautiful on the inside as she was on the outside.

No wonder the Primale adored her. And as much as Cormia had wanted to stake a claim on him around Bella, she found there was no need to exert her First Mate status. The Primale didn't come up as a topic of conversation, and there were no undertones to bump up against.

What she had perceived as a rival had turned out to be a friend.

Cormia went back to what was on her lap. The floppy booklet was big and thin, with glossy pages and lots of what Bella had told her were ads. *Vogue*, it said on the front. "Look at all these different kinds of clothes," she murmured. "How amazing."

"I'm almost done with *Harper's Bazaar*, if you want it—"

The door burst open with such force that Cormia leaped off the bed and sent *Vogue* flapping into the corner like a startled bird. The Brother Zsadist was in the doorway, fresh from fighting, given the stench of baby powder he carried and all the weapons on him.

"What's going on?" he demanded.

"Well," Bella said slowly, "you've just scared the holy hell out of Cormia and me, Tim Gunn has called time for the designers, and I'm getting hungry again, so I'm about to call Fritz and ask for an omelet. Bacon and cheddar cheese. With hash browns. And juice."

The Brother looked around as if he were expecting to see *lessers* behind the drapes. "Phury said you weren't feeling well."

"I was tired. He helped me up the stairs. Cormia started here as a babysitter, but now I think she's staying because she's kind of enjoying herself, aren't you? Or at least she was, right?"

Cormia nodded, but didn't take her eyes off the Brother. With his scarred face and his huge body, he'd always made her feel uncomfortable, not because he was ugly in any way, but because he appeared so fierce.

Zsadist looked over at her, and the oddest thing happened. He spoke in a shockingly kind voice and raised his hand as if to calm her.

"Easy, now. I'm sorry I scared you." His eyes gradually turned yellow and his face softened. "I'm just worried about my *shellan*. I'm not going to hurt you."

Cormia felt the tension in her release and found herself understanding better why Bella was with him. With a bow, she said, "Of course, Your Grace. Of course you are worried for her."

"Are you okay?" Bella asked, looking at her *hellren*'s black-stained clothes. "Is everyone in the family okay?"

"The Brothers are all fine." He went over to his *shellan* and touched her face with a hand that shook. "I want Doc Jane to have a look at you."

"If that would make you feel better, by all means, have her come. I don't think there's anything wrong, but I want to do whatever makes you feel more comfortable."

"Is it the spotting again?" Bella didn't answer. "I'll go get her—"

"It's not much, and it's nothing different from what I've had before. Doc Jane would probably be a good idea, except I doubt there's anything to be done." Bella turned her lips to his palm and kissed him. "But first, please tell me what happened tonight?"

Zsadist just shook his head, and Bella closed her eyes, as if she were used to getting bad news . . . as if she had gotten it so often that words about the exact situations were no longer needed. Speech could add nothing to her sadness or his. Nor could it relieve what they clearly felt.

Zsadist dipped his head and kissed his mate. As their eyes met, the love between them was so intense, it created an aura of warmth Cormia could swear she felt from over where she was standing.

Bella had never shown this kind of connection with the Primale. Ever.

Nor, for that matter, had he toward her. Although perhaps that was just out of discretion.

Zsadist said a few quiet words, then left as if he were on the prowl, brows down, heavy shoulders set like beams for a house.

Cormia cleared her throat. "Would you like me to get Fritz for you? Or put your order in for a repast?"

"I think I'd better wait, if Doc Jane's going to examine me." The female's hand crept up onto her belly and moved in slow circles. "Would you like to come back and watch the rest of the shows with me later?"

"If you'd like—"

"Absolutely. You're very good company."

"I am?"

Bella's eyes were impossibly kind. "Very. You make me feel calm."

"Then I shall be your birth companion. Where I'm from, a pregnant sister always has a birth companion."

"Thank you . . . thank you very much." Bella turned away as fear speared into her eyes. "I'll take any help I can get."

"If I may," Cormia murmured, "what worries you most?"

"Him. I worry about Z." Bella's eyes swung back. "Then I worry about my young. It's so strange. I don't worry about me all that much."

"You are very brave."

"Oh, you don't see me in the middle of the day in the dark. I fall apart plenty, trust me."

"I still think you are brave." Cormia put her hand on her flat stomach. "I doubt I could be so courageous."

Bella smiled. "I think you're wrong about that. I've watched you these past months, and there's an incredible strength in you."

Cormia wasn't so sure about that. "I do hope the examination goes well, and I'll come back later—"

"You don't honestly think it's easy to be what you are, do you? To live under the kind of pressures the Chosen have to? I can't imagine how you deal with it, and I have tremendous respect for you."

All Cormia could do was blink. "You . . . do?"

Bella nodded. "Yeah, I do. And you want to know something else? Phury's lucky to have you. I'm just praying he figures that out sooner rather than later."

Dearest Virgin Scribe, that was not something Cormia had ever expected to hear from anyone, much less Bella, and her shock must have shown because the female laughed.

"Okay, I've made you feel weird, and I'm sorry. But I've wanted to say that to the both of you for the longest time." Bella's eyes shifted over to the bathroom, and she took a deep breath. "Now I guess you'd better go so I can get ready for Doc Jane and her poking. Love that female, I really do, but man, I hate when she snaps on those gloves of hers."

Cormia said a good-bye of sorts and left for her own bedroom, deep in thought.

When she turned the corner next to Wrath's study, she stopped. As if she'd summoned him, the Primale was at the head of the great stairwell, looming large and looking exhausted.

His eyes clung to her.

He must hunger for news of Bella, she thought. "She's feeling better, but I think she's hiding something. The Brother Zsadist has just gone for Doc Jane."

"Good. I'm glad. Thank you for watching over her."

"It was my pleasure. She's lovely."

The Primale nodded; then his eyes traced over her from her hair, which was up high on her head, to her bare feet. It was as if he were reacquainting himself with her, as if he hadn't been around her for ages.

"What ugliness have you witnessed since you left?" she whispered.

"Why do you ask?"

"You stare at me as if it has been weeks since you saw me. What have you seen?"

"You read me well."

"About as well as you avoid my question."

He smiled. "Which would be very well, huh."

"You don't have to speak of—"

"I saw more death. Avoidable death. Such a damn waste. This war is evil."

"Yes. Yes, it is." She wanted to take his hand. Instead, she said, "Would you . . . join me in the garden? I was going to walk among the roses for a bit before the sun comes."

He hesitated, then shook his head. "I can't. I'm sorry."

"Of course." She bowed to avoid his eyes. "Your Grace."

"Be careful."

"I will." She gathered her robing and walked quickly to the stairs he had just mounted.

"Cormia."

"Yes?"

As she looked over her shoulder, his eyes bored into hers. They burned in a way that took her back to the two of them on the floor in his bedroom, and her heart leaped to her throat.

Except then he merely shook his head. "Nothing. Just stay safe."

As Cormia went down the stairs, Phury headed for the hall of statues and the first of the windows that looked out over the back garden.

Going with her to see the roses was so not an option. He was raw right now, stripped of his skin, though he still wore his suit of flesh. Every time he closed his eyes, he saw those bodies in the clinic's corridor and the scared faces in that medicine closet and the bravery of those who shouldn't have had to fight for their lives.

If he hadn't stopped to help Bella up the stairs and then gone to find Zsadist, maybe those civilians wouldn't have been saved. Sure as

hell, no one would have called him as backup, because he wasn't a Brother anymore.

Down below, Cormia emerged on the terrace, her white robe glowing against the dark gray stone pavers. She drifted over to the roses and bent at the waist to bring her nose to the blooms. He could almost hear her breath going in and the sigh of contentment she'd release as the fragrance registered.

His thoughts shifted from the ugliness of war to the beauty of the female form.

And to what males did with females in between satin sheets.

Yeah, it was a big no on being around Cormia right now. He wanted to replace the death and suffering he'd seen tonight with something else, something alive and warm and all about the body, not the head. As he watched his First Mate lavish her attentions on the rosebushes, he wanted her naked and writhing and slick with sweat underneath him.

Ah . . . but she wasn't his First Mate any longer, was she.

Shit.

The wizard's voice drifted through his head. *Could you honestly have done right by her, though? Made her happy? Kept her safe? You spend a good twelve hours a day smoking. Could you light up blunt after blunt in front of her and have her watch you wilt into your pillows and nod off? You want her to see that?*

Do you want her dragging you back into the house at dawn, like you did for your father?

Would you hit her in frustration someday, too?

"No!" he said out loud.

Oh, really? Your father said that to you. Didn't he, mate. Promised you right to your face that he'd never hit you again.

Problem is, the word of an addict is just that. A word. Nothing more.

Phury rubbed his eyes and turned away from the window.

To give himself a purpose, any purpose, he headed for Wrath's study. Even though he wasn't a member of the Brotherhood anymore, the king would want to know what had happened at the clinic. With Z busy with Jane and Bella, and the other Brothers helping out at the new clinic, he might as well make an unofficial report. Besides, he wanted Wrath to know the reason why he'd gone over there in the first place, and reassure the king that he wasn't disregarding his pink slip.

And then there was the whole Lash issue.

The kid was missing.

The tally of heads at the new clinic and the count of the bodies at the old one had revealed only one abduction, and Lash was it. The medical staff indicated he was alive at the time of the raid, having been resuscitated after his vitals crashed. Which was tragic. The kid might have been a bastard, but no one wanted him to fall into the hands of the *lessers*. If he was lucky, he'd died on the way to wherever they were taking him, and there was a good chance he had, given the shape he'd been in.

Phury knocked on Wrath's study. "My lord? My lord, you in?"

When there was no answer, he tried again.

He didn't get any response, so he turned away and headed for his room, knowing damn well he was going to light up and smoke out and take his place once again in the wizard's bleak kingdom.

As if you could be anywhere else, the dark voice in his head drawled.

Across town, at Blaylock's parents' house, Qhuinn was sneaked in through the back service entrance the *doggen* used. He did his best to limp along, but Blay had to carry him up the servants' staircase.

After Blay left his room to go lie about where he'd been and what he'd been doing, John took up sentry duty while Qhuinn settled on his buddy's bed with none of his usual relief. And not just because he felt like a punching bag.

Blay's folks deserved better than this. They'd been good to Qhuinn all along. Hell, a lot of parents wouldn't let their kids near him, but Blay's had been tight from the get-go. And now they were inadver-

tently jeopardizing their station in the *glymera* by harboring a dis-owned, PNG fugitive.

Just the thought of it all made Qhuinn sit up with the intention of taking off, but his belly had other plans for him. A sharpshooter went through his gut, like his liver had picked up a bow and arrow and taken aim at his kidneys. With a groan, he lay back down.

Try to stay still, John signed.

"Roger . . . that."

John's phone went off, and the guy took it out of the pocket of his A & F jeans. As he read whatever it was, Qhuinn thought back to the three of them going to the mall to shop and him fucking that manager in the dressing room.

Everything had changed since then. The whole world was different now.

He felt years older, not days.

John looked up with a frown. *They want me to come home. Something's up.*

"Take off then . . . I'm cool here."

I'll come back if I can.

"No worries. Blay'll keep you looped."

As John left, Qhuinn looked around and remembered all the hours he'd spent lying on the bed in this room. Blay had a sweet crib. The walls were paneled in cherrywood, which made it seem like a study, and the furniture was modern and sleek, not that stuffy antique crap all the members of the *glymera* collected along with ass-wrenching rules on social etiquette. The king-sized bed was covered with a black quilt and had enough pillows to get you comfortable without girling you up. The plasma screen high-def had an Xbox 360, a Wii and a PS3 on the floor in front of it, and the desk where Blay did his homework was as neat and orderly as all the cards to those gamers were. To the left, there was a dorm-sized refrigerator, a black Rubbermaid trash barrel that kind of looked like a cock, to be honest, and an orange bin for bottles.

Blay had gone green a while ago and was big into recycling and reuse. Which was so him. He gave monthly to PETA, ate only free-range meat and poultry, and was into organic food.

If there had been a vampire UN to intern at, or a way for him to volunteer at Safe Place, he would have done it in a heartbeat.

Blay was the closest thing to an angel Qhuinn had ever come near.

Fuck. He had to get out of here before his father got the whole family kicked out of the *glymera*.

As he shifted around to try to ease his lower back, he realized it wasn't all internal injuries that were making him uncomfortable: The envelope his father's *doggen* had given him had stayed put in the waistband of his jeans even through the beating.

He didn't want to see the papers again, but somehow they ended up in his dirty, bloody hands.

Even with his blurry eyesight and his case of the all-over agonies, he focused on the parchment. It was his five-generation family tree, his birth certificate, as it were, and he looked down to the three names on the last line. His was to the left, on the far side of his older brother's and his sister's. His entry was covered by a thick X, and underneath his parents' and siblings' listings were their signatures in the same heavy ink.

Taking him out of the family required a lot of paperwork. His brother's and sister's birth certificates would have to be modified like this, and his parents' marriage scroll would have to be edited, too. The *glymera*'s Princeps Council would also need to receive a declaration of disinheritance, the renunciation of parentage, and a petition for expulsion. After Qhuinn's name was redacted from both the *glymera*'s roll call and the aristocracy's massive genealogical file, the Council's *leahdyre* would then compose a missive that would be sent out to all the *glymera*'s families, formally announcing the exile.

Anyone with a mate-able female of appropriate age needed to be forewarned, of course.

It was all so ridiculous. With his mismatched eyes, it wasn't as if he would have gotten some aristocrat's name carved in his back anyway.

Qhuinn folded up the birth certificate and returned it to the envelope. As he closed the flap, his chest felt as if it were caving in. To be all alone in the world, even as an adult, was terrifying.

But to contaminate those who had been kind to him was worse.

Blay came through the door with a tray of food. "I don't know if you're hungry—"

"I've got to go."

His friend put what he was carrying down on the desk. "I don't think that's a good idea."

"Help me up. I'll be fine—"

"Bullshit," came a female voice.

The Brotherhood's private physician appeared out of thin air, right in front of them. Her doctor's bag was the old-fashioned kind, with two handles at the top and a body like a loaf of bread, and her coat was a white one, just like they wore at the clinic. The fact that she was a ghost was a nonstarter. Everything about her, from her clothes and bag to her hair and perfume, became solid and tangible as she arrived, exactly as if she were normal.

"Thank you for coming," Blay said, ever the good host.

"Hey, Doc," Qhuinn muttered.

"And what do we have here." Jane came over and sat on the corner of the bed. She didn't touch him, just looked him up and down with an intense physician's eye.

"Not exactly a candidate for *Playgirl*, huh," he said awkwardly.

"How many of them were there?" Her voice wasn't joking around.

"Eighteen. Hundred."

"Four," Blay interjected. "An honor guard of four."

"Honor guard?" She shook her head, as if she couldn't understand the race's ways. "For Lash?"

"No, from Qhuinn's own family," Blay said. "And they weren't supposed to kill him."

Well, if that wasn't his new theme song, Qhuinn thought.

Doc Jane opened her bag. "Okay, let's see what's doing under your clothes."

She was characteristically all business as she cut off his shirt, listened to his heart, and took his blood pressure. As she worked, he passed the time looking at the wall, the blank TV screen, her bag.

"Handy . . . *bag* . . . you got there," he grunted as her hands palpated his abdomen and hit a soft spot.

"Always wanted one. It's part of my *Marcus Welby, M.D.*, fetish."

"Who?"

"This hurt, too?" His gasp as she poked him again answered just fine, so he left it at that.

Doc Jane took off his pants, and as he went commando, he quickly pulled some sheets over his privates. She pushed them aside, looked him over professionally front to back, and then asked him to flex his arms and legs. After she lingered over a couple of spectacular black and blues, she covered him again.

"What did they work you over with? Those bruises on your thighs are severe."

"Crowbars. Big, massive—"

Blay cut in. "Clubs. Had to be those ceremonial black clubs."

"That would be consistent with the injuries." Doc Jane took a moment, as if she were a computer processing an information request. "Right, here's where we are. What's going on with your legs is undoubtedly uncomfortable, but the contusions should heal on their own. You have no open wounds, and although it appears your palm was knifed, I'm assuming that happened a little earlier, because it's healing already. And nothing appears broken, which is a miracle."

Except his heart, of course. To be beaten by your own brother—

Shut it, you pantywaist, he told himself.

"So I'm just fine, right, Doc?"

"How long were you out cold?"

He frowned, that vision from the Fade suddenly swooping down out of his memory like a black crow. God . . . had he died?

"Ah . . . I have no idea how long. And I didn't see anything while I was out. It was just blackness, you know . . . I was down for the count." No way he was talking about that little all-natural acid trip. "But I'm good, you know—"

"I'm going to have to disagree with you there. Your heart rate's high, your blood pressure is low, and I don't like that belly of yours."

"It's just a little sore."

"I'm worried something's ruptured."

Great. "I'll be fine."

"And your medical degree is from where?" Doc Jane smiled, and he laughed a little. "I'd like to give you an ultrasound, but Havers's clinic got hit tonight."

"*What?*"

"*What?*" Blay asked at the same time.

"I assumed you knew."

"Were there survivors?" Blay asked.

"Lash is missing."

While the implications of that little news flash sank in, Jane reached into her bag of goodies and took out a sealed needle and a vial with a rubber top. "I'm going to give you something for the pain. And don't worry," she said wryly, "it's not Demerol."

"Why, is Demerol bad?"

"For vampires? Yes." She rolled her eyes. "Trust me."

"Whatever you think sounds good."

When she was finished shooting him up, she said, "This should last you a couple of hours, but I plan to be back way before that."

"Dawn must be close, huh."

"Yup, so we're going to have to move fast. There's a temporary clinic set up—"

"I can't go there," he said. "I can't . . . That would not be a good call."

Blay nodded. "We need to keep his whereabouts on the DL. He's not safe anywhere right now."

Doc Jane's eyes narrowed. After a moment, she said, "Okay. Then I'll figure out where I can get you what you need in a more private setting. In the meantime, I don't want you to move from this bed. And no eating or drinking, in case I have to go in."

As Doc Jane packed up her Marcus-whoever-he-was bag, Qhuinn counted the number of people who wouldn't have come near him, much less try to treat his injuries.

"Thank you," he said in a small voice.

"My pleasure." She put her hand on his shoulder and squeezed. "I'm going to fix you. Bet your life on it."

In that moment, as he looked into her dark green eyes, he honestly believed she could fix the whole wide world, and the wave of relief that washed over him was as if someone had tucked a soft blanket all around his body. Shit, whether it was the fact that his life was in capable hands or the result of whatever she'd pumped into his arm, he didn't really care. He'd take the easing where he found it.

"I feel sleepy."

"That's my plan."

Doc Jane went over and whispered to Blay for a moment . . . and though the guy tried to hide his reaction, his eyes widened.

Ah, so he was in deep shit, Qhuinn thought.

After the doc left, he didn't bother to ask what had been said, because there was no way Blay was going to go there. His face was a closed cupboard.

But there was still plenty of other stuff to cover, thanks to the shit storm they were all in. "What did you tell your parents?" Qhuinn asked.

"You don't have to worry about a thing."

In spite of the exhaustion that was dragging at him, he shook his head. "Tell me."

"You don't—"

"You tell me . . . or I'm going to get up and start doing fucking Pilates."

"Whatever. You've always said that was for pansies."

"Fine. Jujitsu. Talk before I pass out, would you?"

Blay took a Corona out of the little fridge. "My parents guessed it was us coming in. They're just back from the *glymera*'s big party. So Lash's folks must be finding out now."

Fuck. "You tell them . . . about me?"

"Yeah, and they want you to stay." The beer made a gasping sound as Blay opened it. "We're just not going to say anything to anybody. There'll be speculation about where you've gone, but it's not like the *glymera*'s going to do a house search for you, and our *doggen* are discreet."

"I'm only staying today."

"Look, my parents love you, and they're not going to toss you out on your ass. They know what Lash was like, and they also know your parents." Blay stopped there, but the tone he'd used added a lot of adjectives to the words.

Prejudicial, judgmental, cruel . . .

"I'm no one's burden." Qhuinn glowered. "Not yours. Not anyone's."

"It's not a burden, though." Blay's eyes dropped to the floor. "I just have my parents and me. Who do you think I'd go to if something bad happened? John and you are all I have in this world apart from my mom and dad. The two of you are my family."

"Blay, I'm going to jail."

"We don't have any jails, so you're going to need a place to be under house arrest in."

"And you don't think that'll be public record? You don't think I'll have to disclose where I stay?"

Blay swallowed half his beer, got out his phone, and started texting. "Listen, can you stop playing spot-the-obstacle? We're going to have enough problems of our own without you pulling more out of your ass. We'll figure a way for you to stay here, okay?"

There was a beep.

"See? John agrees." Blay flashed the screen, which read, GREAT IDEA on it, then polished off his beer with the satisfied expression of a male who had sorted out both his basement and his garage. "This is all going to be fine."

Qhuinn eyed his friend through lids that had become heavy as tile roofs. "Yeah."

As he passed out, his last thought was that, sure, things were going to work out . . . just not how Blay had it planned.

TWENTY-TWO

Lash, son of the Omega, was reborn on a scream that ripped out of his throat.

In confused madness, he returned to the world as he had come into it twenty-five years before: naked and gasping and bloodied, only this time his body was that of a full-grown male, not an infant.

His quick moment of conscious awareness passed fast, and then he was in agony, his veins filled with acid, every inch of him corroding from the inside out. He put his hands on his stomach, jacked over to the side, and threw up black bile onto a worn wooden floor. Too consumed by the retching, he didn't bother to wonder where he was or what had happened or why he was voiding stuff that looked like old crankcase oil.

In the midst of the swirling disorientation and the crippling heaves and a blind panic he couldn't control, a savior reached out to him. A hand smoothed down his back and stroked him over and over again, the warm palm falling into a rhythm that slowed his racing heart and calmed his head and eased his stomach. When he could, he rolled onto his back again.

In the midst of a blurry visual field, a black translucent figure came into focus. Its face was ethereal, a vision of male beauty in the bloom of its early twenties, but the malevolence behind the shadowy eyes made the visage horrible.

The Omega. It had to be the Omega.

This was the Evil his religion and folklore and training had described.

Lash started to scream again, but the shadowed hand reached out to him and gently touched his arm. He calmed.

Home, Lash thought. *I am home.*

His head flickered in hysteria at the conviction. He was not home. He was . . . Sure as hell he'd never seen this decrepit room before.

Where the fuck was he?

"Be of ease," the Omega murmured. "It shall all come back to you."

And it did, in a rush. He saw the locker room at the training center . . . and John, that frickin' pansy, getting all freaked out when his dirty little secret was exposed. Then it was the two of them pounding it out until . . . Qhuinn . . . Qhuinn had sliced his throat open.

Holy shit . . . he could even feel himself going down onto the floor in the shower, the tiles a hard, wet landing pad. He relived the cold shock and remembered putting his hands to his throat and starting to gasp as a suffocating, choking squeeze overtook his chest . . . his blood . . . he'd been drowning in his own blood . . . but then he'd been stitched up and sent to the clinic, where . . .

Shit, he'd died, hadn't he. The doctor had brought him back, but he had definitely died.

"Which was how I found you," the Omega murmured. "Your death was the beacon."

But why would the Evil want him?

"Because you are my son," the Omega said in a reverent, distorted voice.

Son? *Son?*

Lash shook his head slowly. "No . . . no . . ."

"Look into my eyes."

When the connection was made, more scenes were shown to him, the visions like pages flipped in a picture book. The story that unfolded made him both cringe and breathe easier. He was the son of the Evil. Born of a vampire female held against her will in this very farmhouse over two decades ago. After his birth he had been left at a gathering site for vampires, found by them, and taken to Havers's clinic . . . where he was later adopted by his family in a private exchange that even he didn't know about.

And now, having reached his maturity, he had returned to his sire. *Home.*

As Lash grappled with the implications, a hunger swirled in his belly, and his fangs protruded into his mouth.

The Omega smiled and looked over his shoulder. A *lesser* the size of a fourteen-year-old stood in the far corner of the shitty room, his ratlike eyes trained on Lash, his small body tense as a coiled snake.

"And now for the service you shall provide," the Omega said to the slayer.

The Evil extended his shadowy hand and beckoned the guy forward.

The *lesser* didn't so much walk as move in a block, as if his arms and legs were paralyzed and his body were being lifted and carried upright over the floor. Pale eyes popped wide and rolled with panic, but Lash had other things on his mind than the fear of the man being presented to him.

As he caught the sweet scent of the *lesser*, he sat up, baring his fangs.

"You shall feed my son," the Omega said to the slayer.

Lash didn't wait for consent. He reached up, grabbed that little fucker around the back of the neck, and dragged the guy to his tingling canines. He bit hard and sucked deep, the blood sweet as treacle and just as thick.

It didn't taste like anything he was used to, but it filled his belly and gave him strength, and that was the point.

As he nursed, the Omega started to laugh, softly at first, then louder, until the house shook from the force of mad, murderous glee.

Phury tapped his blunt on the lip of his ashtray and looked at what he'd done with his quill. The drawing was shocking, and not just because of the subject matter.

The damn thing was also one of the best he'd ever put on a piece of paper.

The female form on the creamy expanse was lying back on a bed of satin, with pillows puffed up behind her shoulders and neck. One arm was above her head, her fingers twining in her long hair. The other was down at her side, the hand resting at the juncture of her thighs. Her breasts were taut, her little nipples peaked for a mouth, and her lips were parted in invitation—as were her legs. Both were open, one knee bent up, her foot arched, her toes curled tight, as if she were anticipating something delicious.

She was staring straight out of the page, looking right at him.

What he'd done was no willy-nilly sketch, either. The drawing was fully rendered, painstakingly crosshatched, perfectly shaded to show the female's allure. The result was sex personified in three dimensions, an orgasm about to be realized, all the things a male would want in a sensual partner.

As he took another drag, he tried to tell himself that she wasn't Cormia.

No, this wasn't Cormia . . . this was no one female, just a composite of sexual attributes he'd forgone with all his celibacy. This was the feminine ideal he wished he had been with for his first time. This was the female he would have loved to have been drinking from all

these years. This was his fantasy lover, giving and demanding by turns, soft and yielding sometimes, greedy and naughty at others.

She was not real.

And she was not Cormia.

He exhaled a curse, rearranged the hard cock in his pajama bottoms, and stabbed out the blunt.

He was so full of shit. Full. Of. Shit. This absolutely was Cormia.

He glanced at the Primale medallion over on the bureau, thought of his talk with the Directrix, and cursed again. Great. Now that Cormia wasn't his First Mate, he'd decided that he wanted her. Just his luck.

"Christ."

He leaned over to the bedside table, twisted up another fattie, and lit the fucker. With the hand-rolled between his lips, he started to draw the ivy, beginning at her lovely, curled toes. As he added leaf after leaf and obscured the drawing, he felt as if it were his hands going up her smooth legs and over her stomach and up to her tight, high breasts.

He was so distracted by caressing her in his mind that the choking sensation that usually came when he covered a drawing with the ivy didn't flare up until he got to her face.

He paused. This truly was Cormia and not a half-her, as his drawing of Bella had been the other night. Cormia's features were all there, out in plain view, from the tilt of her eyes to the plump of her lower lip to the lushness of her hair.

And she was looking at him. Wanting him.

Oh, God . . .

He quickly drew the ivy up around her face and then stared at the way he'd ruined her. The shit covered her completely, even overflowing the bounds of her body, burying her without putting her under the ground.

In a flash, he recalled the garden at his parents' house as he had seen it that last time, when he'd gone back to bury them.

God, he could still remember that night with perfect clarity. Especially how the remnants of the fire had smelled.

The grave he had dug was off to the side, the hole in the earth a raw wound in the thick ivy of the garden. He'd put both his parents in it, but there had been only one body to bury. He'd had to burn his mother's remains. When he'd found her, she had decomposed in her bed to such an extent that he wasn't able to carry her out of the basement. He'd set what was left of her on fire down where she'd lain, and had spoken sacred words until the smoke had choked him so badly he'd had to get out.

While the fire raged within her stone room, he had picked up his father and taken the male out to the grave. After the blaze had devoured what it could reach in the basement, Phury had swept up the ashes that were left and placed them in a large bronze urn. There had been a lot of them, because he'd burned the mattress and bedding along with her.

The urn went next to his father's head, and then he had shoveled loose dirt on the top of them.

He'd burned the whole house down after that. Burned it flat to the ground. It was cursed, the whole place, and he was sure that even the fierce temperature of the flames hadn't been enough to cleanse the infection of bad luck.

As he'd left, his last thought had been that it wouldn't be long before the ivy covered up the foundation.

Sure you burned it all, the wizard said in his head. *But you were right, you didn't make the curse go away. All those flames didn't cleanse them or you, did they, mate. Just made you an arsonist as well as a failed savior.*

Putting out the blunt, he wadded up the drawing, attached his prosthesis, and went to his door.

You can't run from me or the past, the wizard murmured. *We're like the ivy on that plot of land, with you always, covering you up, blanketing the curse that is upon you.*

J.R. WARD

Throwing out the drawing, he left his room, suddenly frightened of being alone.

As he stepped out into the corridor, he nearly plowed over Fritz. The butler leaped back in time, protecting a bowl of . . . peas? Peas in water?

Cormia's constructions, Phury thought as what was in the *doggen*'s arms sloshed around.

Fritz smiled in spite of the near miss, his wrinkled, rubbery face pulling into a happy grin. "If you are looking for the Chosen Cormia, she is in the kitchen, taking her Last Meal with Zsadist."

Z? What the hell was she doing with Z? "They're together?"

"I believe the sire wished to speak with her privately about Bella. That is why I am doing chores elsewhere in the house at the moment." Fritz frowned. "Are you all right, sire? May I get you anything?"

How about a head transplant? "No, thanks."

The *doggen* bowed and went into Cormia's room, just as voices drifted up from the foyer. Phury went to the balcony and leaned over the gold-leafed rail.

Wrath and Doc Jane were at the foot of the stairs, and Jane's ghostly expression was as strident as her voice.

"—ultrasound technology. Look, I know it's not ideal, because you don't like people on the grounds, but we don't have a choice here. I went to the clinic, and not only will they not accept him, they demanded to know where he was."

Wrath shook his head. "Christ, we can't just bring him—"

"Yes, we can. Fritz can pick him up in the Mercedes. And before you argue with that, you've had those trainees coming to the compound every week since last December. He won't know where he is. And as for the *glymera* shit, no one needs to know he's here. He could die, Wrath. And I don't want that on John's conscience, do you?"

The king cursed long and low and glanced around, as if his eyes needed something to do while his head churned over the sitch. "Fine.

Arrange for the pickup with Fritz. The kid can have the test and the operation, if need be, in the PT suite, but then he has to be transported back out ASAP. I don't give a rat's ass about the *glymera's* opinions, what I'm worried about is precedent. We can't become a hotel."

"Understood. And listen, I'm going to want to help Havers out. It's too much for him to set up the new clinic and care for patients. Thing is, it's going to involve some days off-site for me."

"Vishous okay with that security risk?"

"Not his call, and I'm telling you only out of courtesy." The female laughed dryly. "Don't give me that look. I'm already dead. It's not like the *lessers* can kill me again."

"That is so not funny."

"Gallows humor is part of having a doctor in the house. Deal with it."

Wrath barked a laugh. "You are such a hard-ass. No wonder V fell for you." The king grew serious. "But let's be perfectly clear. Hard-ass or not, I'm in charge here. This compound and everyone in it is my deal."

The female smiled. "God, you remind me of Manny."

"Who?"

"My old boss. Chief of surgery at St. Francis. The two of you would get along beautifully. Or . . . maybe not." Jane reached out and put her transparent hand on the king's thick, tattooed forearm. As the contact was made, she became solid from head to toe. "Wrath, I'm not stupid, and I'm not going to do anything precipitous. You and I want the same thing, which is for everybody to be safe—and that includes members of the species who don't live here. I'm never going to work for you, or anybody else, because that's not my nature. But I'm sure as hell going to work *with* you, okay?"

Wrath's smile was full of respect, and he nodded once, the closest the king ever came to a bow. "I can live with that."

As Jane took off in the direction of the underground tunnel, Wrath looked up at Phury.

He said nothing.

"That Lash you were talking about?" Phury asked, hoping the kid had been found or something.

"Nope."

Phury waited for a name. When the king just turned and hit the stairs, his long, calm stride eating up the distance two steps at a time, it was clear none was coming.

Brotherhood business, Phury thought.

Which used to be yours, the wizard was kind enough to point out. *Until you lost your napper.*

"I was coming to find you," Phury lied, going over to his king and deciding that an unofficial report about what had happened at the clinic was clearly unnecessary by this time. "There are a couple of Chosen who are going to be stopping by here. They're coming to see me."

The king's brows sank behind his wraparounds. "So you completed the ceremony with Cormia, huh. Shouldn't you be seeing the females over on the Other Side?"

"I will soon enough." Shit, wasn't that the truth.

Wrath crossed his arms over his heavy chest. "I heard you manned up at the clinic tonight. Thanks for that."

Phury swallowed hard.

When you were a Brother, you were never thanked by the king for what you did, because you were just carrying out your duty and your job and your birthright. You might get an *attaboy* for kicking ass, or some awkward, testosterone-scrambled sympathy if you got cracked and were hurt . . . but you were never thanked.

Phury cleared his throat. He couldn't get *you're welcome* out, so he just murmured, "Z was on top of everything . . . and so was Rehv, who happened to be there."

"Yeah, I'm going to thank Rehvenge as well." Wrath turned toward the study. "That *symphath* is proving useful."

Phury watched the double doors slowly close, the pale blue room beyond getting shut out of his sight.

As he himself turned to go, he caught sight of the majestic ceiling of the foyer, those warriors so proud and true.

Now he was a lover, not a fighter, wasn't he.

Aye, the wizard said. *And I bet you'll be just as bad at the sex. Now go run along and find Cormia and tell her how you like her so much you're benching her. Look into her eyes and tell her that you're going to fuck her sisters. All of them. Every one of them.*

Except her.

And tell yourself you're doing the right thing by her as you break her heart. Because that is the reason you're running. You have seen the way she looks at you and you know that she loves you and you are a coward.

Tell her. Tell her everything.

As the wizard started on a true roll, Phury took the stairs down to the first floor, went into the billiards room, and picked up a bottle of Martini & Rossi vermouth and a bottle of Beefeater gin. He grabbed a jar of olives, a martini glass, and . . .

The box of toothpicks made him think of Cormia.

Heading upstairs again, he was still afraid to be alone, but he was equally afraid of being around anyone else.

The only thing he knew was that there was one surefire way of shutting down the wizard, and he was going to work that plan.

Until he passed the fuck out.

TWENTY-THREE

For the most part, Rehv didn't like staying in the studio behind his office at ZeroSum. After a night like tonight, though, he wasn't up for driving out of the city to the safe house where his mother stayed, and his penthouse at the Commodore, with its glass-fronted views, was so not an option.

Xhex had picked him up from the clinic, and on the way back to the club he'd gotten grilled pretty damn good as to why he hadn't called her in for the fighting. But come on, he'd said to her, another half-breed *symphath* in the mix?

Yeah, right. Besides, clinics made her jumpy as hell.

After he'd filled her in on the infiltration, he'd lied and said Havers had given him a look-see and some drugs. She'd known he was talking out of his ass about his arm, but thank fuck it was too close to dawn for them to get into a knock-down-drag-out. Sure, she could have stayed around and continued to argue with him, but Xhex always had to get back to her place. Always.

To the point that he wondered what exactly was waiting at home for her. Or who.

Walking into his bathroom, he kept his sable on even though the dial on the thermostat was cranked all the way up to fireplace. As he got the shower's heat rolling, he thought about what had gone down at the clinic and found that it had been tragically energizing. Fighting to him was like a Tom Ford suit: a perfect fit and something he could sport with pride. And the good news was that his *symphath* side had stayed in control, even with the enticement of all that *lesser* blood getting spilled.

See? He was fine. He really was.

When steam began to waft up all around him, he forced himself to take off his coat and his Versace suit and his Pink shirt. The clothes were utterly trashed, and his sable hadn't fared much better. He put them in a pile for dry cleaning and mending.

On the way to the hot water, he walked by the long mirror over the bank of glass sinks. Turning toward his reflection, he ran his hands down the five-pointed red stars on his chest. Then he went lower and cupped his cock.

Would have been nice to have some sex after all that, or at least cleanse his body's palate with a good hand job. Or three.

As he hefted himself in his palms, he couldn't ignore the fact that his left forearm looked like it had been put through a meat grinder from all his injections.

Side effects just sucked.

He stepped under the water and knew that it was hot only because of the milky, humid air around him and the way his core temperature let out a huge sigh of relief. His skin told him nothing, not how hard the spray was hitting his shoulders, not that the bar of soap he passed over himself was smooth and slippery, not that his palm was broad and warm as it followed the suds and swept them off to the drain below.

He kept it up with the soap routine longer than was necessary.

Thing was he couldn't stand to go to bed with any kind of dirt on him, but more than that, he needed the excuse to stay in the shower. This was one of the few times he was warm enough, and the shock of stepping out was always a bitch.

Ten minutes later, he was naked between the sheets of his king-sized bed and had his thick mink blanket up to his chin like a child. As the inner chill from having toweled off faded, he closed his eyes and willed the lights off.

His club on the other side of the steel-paneled walls would be empty by now. His girls would be home for the day, as most of them had kids. His bartenders and bookies would be grabbing a bite and unwinding somewhere. His backroom scale staff of geeks would be watching *Star Trek: TNG* reruns. And his twenty-person cleaning crew would be finished with the floors and the tables and the bathrooms and the banquettes and be ditching their uniforms and heading off to their next job.

He liked the idea that he was here alone. It didn't happen often.

As his phone went off, he cursed and was reminded that even if he was by himself, there were always people yapping at him.

He sneaked his arm out to answer the thing. "Xhex, if you want to keep arguing, let's TO until tomorrow—"

"Not Xhex, *symphath*." Zsadist's voice was tight as a fist. "And I'm calling about your sister."

Rehv sat up, not caring that the blankets dropped from his body. "What."

When he hung up with Zsadist, he lay back down, thinking this had to be what you felt like when you thought you were having a heart attack, but it turned out just to be indigestion: relieved, but still sick to your stomach.

Bella was okay. For now. The Brother had called because he was keeping to the deal they'd struck. Rehv had promised he wouldn't interfere, but he wanted to be in the loop about how she was doing.

Man, this pregnancy thing was awful.

He pulled the covers up to his chin again. He needed to call his mother and give her the update, but he'd do that later. She would just be retiring for bed, and there was no reason to keep her up all day long worrying.

God, Bella . . . his darling Bella, no longer his baby sister, now a Brother's *shellan*.

The two of them had always had a deep, complicated relationship. In part, it was their personalities, but it was also because she had no idea what he was. No clue either about their mother's past or what had killed her father.

Or who, was more like it.

Rehv had murdered to protect his sister, and he wouldn't hesitate to do so again. For as long as he could remember, Bella had been the only innocence in his life, the only purity. He'd wanted to keep her like that forever. Life had had other plans.

To avoid thinking about her abduction by the *lessers*, which he still blamed himself for, he recalled one of his most vivid memories of her. It had been about a year after he'd taken care of business at home and put her father in the ground. She'd been seven.

Rehv had walked into the kitchen and found her eating a bowl of Frosted Flakes at the kitchen table, her feet dangling from the big-girl chair she'd been sitting in. She'd been wearing pink slippers—the ones she didn't like but had to put on when her favorites, the navy blue ones, were in the wash—and a Lanz flannel nightgown that had strips of yellow roses separated with blue and pink lines.

She'd been such a picture, sitting there with her long brown hair down her back and those little pink slippers and her brow all furrowed as she chased around the last few flakes with her spoon.

"Why you watchin' me, rooster?" she'd piped up, her feet swinging back and forth underneath the chair.

He'd smiled. Even then he'd worn his hair in a Mohawk, and she was the only one who dared to give him a cheeky nickname. And, naturally, he loved her all the more for it. "No reason."

Which had been a lie. As that spoon fished around in the sugary milk, he'd been thinking that this calm, quiet moment had been so worth all the blood he'd gotten on his hands. In fucking spades.

With a sigh, she'd looked over at the cereal box, which was across the way on the kitchen counter. Her feet had stopped their rocking, the little *piff, piff, piff* of the slippers on the chair's lower rung drifting off into silence.

"What are you looking at, Lady Bell?" When she didn't immediately answer, he'd eyeballed Tony the Tiger. As scenes of her father had flashed through his head, he'd been willing to bet she was seeing the same thing he was.

In a small voice, she'd said, "I can have more if I want. Maybe."

Her tone had been hesitant, as if she were dipping her foot in a pond that might have leeches in it.

"Yeah, Bella. You may have as much as you like."

She hadn't leaped up out of the chair. She'd remained still in the manner of children and animals, just breathing, her senses threading out through her environment, testing for danger.

Rehv hadn't moved. Even though he'd wanted to bring the box to her, he'd known that she was the one who needed to cross the glossy red cherry floor in those slippers and bring Tony the Tiger back to her bowl. Her hands had to be the ones to hold the box as another school of flakes got sprinkled into the warming milk. She had to pick up her spoon again and eat.

She had to know that there was no one in the house who would criticize her for getting seconds because she was still hungry.

Her father had specialized in that kind of thing. Like a lot of males of his generation, the piece of shit had believed that females of the *glymera* needed to be "kept trim." As he'd said over and over again, fat on the aristocratic female body was the equivalent of dust accumulating on a priceless statue.

He'd been even harder on their mother.

In silence, Bella had looked down into the milk and weaved her spoon through it, making a wake of waves.

She wasn't going to do it, Rehv had thought, ready to kill that bastard sire of hers all over again. She was still scared.

Except then she'd put the spoon to rest on the plate under the bowl, slipped from the chair, and gone across the kitchen in her little Lanz nightgown. She didn't look at him. Didn't seem to look at Tony's cartoon-vivid puss when she picked up the box, either.

She was terrified. She was courageous. She was tiny and she was fierce.

His vision had run red at that point, but not because his bad side was coming out. As the second serving of Frosted Flakes had been poured, he'd had to go. He'd said something cheery about nothing in particular, walked quickly into the hall bathroom, and shut himself in.

He had wept his tears of blood alone.

That moment in the kitchen with Tony and Bella's second-best pair of slippers had told him he'd done right: The approval for the murder he'd committed had come when that cereal box had been walked across that kitchen by his darling, beloved, precious little sister.

Returning to the present, he thought of Bella now. A grown female with a powerful mate and a young barely in her body.

The demon she faced now was nothing her big, bad brother could help her with. There was no open grave into which he could throw the beaten, bloody remains of fate. He couldn't save her from this particular monster.

Time would tell, and that was that.

Until her abduction, he'd never once considered that she might die before him. During those hideous six weeks when she'd been kept by that *lesser* underground, though, the order of his family's deaths had been all he could think about. He'd always assumed that their mother was going to go first, and in fact, she'd just now started on

the quick decline that carried vampires to the end of their lives. He'd been well aware he'd go next, as sooner or later one of two things was going to happen: Either someone was going to find out about his *symphath* nature and he was going to be hunted down and sent to the colony, or his blackmailer was going to orchestrate his demise in the manner of *symphaths*.

Which was to say, out of the blue and viciously creative—

Right on cue, a musical chord came out of his phone. The ring repeated again. And again.

He knew who was calling without picking up. But such were the connections between *symphaths*.

Speak of the devil, he thought as he answered his blackmailer's call.

When he hung up, he had a date with the Princess the following evening.

Lucky him.

Qhuinn had this long, fucked-up dream that he was at Disney World on a ride with lots of ups and downs. Which was weird, as he'd only seen roller coasters on the TV. 'Cuz you couldn't get on Big Thunder Mountain if you couldn't handle the sun.

When whatever ride he was on ended, he opened his eyes and discovered he was in the PT/first-aid room at the Brotherhood's training center.

Oh, thank fuck.

Obviously he'd gotten cracked in the head while sparring with someone during class, and that shit with Lash and the stuff with his family and his brother honor-guarding him had all been a nightmare. What a relief—

Doc Jane's face appeared in front of his. "Hey, there . . . you're back."

Qhuinn blinked and coughed. "Where . . . I go?"

"You had a little nap. So I could take your spleen out."

Shit. Wasn't a hallucination. Was the new reality. "Am . . . I okay?"

Doc Jane put her hand on his shoulder, her palm warm and weighty even though the rest of her was translucent. "You did very well."

"Stomach still hurts." He lifted up his head and looked down his bare chest to the bandage sashing his waist.

"It would be wrong if it didn't. But you'll be happy to know you can go back to Blay's in an hour. The operation was totally textbook, and you're already healing well. I have no problem with daylight, so if you need me, I can be at his house in a moment. Blay knows what to watch for, and I've given him some meds for you."

Qhuinn shut his eyes, subsumed by some kind of fucked-up sadness.

As he tried to chill, he heard Doc Jane say, "Blay, you want to come over here—"

Qhuinn shook his head, then turned it away. "Need a minute alone."

"Are you sure?"

"Yes."

As the door closed quietly, he put a shaking hand over his face. Alone . . . yeah, he was alone, all right. And not just because there was no one else in the room with him.

He'd really enjoyed thinking the last twelve hours had been a dream.

God, what the fuck was he going to do with the rest of his life?

In a flash he remembered the vision he'd had when he'd approached the Fade. Maybe he should have gone right through that damn door in spite of what he saw. Sure as shit would have made everything easier.

He collected himself for a moment. Or maybe more like half an hour. Then he called out in as strong a voice as he could muster, "I'm ready. I'm ready to go."

TWENTY-FOUR

A house can be empty even when it's full of people. And wasn't that a good thing.

About an hour before dawn, Phury lurched around one of the mansion's countless corners and had to put his hand out to steady himself.

He wasn't truly by himself, though, was he. Boo, the household's black cat, was right there with him, padding along, supervising. Hell, the animal was arguably running the show, as somewhere along the line, Phury had taken to following, not leading.

Leading would so not be a good call. His blood alcohol level was way over the legal limit for anything other than brushing his teeth. And that was before you added on the numbing effects of a haystack's worth of red smoke.

How many blunts? How much hooch?

Well, it was now . . . He had no idea what time it was. Had to be close to dawn, though.

him. He wanted her to use him . . . use him until he was drained dry and every inch of his body was utterly limp, even that ever-ready cock of his.

"Why did you pick the scene, Cormia?"

Her graceful hand went back to the base of her throat. "Because . . . it makes me think of you."

Phury exhaled on a growl. Okay, that was not what he expected her say. And duty was one thing, but man, she didn't have the look of a female worried about living up to tradition. She wanted sex. Maybe even needed it. Just like he did.

And she wanted it with him.

In slow motion, Phury pivoted toward her, his body suddenly very coordinated, the fuzz from all the red smoke and booze totally blown away.

He was going to take her. Here. Now.

He headed down the shallow steps, ready to claim what was his.

Cormia rose up from her chair, in the midst of the blinding light of the Primale's eyes. He was a massive shadow as he came at her, his long strides eating up two of the shallow steps at a time. He stopped when he was but a foot away from her, smelling of that delicious smoky scent and also of dark spices.

"You watch because it makes you think of me," he said in a deep, rough voice.

"Yes . . ."

He reached out and touched her face. "And what do you think about?"

She pulled up her courage and threw out words that made no sense. "I think about how I . . . have certain feelings for you."

His erotic laugh was a dark thrill. "Feelings . . . And where exactly do you feel me, I wonder?" His fingertips drifted from her face to her neck to her collarbone. "Here?"

She swallowed, but before she could answer, his touch drifted

over her shoulder and down her arm. "Here, maybe?" He gave her wrist a squeeze, right at her veins, and then his hand slipped onto her waist and curved around, easing onto the small of her back, pressing in. "Tell me, is it right here?"

Suddenly, he gripped her hips with both hands, leaned toward her ear, and whispered, "Or is it perhaps lower?"

Something swelled in her heart, something warm as the light in his eyes.

"Yes," she said, barely breathing. "But also here. Most of all . . . here." She put his hand to her chest, right over her heart.

He stilled, and she felt the change in him, the hot current in his blood cooling, the flames extinguished.

Ah, yes, she thought. In revealing herself, she had exposed his truth.

Although it had been obvious all along, hadn't it.

The Primale stepped back and drew a hand through his outrageously beautiful hair. "Cormia . . ."

Drawing up her dignity, she squared her shoulders. "Tell me, whatever shall you do with the Chosen? Or is it me in specific whom you do not wish to mate?"

He stepped around her and paced in front of the screen. The frozen image from the movie, of Johnny and Baby lying so closely together, played over his body, and she wished she knew how to turn the movie off. The sight of Baby's leg up on Johnny's hip, his hand gripping her thigh as he ground himself against her, was not what she needed to be seeing at the moment.

"I don't want to be with anyone," the Primale said.

"Liar." As he turned to face her in surprise, she found that the consequences of candor didn't matter to her anymore. "You knew all along you didn't want to lay with any of us, didn't you. You knew it and yet you went along with the ceremony before the Scribe Virgin, even though you were in love with Bella and couldn't bear being with anyone else. You lifted the hopes of forty females of worth on a *lie—*"

"I met with the Directrix. Yesterday."

Cormia's legs went weak, but she kept her voice strong. "Did you. And what have the two of you decided."

"I'm . . . going to let you go. From the position of First Mate."

Cormia fisted her robing so tightly, there was a soft tearing sound. "Going to or have done so."

"Have done so."

She swallowed hard and let herself sink back into the chair.

"Cormia, please know that it's not you." He came over and knelt down in front of her. "You're beautiful—"

"No, it is me," she said. "It's not that you can't mate with any other female, you don't want me."

"I just want you to be free of all this—"

"Don't lie," she snapped, throwing off all pretense of civility. "I told you all along that I would take you within me. I have neither said nor done aught to discourage you. So if you are setting me aside, it is because you don't want me—"

The Primale grabbed her hand and put it palm-first between his legs. As she gasped at the contact, his hips surged and pushed something long and hard into her palm. "The wanting is *not* the problem."

Cormia's lips parted. "Your Grace . . ."

Their eyes met and clung. When his mouth opened slightly, as if he couldn't breathe, she gained the courage to gently wrap her hand around his rigid sex.

His massive body trembled and he let go of her wrist. "It's not about the mating," he said hoarsely. "You were forced into this."

True. In the beginning, she had been. But now . . . her feelings for him were not forced in the slightest.

She looked into his eyes and felt a curious relief. If she wasn't his First Mate, none of this counted, really, did it. Moments like this, with them together—they were just two private bodies, not vessels of immense significance. It was just him and her. A male and a female.

But what about the others, she had to ask herself. What about all

her sisters? He was going to be with them; she could see it in his eyes. There was resolve in that yellow stare of his.

And yet, as the Primale's breath left him on a shudder, she pushed all that out of her mind. She would never truly have him as her own . . . but she had him alone right now.

"I'm not being forced anymore," she whispered, leaning into his chest. Tilting her chin up, she offered what he wanted. "I want this."

He stared down at her for a moment, and then the words he spoke in a guttural voice made no sense: "I'm not good enough for you."

"Untrue. You are the strength of the race. You are our virtue and power."

He shook his head. "If you believe that, I'm not at all who you think I am."

"Yes, you are."

"I'm not—"

She silenced him with her mouth, then pulled back. "You can't change what I think of you."

He reached up and brushed her lower lip with his thumb. "If you truly knew me, everything you believe would change."

"Your heart would be the same. And that is what I love."

As his eyes flared at the word, she kissed him again to get him to stop thinking, and evidently it worked. He groaned and took the lead, taking those soft, soft lips of his and stroking her mouth until she couldn't breathe and didn't care. When his tongue licked at her, she sucked it in on instinct, and felt his body jerk and surge against her.

The kissing went on and on. There seemed to be no end to the ways of it or the different sensations of rasp and drag and thrust and suck, and it wasn't just her mouth that was a part of it . . . Her whole body felt what they were doing, and clearly going by its heat and urgency, so did his.

And she wanted him even more involved. Moving her arm up and back, she rubbed at his sex.

He pulled away sharply. "You might want to be careful with that."

"With this?" As she stroked him through his trousers, he threw his head back and hissed—so she did it some more. She kept at him until he was biting into his lower lip with long fangs and the muscles running up the sides of his throat were straining.

"Why must I be careful, Your Grace?"

His head righted and he brought his mouth to her ear. "You're going to make me come."

Cormia felt something warm pool between her thighs. "Was that what you did when we were in your bed? That first day?"

"Yes . . ." He drew the word out, the *s* drifting.

With a curious, single-minded drive, she found that she wanted him to do that again. Needed him to.

She angled her chin so that she was right at his ear. "Do it for me. Do it now."

The Primale growled deep in his chest, the sound vibrating up between their bodies. Funny, if she'd heard the sound from anyone else she would have been terrified. Coming from him, in this situation, she was thrilled: His leashed power was in the palm of her hand. Literally. And she had the control.

For once in her forsaken life, she was in control.

As he pushed his hips into her palm, he said, "I don't think we should—"

She cranked her hand down on him hard, and he moaned in pleasure. "Don't you take this from me," she demanded. "Don't you *dare* take this from me."

Following an impulse that came from the Virgin Scribe only knew where, she bit down on his earlobe. The response was immediate. He barked out a curse and leaped up, pinning her to the chair, all but mounting her with lust.

Not about to shrink back, she held her hand right to his sex and worked at him, playing counterbalance to the thrusting of his lower body. He seemed to relish the friction, so she kept at it even as he took her chin and forced her head toward his.

"Let me see your eyes," he bit out. "I want to be looking in your eyes when I—"

He released a wild groan as their stares met, and his body went tense all over. His hips jerked once . . . twice . . . three times, each spasm punctuated by a moan.

As his body expressed its pleasure, the Primale's rapt face and straining arms were the most beautiful things she'd ever seen. When he finally settled, he swallowed hard and didn't move away from her. Through the fine wool twill of his slacks, she felt a wetness on her hand.

"I like it when you do that," she said.

He let out a brief laugh. "I like it when you do that to me."

She was about to ask him if he wanted to try it again, when his hand brushed her hair back from her cheek. "Cormia?"

"Yes . . ." Funny, she drew out the word just as he had.

"Would you let me touch you a little?" He looked down at her body. "I can't promise you anything. I'm not . . . well, I can't promise you the same thing you gave me. But I would love to touch you. Just a little."

Desperation stole the air out of her lungs and replaced it with fire. "Yes . . ."

The Primale closed his eyes and seemed to gather himself. Then he bent down and pressed his lips to the side of her throat. "I do think you're beautiful, never doubt that. So beautiful . . ."

As his hands drifted to the front of her robe, the tips of her breasts grew so tight, she twisted under him.

"I can stop," he said, hesitating. "Right now—"

"No." She grabbed onto his shoulders, holding him in place. She didn't know what was going to happen next, but she needed it, whatever it was.

His lips moved up higher on her neck, then lingered on her jaw. Just as he pressed his mouth to hers, a featherlight brush ran over the robe . . . to one of her breasts.

As she surged up, her nipple pushed into his hand and they both groaned.

"Oh, Jesus . . ." The Primale eased back a little and carefully, reverently pulled the lapel of her robe away from her breast. "Cormia . . ." His deep, approving tone was like a caress, nearly tangible and all over her body.

"Can I kiss you here?" he groaned, his touch circling her nipple. *"Please."*

"Sweet Virgin, *yes* . . ."

His head went down and his mouth covered her, warm and moist, pulling gently, suckling.

Cormia threw her head back and thrust her hands deep into his hair, her legs parting for no reason and every reason. She wanted him at her sex, in any way he would come at her—

"Sire?"

Fritz's respectful intrusion from the far end of the theater snapped them both to attention. The Primale quickly straightened and covered her up, even though the chair prevented the butler from seeing anything.

"What the hell is it?" the Primale said.

"Forgive me, but the Chosen Amalya is here with the Chosen Selena to see you."

An ice wave went through Cormia, freezing out all the heat and the urgency in her blood. Her sister. Here to see him. How perfect.

The Primale got to his feet, uttering a horrid word Cormia couldn't help but echo in her own head, and he excused Fritz with a quick movement of his hand. "I'll be there in five minutes."

"Yes, sire."

After the *doggen* left, the Primale shook his head. "I'm sorry—"

"Go do what you need to do." As he hesitated, she said, *"Go.* I'd like to be alone."

"We can talk later."

No, not really, she thought. Talk wasn't going to solve any of this.

"Just go," she said, tuning out whatever else he spoke.

When she was alone once more, she stared at the frozen picture on the screen until all of a sudden it was replaced by a black wash, and a little grouping of English letters reading *Sony* flashed here and there.

She felt wretched, inside and out. Apart from the ache in her chest, her body had hunger pangs as if from a meal denied or a vein left untapped.

Except it wasn't food that she needed.

What she needed had just walked out the door.

Into the arms of her sister.

TWENTY-FIVE

Far upstate in the Adirondacks, on the verge of dawn's arrival over Saddleback Mountain, the male who had taken the deer down the night before was tracking another. Slow and uncoordinated, he knew the hunter role he was playing was a joke. The strength he got from the animal blood just wasn't enough anymore. Tonight as he'd left his cave, he was so weak he wasn't sure whether he could dematerialize at all.

Which meant he probably wasn't going to be able to get close enough to his prey. Which meant he wasn't going to feed. Which meant . . . the time had finally come.

It was so odd. He'd wondered, as he imagined everyone did from time to time, how exactly he was going to die. What would the circumstances be? Would it hurt? How long would it take? He'd assumed, given what his line of work had been, that it would have been fighting.

Instead, it was going to be here in this quiet forest by the hand of dawn's burning glory.

Surprise.

Up ahead, the buck lifted its heavy rack and prepared to bound away. Gathering what little energy he had, the male willed himself to cross the distance between their two bodies . . . and nothing happened. His corporeal form flickered in space, blinking on and off as if his light switch were being triggered, but he didn't change positions, and the deer shot off, white tail flicking as it crashed through the underbrush.

The male let himself fall back on his ass. As he looked at the sky, his regrets were many and deep, and most involved the dead. Not all, though. Not all.

Although he was desperate for the reunion he expected to find in the Fade, though he hungered for the embrace of the ones he'd lost so recently, he knew he was leaving a part of himself behind here on earth.

It couldn't be helped. The leaving behind, that was.

His only solace was that his son had been left in very good hands. The best. His brothers would look after his son, as was the proper way of things in families.

He should have said good-bye, though.

He should have done a lot of things.

But the shoulds were over now.

Ever mindful of the suicide legend, the male made a couple of attempts to stand, and when they failed, he even tried to drag his deadweight body in the direction of his cave. He got nowhere, and it was with a slice of joy through his dark heart that he finally allowed himself to collapse onto the pine needles and leaves.

The male lay there facedown, the cool, dewy forest bed filling his nose with smells that were clean even though they came from the dirt.

The first rays of the sun came from behind him, and then he felt the blast of the heat. The end had arrived, and he welcomed it with open arms and with eyes that were closed in relief.

His last sensation before he died was his liberation from the ground, his broken body being drawn up into the brilliant light, drawn unto the reunion it had taken eight horrible months for him to find.

TWENTY-SIX

s night fell some sixteen hours later, Lash stood at the foot of a rolling lawn that led up to a sprawling Tudor house . . . and turned the ring the Omega had given him round and round.

He had grown up here, he thought. Been raised and fed and tucked into bed here as a young. When he was older, he'd stayed up to watch movies and read books with dirty shit in them, and surfed the Net and eaten junk food here.

He'd gone through his transition and had sex for the first time up in his room on the third floor.

"Y'all want some help?"

He turned and looked at the *lesser* who was behind the wheel of the Ford Focus. It was the little slayer, the one he'd drunk from. The guy had pale hair like Bo from *The Dukes of Hazzard*, all curling up around the cowboy hat he wore. His eyes were a faded cornflower blue, suggesting that before he'd been inducted he'd been a real middle-America white boy.

The guy had survived the feeding, thanks to some true depravity on the Omega's part, and Lash had to admit he was glad. He needed help understanding where he was at, and he wasn't threatened by Mr. D.

"Hello?" the *lesser* said. "Y'all okay there?"

"You stay in the car." It felt good to say that and know there wasn't going to be any discussion. "I won't be long."

"Yes, suh."

Lash looked back up at the Tudor palace. Lights glowed yellow in windows made of diamond-paned glass, and the house was spotlit from the ground like a beauty queen on a stage. Inside, people moved around, and he knew who they were by the shapes of their bodies and where they were.

On the left, in the sitting room, were the two who had raised him as their own. The one with the broad shoulders was his father, and the male was pacing, hand going up and down to his face as if he were drinking something. His mother was on the couch, all bobble-head proportioned with her elaborate chignon and her slender neck. She kept touching her hair, as if trying to make sure everything was in place even though it was no doubt sprayed stiff as a boxwood shrub.

To the right, in the kitchen wing, several *doggen* scurried around, moving from stove to cabinet to refrigerator to counter to stove.

Lash could practically smell the dinner, and his eyes watered.

By now, his parents must know about what had happened in the locker room and then at the clinic. They must have been told. They'd been out at the *glymera*'s ball last evening, but they'd been home all day, and both appeared to be unsettled.

He glanced at the third floor and the seven windows that marked his room.

"You going in?" the slayer asked, making him feel like a pussy.

"Shut the fuck up before I cut your tongue out."

Lash unsheathed the hunting knife that hung from his belt and walked forward over the cropped grass. The lawn was soft under the new combat boots he had on.

He'd had to have the little *lesser* get him some clothes, but he didn't like what he was wearing. It was all from Target. Cheap.

As he came up to the mansion's front door, he put his hand to the security pad . . . but paused before he entered the code.

His dog had died a year ago. Of old age.

The thing had been a pedigreed rottweiler, and his parents had gotten it for him when he was eleven. They hadn't approved of the breed, but Lash had been adamant, so they'd adopted one that was about a year old. First night in the house, Lash had tried to pierce the thing's ear with a safety pin. King had bitten him so hard, the dog's fangs had punctured his arm and come out the other side.

They'd been inseparable after that. And when that mean old dog had kicked it, Lash had cried like a little bitch.

He reached out and entered the pass code, then put his left hand on the door latch. The light over the door flashed on his knife's blade.

He wished the dog were still alive. He would have liked to have one thing from his old life to carry forward into his new one.

He stepped into his house and headed for the sitting room.

When John Matthew came up to the doors of Wrath's study, he was about as relaxed as a golfer in a thunderstorm, and the sight of the king made the anxiety worse. The male was sitting behind his delicate desk, frown on his face, fingers drumming, stare locked on the phone like bad news had just come in. Again.

John tucked what was in his hand under his arm and knocked quietly on the jamb. Wrath didn't look up. "What's doing, son."

John waited for the king to glance across the way, and when he did, John signed with care. *Qhuinn got kicked out of his family.*

"Yeah, and I heard the beat-down was from an honor guard cour-

tesy of them." Wrath leaned back in his chair, the slender bones of
the thing squeaking. "That father of his . . . typical *glymera*."

The tone suggested that was a compliment along the lines of *ass-
wipe*.

He can't stay at Blay's forever, and he has nowhere to go.

The king shook his head. "Okay, I know where you're going with
this, and it's a no. Even if this were a normal household, and it's not,
Qhuinn killed a trainee, and I don't give a shit what you think Lash
might have done to deserve it. I know you talked to Rhage and told
him what happened, but not only is your boy out of the program,
he's going to be up on charges." Wrath leaned to the side and looked
around John. "You get Phury out of bed yet?"

John looked over his shoulder. Vishous was standing in the doorway.

The Brother nodded. "He's getting dressed. So is Z. You sure you
don't want me to handle this?"

"The two of them were Lash's teachers, and Z was a witness to the
aftermath of what went down at the clinic. Lash's parents want to
talk to them and only them, and I promised that they'd be over to
that house ASAP."

"Okay. Keep me posted."

The Brother took off, and Wrath put his elbows on the desk.
"Look, John, I know Qhuinn's a buddy of yours, and I do feel bad
about a lot of his circumstances. I wish I were in a position to help
him, but I'm not."

John pushed, hoping he wouldn't have to go to his last resort.
What about Safe Place?

"The females there aren't comfortable around males for good reason. Especially ones with violent histories."

*But he's my friend. I can't just sit back knowing he's got no place to
go, no job, no money—*

"None of that is going to matter, John." The words *jail time* hovered in the air. "You said it yourself. He took deadly force into what

was your basic argument between two hotheaded guys. The right response was peeling you and Lash apart. It was not popping a knife and slicing his first cousin's throat open. Did Lash come at you with a deadly weapon? No. Could you honestly say that the kid was going to kill you? No. It was an inappropriate use of force, and Lash's parents are arguing assault with a deadly with intent to kill, and proximal murder under the old law."

Proximal murder?

"The medical staff swear Lash had been resuscitated when that raid took place. His parents are assuming he doesn't survive his capture by the *lessers* and are going with but-for causation. But for Qhuinn's actions, Lash wouldn't have been at the clinic and he wouldn't have been abducted. Therefore, it's proximal murder."

But Lash worked there. So he could have been in the clinic at any rate that night.

"Except he wouldn't have been in one of the beds as a patient, would he?" Wrath's blunt fingers drummed on the delicate desk. "This shit is heavy-duty, John. Lash was the only son of his parents, both of whom are from founding families. It's not going to go well for Qhuinn. That honor guard is the least of his problems at this point."

In the silence that followed, John's lungs got tight. He'd known all along that they were going to reach this impasse, that what he'd told Rhage wouldn't go far enough to save his friend. And sure, he'd have done anything to avoid this, but he'd come prepared.

John went back to the double doors and closed them, then approached the desk. His hand shook as he took the file he had under his arm and placed his trump card on the king's blotter.

"What's this?"

With John's stomach using his pelvic cradle as a bouncy castle, he slowly pushed his medical record toward the king.

Me. What you need to see is the first page.

Wrath frowned and picked up the magnifying glass he had to use to be able to read. Opening the folder, he bent down over the report that detailed the therapy session John had had at Havers's. It was clear when the king got to the salient part, because the male's heavy shoulders tightened under his black T-shirt.

Oh, God . . . John thought, he was so going to throw up.

After a moment, the king closed the file and put the magnifying glass back down on the blotter. In silence, he took care to arrange the two things so they were side by side and positioned perfectly, the ivory handle of the magnifier in line with the bottom of the file.

When Wrath finally looked up, John did not move his eyes away, even though he felt as if every inch of him were dripping with filth. *That was why Qhuinn did it. Lash read my file because he was working at Havers's, and he was going to spill it to everyone. Everyone. So it was hardly your basic argument between hotheads.*

Wrath popped up his sunglasses and rubbed his eyes. "Jesus . . . Christ. I can understand why you weren't in a big hurry to come forward with this." He shook his head. "John . . . I'm so sorry about what happ—"

John stomped his foot to bring the king's head up. *I'm not letting you know for any other reason than Qhuinn's situation. I am not talking about it.*

Then, in quick, jerky movements of his hands, because he had to get this shit over with, he signed, *When Qhuinn took out the knife, Lash had me pinned to the wall in the shower and he was taking my pants down. My friend did what he did not just to keep Lash from talking—feel me? I . . . I froze and . . . I froze. . . .*

"Okay, son, it's okay . . . you don't have to go any further."

John linked his arms around his body and tucked his shaky hands against his sides. Squeezing his eyes shut, he couldn't bear to see Wrath's face.

"John?" the king said after a moment. "Son, look at me."

John could hardly manage to open his eyes. Wrath was so masculine, so powerful—the leader of the whole race. To admit to such a

male that this shameful, violent thing had happened was nearly as bad as going through it in the first place.

Wrath tapped the file. "This changes everything." The king reached over and picked up the phone. "Fritz? Hey, buddy. Listen, I want you to go pick Qhuinn up at Blaylock's and bring him to me. Tell him it's a command performance."

As the phone was set back down, John's eyes started to burn as if he were tearing up. In a panic, he grabbed his folder, wheeled around, and all but ran to the door.

"John? Son? Please don't go yet."

John didn't stop. He just couldn't. He shook his head, broke out of the study, and beat feet to his room. After he shut his door and locked it, he went to the bathroom, knelt in front of the toilet, and threw up.

Qhuinn felt like a heel as he stood over Blay's sleeping form. The guy slept as he always had ever since he was a kid: head wrapped in a blanket, covers pulled up to below his nose. His huge body was a mountain rising off the flat plane of the bed, no longer the little molehill of a pretrans—but his position was still the same.

They had been through so much together . . . all the big firsts in life, from drinking to driving to smoking to the change to sex. There was nothing they didn't know about each other, no inner thought that they hadn't broached one way or another.

Well, that wasn't entirely true. He knew some things Blay wouldn't admit.

Not saying good-bye felt like something close to robbery, but that was the way of it. Where he was headed, Blay couldn't follow.

There was a vampire community out West; he'd read about it on one of the bulletin boards on the Net. The group was a faction that had broken off from mainstream vampire culture, like, two hundred years ago, and formed an enclave far away from the race's seat of Caldwell.

No *glymera* types there. Most of them were outlaws, as a matter of fact.

He figured he could make it there in one night by dematerializing a couple hundred miles at a time. He'd be a wreck by the time he landed, but at least he'd be with his kind. Outcasts. Roughnecks. AWOLs.

The laws of the race were going to catch up with him at some point, but he had nothing to lose in making the powers that be work to find him. He was already disgraced on every level, and the charges that were going to get laid against him couldn't get any worse. He might as well finally have a taste of freedom before he was boxed and mailed to jail.

The only thing he worried about was Blay. The guy was going to have a hard time being left behind, but at least John was going to be there for him. And John was good peeps all around.

Qhuinn turned away from his friend, slung his duffel over his shoulder, and quietly went out the door. He'd healed up like a charm, the rapid recovery being the one and only legacy his family couldn't strip him of. The surgery had left nothing but a stitch in his side, and the bruising was mostly gone—even from his legs. He felt strong, and though he was going to need to feed soon, he was good to go.

Blay's house was a grand antique, but it was done with a modern twist, which meant there was wall-to-wall carpeting down the hall to the back stairs—thank fuck. Qhuinn ghosted along, making no sound at all as he headed for the underground tunnel that led out from the basement.

As he came into the cellar, the place was neat as a pin, and as always smelled like Chardonnay for some reason. Maybe it was the regular whitewashing of the old stone walls?

The hidden entrance to the escape tunnel was all the way in the far corner to the right and it was shielded by bookshelves that were on a slide. You simply reached out, pulled the copy of *Sir Gawain*

and the Green Knight forward, and a latch released, causing the partition to retract and reveal—

"You are such a moron."

Qhuinn jumped like an Olympian. There, in the tunnel, seated in an outdoor lounger like he were getting a tan, was Blay. He had a book on his lap, a battery-operated lamp on a little table, and a blanket over his legs.

The guy calmly lifted a glass of orange juice up in toast, then took a sip. "Helllllllo, Lucy."

"What the fuck? You're like lying in wait for me or some shit?"

"Yup."

"What was in your bed?"

"Pillows and my head blankie. I've had a nice little chill sesh hanging here. Good book, too." He flashed the cover of *A Season in Purgatory.* "I like Dominick Dunne. Good writer. Great glasses."

Qhuinn looked beyond his friend at the low-lit tunnel that disappeared into what appeared to be an infinite dark distance. Kind of like the future, he thought.

"Blay, you know I have to leave."

Blay lifted his phone. "Actually, you can't. Just got a text from John. Wrath wants to see you, and Fritz is coming for you as we speak."

"Shit. I can't go—"

"Two words: Command. Performance. You bolt now and you're not only a fugitive from the *glymera*, you're on the king's list of things to do. Which means the Brothers will be going after you."

They were going to do that anyway. "Look, this thing with Lash is heading for a royal tribunal. That's what the message from John is all about. And they're going to put me away somewhere. For a long, long time. I'm just leaving for a while."

Read: for as long as I can stay hidden.

"You're going to defy the king?"

"Yeah, yeah, I am. I have nothing to lose, and maybe it will be years before I'm found."

Blay moved the blanket from his legs and stood up. He was dressed in jeans and a fleece, but somehow looked as if he were wearing a tuxedo. Blay was like that: formal even in his scrubbies.

"You take off, I'm going to go with you," he said.

"I don't want you to."

"Tough. Shit."

As Qhuinn pictured the land of outlaws that he was headed for, he felt a buildup of pressure in his chest. His friend was so steadfast, so true, so honorable and clean. There was still an essential, optimistic innocence to him, though he was fully a male now.

Qhuinn took a breath and squeezed out, "I don't want you knowing where I end up. And I don't want to see you again."

"You can't be serious."

"I know . . ." Qhuinn cleared his throat and forced himself to go on. "I know the way you watch me. I've seen you looking at me . . . like when I was with that chick in the dressing room at A and F? You weren't looking at her, you were looking at me, and it was because you were jonesing for me. Weren't you." Blay took a stumbling step back, and, like they were in a fistfight, Qhuinn hit harder. "You've wanted me for a while, and you think I haven't noticed. Well, I have. So don't follow me. This shit between us ends here, tonight."

Qhuinn turned away and started walking, leaving his best friend, the male he cared about most in the world, more even than John, in that chilly tunnel. Alone.

It was the only way to save the guy's life. Blay was exactly that flavor of noble idiot who would follow those he loved right off the Brooklyn Bridge. And since you couldn't talk him out of anything, you had to cut him off.

Qhuinn walked fast and then even faster, heading away from the light. As the tunnel went right, Blay and the glow from the basement were lost and he was by himself in the dim, steel cage deep in the earth.

He saw Blay's face clear as day the whole way along. With each

step he took, his friend's crushed expression was the beacon he followed.

It was going to stay with him. Forever.

By the time he reached the end of the tunnel, put in the pass code, and opened the way into a gardening shed about a mile away from the house, he realized he did have something to lose after all . . . that there was a level lower than he thought he'd bottomed out at: He'd shredded Blay's heart and crushed it under his boot, and the regret and pain he felt were almost more than he could bear.

As he stepped out into a stand of lilacs, he came to a change of mind. Yes, he was disgraced by birth and circumstance. But he didn't have to make that worse.

He took out his phone, which by now had only one bar of battery left on the screen, and texted John where he was. He wasn't sure whether he still had service—

John hit him right back.

Fritz would be there to pick him up in ten minutes.

TWENTY-SEVEN

Up in her bedroom in the Brotherhood's mansion, Cormia sat on the floor in front of the construction she'd started the night before, a box of toothpicks in her hand, a bowl of peas next to her. She wasn't putting either to use. All she'd been doing for the good Virgin knew how long was flicking the box's lid flap open and closed . . . open and closed . . . open and closed.

Stalled out and all but immobile, she'd been at the flicking for quite some time now, and her thumbnail was wearing a patch in the lip.

If she was no longer First Mate, she had no reason to stay on this side. She was serving no official function, and by all that was manifest, she should be back in the Sanctuary meditating and praying and serving the Scribe Virgin with her sisters.

She didn't belong in this house or this world. She never had.

Shifting her focus from the box to the structure she'd put together, she measured the units and thought of the Chosen and their

network of functions, from the keeping of the spiritual calendar to the worshiping of the Scribe Virgin to the recording of Her words and Her history . . . to the birthing of Brothers and future Chosen.

As she pictured herself living in the Sanctuary, she felt as if she were going backward, not returning home. And strangely, what should have bothered her the most—that she had failed as First Mate—wasn't what upset her.

Cormia tossed the box of toothpicks to the ground. When it landed, the lid flipped open and a bunch of the blond sticks popped out and scattered in a tangle.

Discord. Disorder. Chaos.

She picked up what had spilled, making right out of the mess and deciding she needed to do the same with her life. She would speak to the Primale, pack up her three robes, and go.

As she put the last toothpick into the box, there was a knock at the door.

"Come in," she said without bothering to get up.

Fritz put his head around the jamb. "Good evening, Chosen, I carry a message from Mistress Bella. She is inquiring whether or not you would wish to join her for First Meal in her bedroom?"

Cormia cleared her throat. "I'm not sure—"

"If I may," the butler murmured. "Physician Jane just left her once again. I gather that the examination raised questions. Perhaps the Chosen's presence would calm our *mahmen*-to-be?"

Cormia looked up. "Another exam? You mean after last evening?"

"Yes."

"Tell her I will be there right away."

Fritz's head dipped reverently. "Thank you, madam. Now, I must needs perform a pickup, but I shall be back and shall cook for you. I shan't be gone long."

Cormia took a quick shower, dried and coiled her hair, and changed into a freshly pressed robe. As she came out of her room, she heard the sounds of boots on the foyer and looked over the balcony. The Primale was down below, striding across the mosaic apple tree on the floor. He was dressed in black leathers and a black shirt, and his hair, that wonderful, soft profusion of color, was bright in the lights and against the dark width of his shoulders.

As if he sensed her, he stopped and glanced up. His eyes flashed like citrines, sparkling, captivating her.

And she watched the glow in them dim.

Cormia was the one who pivoted away, because she'd quite had it with being the one who was left. Just as she turned, she saw Zsadist coming around the corner of the hall of statues. His eyes were black as they shifted to her, and she didn't have to ask how Bella was. Words weren't necessary, given his dark expression.

"I was going to stay with her," she said to the Brother. "She asked for me."

"I know. I'm glad. And thank you."

In the beat of silence, she measured the daggers crisscrossing over the warrior's chest. And there were other weapons on him, she thought, though she couldn't see them.

The Primale had had none. No daggers, no bulges under his clothes.

She wondered where he was going. Not the Other Side, as he was dressed for this world. Where then? And for what?

"Is he down there waiting for me?" Zsadist asked.

"The Primale?" When the Brother nodded, she said, "Er . . . yes, yes, he is."

Odd to be the one who knew where he was . . . and the one to be asked.

She thought of his lack of weapons.

"Take care of him," she demanded without apology. "Please."

Something tightened Zsadist's face, then he inclined his head once. "Yeah, I'll do that."

As Cormia bowed and turned to the hall of statues, Zsadist's low voice stopped her dead: "The baby's not moving very much. Not since whatever happened last night."

Cormia looked over her shoulder and wished there were more she could do. "I'll purify the room. That is what we do on the Other Side when . . . I'll purify the room."

"Don't tell her you know."

"I won't." Cormia wanted to reach out to the male. Instead, she said, "I'll take care of her. Go and do your business with him."

The Brother bowed his head and took off down the stairs.

Below in the foyer, Phury rubbed his chest and then stretched, trying to get rid of the ache between his pecs. He was surprised at how difficult it was to see Cormia turn away from him.

Curiously brutal, as a matter of fact.

He thought of the Chosen he'd met at dawn. The difference between her and Cormia was obvious. Selena was eager to be First Mate, her eyes shining as she looked him over as if he were a prize bull. It had taken all the manners he had just to stay in the same room with her.

She wasn't a bad female and was more than beautiful enough, but her affect . . . man, it was like she wanted to crawl into his lap right then and there and get down to it. Especially as she'd assured him that she was more than ready to serve him and her tradition . . . and that "every bone in her body wanted this."

This clearly meaning his sex.

And there was another coming at the end of tonight.

Sweet. Jesus.

Zsadist appeared at the head of the stairwell and came down quickly, his windbreaker in his hand. "Let's go."

As he measured his twin's tight brow, Phury thought, Bella wasn't doing well.

"Is Bella—"

"Not going there with you." Z marched across the foyer, passing by without so much as a glance. "We're just about business, you and me."

As Phury frowned and then followed behind, their footsteps echoed up as if one person, not two, were walking along. Even with Phury having the prosthesis, he and Z had always had the same long stride, the same way of going heel to toe, the same swing in their arms.

Twins.

But the similarities ended with biology, didn't they. In life, they'd gone in two separate directions.

Both of which had sucked.

With a sudden shift in logic, Phury saw things in a different light.

Shit, all along he'd tortured himself about Z's fate . . . all along he'd lived in the cold, pervasive shadow of their family's tragedy. He had suffered, goddamn it . . . he had suffered, too, and suffered still. And while he respected the sanctity of his twin's mating with Bella, something popped in his head at getting closed out as if he were an absolute stranger. And a hostile one at that.

When he stepped out into the pebbled courtyard, he stopped dead. "Zsadist."

Z kept on walking toward the Escalade.

"Zsadist."

His twin paused, put his hands on his hips, and didn't turn around. "If this is about you and the *lesser* shit, don't try to apologize again."

Phury reached up and loosened the collar on his shirt. "It's not."

"I don't want to hear about the red smoke, either. Or your getting kicked the fuck out of the Brotherhood."

"Turn around, Z."

"Why."

There was a long pause. Then he gritted out in a hard voice, "You never said thank you."

Z's head shot over his shoulder. "Excuse me?"

"You. Never. Thanked. Me."

"For what?"

"For saving you. God*damn* it, I saved you from that whore Mistress of yours and what she did to you. And you *never thanked me.*" Phury walked up to his twin, his voice getting louder and louder. "I searched for you for a *fucking* century, and then I got your ass out of there and saved your *fucking* life—"

Zsadist leaned forward on his shitkickers, pointing his finger out like a gun. "You want credit for rescuing me? Don't hold your breath. I never asked you for the fucking favor. That was all about your Good Samaritan complex."

"If I hadn't gotten you out, you wouldn't have Bella!"

"And if you hadn't, she wouldn't be in danger of dying right now! You want gratitude? Better pat yourself on the back, because I'm not feeling it at the moment."

The words drifted off into the night as if looking for other ears to fill.

Phury blinked, then found words coming out of his mouth, words he'd wanted to say for a long time. "I buried our parents by myself. I was the only one who took care of their bodies, who smelled the smoke of the burning—"

"*And I never knew them.* They were strangers to me, and so were you when you showed up—"

"They loved you!"

"Enough to stop looking for me! Fuck them! You think I didn't know he stopped? I went back and traced the trail from that house you burned down. I know how far our father went before he gave up. You think I give a shit about him? *He let me go!*"

"You were more real to them than I was! You were everywhere in that house, you were everything to them!"

"Boo-fucking-hoo, Phury," Z snapped. "Don't you dare poor-me it with me. Do you have *any* idea what my life was like?"

"I lost my fucking leg for you!"

"You chose to come after me! If you don't like the way things worked out, don't bitch to me about it!"

Phury exhaled hard, absolutely stunned. "You ungrateful bastard. You ungrateful mother*fucker* . . . You mean to tell me you would rather have stayed with the Mistress?" When there was nothing but silence, he shook his head. "I'd always thought the sacrifices I'd made were worth it. The celibacy. The panic. The physical costs." Anger resurged. "Not to mention the royal head fuck I got from the number of the times you asked me to beat the living shit out of you. And now you tell me you would rather have *stayed* a blood slave?"

"Is that what all this is about? You want me to justify this self-destructive savior streak you got going on by being *grateful*?" Z laughed low and hard. "Whatever. You think I'm having a party watching you smoke and drink yourself into an early grave? You think I like what I saw the other night in that alley?" Z cursed. "Fuck it, I'm so not playing this. Wake up, Phury. You're killing yourself. Quit searching for crutches and spouting lies, and take a good long look at yourself."

On some dim inner level Phury realized that this collision between the two of them had been overdue. And that his twin had a point.

But so did he.

He shook his head again. "I don't think I'm wrong to ask for some acknowledgment. I've been invisible in this family all my life."

There was a stretch of silence.

Then Z spat, "For fuck's sake, get off the cross. Someone else needs the wood."

The dismissive tone sparked the anger again, and Phury's arm swung of its own volition, his fist catching Z on the thick of the jaw, the crack like a homer hit off a wooden bat.

Z went on a flying spin and landed on Rhage's GTO like a tarp.

As the Brother righted himself, Phury fell into a fighting stance

and shook out his knuckles. In another second and a half, they were going to be locked in a vicious bodily argument, fists instead of nasty words being traded back and forth until one or both of them collapsed.

And exactly where the hell was that going to get them?

Phury slowly lowered his arms.

At that moment, Fritz's Mercedes came through the courtyard's gates.

In its headlights, Zsadist rearranged his jacket and calmly walked over to the driver's-side door of the Escalade. "If it weren't for what I just promised Cormia, I'd bust your mouth open."

"What?"

"Get in the fucking car."

"What did you say to her?"

As Z got behind the wheel, his black eyes cut through the night like knives. "Your girlfriend is worried about you, so she made me promise I'd take care of you. And unlike some people, I keep my word."

Ouch.

"Now get in." Z slammed the SUV's door shut.

Phury cursed and went over to the passenger side while the Merc came to a halt and Qhuinn got out of the backseat. The kid's eyes went saucer as he looked up at the mansion.

Clearly he was here for his trial, Phury thought as he slid into shotgun next to his deathly silent twin.

"You know where Lash's parents' house is, right?" Phury said.

"Of course I do."

The *shut up* went unsaid.

As the Escalade headed for the gates, the wizard's voice was dead serious as it banged around in Phury's head: *You have to be a hero to earn gratitude, and you are not one of the knight-in-shining-armor types. You just want to be.*

Phury looked out the window, the angry words he and Z had just exchanged echoing like gunshots in an alley.

Do them all a favor and walk away, the wizard said. *Just walk away, mate.*

You want to be a hero? Make it so they don't have to deal with you ever again.

TWENTY-EIGHT

huinn was absolutely sure his nuts were on Wrath's menu tonight, but even so, he was amazed at the sight of the Brotherhood's training center. The thing was the size of a small city, made up of blocks of stone that were big as a male's torso, with windows that looked like they were reinforced with titanium or some shit. The gargoyles around the roof and all the shadows were perfect. Exactly what you'd expect.

"Sire?" the butler said as he indicated the cathedral-worthy front door. "Shall we go in? I must needs get to my cooking."

"Cooking?"

The *doggen* slowed his speech down as if he were addressing a moron. "I cook for the Brotherhood as well as tend to this, their home."

Holy shit . . . This wasn't the training center; this was the Brotherhood's digs.

Well, duh. Check out the security. There were cameras mounted over the doors and under the roof, and the retaining wall of the courtyard was like something out of a movie about Alcatraz. Hell, he expected a fleet of Dobermans to come trucking around the corner with their chompers showing.

Then again, the dogs were probably still gnawing on the bones of the last guest they'd turned into pulled pork.

"Sire?" the butler repeated. "Shall we?"

"Yeah . . . yeah, sure." Qhuinn swallowed hard and walked forward, prepared to face the music with the king. "Ah, listen, I'm just going to leave my stuff in the car."

"As you wish, sire."

Man, thank God Blay didn't have to see what was about to go down—

One side of the mammoth double doors opened and a familiar friend lifted a hand.

Oh. Great. Blay would miss the show, but John was having a front-row seat, evidently.

The guy was dressed in the blue jeans and one of the deconstructed button-downs they'd gotten at Abercrombie. His bare feet were pale on the black stone stairs, and he seemed relatively calm, which was kind of irritating. The bastard could at least have had the grace to sport a cold sweat or a case of the sympathy shits.

Hey, John signed.

"Hey."

John stepped back, clearing the way. *How are you doing?*

"I wish I were a smoker." Because then he could put this off for the duration of a cig.

No, you don't. You hate smoking.

"When I face the firing squad, I may rethink that hard line."

Shut up.

Qhuinn walked through a vestibule that made him feel totally underdressed, what with its black-and-white marble floor and its chandelier—was that made of real gold? Probably—

Holy fuck, he thought as he stopped dead.

The foyer in front of him was palatial. Total Russian royalty, with its brilliant colors and its incredible gold-leafed everything and its mosaic floor and its painted ceiling . . . or, shit, maybe it was more like something out of a Danielle Steel novel, with all its romantic marble columns and arching expanse.

Not that he'd read any of her books.

Well, okay, there had been that one, but he'd been twelve and sick and had focused just on the sex parts.

"Up here," a deep, echoing voice said.

Qhuinn looked to the top of an ornate staircase. Standing with shitkickers planted like he owned the world, dressed in black leathers and a black T-shirt, was the king.

"Come on, let's do this," Wrath commanded.

Swallowing hard, Qhuinn followed John to the second floor.

As they got to the top, Wrath said, "I just want Qhuinn. John, you stay here."

John started to sign, *I want to be his witness—*

Wrath turned away. "Nope. There's going to be none of that."

Shit, Qhuinn thought. He wasn't going to be allowed any defense testimony?

I'll be waiting, John signed.

"Thanks, man."

Qhuinn stared beyond the open doors the king had gone through. The room before him was . . . well, it looked like the kind of place his mother would have liked: pale blue, with spindly, girly furniture and drippy crystal light fixtures that looked like earrings.

Not exactly what you'd expect Wrath to hang out in.

As the king went in and planted it behind a delicate desk, Qhuinn stepped inside, shut the doors, and linked his hands in front of himself. As he waited, the whole thing struck him as surreal. He could not possibly fathom how his life had come down to this.

"Did you mean to kill Lash?" Wrath asked.

So much for opening statements. "Ah . . ."

"Did you or didn't you?"

In quick succession Qhuinn reviewed his answers: *No, of course not, the knife was acting of its own volition, I was actually trying to stop it. . . . No, I only meant to give him a shave. . . . No, I didn't realize that slicing open someone's jugular was going to lead to death. . . .*

Qhuinn cleared his throat once. Twice. "Yeah. I did."

The king crossed his arms over his chest. "If Lash hadn't gone for John's pants, would you have done the same thing?"

Qhuinn's lungs stopped working for a moment. He shouldn't have been surprised the king knew exactly what had gone down, but shit, hearing the words was kind of shocking. Plus, talking about the whole thing was hard, given what Lash had said and done. It was, after all, John.

"Well?" came the demand over the desk. "If Lash hadn't gone for his pants, would you have throated him?"

Qhuinn gathered his thoughts. "Look, John told me and Blay to stay out of it, and as long as it was a fair fight I was prepared to let it ride. But . . ." He shook his head. "Nah. That shit Lash pulled wasn't fair. It was like using a concealed weapon."

"But you didn't have to kill him, did you. You could have peeled him off John. Clocked him a couple of times. Rolled him out."

"True."

Wrath stretched his arm to the side as if to loosen it, and his shoulder let out a crack. "You're going to be totally fucking honest with me now. If you lie, I'll know it, because I'll smell it." Wrath's eyes burned behind his wraparounds. "I'm well aware you hated your cousin. Are you sure you didn't use deadly force for your own agenda?"

Qhuinn dragged his hand through his hair and remembered all that he could about what had gone down. There were holes in his memory, blank spaces carved by the tangle of emotions that had had him palming the knife and lunging forward, but he remembered enough.

"To be honest . . . shit, I couldn't let John get hurt and humiliated like that. See, he froze. When Lash went for his pants, he froze. The two of them were in the shower and John was up against the tile and all of a sudden he went dead still. I don't know whether Lash would have followed through with . . . well, you know . . . because I wasn't in his head, but he was just the type who would try it." Qhuinn swallowed hard. "I saw it happen, saw that John couldn't do anything and . . . it was like everything went blank . . . I just—fuck—the knife was in my hand and then I was on Lash and the slice was quick. For real? Sure, I hated Lash, but I don't give a fuck who pulled that shit on John. I would have gone gunning for them. And before you ask it, I know what your next question is going to be."

"And your answer is."

"Yeah, I would do it again."

"Would you now."

"Yes." Qhuinn looked around at the pale blue walls and thought it didn't seem right to be talking about such ugliness in a room that was so fricking lovely. "Guess that makes me an unrepentant mur-derer, huh . . . so what are you going to do to me? Oh, and you probably know this already, but my family has disowned me."

"Yeah, I've heard that."

There was a long silence, and Qhuinn passed the time looking at his New Rocks and feeling his heart skip in his chest.

"John wants you to stay here."

Qhuinn's eyes shot to the king. "What?"

"You heard me."

"Shit. You can't approve that. No way can I stay here."

Black eyebrows crashed down. "Excuse me?"

"Er . . . sorry." Qhuinn clammed up, reminding himself that the Brother was king, which meant he could do whatever the fuck he wanted, including but not limited to renaming the sun and the moon, declaring that people had to salute him with their thumbs up their asses . . . and taking roadkill like Qhuinn under his roof if he were so inclined.

King was spelled c-a-r-t-e b-l-a-n-c-h-e in the vampire world.

Plus, why the fuck say no to something that would help him? *Duh.*

Wrath stood up, and Qhuinn had to fight not to take a step back even though they were separated by about twenty-five feet of Aubusson.

Jesus, the male towered, though.

"I spoke to Lash's father about an hour ago," Wrath said. "Your family has indicated to him that they're not going to pay the restitution. As they've disowned you, they say that you owe the money. Five million."

"Five *million?*"

"Lash was abducted by the *lessers* last night. No one thinks he's coming back. You're up for proximal murder, as the assumption is that the slayers wouldn't have bothered snatching a dead body."

"Whoa . . ." God, Lash . . . and, shit, that was a lot of green. "Look, I got the clothes on my back and a spare set in my duffel. They're welcome to the shit if they want it—"

"Lash's father is aware of your financial situation. In light of it, he wants you to become an indentured servant in their household."

The blood rushed out of Qhuinn's head. A slave . . . for the rest of his life? For Lash's parents?

"This would," Wrath tacked on, "be after you went to prison, of course. And actually, the race still has one in operation. Up north of the Canadian border."

Qhuinn just stood there, utterly numb. Man, your life could end in so many different ways, he thought. Death wasn't the only way out of it.

"What do you say about all this?" Wrath murmured.

Prison . . . in God only knew where for God only knew how long. Slavery . . . in a household that would forever hate him until he kicked it.

Qhuinn thought of that walk through the tunnel at Blay's and the decision he had come to on the far side.

"I have mismatched eyes," he whispered, lifting his fucked-up stare to the king. "But I have honor. I'll do whatever has to be done to make it right . . . *provided*," he said with sudden strength, "that no one makes me apologize. That . . . I can't do that. What Lash did was beyond wrong. It was intentionally cruel and done to ruin John's life. I. Am. Not. Sorry."

Wrath came around the desk and strode across the room. As he passed by, he said briskly, "Right answer, son. Wait out there with your boy. I'll be with you in a few."

"Excuse . . . What?"

The king opened the door and impatiently nodded. "Out. There."

Qhuinn stumbled from the room.

How'd it go? John signed as he jumped up from a chair that was against the hall wall. *What happened?*

As Qhuinn looked at his friend, he was not about to tell the guy that he was going to jail and then being released into the custody of Lash's parents to be tortured for the rest of his days. "Ah, not too bad."

You lie.

"Do not."

You're the color of fog.

"Well, hello, I had surgery, like, yesterday."

Oh, please. What's happening?

"To tell you the truth, I have no clue—"

"'Scuse me." Beth, the queen, came up with a grave expression. In her hands was a long, flat leather box. "Boys? I need to get in there."

As they stepped apart, she ducked into the study and shut the door.

John and Qhuinn waited. Then waited some more . . . and some more.

God only knew what was doing. Guess it took a while for the

king and queen to draw up his *Go to Jail, Do Not Pass Go, Do Not Collect $500* papers.

John took out his phone, like he needed something to do with his hands, and frowned as he checked the thing. After he texted someone, he put it back in his pocket.

Weird that Blay hasn't checked in yet.

Not really, Qhuinn thought, feeling like a son of a bitch.

The king threw the doors wide. "Getcha asses back in here."

There was a scramble of their feet, and then Wrath shut them all in together. The king returned to his desk, parked it in the doll-like chair, and propped his huge shitkickers on the mound of paperwork. When Beth fell in by the side of where he sat, he reached up and took her hand.

"You boys familiar with the term *ahstrux nohtrum?*" When the two of them shook their heads like idiots, Wrath smiled a cold, nasty little grin. "It's an antiquated position. It's like a private guard, only they're allowed to use deadly force when protecting their master. They're killers with a pass."

Qhuinn swallowed hard, wondering what the hell that had to do with him and John.

The king continued. "*Ahstrux nohtrum* may be commissioned only by royal decree, and the standard is kind of like the U.S. Secret Service's for protection. The subject must be a person of interest, and the guard must be capable." Wrath kissed his queen's hand. "A person of interest is someone whose presence is significant as judged by the king. Which is me. Now . . . my *shellan* here, she's the most precious thing in the world, and there is nothing that I won't do to make sure her heart is protected. Also, in terms of the race as a whole, she is queen. Therefore her only brother most definitely falls into the person-of-interest category.

"As for the qualified-guard part . . . I happened to know, Qhuinn, that out of the training class, you were the best fighter, aside from John. You're vicious with the hand-to-hand, a great shot on the

range"—the king's voice grew wry—"and we're all aware of how good you are with a knife, aren't we."

Qhuinn felt a weird rush go through him, like some kind of fog had lifted and revealed an unexpected path out of the wilderness. He reached for John's arm to steady himself even though it totally slapped the *Hello! My Name Is Nancy* tag on him.

"One thing, though," the king said. "*Ahstrux nohtrum* are expected to sacrifice their own lives for the one they protect. If shit comes down to it, they will take a mortal hit. Oh, and it's a lifelong commitment, unless I say different. I'm the only one who can issue a pink slip, feel me?"

Qhuinn's mouth talked of its own accord: "Of course. Absolutely."

Wrath smiled and reached over to the box Beth had carried in. He took out a thick sheaf of paper, at the bottom of which was a gold seal with red and black satin ribbons. "Gee, would you look at this."

He casually tossed the official-looking document to the far edge of the desk.

Qhuinn and John leaned in together. In the Old Language, the thing stated that . . .

"Holy . . . fuck," Qhuinn breathed, then abruptly looked up at Beth. "I'm sorry, I didn't mean to use foul language."

She smiled and kissed the top of her *hellren*'s head. "It's okay. I've heard worse."

"Look at the date," Wrath said.

It was backdated . . . the fucker was backdated to two months ago. According to the document, Qhuinn, son of Lohstrong, had been functioning as John Matthew, son of Darius, son of Marklon's *ahstrux nohtrum* since late June.

"I'm really rat-ass awful at paperwork," Wrath drawled. "I just forgot to tell you two what was doing. My bad. Now, of course, this means that you, John, are responsible for the restitution, because the subject being guarded has to settle all debts incurred as a result of protection."

John immediately signed, *I'll pay—*

"No, wait," Qhuinn cut in. "He doesn't have that kind of money—"

"Your buddy's worth about forty million at this point, so he can handle it just fine."

Qhuinn looked over at John. "What? Why the hell are you working in the office for clothes money?"

Who do I make the check out to? John signed, ignoring him.

"Lash's parents. Beth, as the Brotherhood's CFO, will tell you which account it comes out of, right, *leelan*?" Wrath squeezed the queen's hand and smiled up at her. When he refocused on Qhuinn and John, the loving expression was gone. "Qhuinn's moving into the house effective now, and he's going to have a salary of seventy-five thousand a year, which you will pay. And, Qhuinn, you're so totally out of the training program, but that doesn't mean the Brothers and I won't . . . oh, I don't know, spar with your ass to keep your skills sharp. After all, we take care of our own. And you're one of us now."

Qhuinn took a deep breath. And then another. And then— "I need . . . I need to sit down."

Like a complete flippin' lightweight, he stumbled over to one of the pale blue couches. With everyone staring at him like they were about to offer him either a paper bag to breathe into or some Kleenex, he put his hand to where he'd been operated on in hopes of making it seem like he was overcome by his injury, not his emotions.

Trouble was . . . he couldn't seem to draw any air into his lungs. He wasn't sure what the fuck was going into his mouth, but whatever the shit was, it wasn't doing a damn thing to clear the dizziness in his head or the burning sensation around his rib cage.

Curiously, the one who came over and crouched down in front of him wasn't John or the queen. It was Wrath. The king suddenly ap-

peared in his watery vision, those sunglasses and that cruel face at total odds with the soft voice that he used.

"Put your head between your knees, son." The king's hand landed on his shoulder and gently pushed him down. "Go on now."

Qhuinn did as he was told, and started to shake so badly that if it hadn't been for Wrath's big palm holding him steady, he would have fallen on the floor.

He would not cry. He refused to let one single tear out. Instead, he gasped and he shook and he grew drenched in a cold sweat.

Quietly, so only Wrath would hear, he whispered, "I thought . . . was all alone."

"Nah," Wrath answered just as softly. "Like I said, you're one of us now, feel me?"

Qhuinn lifted his eyes. "But I'm no one."

"Ah, to hell with that." The king shook his head slowly. "You saved John's honor. So like I said, you're family, son."

Qhuinn shifted his eyes over to Beth and John, who were standing side by side. Through his unshed tears, he saw the resemblance in their dark hair and deep blue eyes.

Family . . .

Qhuinn steeled his spine, got to his feet, and pulled himself up to his full height. Straightening his shirt and then his hair, he became completely and utterly composed as he walked over to John.

With set, straight shoulders, he put his hand out to his friend. "I'll lay my life down for you. With or without that piece of paper."

As the words came out of his mouth, he realized it was the first thing he'd ever said as a full-grown male, the first vow he'd ever taken. And he couldn't think of a better person to offer it to, except for maybe Blay.

John glanced down, then clasped the palm that was presented to him, his grip firm and strong. They didn't hug, they didn't speak.

And I for you, John mouthed as their eyes met. *And I . . . for you.*

*   *   *

"You can ask me about Phury if you want. When you're finished with that."

Cormia straightened from the white candle she was lighting and glanced over her shoulder. Bella was lying on her back in the big bed across the room, her thin, pale hand on her rounded belly.

"Really, you can," the female said with a small smile. "It'll give me something else to think about. And right now I need that."

Cormia blew out her match. "How did you know he was on my mind?"

"You have what I call a 'male brow.' Which is a frown brought on when you're thinking about your male and you either want to boot him in the ass or wrap your arms around him and hold him 'til he can't breathe."

"The Primale is not mine." Cormia took the gold incense burner in her hand and moved it three times around the candle. The chant she recited was soft but insistent, calling upon the Scribe Virgin to watch over Bella and her young.

"He doesn't love me," Bella said. "Not really."

Cormia put the burner on a table in the easternmost corner of the room and double-checked that the three candles had good, strong flames.

Past, present, and future.

"Did you hear what I said? He doesn't love me."

Cormia squeezed her eyes shut. "I do believe you are wrong about that."

"He just thinks he does."

"With all due respect—"

"Do you want him?"

Cormia flushed as what had happened in the movie theater came back to her. She relived the feel of him . . . the power she'd had with his sex in her hand . . . the way his mouth had moved against her breast.

Bella laughed softly. "I'll take that blush as a yes."

"Dearest Virgin, I have no idea what to say."

"Sit with me." Bella patted the bed next to her. "Let me tell you about him. And why I'm sure that he's not in love with me."

Cormia knew that if she went over and listened to how the Primale couldn't possibly feel as he believed he did, she was just going to get more lost to him.

So naturally she sat down beside Bella on the comforter.

"Phury's a good male. A great male. He loves deeply, but that doesn't mean he's in love with everyone he cares about. If you two just take a little time—"

"I'm going back soon."

Bella's brows went up. "To the Other Side? Why?"

"I've been here a long time." It was too hard to say she'd been passed over. Especially to Bella. "I've been here . . . long enough."

Bella looked saddened. "Will Phury be leaving too?"

"I don't know."

"Well, he'd have to come back to fight."

"Ah . . . yes." Clearly the female didn't know he'd been removed from the Brotherhood yet, and now was not the time for her to have any unpleasant shocks.

Bella's hand smoothed over her belly. "Has anyone told you why Phury became the Primale? Instead of Vishous, that is."

"No. I didn't even know there was a substitution until the Primale was the one who was with me in the temple."

"Vishous fell in love with Doc Jane right about the time it was all going down. Phury didn't want them to be parted, so he stepped in." Bella shook her head. "The thing about Phury is, he'll always put others before himself. Always. It's his nature."

"I know. That's why I admire him so. Where I am from . . ." Cormia struggled to find the words. "To the Chosen, selflessness is the greatest of all values. We serve the race and the Scribe Virgin, and in doing so we joyfully put the whole before ourselves. It is the highest order of virtue to sacrifice yourself to the greater good, to that which is of more importance than the self. The Primale does that. I believe that is . . ."

"Is . . . ?"

"That is why I respect him so. Well, that and his . . . his . . ."

Bella laughed in a throaty way. "His keen mind, right? It's clearly got nothing to do with the yellow eyes or all that wonderful hair?"

Cormia figured that if her blush had spoken for her once already, it could do it again.

"You don't have to answer," Bella said with a smile. "He is a special male. But back to the selfless stuff? Here's the thing. If you spend too much time focusing outward, you lose yourself. That's why I worry about him. And that's why I know he doesn't truly love me. He believes I saved his twin in ways he couldn't. It's gratitude he feels. Intense gratitude and idolization. But it's not true love."

"How do you know this, though?"

There was a hesitation. "Ask him about his relationships with females. You'll understand."

"Has he been in love often?" She braced herself for the answer.

"Absolutely, positively no." Bella's hand went round and round her belly. "This isn't any of my business, but I'm going to say it anyway. Save my *hellren*, there isn't a male I hold in higher esteem than Phury, and I like you a lot. If he continues to stay here, I hope you do, too. I like the way you look at him. And I really like the way he looks at you."

"He's passed me over."

Bella's head came up. "What?"

"I am no longer the First Mate."

"God . . . damn."

"So I really should go back to the Sanctuary. If only to make things easier on whomever he chooses to replace me."

It was the right thing to say, but she didn't really believe it. And her feelings showed in her voice. Even she could hear the strain.

Funny, the practice of saying one thing while keeping what she

truly thought to herself was a skill she'd honed over the span of her life on the Other Side. When she'd been over there, lying had been as easy and comfortable as the white robe she wore and the pre-scribed way she did her hair and the rote recitation of ceremonial text.

Now it was hard.

"No offense," Bella said, "but my bullshit meter is going off."

"Bullshit . . . meter?"

"You're lying to me. Look, may I offer you some unsolicited ad-vice?"

"Of course."

"Don't allow yourself to get swallowed up and lost in this Chosen thing. If you truly believe what you've been taught, then that's fine. But if you find yourself fighting an inner voice in your head all the time, then it's not where you're supposed to be. Being a good liar is not a virtue."

That was it, wasn't it, Cormia thought. That was precisely what she had always had to do. Lie.

Bella shifted on the pillows, pulling herself up. "I don't know how much you've heard about me, but I have a brother. Rehvenge. He's a hardheaded handful, always has been, but I love him and we're very close. My father died when I was four, and Rehv stepped in as head of the household for my mother and me. Rehv took great care of us, but he also was controlling as hell, and eventually I moved out of the family house. I had to. . . . He was driving me nuts. Jesus, you should have heard the fighting. Rehv meant well, but he's old-school, very traditional, and that meant he wanted to make all the decisions."

"He sounds like a male of worth, though."

"Oh, he absolutely is. But the thing was, after twenty-five years under him, I was just his sister, not me, if that makes any sense." Bella reached out and took Cormia's hand. "The best thing I ever did for myself was get away and get to know myself." A haunted light came into her eyes. "It was not easy, and there were . . . consequences.

But even with what I had to go through, I highly recommend figuring out who you are. I mean, do you know who you are as a person?"

"I am a Chosen."

"And what else."

"That's . . . all."

Bella's hand gave a squeeze. "Give *you* some thought, Cormia, and start small. What's your favorite color? What do you like to eat? Are you an early riser? What makes you happy? Sad?"

Cormia looked across the room at the incense burner and thought about all the prayers she knew, prayers that covered every eventuality. And the chants. And the ceremonies. She had a whole spiritual vocabulary at her disposal, not just of words but of actions.

And that was about it. Or was it?

She shifted her eyes to meet Bella's. "I know . . . I like lavender tea roses. And I like to build things in my head."

Bella smiled and then hid a yawn with the back of her hand. "That, my friend, is a good start. Now, you want to finish *Project Runway?* With the TV on, you'll feel less awkward about being in your head while you're with me, and Fritz won't be here with dinner for another twenty minutes."

Cormia eased back into the pillows beside her . . . friend. Not her sister, her . . . friend. "Thank you, Bella. Thank you."

"You're welcome. And I love the incense. Very calming."

Bella pointed the remote at the flat screen and pushed some buttons, and Tim Gunn appeared in the sewing room, his silver hair as neat as pressed cloth. In front of him, one of the designers was shaking her head and looking at her partially constructed red dress.

"Thank you," Cormia said again, without looking over.

Bella just reached out and gave Cormia's hand a squeeze, and they both focused on the screen.

TWENTY-NINE

Lash stumbled out of his parents' home with blood on both his hands. His knees were unhinged, his stride jerky. As he tripped over his own feet, he looked down. Oh, God, the stuff was on his shirt and his boots, too.

Mr. D popped up out of the Focus. "You hurt?"

Lash couldn't find any words to answer. Limp and shaky, he could barely stand. "It took . . . so much longer than I thought."

"Here, now, suh, let's get you in the car."

Lash allowed the little guy to take him around to the passenger side and settle him in the seat.

"Whatchu got in your hand there, suh—"

Lash shoved the *lesser* to the side, bent over, and dry-heaved a couple of times over the ground. Something black and oily came out of his mouth and dribbled down his chin. He wiped it off and looked at it.

Not blood. At least, not the kind . . . "I killed them," he said hoarsely.

The *lesser* knelt down in front of him. "'Course you did, and you made your daddy proud. Them bastards ain't your future. We are."

Lash tried to stop the scenes from replaying in his head. "My mother screamed the loudest. When she saw me kill my father."

"Not your father. Not your mother. Animals. Those things were animals in there. Like taking down a deer . . . or, yeah, like a rat, you know? A vermin." The slayer shook his head. "They wasn't you. You just thought they was."

Lash looked down at his hands. The knife was in one. A chain in the other. "So much blood."

"Yeah, they done bleed a ton, those vampires."

There was a long silence. Like, one that lasted for a year.

"Say, there, suh, you got like a pool thing 'round this place?" When Lash nodded, the *lesser* said, "'Round back?" Lash nodded again. "Okay, we gonna take you there and let you wash up. We got you some fresh clothes in the back of this here car and you gonna put 'em on."

Before Lash knew it, he was in the estate's pool house under a shower, washing the remnants of his parents away from his skin and watching the red funnel down the drain at his feet. He rinsed off the knife and the chain as well, and when he stepped out to towel off, he put the stainless-steel link around his neck first.

There were two dog tags hanging off the thing. One was his rott-weiler's last license, and the other the record of King's final rabies shot.

Lash's change of clothes went on quick enough, and he trans-ferred his father's wallet from the soiled pants he'd had on to the clean ones Mr. D had gotten for him. He was going to have to keep using the boots, but the stains were browning up, looking less red, which made it more bearable.

He came out of the pool house and found the little slayer sitting on one of the glass-topped tables by the lawn chairs.

The *lesser* hopped down off it. "You want me to call for the backup now?"

Lash looked at the Tudor. Driving over here, he'd intended to ransack the place. Take anything that was worth a dime. Use a fleet of what the Omega had told him were his troops to strip the place down to its wallpaper and floorboards.

It seemed like the Conan thing to do. The perfect declaration of his new status. You don't just crush your enemies, you take their horses and burn their huts and hear the lamentations of their women. . . .

Trouble was, he knew what was inside that house. With the bodies of his parents and the *doggen* in it, he was staring at a mausoleum, and the idea of desecrating the place, of sending in a swarm of *lessers* to defile it, was too wrong.

"I want to get out of here."

"We'll come back then?"

"Just get me the fuck out of here."

"Whatever you like."

"Right answer."

Moving like an old man, Lash walked back around to the front of the house and kept his eyes straight ahead, avoiding the windows he passed.

When he'd slaughtered the *doggen* in the kitchen, there had been a roasting chicken in the oven, the kind that had one of those little popup thingies that let you know when it was done. After he'd bled out the last of the servants, he'd stopped by the Viking stove and turned the light on. The chicken's popper had gone off.

He'd opened the slim drawer to the left of the stove and taken out two white-and-red-striped oven mitts that had Williams-Sonoma tags on them. Turning the oven off, he'd slid the roasting pan from the heat and put it on the gas burners. Golden brown with corn-bread stuffing. Giblets were in the bottom, on their way to spicing up the gravy.

He'd turned off the potatoes that were boiling in water, too.

"Get me out of here," he said as he slid into the car. He had to move his legs inside using his hands.

A moment later, the Focus's sewing-machine engine turned over, and they started down the driveway. In the dense silence of the shit box, Lash took his father's wallet out of his fresh cargo pants, flipped the thing open, and checked through the cards. ATM, Visa, Black AmEx . . .

"Where you want to go?" Mr. D asked as they came to Route 22.

"I don't know."

Mr. D glanced over. "I kilt my cousin. When I was sixteen. He was a bastard, and I liked it while it was happening and it was the right thing to do. But afterward, I felt bad. So you got nothing to apologize for if you done feel like you wronged 'em."

The idea that someone knew even a little about what he was going through made the whole thing seem less like a nightmare. "I feel . . . dead."

"It'll pass."

"No . . . I'm never not going to feel like— Oh, fuck it, just shut up and drive, okay?"

Lash slipped the last card free as they took a right on Route 22. It was his father's fake driver's license. As his eyes hit the picture, his stomach rolled. "Pull over!"

The Focus shot onto the shoulder. As a massive SUV passed them, Lash opened the door and heaved some more black shit onto the ground.

He was lost. Utterly lost.

What the hell had he just done? Who was he?

"I know where to take you," Mr. D said. "If y'all just shut the door, I can get you to where you'll feel better."

Whatever, Lash thought. At this point, he would take suggestions from a bowl of Rice Krispies. "Anywhere . . . but here."

The Focus pulled a U-ie and headed toward downtown. They'd gone a couple of miles when Lash glanced over at the little *lesser.* "Where we headed?"

"Place where you can catch your breath. Trust me."

Lash looked out of the window and felt like a total pussy. Clearing his throat, he said, "Tell a squadron to go back there. And take everything that isn't nailed down."

"Yes, suh."

As Z pulled the Escalade up to the Tudor mansion Lash and his parents lived in, Phury frowned and sprang his seat belt free. *What the hell?*

The front door was wide-open to the summer night, the light from the chandelier in the front foyer casting a golden yellow glow over the stoop and the pair of topiaries standing at attention on either side of the entrance.

Okay, this was just wrong. You expected colonials with porch pots and gnomes in their flower beds to have their doors languishing open like that. Or maybe ranch houses with bikes in front of the garage and chalk drawings on the sidewalks. Or, hell, even trailers with busted windows and decrepit plastic chairs dotting their weed lawn.

But Tudor mansions on manicured grounds didn't look right with their grand front doors wide open to the night. It was like a debutante flashing her bra thanks to a wardrobe malfunction.

Phury got out of the SUV and cursed. The smell of fresh blood and *lessers* was all too familiar.

Zsadist palmed one of his guns as he shut his door. "Shit."

As they walked forward, it was pretty damn evident they were not going to be talking to Lash's parents about what had happened to their son. Chances were good he and Z were going to be finding bodies.

"Call Butch," Zsadist said. "This is a crime scene."

Phury already had his phone in his hand and was dialing. "I'm on it." When the Brother answered, he said, "We need backup here, stat. There's been an infiltration."

Before the pair of them walked into the house, they paused to check out the door. The lock hadn't been busted open, and the security system wasn't blaring.

Made no sense. If a slayer had come to the door and rung the bell, he wouldn't have been let in by a *doggen*. No way. So the *lessers* must have broken in by some other route and left through the front door.

And sure as shit they'd been busy. There was a path of blood on the grand Oriental rug in the marble foyer—and it wasn't made up of drops; it was like someone had used a paint roller with the shit.

The red streak ran between the study and the dining room.

Z went left toward the study. Phury pulled a rightie and went into the dining—

"I found the bodies," he said gruffly.

He knew when Z saw what he was looking at, because the Brother growled, "Holy motherfucker."

Lash's slaughtered parents were sitting upright in chairs at the far end of the table, their shoulders tied back so they'd stay upright. Blood had leaked from stab wounds in their chests and necks, pooling on the glossy floor at their feet.

Candles were lit. Wine was poured. On the table between the bodies was a beautiful roasted chicken, so fresh from the oven you could smell the meat over the stench of blood.

The bodies of two *doggen* were seated in chairs to the left and the right of the sideboard, the dead to serve the dead.

Phury shook his head. "How much you want to bet there are no other bodies in the house. Or they'd be lined up here as well."

The fine clothes of Lash's parents had been carefully straightened, his mother's three strands of pearls lying as they should, his father's tie and jacket all arranged. Their hair was a mess and their wounds

were Rob Zombie raw, but their bloodstained clothes were perfect. They were like two morbid Kewpie dolls.

Z pounded his fist into the wall. "Sick fucking bastards . . . those fucking *lessers* are ill."

"For real."

"Let's go through the rest of the place."

They checked the library and the music room and found nothing. The butler's pantry was untouched. The kitchen showed evidence of a struggle consistent with two killings, but that was all—there was no sign of where the break-in had occurred.

The second floor was clean, the lovely bedrooms right out of *House Beautiful* with their toile drapes and their antiques and their luxurious duvets. On the third floor, there was a suite worthy of a king that, going by the textbooks on guns and martial-arts fighting, as well as the computer shit and the stereo system, had been Lash's crib. It was neat as a pin.

In the whole house, save for where the killings had been committed, nothing was disturbed. Nothing was stolen.

They went back downstairs, and Zsadist quickly examined the bodies while Phury ran a check on the security system's master board out by the garage.

When he was finished, he went back to his twin. "I hacked into the alarms. Nothing was triggered or circumvented either through a code or a power outage."

"Wallet's not on the male," Z said, "but the guy's Ebel is still on his wrist. Female has her diamond on her finger and a pair of dime-sized flashers in her earlobes."

Phury put his hands on his hips and shook his head. "Two infiltrations, here and at the clinic. Both with no looting."

"At least we know how they found this place. I mean, shit, Lash was abducted and tortured until he talked. Only way. He wouldn't have had ID on him when he was taken from the clinic, so the addy had to have come from his own mouth."

Phury looked around at all the art on the walls. "Something's just not right here. Normally they'd be looting."

"But assuming they took the father's wallet, the real assets are no doubt in the bank. If they can get access to those accounts, it would be a cleaner way to rob."

"But why leave all this shit?"

"Where are you?" Rhage's voice echoed through the foyer.

"In here," Z called out.

"We have to let the other families in the *glymera* know," Phury said. "If Lash has given up his own address, God only knows what else was peeled out of him. This could be a leak of unprecedented implications."

Butch and Rhage walked into the room and the cop shook his head. "Shit, this takes me right back to Homicide."

"Man . . ." Hollywood sighed.

"Do we know how they got in?" the cop asked, walking around the table.

"No, but let's go through the house again," Phury said. "I just can't believe they walked right through the front door."

When the four of them got upstairs to Lash's room, they were all shaking their heads.

Phury looked around the room, his brain churning. "We've got to get word out."

"Well, look at this," Z murmured, nodding to a window.

Down at the foot of the driveway, a car turned in. Then another. Then a third.

"There's your looters," the Brother said.

"Fuckers," Rhage bit out with a grim smile. "But at least they have good timing—I need to work off dinner."

"And it'd be so damn rude not to greet them at the door," Butch muttered.

Instinctively, Phury reached to open his coat, but then remembered there were no guns or daggers to get to.

There was a split second of awkwardness, during which no one would look at him, so he said, "I'll go back to the compound and contact the other families in the *glymera*. I'll also let Wrath know what's doing."

The three nodded and jogged for the stairs.

As they pounded down to welcome-wagon the *lessers*, Phury took one last look around the bedroom, thinking that he wanted to be with the others, killing the sons of bitches who had done this.

The wizard faced off at him in his mind. *They won't fight with you anymore because they can't trust you. Soldiers don't want to be backed up by someone they have no faith in.*

Face it, mate, you're finished on this side. The question is, how long until you ruin it with the Chosen?

Just as Phury was about to dematerialize, he frowned.

Across the way, on the dresser, there was a smudge of something on one of the brass drawer pulls.

He went over for a closer look. Dark brown . . . it was dried blood.

When he opened the drawer, there were bloody fingerprints on the objects inside: the Jacob & Co. iced-out watch Lash had worn before his transition had smudges on it, and so did a diamond chain and a heavy stud earring. Something had obviously been taken out of the little drawer, but why would a *lesser* leave such expensive things behind? It was hard to imagine what would be worth more than all those diamonds and still fit in a small space.

Phury glanced around at the Sony VAIO laptop and the iPod . . . and the dozen other drawers in the room that were divvied up between the desk and the bureau and the bedside tables. All of them were closed tight.

"You have to leave."

Phury turned around. Z was standing in the doorway, gun drawn.

"Get the fuck out of here, Phury. You're not armed."

"I could be." He glanced over at the desk where a couple of knives lay on the textbooks. "In a heartbeat."

"Go." Z bared his fangs. "You're not helping here."

The first sounds of the fighting drifted up the staircase in a series of grunts and barked curses.

As his twin took off to defend the race, Phury watched Z go. Then he dematerialized from Lash's bedroom, bound for the desk in the training center's office.

THIRTY

"You need to rest," Cormia said as Bella yawned again.

Fritz had just come in and taken away their First Meal dishes. Bella had had steak and mashed potatoes and mint-chocolate-chip ice cream. Cormia had had the potatoes . . . and some of the ice cream.

And she'd thought the M&M's had been delightful?

Bella snuggled more deeply into her pillows. "You know, I think you're right. I am tired. Maybe we can finish up the marathon later tonight?"

"Sounds lovely." Cormia slid off the bed. "Do you need anything?"

"No." Bella's eyes closed. "Hey, before you go. What are those candles made of? They are incredibly soothing."

The female seemed awfully pale against her white lace pillowcase. "They're made of sacred things from the other side. Sacred, healing things. Herbs and flowers mixed with a binding made with water from the Scribe Virgin's fountain."

"I knew they were special."

"I'm not going to be far," Cormia blurted.

"Which is good."

As Cormia stepped out of the room, she was careful to shut the door quietly.

"Madam?"

She looked behind her. "Fritz? I thought you'd left with the tray."

"I did." He lifted the bouquet he was holding. "I needed to deliver these."

"What lovely flowers."

"They are for the second-floor sitting room." He plucked out a lavender rose and offered it forward. "For you, mistress."

"Why, thank you." She took the delicate petals to her nose. "Oh, how lovely."

Cormia jumped as something brushed her leg.

Bending down, she ran her hand over the black cat's silky, resilient back. "Why, hello, Boo."

The cat purred and leaned into her, his surprisingly strong body shifting her weight.

"Do you care for roses?" she asked him, offering him the bloom.

Boo shook his head and nudged at her free hand, demanding more attention.

"I adore this cat."

"And he adores you," Fritz said, then hesitated. "Mistress, if I may . . ."

"What is it?"

"The master Phury is down in the training center's office, and I believe he could use some company. Perhaps you would—"

The cat let out a loud meow, trotted over in the direction of the grand staircase, and flicked his tail. It seemed as if, had he had arms and hands, he would have been pointing down to the foyer.

The butler laughed. "I think his lordship Boo agrees."

The cat meowed again.

Cormia tightened her grip on the rose's stem as she stood up. Maybe this was a good thing. She needed to tell the Primale that she was leaving. "I should like to see His Grace, but are you sure now is the—"

"Good, good! I shall take you to him."

The butler trotted off to the sitting room and returned a moment later. As he came back, there was a spring in his step and a glow to his face, as if he were doing a job he enjoyed.

"Come. Let us descend, mistress."

Boo meowed again and led the way down the stairs and to the left, then over to a black-paneled door tucked in a corner. The butler entered a code on a numerical pad and opened what turned out to be a six-inch-thick steel panel. Cormia followed Fritz down a couple steps . . . and found herself in a tunnel that seemed to go on forever in both directions.

Looking around, she pulled the lapels of her robe more closely together. It was strange to feel claustrophobic in the midst of so much space, but she was abruptly conscious that they were underground and trapped inside.

"The code, by the way, is 1914," the butler said as he closed them all in and checked to make sure the lock was properly engaged. "That would be the year the house was built. You just enter it here on these pads to get through any of the doors along the way. The tunnel is made up of concrete and steel, and is sealed at all ends. And everything in it is monitored by a security system. There are cameras"—he pointed to the ceiling—"and other monitoring devices. You are as safe here as you would be on the grounds or in the house itself."

"Thank you." She smiled. "I was feeling . . . a bit unnerved."

"Perfectly understandable, madam." Boo brushed against her as if he were taking her hand and giving it a little squeeze of reassurance.

"We go this way." The butler walked in a shuffle, his wrinkled face beaming. "The master Phury will love to see you."

Cormia held on to her rose and followed. As she went along, she tried to cast the proper good-bye in her head, and found herself tearing up a little.

She had fought this destiny of hers in the beginning, fought against being First Mate. Yet now, as she was getting what she wanted, she mourned the loss that came with her relative freedom.

Upstairs in the hall of statues, John opened the second door down from his room and turned on the light.

Qhuinn entered the bedroom with care, like he hoped there was no mud on the soles of his New Rocks. "Nice crib."

I'm right next door, John signed.

Both of their phones went off at the same time, and the text was from Phury: *Classes canceled for the coming week. Please log on to secured Web site for more information.*

John shook his head. Classes canceled. Clinic sacked. Lash abducted . . . and likely tortured. The fallout from what had happened in the locker room continued.

Bad news . . . bad news was coming in more than threes.

"No more classes, huh," Qhuinn murmured as he seemed to get a little too busy putting his duffel bag down. "For anyone."

We need to hook up with Blay, John signed. *I can't believe he hasn't texted since night fell. Maybe we should go over there now?*

Qhuinn walked to one of the floor-to-ceiling windows and pulled back the heavy drapery. "I don't think he's going to want to see me anytime soon. And I know you're signing *why* behind my back. Just trust me. He's going to need some serious space."

John shook his head and texted Blay: *ZeroSum 2nite cuz no class? Hav news bout me n Q.*

"He'll say he can't go. Assuming you're texting him to meet up with us."

Qhuinn looked over his shoulder just as the phone beeped. Blay's text read: *Cant 2nite busy w fam. will hitchu l8r.*

John put his phone in his pocket. *What happened?*

"Nothing. Everything . . . I don't know—"

The heavy knock on the door was clearly made by a fist the size of a male's head.

"Yeah?" Qhuinn called out.

Wrath strode in. The king seemed even grimmer than he had been earlier, as if more bad news had come in again over the Brotherhood's transom. In his hand was a black metal briefcase and a tangle of leather.

He lifted both up and looked hard at Qhuinn. "I don't need to tell you not to be an asshole with these, do I?"

"Ah, no . . . sir. What are they, though?"

"Your two new best friends." The king put the case on the bed, flipped two black locks free, and popped the lid.

"Whoa."

Whoa, John mouthed.

"You're welcome."

Inside, nestled in gray egg-carton padding, were a pair of stinger-lethal Heckler & Koch forty-five-millimeter autoloaders. After checking the chamber on one, Wrath handed the black weapon to Qhuinn by the muzzle.

"V's going to draw up some ID on you in the Old Language. If shit gets critical, you will flash it, and whoever is up in your grille has to deal with me. Fritz is going to order you up enough ammo to make a squad of Marines get a case of the jels." The king tossed what turned out to be a chest harness at Qhuinn. "You are never not armed when you're with him. Even in this house. Are we clear? That is the way it works."

As Qhuinn hefted the pistol in his palm, John expected his buddy to make a crack about how it was good to have big loads. Instead, he said, "I want free access to the gun range. I'm going to want to be down there at least three times a week. Minimum."

Wrath's mouth lifted on one side. "We'll name the bitch after you, how about that?"

John felt like a voyeur standing between the two of them and saying nothing, but he was fascinated by the change in Qhuinn. Gone was the jocular front. He was all business, suddenly more hard-core than his hard-core clothes.

Qhuinn pointed to a door. "Does that open into his bedroom?"

"Yup."

"Evening, ladies."

Vishous walked into the room, and Qhuinn's eyes weren't the only ones that flared. In the Brother's hands were a length of heavy chain with a tag on the end, a pair of pliers, and a tackle box.

"Sitchass down, boy," V said.

"Go on." Wrath nodded at the bed. "Time to get chained—that dangler has John's crest on it. You're also getting tattooed. This is for life, like I told you."

Qhuinn sat without a word, and V came up behind him, linked the heavy weight around his throat, and then cranked the open link closed. The medallion hung just a little lower than his collarbones.

"Comes off only if you're dead or you get fired." V knocked Qhuinn in the shoulder. "By the way, if you get fired, under the old laws, your pink slip's a guillotine, true? That's how we get the chain off. If you just kick it, though, we'll break one of the links. 'Cuz defiling the dead's tacky. Now for your tat."

Qhuinn started to take his shirt off. "I've always wanted one—"

"You can leave that on." As V popped open his tackle box and took out a tattooing gun, Qhuinn pushed one sleeve up to his shoulder. "Nope, I don't need your arm either."

As Qhuinn frowned, Vishous plugged in the cord and snapped on two black latex gloves. Over on the bedside, he opened one little black jar and one little red one and a larger container that had a clear solution in it.

"Turn around and face me." The Brother took out a stretch of white cloth and a sterilizing pack as Qhuinn swung his New Rocks around and put his hands on his knees. "Look up."

On his *face*? John thought as V wiped off the top of Qhuinn's left cheek.

Qhuinn didn't budge. Not even when the whirring needle came at him.

John tried to see what was getting inked and couldn't manage it. Odd that red was being used. He'd heard that black was the only color that was allowed—

Holy . . . shit, John thought as V pulled back.

It was a single red teardrop outlined in black.

Wrath spoke up. "Symbolizes that you're willing to shed your own blood for John. Also lets everyone know, in no uncertain terms, what your position is. If John dies, it will be filled in with black ink, signifying you served someone of interest honorably. If it doesn't work out, it will be boxed with an X to show your shame to the race."

Qhuinn stood and went to the mirror. "I like it."

"Good thing," V said dryly as he came over and smoothed some clear ointment over the ink.

"Can you do one other for me?"

V glanced over at Wrath, then shrugged. "Whatchu got?"

Qhuinn pointed to the back of his neck. "I want 'August eighteenth, 2008,' in the Old Language here. And don't make it small."

Today's date, John thought.

V nodded. "Okay. I can do that shit. Hafta be in black, though. That red is only for specials."

"Yeah. Good." Qhuinn went back to the bed and shuffled around so he was sitting cross-legged on the edge of the mattress. Bending his head, he bared his nape. "And spell out the numbers, please."

"Gonna be big."

"Yup."

V laughed. "I like you, true. Now hold your chain up and let me get to work."

It went relatively quick, the whine of the ink gun fluctuating like a car engine, revving and settling, revving and settling. V added a nice artistic swirl underneath the design, then ran it all around, so the tattoo looked like a fancy plaque.

This time, John stood behind V and watched the whole thing. The three lines of text were gorgeous, and given how long Qhuinn's neck was and how short he kept his hair, they would always show.

John wanted one. But what would it be?

"You're solid," V said as he wiped the skin with the once-white cloth, which was now covered with smudges.

"Thank you," Qhuinn said as V smoothed on more of that ointment, the fresh ink vivid against his golden skin. "Thank you very much."

"You haven't seen it yet. For all you know, I could have inked 'jackass' back here."

"Nah. I never doubt you," Qhuinn said, grinning up at the Brother.

Vishous smiled a little, his hard face with its tattoos showing approval. "Yeah, well, you aren't a flincher. Flinchers get fucked. The steady ones get the goods."

V clapped palms with the guy, then packed up and took off while Qhuinn went into the bathroom and used the hand mirror to see the work.

It's beautiful, John signed from behind him. _Really beautiful._

"It's exactly what I wanted," Qhuinn murmured as he looked at the ink that covered the whole back of his neck.

When the two of them returned to the bedroom, Wrath put his hand in his back pocket, took out a set of car keys, and gave them to Qhuinn. "These are to the Mercedes. You go anywhere with him, you take that car until we can get you other wheels. The thing's bulletproof, and faster than anything else on the road."

"Can I still take him to ZeroSum?"

"He's not a prisoner."

John stamped his foot and signed, _I'm also not a pussy._

Wrath barked a laugh. "Never said you were. John, give him the passwords to all the doors and the tunnel and the gates."

"What about classes?" Qhuinn asked. "When they start up again, do I stay with John then, even though I'm kicked out?"

Wrath went over to the door and paused. "We'll cross that bridge when we get to it. Future's kind of unclear. As fucking usual."

After the king left, John thought about Blay. The guy really should have been with them for all of this.

I'd like to go to ZeroSum, he signed.

"Why? 'Cause you think it's going to get Blay out?" Qhuinn went over to the briefcase and loaded the other gun, the clip sliding into place with a whisper and a click.

You need to tell me what's doing. Now.

Qhuinn put on the holster and plugged the weapons in under his armpits. He looked . . . powerful. Deadly. With his cropped dark hair and those piercings in his ear and that tat underneath his blue eye, if John hadn't known the guy, he would have sworn he was looking at a Brother.

What happened between you and Blay?

"I cut him loose, and I was cruel about it."

Good God . . . Why?

"I was on the way to jail for murder, remember? He'd have eaten himself alive worrying about me. It would have ruined his life. Better that he hate me than be lonely for the rest of his days."

No offense, but are you really that important to him?

Qhuinn's mismatched eyes drilled into John's. "Yes. I am. And don't ask any questions about that."

John knew a boundary when he saw it: Conversationally speaking, he'd just run into a concrete wall with barbed wire around it.

I still want to go to ZeroSum, and I still want to give him a chance to meet us out.

Qhuinn pulled a light jacket from his bag and seemed to gather himself as he put it on. When he turned back around, his characteristic smart-ass smile was back in place. "Your wish is my command, prince of mine."

Don't call me that.

As John headed for the exit, he texted Blay, hoping the guy would show eventually. Maybe if he was bugged enough he'd relent?

"So what should I call you?" Qhuinn said as he leaped ahead to open the door with a flourish. "Would you prefer 'my liege'?"

Give it a rest, would you.

"How about good ol'-fashioned 'master'?" When John just glared over his shoulder, Qhuinn shrugged. "Fine. I'll go with fathead then. But that's your damage, I gave you options."

THIRTY-ONE

There were two things the *glymera* liked above all else: a good party and a good funeral.

With the slaughter of Lash's parents, they had both.

Phury sat in front of the computer in the training center's office, a headache directly behind his left eyeball. He felt like the wizard was taking an ice pick to his optic nerve.

Actually, it's a drill, mate, the wizard said.

Right, Phury thought. Of course it is.

Is that sarcasm? the wizard said. *Ah, right. You'd planned to be a washed-up junkie and a disappointment to your brothers, and now that you've succeeded you're getting cheeky. You know, perhaps you should start a seminar for others. Phury, son of Ahgony's ten steps to success at being an utter, irredeemable failure.*

Shall I get the ball rolling? Let's start with the basics: being born.

Phury planted his elbows on either side of the laptop and rubbed his temples, trying to stay grounded in the real world instead of the wizard's boneyard.

The computer screen in front of him glowed, and as he stared at it, he thought of all the shit that was coming into the Brotherhood's general e-mail box. The *glymera* just wasn't getting it. In the message he'd sent out to them, he'd reported on the attacks and urged the aristocracy to get out of Caldwell and take shelter in their safe houses. He'd been careful with the wording, trying not to incite panic, but evidently, he hadn't been dire enough.

Although you'd think the slaughter of their *leahdyre* and his *shellan* in their own home would be enough.

God, there had been so much death from the Lessening Society last night and tonight . . . and given the *glymera's* responses, there was going to be more. Soon.

Lash knew where every single aristocratic family lived in town, so there was a chance that a significant portion of the *glymera* was at risk for exposure. And the poor kid didn't have to give each of the addresses out under duress, either. If the *lessers* got into just a couple of those homes, they'd find clues to so many others—address books, party invitations, meeting schedules. Lash's leaks were going to be like an earthquake hitting a fault line, blowing the whole landscape apart.

But was the *glymera* going to be smart about the threat? No.

According to the e-mail he'd just gotten from the Princeps Council's treasurer, the idiots were not going to their safe houses. Instead, they had to mourn this "staggering loss of such a well-appointed male and female of worth" by throwing another party.

No doubt so that they could wage a power struggle for who would be the next *leahdyre*.

And in closing? The guy had tacked on a little ditty that the *glymera's* Council would be collecting on the debt owed to Lash's family as a result of Qhuinn's actions.

Well, weren't they givers. It wasn't like they wanted the cash for

themselves to . . . say . . . fete a new *leahdyre*. Oh, hell, no. They were "safeguarding the important precedent of ensuring that bad deeds were punished."

Sure they were.

Thank God Qhuinn was free of them, although Wrath's appointment of the kid as John's *ahstrux nohtrum* was a shocker. Bold move, especially as it was retroactive. And just over what appeared to be a fight that Qhuinn had stopped in an inappropriate way? There had to be something more to what had happened in that shower, something that was being kept on the down-low. Otherwise, it made no sense.

The *glymera* was going to know Wrath was protecting Qhuinn, and the appointment was going to come back to bite the king at some point. Even so, Phury was glad that was the way it had all shaken out. John, Blay, and Qhuinn had been the cream of the trainee crop, and Lash . . . well, Lash had always been trouble.

Qhuinn might have had the mismatched eyes, but Lash had had the defect. There had always been something off with that kid.

The computer beeped as another e-mail landed in the Brotherhood's inbox. This time it was the late *leahdyre*'s right-hand man. And what do you know, the guy advocated a "strong stance against what is a tragic series of losses, but ultimately a low threat to our secured abodes. It is best at this time that we come together and go through the appropriate mourning rituals for our dearly departed. . . ."

Okay, talk about stupid. Anyone with half a brain would pack up their matched sets of LV and hightail it out of town until the dust settled. But no, they'd rather get their spats and their gloves out and make like they were in a Merchant-Ivory movie, with all the black clothes and the ceremonial expressions of condolence. He could just hear the elaborate, phony-ass sympathy exchanges they'd volley back and forth to one another while mushroom puffs were passed by *doggen* in uniform and a polite fight for political control ensued.

He only hoped they would come to their senses, because even though they pissed him off, he didn't want them waking up dead, so to speak. Wrath could try to order them out of Caldwell, but chances were that would just make them dig their heels in even harder. The king and the aristocracy were not friends. Hell, they were barely allies.

Another e-mail came in, and it was more of the same. *We're staying and throwing a party.*

Man, he needed a blunt.

And he needed . . .

The closet door swung open, and Cormia stepped out of the secret passageway to the tunnel. There was a lavender rose in her elegant hand and a graceful reserve to her face.

"Cormia?" he said, then felt ridiculous. Like she'd changed her name to Trixie or Irene sometime in the last day? "Is there something wrong?"

"I don't mean to bother you. Fritz suggested . . ." She turned around as if she expected the butler to be right behind her. "Ah . . . he brought me here."

Phury stood up, thinking this might just be payback from the butler for his untimely interruption the night before. And didn't that make the *doggen* a hero. "I'm glad."

Well, maybe *glad* wasn't exactly the right word. Unfortunately, his urge to smoke was replaced with the urgent need to do something else with his mouth. Although sucking would still be involved.

Another e-mail came through, and the laptop let out a peep. They both looked at the computer.

"If you're busy, I can go—"

"I'm not." The *glymera* was like a brick wall, and considering he already had a headache, there was no reason to keep banging his brain up against their stubbornness. Tragically, there was nothing he could do until the next bad thing rolled out and he e-mailed . . .

Although it wouldn't be him though, would it. He'd been riding the keyboard only because everyone else's hands were busy doing dagger business.

"How are you?" he asked to shut himself up. And because the answer mattered.

Cormia looked around the office. "I would never have guessed this was down here."

"Would you like a tour of the place?"

She hesitated and brought forward the perfect lavender rose . . . which was the color of the bracelet John Matthew had given to her. "I think my flower needs a drink."

"I can fix that." Wanting to give her something, anything, he reached over to a twenty-four-pack of Poland Spring and pulled a bottle out. Cracking the lid, he took a swig to lower the level and then put it on the desk. "Plenty in here to keep her happy."

He watched Cormia's hands as she put the rose in the makeshift vase. They were so lovely and pale and . . . they really needed to be on his skin.

All over him.

Phury untucked his shirt as he stood up and came around the desk, making sure that the tails covered the front of his slacks. He hated sloppy dressing, but better to schlub it than run the risk of her seeing that he was aroused.

And he was. Totally. He had a feeling that it was always going to be like this around her: Something about his coming into her palm the night before had changed everything.

He held open the door into the hall. "Come see our training facility."

She followed him out of the office and he took her all around, narrating the things that were done in the gym and the equipment room and the PT facility and the shooting range. She was interested but mostly silent, and he had the feeling she had something to say to him.

He could guess what it was.

She was going to go back to the Other Side.

He paused at the locker room. "This is where the boys shower and change. The classrooms are down here."

Christ, he didn't want her to go. But what the hell did he expect her to do? He'd left her with no role here.

You *have no role here*, the wizard pointed out.

"Come on, let me show you a classroom," he said to draw things out.

He walked her into the one he used, feeling a curious pride at showing her where he worked.

Had worked.

"What's all that?" she asked, pointing to the blackboard, which was covered with figures.

"Oh . . . yeah . . ." He walked over and picked up a felt eraser, quickly running it over the casualty analysis on a bomb detonating in downtown Caldwell.

She crossed her arms over her chest, but it was more like she was holding herself than a big defensive thing. "Do you think I don't know what the Brotherhood does?"

"Doesn't mean I want you reminded of it."

"Are you going to go back into the Brotherhood?"

He froze and thought, *Bella must have told her.* "I didn't know you'd heard I was out of it."

"I'm sorry, it's none of my concern—"

"No, it's fine . . . and, yeah, I think my fighting days are done." He glanced over his shoulder and was struck by how perfect she looked, with her backside braced against one of the tables the trainees sat at and her arms intertwined. "Hey . . . mind if I draw you?"

She flushed. "I suppose . . . well, if you wish. Do I need to do anything?"

"Just stay where you are." He put the eraser back on the blackboard's lip and picked up a piece of chalk. "Actually, would you take your hair down?"

When she didn't reply, he looked back at her and was surprised to find her hands up at her hair, working at the gold pins. One by one,

sections of blond waves came down and framed her face, her neck, her shoulders.

Even under the dulling fluorescent lights of the classroom, she was radiant.

"Sit up on the table," he said in a hoarse voice. "Please."

She did as he asked and crossed her legs . . . and, holy hell, didn't that robe of hers fall open, splitting wide up to her thigh. When she tried to close the gap, he whispered, "Leave it."

Her hands stilled, then shifted back and flattened on the table to support her upper weight. "Is this all right?"

"Don't. Move."

Phury took his time as he drew her, the chalk becoming his hands going over her body, lingering on her neck and the swell of her breasts and the curve of her hip and the long, smooth expanse of her legs. He made love to her as he transferred her image onto the black-board, the sound of the chalk a rasping noise.

Or maybe that was his breath.

"You're very good," she said at one point.

He was too busy and greedy with his eyes to answer her, too pre-occupied with what he imagined himself doing to her when he was finished.

After an eternity that lasted only a moment, he stepped back and measured his work. Perfection. It was her, but more—although there was a sexual undertone to the composition that even she had to see. He didn't want to shock her, but he couldn't have changed that as-pect of the work. It was in every line of her body and her pose and her face. She was the feminine sexual ideal. At least for him.

"It's done," he said roughly.

"Is that . . . who I am?"

"It's how I see you."

There was a long silence. Then she said with a kind of astonish-ment, "You think I'm beautiful."

He traced the lines he'd drawn. "Yes. I do." Silence expanded the distance between them, making him feel awkward. "Well, now . . ." he said. "We can't leave it up like this—"

"Please! No!" she said, putting her hand out. "Let me look at me a little longer. Please."

Okay. Fine. Whatever she wanted. Hell, at this point, she could have told his heart not to beat, and the thing would have complied with the order quite cheerfully. She had become his control tower, his body's master, and anything she told him to do or say or get for her, he would. No questions asked. No care of the means.

In the back of his mind, he knew that all of this was characteristic of a bonded male: Your female commanded you and that was that. Except he couldn't have bonded with her. Right?

"It's so beautiful," she said, her green eyes on the board.

He turned to face her. "That is you, Cormia. You're like that."

Her eyes flared, and then, as if she felt uncomfortable, her hands went to the slit in her robe and closed it.

"Please, no," he whispered, repeating her words. "Let me look a little longer. Please."

Tension boomed between them, positively pounded.

"I'm sorry," he said, annoyed with himself. "I didn't mean to make you feel—"

Her hands released, and that luscious white fabric fell open with such complete obedience, he wanted to pat it on the head and give it a bone.

"Your scent is so strong," she said in a deep voice.

"Yes." He put the chalk down and inhaled, smelling jasmine. "So is yours."

"You want to kiss me, don't you."

He nodded. "Yeah. I do."

"You untucked your shirt. Why?"

"I'm hard. I got hard the moment you came into the office."

She hissed at that, her eyes traveling down his chest to his hips. As her lips parted, he knew exactly what she was thinking about: him coming into her hand.

"It's amazing," she said softly. "When I'm around you like this, nothing seems to matter. Nothing but . . ."

He walked toward her. "I know."

As he stopped in front of her, she looked up. "Are you going to kiss me?"

"If you'll let me."

"We shouldn't," she said, her hands going up to his chest. She didn't push him away, though. She gripped his shirt as if it were a lifeline. "We should not."

"True." He brushed a strand of hair back behind her ear. His desperation to get in her in some way, any way, shorted out his frontal lobe. What he felt as he stood before her was all about the base core of him, the base needs of a male. "But this can be private, Cormia. This can be just you and me."

"Private . . . I like private." She tilted her chin up, offering him what he wanted.

"Me, too," he growled as he sank down onto his knees.

She seemed confused. "I thought you wanted to kiss me. . . ."

"I do." He slipped his palms around her ankles and ran them up and down her calves. "I'm dying to."

"But then why—"

He gently uncrossed her legs, and bless that damn robe's heart, but didn't it fall completely to the sides, showing him everything: Her hips and her thighs and the little slit he needed so badly.

Phury licked his lips as he slid his hands up the inside of her legs, spreading them slowly, inexorably. With an erotic sigh, she leaned back to give him room, reassuring him that she was right there with this, ready for it just as he was.

"Lie back," he said. "Lie back and stretch out."

Oh, fuck . . . She was smooth as cream for him, easing back until she was lying down on the table.

"Like this?"

"Yeah . . . exactly like that."

He ran his palm down the back of one of her legs and extended her foot so it rested on his shoulder. The kissing started at her calf and followed the path that his hands caressed, going higher and higher. He paused at midthigh and double-checked to see if she was truly okay. She was watching him with huge green eyes, her fingers up to her lips, her breath going in and out on a pant.

"You all right with this?" he asked in a low rasp. "Because once I start, it's going to be hard to stop, and I don't want to scare you."

"What are you going to do to me?"

"The same thing you did to me last night with your hand. Except I'm going to use my mouth."

She moaned, her eyes rolling back. "Oh, dearest Virgin Scribe . . ."

"Is that yes?"

"Yes."

He reached up for the robe's tie. "I'm going to take care of you. Trust me."

And, shit, yeah, he knew he would. Some part of him knew with absolute certainty that he was going to pleasure her, even though he hadn't done this before.

He released the tie and parted her robe.

Her body was revealed to him, from her high, tight breasts to the flat expanse of her stomach to the lovely pale lips of her sex. As her hand went down and rested on the mound of her sex, she was the drawing he'd done the day before, everything sexual and feminine and powerful . . . only she was flesh-and-blood real.

"Jesus . . . Christ." His fangs punched out into his mouth, reminding him that he hadn't fed in a while. As a noise came up his throat that was both a demand and a plea, he wasn't sure how much of the moan was because of her sex and how much was because of her blood.

Although did the divisions really matter?

"Cormia . . . I need you."

The way she shifted her legs apart was a gift like nothing that had

ever been wrapped and tagged for him: As she opened herself a little further, he could see the pink core that he was after. She was glistening already.

He was going to add to that.

With a growl, he lunged down and put his mouth to her, going right for the heart of her body.

They both cried out. As her hands speared into his hair, he gripped her thighs hard and moved in even further. She was so warm against his lips, warm and wet, and he made her warmer and wetter as he French-kissed her sex. While she moaned, instinct overtook them both, paving the way for him to lap at her and for her to roll her hips.

God, the sounds were incredible.

The tasting was even more so.

As he looked up over her stomach to her breasts, he had to get at her little nipples. Reaching forward, he pinched them gently then soothed them with his thumbs.

The way she arched nearly had him orgasming. It was just too much.

"Move your hips faster," he said. "Please . . . God, move your hips against me."

As her pelvis started to rock, he extended his tongue and let her ride it as she wanted, using his flesh to pleasure herself. He didn't last long like that, though. He needed to get even closer. Trapping her hips in his palms, he pressed his face from chin to nose against her, and she became all that he tasted and smelled and knew.

And then it was time to get really serious.

He moved up and started an insistent flicking at the top of her sex, knowing he had the right place by the gasping sound she made. When she began to pump her hips with increasing thrall, he reached for her hand to reassure her. She grabbed onto the palm he offered so strongly, she was going to leave marks with her nails, and that was just fantastic. He wanted those crescents in his back as well . . . his ass, too, as he drilled into her.

He wanted to be all over her, inside of her.

He wanted to do some marking of his own.

Cormia knew that her body was doing exactly what the Primale's had the day before. The gathering storm and the urgency she felt and the heat roaring through her told her she was where he had been.

On the brink.

The Primale was huge between her legs, his broad shoulders stretching her wide. His gorgeous multicolored hair was all over her thighs, and his mouth was like on like against her core, lips meeting lips, slippery tongue against slick folds. It all seemed so glorious and scary and inevitable . . . and the only reason she wasn't completely overwhelmed was his hand on hers.

The touch was better than any words of reassurance on so many levels—but mostly because if he'd tried to speak to her, he would have had to stop what he was doing, and that would have been a crime.

Just when she thought she would fragment apart, a wave of energy crashed down all over her, sweeping her up and away to some other place as her body rhythmically surged. As all that wonderful tension snapped free, the release was so satisfying tears sprang to her eyes, and she cried out something—or maybe it was nothing, just an explosion of breath.

When it was over, the Primale lifted his head, his tongue taking on one last lingering upstroke before flicking free of her core.

"Are you okay?" he asked, his eyes wild and yellow.

She opened her mouth to speak. When nothing coherent came out, she nodded.

The Primale licked his lips nice and slow, flashing the tips of fangs that were visible . . . and became even more pronounced as he looked at her neck.

Shifting her head to the side and offering him her vein was the most natural thing in the world to do.

"Take from me," she said.

His eyes flared and he prowled up her body, kissing her stomach and pausing at one of her nipples, giving it lapping attention. And then his fangs were over her throat. "Are you sure?"

"Yes—*oh, GOD!*"

His strike was hard and deep, and it happened so fast . . . just as she'd imagined it would. He was a Brother in need of what sustained them all, and she was nothing fragile to be broken. She gave and he took and another surge of that wild tension began to build in her again.

She shifted on the table, spreading her legs. "Take me. Whilst you do this . . . be in me."

Without breaking the seal on her throat, he growled wildly and worked at his pants, the belt buckle clanging against the table. He shifted her down to the end roughly, clapped his hands behind her knees, and eased her open.

She felt a hot, hard probe—

But then he stopped.

The sucking drifted off to a soft lapping and then to little kisses, and then he grew motionless except for his breathing. She could still sense the sex in his blood, could still smell his dark scent, could still feel the need for her vein, but he didn't move even though she was spread for his use.

He let go of her legs, gently put them down, and gathered her up, tucking his head into her shoulder.

She held him gently, the tremendous weight of his muscles and bones balanced between the floor and the table so he didn't crush her.

"Are you all right?" she said into his ear.

His head shook back and forth and inched even closer to her. "I need you to know something."

"What ails you?" She stroked his shoulder. "Talk to me."

He said something that she didn't catch. "What?"

"I'm . . . a virgin."

THIRTY-TWO

"Tonight?" Xhex asked. "You're going up north tonight?"

Rehv nodded and went back to reviewing the construction plans for his new club. The sheaves of paper were stretched out across his desk, the blue architectural renderings overtaking all his other paperwork.

Nope. This was not what he wanted. The flow wasn't right—it was too open. He wanted a layout that was full of small spaces where people could get off in the shadows. He wanted a dance floor, sure, but not a square one. He wanted unusual. Creepy. Vaguely threatening and very elegant. He wanted the club to be Edgar Allan Poe and Bram Stoker and Jack the Ripper, only done in nickel-plated chrome and a lot of glossy black. Victorian meets modern Goth.

The shit he was looking at was like every other club in town.

He pushed the plans away and checked his watch. "I gotta go."

Xhex crossed her arms and stood in front of the office's door.

"And no, you're not," he said.

"I want to come."

"Am I having a nasty flashback? Because didn't we just do this the night before last? As well as a hundred other times? The answer is and always will be no."

"Why?" she snapped. "I've never understood why. You let Trez go."

"Trez is different." Rehv pulled on his sable coat and opened the drawer of the desk. The new pair of Glock forties he'd just bought fit perfectly into the holster he'd put on with his Bottega Veneta suit.

"I know what you do. With her."

Rehv froze. Then continued slipping the guns into their sleeves. "Of course you do. I meet with her. Give her the money. Leave."

"That's not all you do."

He flashed his fangs at her. "Yes. It is."

"No, it isn't. Is that what you don't want me to see?"

Rehv bit down on his molars and glared at her from across the office. "There is nothing to see. Period."

Xhex didn't back down often, but she had the good sense not to push him any further. Even though her anger simmered in her eyes, she said, "Changes in schedule are not good. She tell you why?"

"No." He headed for the door. "But this is just going to be business as usual."

"It's never business as usual. You've just forgotten that."

He thought of the years of this dirty shit and the fact that the future held only more of the same. "You're so wrong about the forgetting part. Trust me."

"Tell me something. If she tried to hurt you, would you shoot to kill?"

"You did not just ask me that."

The topic of conversation alone was enough to make him want to peel his skin off and send the shit to a dry cleaner. The idea that Xhex was calling him out on something he didn't want to look too closely at was beyond the pale.

The truth was, a part of him loved what he did once a month, too.

And that reality was totally unbearable when he was in the world he mostly inhabited, the world the dopamine allowed him to live in, the world that was relatively normal and healthy.

That little slice of ugliness in his heart was something he sure as fuck wasn't sharing with anybody.

Xhex put her hands on her hips and kicked up her chin, her classic pose whenever they argued. "Call me when it's done."

"I always do."

He gathered together the plans for the club, picked up his overday bag, and stepped out of his office and into the alley. Trez was waiting in the Bentley, and when he saw Rehv, he vacated the driver's seat.

The Moor's voice appeared in Rehv's head, deep, melodic. *I'LL BE THERE IN ABOUT A HALF HOUR TO SCOPE THE ENVIRONS AND CHECK THE CABIN.*

"Good deal."

TELL ME YOU'RE UNMEDICATED.

Rehv clapped the guy on the shoulder. "As of an hour ago. And yes, I have the antivenom."

GOOD. DRIVE SAFELY, ASSHOLE.

"No. I'm going to aim for logging trucks and stray deer."

Trez shut the door and took a step back. As he crossed his arms over his massive chest, he cracked a rare smile, his white fangs glowing against his dark, beautiful face. For a split second, his eyes flashed brilliant peridot green—the Moorish equivalent of a wink.

As Rehvenge took off, he was glad Trez backed him up. The Moor and his brother, iAm, had a bag of fancy tricks that would challenge even a *symphath*. They were, after all, royal members of the s'Hisbe of Shadows.

Rehv glanced at the Bentley's clock. He was due to meet the Princess at one a.m. Considering it was a two-hour trip north and it was now eleven fifteen, he was going to have to drive like a bat out of hell.

As he took off, he thought about Xhex. He didn't want to know

how she knew about the sex . . . hoped like hell she continued to respect his wishes and not show up and hang in the shadows.

He hated that she knew he was nothing but a whore.

On one hand, Phury couldn't believe that the words "I am a virgin" had come out of his mouth. On another, he was glad he'd said them.

He had no idea what Cormia thought, though. She was dead quiet.

He pulled back just enough so he could stuff his sex back in his pants and zip up, then he righted her robe, bringing the two halves together and covering her beautiful body up.

In the silence between them, he paced around the room, going from the door to the far wall and back.

Her eyes watched his every move. God, what the hell was she thinking?

"I suppose it shouldn't matter," he said. "I don't know why I brought it up."

"How is it possible . . . I'm sorry. That's so inappropriate—"

"No, I don't mind explaining." He paused, unsure as to whether she'd read about Zsadist's past. "I took a vow of celibacy when I was young. To make me stronger. And I stuck to it."

Not quite, mate, the wizard chimed in. *Tell her about the whore, why don't you. Tell her about the prostitute that you bought at ZeroSum and took into a bathroom and couldn't finish with.*

How typical of you to be exceptional in that manner. The only soiled virgin on the planet.

Phury stopped in front of his drawing on the blackboard. He'd ruined everything.

Picking up a piece of chalk, he started at her feet, beginning to draw the ivy leaves.

"What are you doing?" she said. "You're ruining it."

Ah, lass, the wizard answered. *However good he is at drawing, he's better at ruination.*

Before long, the stunning figure of her was covered with a blanket of ivy leaves. When he was finished, he stepped back from the board. "I tried sex once. And it didn't work out."

"Why not?" she asked in a tight voice.

"It wasn't right. It wasn't a good choice. I stopped."

There was a pause and then a shuffling sound as she got off the table. "Just as it was now with me."

He spun around. "No, that isn't—"

"You stopped, didn't you. You chose not to go on."

"Cormia, it's not that—"

"Who are you saving yourself for?" Her eyes were smart as hell as she looked at him. "Or is it more like what? Is it the fantasy you have of Bella? Is that what's stopping you? If it is, I feel sorry for the Chosen. But if the celibacy is to keep yourself insulated and safe, I feel sorry for you. That strength is a lie."

She was right. Fuck him, but she was so right.

Cormia coiled up her hair and regarded him with a queen's dignity as she pinned it in place. "I'm going back to the Sanctuary. I wish you well."

As she turned away, he jogged over to her. "Cormia, wait—"

She took her arm away when he tried to take it. "Why should I wait? What precisely is going to change? Nothing. Go be with the others. If you can. And if you can't, you need to step down so someone else can be the strength the race needs."

She clapped the door shut behind her.

Standing in the empty classroom, with the wizard's laughter ringing in his ears, Phury closed his eyes and felt the world shrink down all around him until his past and his present and his future were choking him of breath . . . turning him into one of the statues in his family's overgrown, dead garden.

That strength is a lie. . . .

In the silence that surrounded him, her words just kept replaying in his head, over and over again.

THIRTY-THREE

"This is just a club," the Omega's son said, his voice at once defeated and annoyed.

Mr. D turned off the Focus's wheezer of an engine and looked over. "Yup. And we're going to get you what you need here."

They'd been driving around aimlessly for quite a while, because the Omega's son couldn't stop throwing up. The last heaving session had been about forty minutes ago, though, so Mr. D was pretty sure things had done settled some. Hard to know whether the pukin' were because of what the son had had to do or on account of his induction. Either way, Mr. D had taken care of him, even holding the son's head up at one point, because the guy had been too weak to do it himself.

Screamer's was the right place for them to be hauntin'. Even though the son of the Evil wouldn't be able to eat or have sex, there was one sure thing they would find here: drunken human males what could be used as punching bags.

Tired and overwrought as the son was, he had power in his veins, power that needed to be triggered. The club and its idiots were the gun. The son was the bullet.

And a fight would revive things real good. "Come on, now," Mr. D said, getting out.

"This is bullshit." The words mighta sounded strong, but the tone was still that of a guy whose grain silo was empty.

"It ain't." Mr. D walked around, opened the son's door, and helped him out. "Y'all gotta trust me."

They walked across the street to the club, and when the bouncer at the head of the wait line glared at Mr. D, he slipped the big man a fifty, which got them in.

"We gonna just have a hang-around," Mr. D said as he took them through the crowd and over to the bar.

All through the club, hard-core rap thumped, while women dressed in bits of leather paraded by on cock patrol and men glared at one another.

He knew he'd done right when the son's eyes rifle-sighted a group of college-y guys who was barking loudly and sucking back hot sauce in martini glasses.

"Yup, we just havin' ourselves a little breather," Mr. D said with satisfaction.

The bartender came by. "Whatchu want?"

Mr. D smiled. "Nothing for us—"

"Shot of Patrón," the son said.

As the bartender went off, Mr. D leaned in. "You can't eat no more. No drinking 'n' no sex neither."

The son's pale eyes shot over to him. "What? Are you fucking kidding me?"

"No, suh, that's the way—"

"Yeah, fuck that." When the shot glass came down for a landing, the son said to the bartender, "Start a tab."

Lash tossed back the tequila while glaring at Mr. D.

Mr. D shook his head and started scouting for the bathroom.

Yeah, boy, when he'd tried the food routine he'd ended up hurling for an hour, and hadn't they already done enough of that tonight?

"Where's my second," Lash barked out to the bartender.

Mr. D swiveled his head back around. The Omega's son was standing there, happy as you please, tapping his fingers on the bar. The second shot came. Then the third.

After the fourth was ordered, Lash's pale eyes slid over, aggression flaring in them. "So what was this about no eating and no drinking?"

Mr. D couldn't decide whether he was looking at a bomb about to go off . . . or a miracle. No *lessers* were able to take food and drink once they'd been turned. The Omega's black blood nourished them and was incompatible with anything else. All they needed to survive was a couple of hours of rest every day.

"I guess you is different," Mr. D said with respect in his voice.

"Damn straight I am," the son muttered, and then ordered a hamburger.

As the guy ate and drank, you could see the color come back into his face and the spaced-out look get replaced by confidence. And while watching that hamburger and fries and all that tequila go down into Lash's gullet, Mr. D had to wonder whether the son would pale out as the rest of the *lessers* did. The regular rules were clearly not applying here.

"And what is this shit about no sex?" the son said as he wiped his mouth on a black paper napkin.

"We is impotent. You know, can't get—"

"I know what it means, Professor."

The son eyed a blond loose goose at the end of the bar. The woman was no one Mr. D would have had the guts to go after, even if he'd been able to get it up. With her *Playboy* body and her prom-queen face, he woulda given her a pass as out of his league. Not that she'd have noticed him to begin with.

She noticed the son, though, and the way she were looking at the guy made Mr. D measure his new boss right careful. Lash was a handsome sonofa, true 'nough, with his cropped blond hair and his chiseled face and those gray eyes. And he had the kind of body the women done go for, big and muscled, his torso an inverted triangle sitting on his hips, ready for all kinds of action.

It dawned on Mr. D that if they was still in school, he'd be proud to be seen with the son. And likely on the outs with the kind of people the son hung with.

But this weren't school, and Lash needed him. Knew it, too.

The girl across the way smiled at the son, picked the cherry out of her blue drink, and swirled her pink tongue around the dangler.

You could kind of imagine her doing that to a set of balls and Mr. D had to look away. Oh, yes'm, he'da been blushing right good if he'd still been human. He'd always been a blusher when it came to girls.

The son shifted off his bar stool. "No food. No sex. Yeah, right. Wait here, motherfucker."

The son turned away and headed for the woman.

As Mr. D got left at the bar with an empty shot glass and a plate with smudges of ketchup and grease on it, he supposed he'd done good. He'd wanted to get the Omega's son thinking about something other than slaughtering his vampire parents . . . he'd just figured it was going to be a good fistfight.

Instead, the son had a nice little meal and got hisself some booze. And was now going to top things off by banging the experience out of his memory.

Mr. D shook his head at the bartender when he was asked if he wanted something. Damn shame he couldn't drink no more. He'd liked his SoCo. Could have used the hamburger, too. He'd loved his burgers, he really had.

"You got anything for me, Sam-dog?"

Mr. D glanced over. A big guy with a jackass smile and a dump-truck worth of ego had draped himself over the bar and was looking at the bartender. Under his black leather jacket, which had a terrific eagle embroidered on the back, he was dressed in jeans that were

three sizes too big and construction boots. Around his neck were some diamond chains, and he had a flashy watch on.

Mr. D weren't into the jewelry, but he did jones the guy's class ring. It was yellow gold, unlike the rest of his stuff, and had a pale blue stone in the middle.

Mr. D would have liked to be graduated from high school.

The bartender came over. "I got some, yeah." He nodded at the group of guys what had pissed off the son a little bit ago. "Told them who to look for."

"Nice." Big Guy took something out of his pocket and the two shook hands.

Cash, Mr. D thought.

Big Guy grinned and straightened his leather jacket, that class ring flashing bright blue. He approached the guys from the side, then turned as if he was showing them the back of his coat.

There was a hoot and holler and then a lot of hands went in pockets and palms were shook and there was some more with the pockets.

Not smooth. Other people were looking over, and it was pretty obvious that they wasn't exchanging no business cards.

He weren't going to last long in the business, Mr. D thought.

"You sure you don't want anything?" the bartender asked Mr. D.

Mr. D glanced toward the bathroom Lash had taken the blonde into. "Nah, thanks. I'm just waitin' on my friend."

The bartender grinned. "Betcha he's going to be a while. She looks like she gives a nice ride, that one."

Upstairs in her bedroom, Cormia packed up everything . . . which wasn't much.

Staring at the small pile of robes, prayer books, and incense burners that she'd gathered together, she realized with a curse that she'd left her rose in the office. Then again, she wouldn't have been able to take it with her to the Sanctuary. The only things from this side that were allowed in were those of historical importance.

In the larger sense, of course.

She glanced over at her latest—her last—construction of tooth-picks and peas.

She was such a hypocrite, criticizing the Primale for seeking strength in separation, when what was she doing? Leaving this world that challenged her so, with the intention of seeking a seclusion that was even deeper than the one she'd had before as a Chosen.

Tears came into her eyes—

The knock on her door was soft.

"One moment!" she called out, trying to calm herself. When she finally went over and answered the door, her eyes widened and she pulled the lapels of her robe together, hiding the bite mark on her neck. "My sister?"

The Chosen Layla was on the other side, looking as lovely as ever. "Greetings."

"Greetings, indeed."

They exchanged lingering deep bows, which was as close to hug-ging as Chosen were permitted.

"Whither thou come?" Cormia asked as they straightened. "Are you to be of blood service to the Brothers Rhage and Vishous?"

Funny, the formality of her words seemed odd to her now. She'd grown used to more informal discourse. More comfortable with it.

"Indeed, I am to see the Brother Rhage." There was a pause. "And as well I sought to inquire after you. May I come in?"

"But of course. Please avail yourself of my quarters."

Layla entered and brought with her an awkward silence.

Ah, so the news had made it to the Sanctuary, Cormia thought. All the Chosen knew she had been passed over as First Mate.

"What is this?" Layla asked, pointing to the latticework in the corner of the room.

"Oh, it's just a hobby."

"Hobby?"

"When I have time on my hands, I . . ." Well, that was an admis-

sion of guilt, wasn't it. She should have been praying if she had nothing else to do. "Anyway . . ."

Layla didn't cast condemnation in expression or words on the revelation. And yet her presence alone was enough to make Cormia feel bad.

"So, my sister," Cormia said with sudden impatience, "I am guessing it is known that another shall be elevated to First Mate?"

Layla went over to the toothpicks and the peas and ran a delicate finger down one of the sections. "Do you recall when you found me hidden by the Reflecting Pool? It was after I had seen John Matthew through his transition."

Cormia nodded, remembering how the Chosen had been crying softly. "You were quite upset."

"And you were so kind to me. I sent you away, but I was so grateful, and it is in that spirit that I . . . I have come here to return the gentleness you proffered unto me. The burdens we carry as Chosen are weighty and not always understood by others who are not one among us. I want you to know that, having felt as you do now, I am your sister in the heart at this moment."

Cormia bowed low. "I am . . . touched."

She was a lot of other things too. Amazed, for one thing, that they were speaking of this at all. The candor was unusual.

Layla looked back to the construction. "You do not wish to return unto the fold, do you."

After weighing her options, Cormia decided to trust the Chosen with a truth she could barely admit to herself. "You read me well."

"There are others of us who have sought another way. Who have come to pass their lives on this side. There is no shame."

"I'm not so sure of that," Cormia said dryly. "Shame is like the robes we wear. Always with us, ever clothing us."

"But if you shed the robe, you are free of the burdens and the choice is yours."

"Are you sending me a message, Layla?"

"Nay. Verily, if you return to the fold, so shall you be welcomed back with full hearts by your sisters. The Directrix made it plain of sight that there is naught of impropriety in the change of First Mates. The Primale holds you in his highest esteem. She said so."

Cormia started pacing. "That is the official stance, of course. But honestly . . . you must know what the others think in their quiet moments. There are but two explanations. Either I was found wanting by the Primale or I denied him. Both are unacceptable and equally egregious."

The silence that followed told her she'd drawn the correct conclusion.

She paused by the window and looked out over the pool. She wasn't sure she had the strength to leave her sisters, she thought. Moreover, where would she go?

As she thought of the Sanctuary, she told herself that there had been enjoyable days there. Times when she had felt a sense of purpose and been nourished by being part of a greater good. And if she became a sequestered scribe, as she intended to be, she could avoid contact with the others for whole cycles at a time.

Privacy struck her as a grand thing.

"Is it true you care naught for the Primale?" Layla asked.

No. "Yes." Cormia shook her head. "I mean, I care for him as I should. In the same manner you do. I shall be joyous for whoever shall become the next First Mate."

Apparently, Layla didn't have a bullshit meter like Bella's, because the lie floated out into the air and the Chosen didn't question a syllable of it—she just bowed in acknowledgment.

"May I inquire after something then?" Layla asked as she straightened.

"Of course, sister."

"Has he treated you well?"

"The Primale? Yes. He has been very solicitous."

Layla went over to the bed and picked up one of the prayer books.

"I read in his biography that he is a great warrior and that he saved his twin from a horrible fate."

"He is a great warrior." Cormia looked down at the rose garden. She imagined that all the Chosen had read his volumes in the Brotherhood's special section of the library by now—and she wished she had done the same before he'd brought her here.

"Does he speak of that?" Layla prompted.

"Of what?"

"How he rescued his twin, the Brother Zsadist, from an unlawful blood slavery? That is how the Primale lost his leg."

Cormia's head whipped around. "Truly? That is how it happened?"

"He has never spoken to you of it?"

"He has not, no. He is a most private individual. At least with me."

The information was a shock, and she thought of what she had said to him, that he loved the fantasy of Bella. Was that true of herself with the Primale? She knew so little of his history, so little of what had shaped him as the male he was.

Ah, but she knew his soul, didn't she.

And she loved him for that.

There was a knock at the door. When she called out, Fritz put his head in.

"Pardon me, but the sire is ready for you," he said to Layla.

Layla's hands went to her hair and then smoothed over her robe. As Fritz ducked out of the room, Cormia thought that the Chosen was taking special care with her—

Oh . . . no . . .

"You are . . . going to see him? The Primale?"

Layla bowed. "I am to see him now, yes."

"Not Rhage."

"I am to serve him afterward."

Cormia stiffened as ice ran through her. But of course. What had she expected. "You'd better go then."

Layla's eyes narrowed, then flared wide. "My sister?"

"Go on. Better not keep the Primale waiting." She turned away to the window, suddenly ready to scream.

"Cormia . . . ," her sister whispered. "Cormia, you care for him. Verily, you care for him deeply."

"I never said that."

"You don't have to. It is in your face and your tone. Sister mine, why ever . . . why are you stepping aside?"

As Cormia pictured the Primale with his head between her sister's thighs, his mouth making Layla arch in pleasure, her stomach rolled. "I wish you very well in your interview. I hope that he chooses well and chooses you."

"Why are you stepping aside?"

"I was *cast* aside," she bit out. "The decision was not mine. Now, please do not keep the Primale waiting. After all, God forbid, we can't have that."

Layla paled. "God?"

Cormia waved her hand back and forth. "It's just an expression they use here, not an indication of my faith. Now, please, go."

Layla seemed to need a moment to collect herself after the spiritual slip. Then her voice became gentle. "Rest assured he will not pick me. And know that should you ever need a—"

"I won't." Cormia turned away and stared out the window with total fixation.

When the door finally clicked shut, she cursed. Then marched across the room and kicked the ever-living crap out of her construction. She ruined every last section, breaking every single neat little box until the order that had been was rubble on the carpet.

When there was nothing else to destroy, her tears christened the mess, as did the blood on the soles of her bare feet.

THIRTY-FOUR

Downtown at Screamer's, Lash was putting one of the private bathrooms to good use.

And not because he was taking a nice long piss.

He was buried to the balls in that blonde from the bar, nailing her from behind as she braced herself against the sink. Her black leather skirt was pushed up to her hips, her black thong shoved over, her black V-neck pulled wide and held that way by her breasts. She had a precious little pink butterfly tattooed on her hip, and a heart on a chain around her throat, and both were getting banged around to the beat of his thrusting.

It was fun, especially because, in spite of her tough slut clothes, he had a feeling she was out of her league with this kind of sex: no implants, lipstick wasn't smudge-proof, and she'd tried to get him to wear a condom.

Right before he came, he pulled out, spun her around, and forced her onto her knees. He roared as he orgasmed in her mouth, thinking that little shit Mr. D had been right: This was exactly what he'd needed. A sense of mastery, a reconnection with what had been normal for him.

And sex was still good.

As soon as he was finished, he zipped up, not caring whether she spit or swallowed.

"What about me?" she asked, wiping her mouth.

"What about you?"

"I'm sorry?"

Lash cocked an eyebrow as he checked his hair in the mirror. Hmm . . . maybe he should grow it out again. He'd done the whole military shear after his transition, but he'd liked his ponytail. He had good hair.

God, King's dog collar looked hot on him—

"Hello?" the girl demanded.

Annoyed, he glanced at her in the glass. "You don't honestly expect me to care whether you get off."

For a moment, she seemed confused, like the movie she'd rented at Blockbuster had had a different DVD inside the sleeve. "Excuse me?"

"What didn't you understand?"

Shock made her blink like a fish. "I don't . . . get it."

Yeah, evidently *Debbie Does Dallas* was showing on her screen, not *Pretty Woman*.

He looked around the bathroom. "You let me take you in here and push your skirt up and fuck you. And you're surprised I don't care? Exactly what did you think was going to happen?"

The last of the excited, I'm-a-good-girl-doing-a-bad-thing drained from her expression. "You don't have to be rude."

"Why is it bitches like you are always surprised?"

"Bitches?" Self-righteous anger distorted her face, taking her from pretty into gorgon territory—and yet making her somewhat more intriguing. "You don't know me."

"Yeah, I do. You're a slut who lets a guy she's never met before

come in her mouth in a bathroom. Please. I'd have more respect for a prostitute. At least they get paid in something other than spunk."

"You are such a bastard!"

"And you are boring me." He reached for the knob.

She grabbed his arm. "Watch it, asshole. I can make things bad for you in a heartbeat. Do you know who my father is?"

"Someone who didn't do his job of raising you properly?"

Her free palm hit him square in the face. "Fuck you."

Okay, the fighting definitely made her more interesting.

As his fangs punched out into his mouth, he was ready to bite through her throat like it was a Twizzler fresh out of the bag. Except someone pounded on the door and reminded him he was in public and she was human and cleanup was always a bitch.

"You're gonna be sorry," she spat at him.

"Oh, yeah?" He leaned in and was surprised when she held her ground. "You can't touch me, girlie."

"Watch me."

"You don't even know my name."

Her smile was icy, adding years to her age. "I know plenty—"

The pounding on the door started up again.

Before she teed up for another slap and he couldn't stop himself from retaliating, Lash ducked out of the bathroom, his parting salvo a quick, "Pull your skirt down, why don't you."

The guy who'd been knock-knock-knockin' on the other side took one look at him and stepped way back. "Sorry, man."

"No problem," Lash said, rolling his eyes. "You probably saved that bitch's life."

The human laughed. "Stupid whores. Can't live with 'em, can't shoot 'em." The bathroom next door opened and the guy turned away, flashing a righteous eagle embossed on the back of his leather jacket.

"Nice bird you got there," Lash said.

"Thanks."

Lash went over to the bar and nodded at Mr. D. "Time to go. I'm done."

He took his wallet from his back pocket—and froze. The billfold wasn't his. It was his father's. He quickly slipped a fifty out, then buried the thing back where it had been.

He and Mr. D left the crowded, noisy club and when he stepped onto Trade Street's sidewalk, he took a long, deep breath. Alive. He felt totally alive.

On the way over to the Focus, Lash said, "Give me your phone. And the numbers of four straight-up killers."

Mr. D handed the Nokia over and recited some digits. As Lash called the first one and gave the slayer an address in a high-rent part of town, he could practically hear the bastard's suspicion—especially as the *lesser* asked who the fuck was calling him on Mr. D's phone.

They didn't know who he was. His men didn't know who he was.

Lash handed the fucking phone back to Mr. D and barked for the *Fore-lesser* to give confirmation. Man, he shouldn't have been surprised at the doubting thing, but that shit was so going to change. He was going to give his troops a few places to hit tonight to gain himself some cred, then the Lessening Society was going to have a come-to-Jesus meeting in the morning.

They would follow him or meet their maker. Period.

After he and Mr. D did the cell phone handoff three more times, Lash said, "Now take me to Twenty-one Fifteen Boone Lane."

"You want me to call more men in to hit it with us?"

"For our next house, yeah. But this first one is personal."

His dear old cousin Qhuinn was about to eat his own ass for lunch.

After five months of being the Primale, Phury was used to not feeling comfortable. The whole goddamn thing had been one ill-fitting suit after another, a whole wardrobe of I-don't-want-to-do-this.

And yet interviewing Layla for the position of First Mate felt especially wrong.

Viciously wrong.

As he waited for her in the library, he prayed to God she didn't drop her robe like the others had.

"Your Grace?"

He looked over his shoulder. The Chosen was standing in the open double doors of the room, her white robe falling to the floor in folds, her slender body held with regal grace.

She bowed deeply. "It is my wish for you to fare well this evening."

"Thank you. I hope the same for you."

As she straightened, her eyes met his. They were green. Like Cormia's.

Shit. He needed a blunt. "Would you mind if I light up?"

"Of course not. Here, let me bring you the flame." Before he could tell her not to bother, she picked up a crystal lighter and came over to him.

Putting a hand-rolled between his lips, he stopped her as she flipped the lid free. Taking the heavyweight from her, he said, "Not to worry. I can do it."

"Of course, Your Grace."

The flint rasped and the flame popped up yellow and she stepped back, her eyes moving around the room. "This reminds me of home," she murmured.

"How so?"

"All of the books." She went across the way and touched some of the leather spines. "I love books. If I hadn't been trained as an *ehros*, I would have wanted to be a sequestered scribe."

She seemed so laid-back, he thought, and for some reason that made him anxious. Which was nuts. With the others, he'd felt like a lobster in the lobby of a seafood restaurant. With her, they were just two people talking.

"May I ask you something?" he said as he exhaled.

"Of course."

"Are you here freely?"

"Yes."

Her answer was so level, it seemed rote. "You sure about that?"

"I have long wanted to serve the Primale. I have been steadfast always in this desire."

She seemed totally sincere . . . but something was off.

And then he figured out what it was. "You don't think I'm going to choose you, do you."

"No."

"And why is that?"

Now the emotion came out in her, her head dropping, her hands coming up, her fingers entwining. "I was brought here to see Master John Matthew through his transition. I did so, but he . . . denied me."

"How?"

"After he'd been through the change, I washed him, but he denied me. I have been trained to serve sexually and was prepared to do so, and he denied me."

Whoa. Okay. TMI. "And you think that means I won't choose you?"

"The Directrix insisted that I come to you, but it was a measure of respect for you, to give you leave over all Chosen. Neither she nor I expect you to elevate me to First Mate."

"Did John Matthew say why he didn't . . . ?" Because most males were horny as hell right after their changes.

"I left when I was asked to. That is all." Her eyes flipped up to Phury's. "Verily, the Master John Matthew is a male of worth. It is not in his nature to detail the faults of another."

"I'm sure it wasn't because of—"

"Please. May we depart from this subject, Your Grace?"

Phury exhaled a stream of coffee-scented smoke. "Fritz said you were up in Cormia's room. What were you doing there?"

There was a long pause. "That would be between sisters. Of course, I would tell you . . . should you order me to do so."

He couldn't help but approve of the quiet reserve in her voice.

"No, that's okay." He was tempted to ask if Cormia was all right, but he knew the answer to that one. She wasn't. Any more than he was.

"Would you like me to go?" Layla asked. "I know the Directrix has two of my sisters prepared for you. They are eager to come over and greet you."

Just like the other two who'd been to see him the night before. Excited. Ready to please. Honored to meet him.

Phury brought the blunt to his lips again and inhaled long and slow. "You don't seem too thrilled with this."

"With my sisters coming to see you? Of course I—"

"No, with meeting me."

"On the contrary, I am eager to be with a male. I have been trained for mating and I want to serve as more than a blood source. Rhage and Vishous do not require all my services, and it is a burden to be unused. . . ." Her eyes went to the books. "Indeed, I feel as though I am shelved. That I have been given the words to the story of my life, but that I remain largely unread, as it were."

God, he so knew what that was like. He felt as though he had been waiting forever for things to settle down, for the drama to end, for him to be able to take a deep breath and start living. How ironic. It sounded as if Layla was feeling the way she was because nothing was happening in her life. He felt unread because too much had been going on for too long.

Either way, the end result was the same.

Neither of them was doing more than just getting through the day.

Well, cry me a river, mate, the wizard drawled.

Phury went over to an ashtray and stabbed out the blunt. "Tell the Directrix she doesn't need to send anyone else to me."

Layla's eyes shot to his. "I beg your pardon?"

"I choose you."

Qhuinn pulled the black Mercedes up in front of Blay's house and put the thing in park. They'd waited for hours at ZeroSum, with

John texting Blay every now and again. When they kept hearing nothing back, John had pulled up stakes and here they were.

"You want me to open your door," Qhuinn said dryly as he cut the engine.

John looked over. *If I say yes, would you do it?*

"No."

Then by all means, open my door.

"Damn you." Qhuinn got out of the driver's seat. "Ruining my fun."

John shut his door and shook his head. *I'm just glad you're so manipulate-able.*

"That's not a word."

Since when have you been in bed with Daniel Webster? Hello? "Gigunda"?

Qhuinn glanced to the house. He could just hear Blay's voice filling in, *That would be Merriam-Webster.* "Whatever."

The two of them went around to the back of the house, going up to the door that went into the kitchen. The place was a big brick colonial, real formal-looking in front, but it had a cozy rear side, with kitchen windows than ran from floor to ceiling, and a stoop with a friendly wrought-iron lantern that hung down.

For the first time in his life, Qhuinn knocked and waited for an answer.

Guess it was a humdinger of a fight, huh, John signed. *Between you and Blay.*

"Oh, I don't know. Sid Vicious behaved worse than I did, for example."

Blay's mom answered the door, looking exactly as she always did, all Marion Cunningham from *Happy Days*, from the red hair to the skirt. The female was everything that was round and lovely and warm about the fairer sex, and Qhuinn realized as he stared at her now that she, not his chilly swizzle stick of a mother, was the standard that he held females up to.

Yeah . . . it was fine and dandy to ball chicks and guys in bars, but

he would mate someone like Blay's mother. A female of worth. And he would stay true to her until the end of his days.

Assuming he could find someone who would have him.

Blay's mother stepped back to let them in. "You know you don't have to knock—" She looked at the platinum chain around Qhuinn's throat, then at the new tat on his cheek.

Glancing at John, she murmured, "So that's how the king fixed it."

Yes, ma'am, John signed.

She turned to Qhuinn, threw her arms around him, and hugged him so hard his spine shifted. Which was so what he needed. As he held on to her, he took his first deep breath in days.

In a whisper, she said, "We would have kept you here. You didn't have to go."

"Couldn't do that to you."

"We're a stronger lot than you think." She loosened her hold on him and nodded to the rear staircase. "Blay's upstairs."

Qhuinn frowned as he saw a stack of luggage next to the kitchen table. "Going somewhere?"

"We have to get out of the city. Most of the *glymera* are staying, but with . . . what's happened, it's too dangerous here."

"Wise idea." Qhuinn shut the kitchen door. "You going upstate?"

"Blay's father is looking for some vacation time, so the three of us are going to make the rounds of family down south—"

Blay appeared at the bottom of the stairs. Crossing his arms, he nodded at John. "Wassup."

As John signed a greeting back, Qhuinn couldn't believe his buddy hadn't mentioned anything about leaving the city. *Shit.* Was he just going to take off and not say where he was going or when he was due back?

Well, duh. Wasn't that the pot calling the kettle black?

Blay's mom squeezed Qhuinn's arm and whispered, "I'm glad you came before we left." In a louder voice, she said, "Okay, I've cleaned out the fridge, and there's nothing perishable in the pantry. I think I'll go get my jewelry out of the safe."

Jesus, John signed as she took off. *How long are you guys going to be gone?*

"Don't know," Blay said. "A while."

In the long pause that followed, John looked back and forth between the two of them. Eventually he made a snorting noise and signed, *Okay, this is stupid. What the fuck happened between you two?*

"Nothing."

"Nothing." Blay nodded over his shoulder. "Listen, I gotta go up and finish packing—"

Qhuinn quickly jumped in. "Yeah, we hafta get go—"

Oh, hell, no. John marched over to the stairs. *We're going to your room and sorting this out. Right now.*

As John put sole to step, Qhuinn had to follow the guy, thanks to his new job, and he figured Blay went along probably because his inner Emily Post couldn't handle not being a good host.

Upstairs, John shut the bedroom door behind them all and put his hands on his hips. As his stare went back and forth, he was like a parent standing over two recalcitrant children and a mess on the floor.

Blay went over to his closet, and as he opened it, the full-length mirror on the back side caught Qhuinn's reflection. Their eyes met for a moment.

"Nice new piece of jewelry there," Blay murmured, looking at the chain that marked Qhuinn's new station.

"Not jewelry."

"No, it isn't. And I'm happy for you two. I really am." He took out a parka . . . which meant the family was either going "down south" as in Antarctica, or the guy intended to be away a long time. Like, into winter.

John stamped his foot. *We're running out of time here. Hello? Assholes?*

"I'm sorry," Qhuinn murmured to Blay. "For what I said in the tunnel."

"You tell John about it all?"

"No."

Blay dropped his coat on his Prada duffel bag and looked at John. "He thinks I love him. As in . . . in love with him."

John's mouth slowly fell open.

Blay's laugh flared and stopped short, as if his throat got tight. "Yeah. Go fig. Me in love with Qhuinn . . . a guy who, when he's not moody, is a slut and smart-ass. Except you want to know what the most fucked-up thing is, though?"

Qhuinn tensed as John nodded.

Blay glanced down at his duffel. "He's right."

Well, didn't John look like he'd been nailed in the foot with a spike.

"Yup," Blay said. "That's why I could never get into the females all that much. None of them compared to him. No other guys do either, by the way. So I'm fucked royal, but then, that's my biz and not his or yours."

Christ, Qhuinn thought. Wasn't this the week for revelations.

"I'm sorry, Blay," he said, because he had no idea what else to do.

"Yeah, I bet you are. Makes things hella awkward, huh." Blay palmed the parka and slung the Prada bag up onto his shoulder. "But it's all good. I'm getting out of town for a while, and you two are solid. So cool. Now I gotta go. I'll text you in a couple of days."

Qhuinn was more than willing to bet that the *you* there was referring only to John.

Shit.

Blay turned away. "Later."

As his best friend in all the world showed them his back and headed for the door, Qhuinn opened his useless lips and prayed that the right thing would come out. When nothing did, he prayed that something would jump free. Anything—

The scream that came up from the first floor was high-pitched.

Blay's mother.

The three of them were out of that bedroom like a bomb had gone off in it, shooting down the hall, thundering down the stairs. In the kitchen, they found that the nightmare of the war had come home.

Lessers. Two of them. In Blay's motherfucking house.

And one of them had his mother up against his chest in a choke hold.

Blay let out a primal yell, but Qhuinn caught him before he surged forward. "There's a knife against her throat," Qhuinn hissed. "He'll slice her where she stands."

The *lesser* smiled as he dragged Blay's mom across the kitchen and out of the house, toward a minivan that was parked by the garage.

As John Matthew dematerialized out of sight, another slayer came in from the dining room.

Qhuinn let Blay go, and the two of them went on the attack, plowing first into that slayer and then engaging another as it walked in the back door.

While the hand-to-hand went wild and the kitchen got trashed, Qhuinn prayed like hell that John had taken form inside the open van and was rolling out one fuck of a two-fisted welcome.

Please let Blay's mom not get taken down in the cross fire.

As yet another slayer came through the door, Qhuinn head-butted the *lesser* he was trading punches with, palmed one of his brand-new spanking forty-fives, and rammed the muzzle under the bastard's chin.

The bullets decimated the fucker's head, blowing the top of it clear off—which gave Qhuinn plenty of time to stab the thing in the heart with the knife he had at his hip.

Pop! Pop! Fizz-fizz! Oh, what a relief it is.

As the thing disappeared in a flash of light, Qhuinn didn't pause to enjoy his first *lesser* kill. He spun around to check on Blay and was

shocked to his balls. The guy's father had come pounding into the room and the two were hauling ass. Which was kind of a surprise, as Blay's dad was an accountant.

Time to back up John.

Qhuinn beelined it out the back door, and just as his boots hit grass, a brilliant flash of light from the minivan told him that help wasn't going to be necessary.

In a smooth move, John jumped out of the Town & Country and slammed the door shut; he pounded on the quarter panel and the thing reversed at a dead run. Qhuinn caught a brief impression of Blay's mom white-knuckled behind the wheel as she shot backward down the driveway.

"You okay, J-man?" Qhuinn said, hoping like hell that John Matthew didn't get killed on Qhuinn's first night as his *ahstrux nohtrum*.

Just as John lifted his hands to sign, there was a crash of glass.

The two of them wheeled around to the house. Like something out of a movie, a pair of bodies flew out of the family room's picture window. Blay's was one of them, and he landed on top of the *lesser* he'd tossed out the house like a stained mattress. Before the slayer could recover from the impact, Blay grabbed on to its head and cracked the fucker's neck like a chicken.

"My father's still fighting in the house!" he yelled as Qhuinn tossed him the knife. "Down in the cellar!"

As John and Qhuinn shot back inside, a third flare of light went off, and then Blay caught up with them at the basement stairs. The three of them rushed to where new sounds of fighting came from.

When they got to the bottom of the stairwell, they stopped dead. Blay's father was facing off with a *lesser*, a Civil War sword in one hand, a dagger in the other.

Behind his Joe Friday glasses, his eyes were lit like torches, and they flicked over for a split second. "Stay out of this. This one's mine."

The shit was done faster than you could say *Ninja Dad*.

Blay's father went Ginsu on the slayer, carving the thing up like a turkey, then stabbing it back to the Omega. As the glare from the extermination faded, the male looked up with frantic eyes.

"Your mother—"

"Got away in their van," Qhuinn answered. "John got her free."

Both Blay and his father sagged at that news. Which was when Qhuinn noticed Blay was bleeding from a cut on the shoulder and one across his abdomen and another on his back and . . .

His father wiped his brow with his arm. "We've got to get ahold of her—"

John held up his phone, a ringing coming out over the speaker.

When Blay's mother answered, her voice cracked, but not because the connection was bad. "John? John is—"

"We're all here," Blay's father said. "Keep driving, darling—"

John shook his head, handed the phone over, and signed, *What if there's a tracking device in the van?*

Blay's father muttered a curse. "Darling? Pull over. Pull over and get out of the van. Dematerialize up to the safe house, and call me when you're there."

"Are you sure—"

"Now, dearest. *Now.*"

There was the sound of an engine decelerating. The slam of a car door. Then silence.

"Darling?" Blay's father grabbed for the phone. "Darling? Oh, Jesus . . ."

"I'm here," came her voice. "Here at the safe house."

Everyone took a deep breath.

"I'll be right there."

Other words were said, but Qhuinn was busy listening for sounds of footsteps up the stairs. What if more *lessers* came? Blay was injured, and the guy's father looked wiped.

"We really gotta get out of here," he said to no one in particular.

They went upstairs, put the suitcases in Blay's father's Lexus, and

before Qhuinn could count one, two, three, Blay and his father were off into the night.

It all went so fast. The attack, the fighting, the evac . . . the goodbye that was never spoken. Blay just got in the car with his father and took off with their luggage. But what else was going to happen? Now was hardly the time for a long, drawn-out thing, and not just because the *lessers* had come for a little house tour ten minutes ago.

"I guess we should take off," he said.

John shook his head. *I want to stay here. More are going to come when the ones we killed don't check in.*

Qhuinn looked at the family room, which was now a porch thanks to Blay's Hollywood-stuntman routine. There was a lot to loot in the house, and the idea that even a box of Kleenex from Blay's might fall into the Lessening Society's hands pissed him off royally.

John started texting. *I'm telling Wrath what happened and that we're hanging here. We trained for this. It's time we get into the action.*

Qhuinn couldn't agree more, but he was pretty damn sure Wrath wasn't going to approve.

John's phone went off a moment later. He read what it was to himself, and then slowly smiled and turned the screen around.

The text was from Wrath. *Agreed. Call if you need backup.*

Holy shit . . . They'd joined the war.

THIRTY-FIVE

Rehv parked the Bentley at the southeast entrance of Black Snake State Park. The gravel lot was small, big enough for only ten cars, and whereas the other lots were chained off after hours, this one was always open because it had trails to the rentable cabins.

As he got out of the car, he took his cane, but not because he needed it for balance. His vision had gone red about halfway through the drive and now his body was alive and humming, warmed up, with sensation everywhere.

Before he locked up the Bentley, he stashed his sable coat in the trunk, because the car was noticeable enough without twenty-five thousand dollars' worth of Russian fur in plain view. He also double-checked that he had the antivenom kit with him and plenty of dopamine.

Yup. Yup.

He shut the trunk, hit the alarm, and turned to the thick line of

shorter trees that formed the park's outer boundaries. For no good reason, the birches and oaks and poplars around the man-made lot reminded him of a crowd penned in at a parade, all of them packed in tight at the edge of the gravel, their branches overlapping out-of-bounds even as their trunks stayed where they should.

The night was still except for a crisp, dry breeze that was all about fall's impending arrival. Funny, this far upstate, August could get downright cold, and as his body was now, he liked the chill. Thrived on it, even.

He walked over to the main trailhead, going past an unmanned check-in and a series of signs for hikers. A quarter mile in there was an offshoot into the forest, and he took the dirt path deeper into the park. The log cabin was a mile farther, and he was about two hundred yards away from the thing when a tangle of leaves scampered by his feet. The shadow that carried them forward was tropical-hot around his ankles.

"Thanks, man," he said to Trez.

I'll meet you there.

"Good."

As his bodyguard misted across the ground, Rehv straightened his tie for no good reason. Shit knew the thing wasn't going to stay around his neck for much longer.

The clearing where the cabin was located was awash in moonlight, and he couldn't tell which of the shadows among the trees was Trez. But that was why his bodyguard was worth his tremendous weight in gold. Even a *symphath* couldn't tease him out of the landscape when he didn't want to be seen.

Rehv went up to the rough-hewn door and paused, looking around. The Princess was here already: All around the ostensibly bucolic spot was a dense, invisible cloud of dread—the kind that kids felt when they looked at abandoned houses on dark, windy nights. It was the *symphath* version of *mhis*, and it guaranteed that the two of them wouldn't be disturbed by humans. Or other animals, for that matter.

He wasn't surprised she'd come early. He could never predict whether she would be late, early, or on time, and therefore he was never off his game, no matter when she showed.

The cabin door opened with its familiar creak. As the sound went right into the cringe center of his brain, he covered up his emotions with the picture of a sunny beach he'd once seen on TV.

From out of the shadows in the corner of the open space, accented words drifted over thick and low. "You always do that. Makes me wonder what you hide from your love."

And she could keep guessing. He could not allow her to get into his head. Aside from the fact that self-protection was critical, shutting her out drove her crazy, and that made him glow with satisfaction like a fucking spotlight.

As he closed the door, he decided to play the jilted romantic tonight. She would expect him to be wondering what the hell had happened to their reg/sched and she'd hold him hostage for the info as long as she could. But charm worked, even on *symphaths*—although naturally in a fucked-up, roundabout way. She knew he hated her and that it cost him to pretend to be in love with her. His grind and chafe at speaking pretty lies would be what would put him in her good graces, not the lies themselves.

"How I've missed you," he said in a deep, intent voice.

His fingers went to the tie he'd just straightened and slowly worked the knot free. Her response was instantaneous. Her eyes flashed like rubies in front of a bonfire, and she did nothing to hide the reaction. She knew it made him sick.

"You missed me? Of course you missed me." Her voice was like that of a snake, the *S*'s lingering through long exhales. "But by how much?"

Rehv kept the beach scene in the forefront of his mind, nailing the sucker to his frontal lobe, keeping her out of him. "I missed you to distraction."

He put his cane aside, shed his jacket, and let loose the top button

on his silk shirt . . . then the next . . . and the next, until he had to pull the tails out of his slacks to finish the job. As he shrugged his shoulders and let the silk fall to the floor, the Princess hissed for real and his cock swelled.

He hated her and he hated the sex, but he loved that he had the power over her that he did. Her weakness gave him a sexual thrill that was damn close to when you were actually attracted to someone. Which was how he managed to get it up even as his skin crawled like it was draped in a blanket of worms.

"Keep your clothes on," she said in a sharp voice.

"No." He always took them off when he wanted to, not when she said. His pride demanded it.

"Keep your clothes on, whore."

"No." He undid his belt and snapped it free from his hips, the supple leather cracking in the air. He dropped it as he had the shirt, without care.

"The clothes stay on . . ." Her words drifted because her strength was weakening. Which was the fucking point.

With a deliberate hand, he cupped himself, then unzipped his fly, freed the fastener, and felt his pants fall down to the rough floor in a rush. His erection stood straight out from his hips, and pretty much summed up their relationship. He was viciously angry at her, and he hated himself, and he despised the fact that Trez was outside witnessing this all.

And as a result his cock was rock-hard and glistening at the tip.

For *symphaths*, a trip into mental illness was better than any Agent Provocateur splurge, and that was why this whole thing worked. He could give that sick shit to her. He could give her something else, too. She craved the sexual combat they had. *Symphath* mating was a civil chess match with an exchange of body fluids at the end. She needed the carnal grunt and grind only his vampire side could give her.

"Touch yourself," she breathed. "Touch yourself for me."

He didn't do as she asked. With a growl, he kicked off his loafers and stepped away from the pile of his clothes. As he walked forward, he was damn aware of the picture he made, all hard and heavy. He stopped in the middle of the cabin, a slice of moonlight streaming through the window and running over the planes of his body.

He hated to admit it, but he craved this bad shit with her, too. It was the only time in his life that he could be who he really was, that he didn't have to lie to the people around him. The ugly truth of it was, part of him needed this sick, twisted relationship, and that, more than the threat to him and Xhex, was what kept him coming back month after month.

He wasn't sure whether the Princess knew his weakness. He was always careful not to tip his hand, but you could never be too sure what a *symphath* had on you. Which, of course, made the maneuvering all the more interesting because the stakes were higher.

"I thought we would start off tonight with a little show," he said, turning around. With his back to her, he started to pleasure himself, taking his thick cock into his big hand and stroking it.

"Boring," she said breathlessly.

"Liar." He squeezed the head of his arousal so hard a gasp shot out of him.

The Princess moaned at the sound he made, his pain drawing her even further into the game. As he looked down at what he was doing, he felt a brief, troubling displacement, like it was someone else's cock and someone else's arm moving up and down. But, then, the distance from the act was necessary, the only way his decent vampire nature could handle this thing they did. The good part of him wasn't here. He checked it at the door when he stepped inside.

This was the land of the Sin-eater.

"What are you doing," she groaned.

"Stroking myself. Hard. The moonlight looks good on my cock. I'm wet."

She sucked in sharply. "Turn around. Now."

"No."

Even though she made no sound, he knew she came forward at that moment, and the triumph he felt wiped out the disassociation. He lived for breaking her. It was fucking heroin in his veins, this power coursing through him. Yeah, afterward he would feel dirty as fuck, and, sure, he lived with nightmares because of all this, but right now he was seriously getting off.

The Princess came around in the shadows, and he knew when she saw what he was up to, because she moaned out loud, not even her *symphath* reserve strong enough to hold in her response.

"If you're going to look at me"—he squeezed the head of his cock again until it went purple and he had to arch his back from the pain—"I want to see you."

She stepped into the moonlight, and he lost his rhythm for a moment.

The Princess was dressed in a brilliant red gown, the rubies at her throat glowing against her paper white skin. Her blue-black hair was coiled on her head, her eyes and lips the same color as the bloodred stones around her neck. From her earlobes, two albino scorpions hung from their stinger tails, watching him.

She was hideously beautiful. An upright reptile with hypnotic eyes.

Her arms were crossed in front of her waist and tucked into the floor-length sleeves of her dress, but she dropped them now, and he didn't look at her hands. Couldn't. They disgusted him too much, and if he caught sight of them he would lose his erection.

To keep himself aroused, he slipped his palm under his balls and stretched them up so they framed his cock. As he let both parts of his sex fall back into place, they bobbed with potency.

There was so much she wanted to see of him that her eyes didn't know where to go. As they traced over his chest, they lingered on the pair of red stars that marked his pecs. Vampires thought they were just decoration, but to *symphaths*, they were evidence of both his royal blood and the two murders he'd committed: Patricide got you stars, as opposed to matricide, which got you circles. Red ink meant he was a member of the royal family.

The Princess did away with her gown, and beneath its lush folds her body was covered in a red satin netting that dug into her skin. In keeping with the largely sexless appearance of her kind, her breasts were small and her hips smaller. The only way you could be sure she was female was the tiny slit between her legs. The males were likewise androgynous, with their long hair that they wore up as the females did and their identical gowns. Rehv had never seen one of the males naked, thank fuck, but he assumed their cocks had the same little anomaly his own did.

Oh, the joy.

His anomaly was, of course, another reason he liked fucking the Princess. He knew it hurt for her at the end.

"I'm going to touch you now," she said, coming up to him. "Whore."

Rehv steeled himself as her hand closed around his arousal, but he gave her only a moment of contact. Stepping back sharply, he popped his cock out of her grip.

"Are you going to end our relationship?" he drawled, hating the words he spoke. "Is that why you blew me off the other night? This shit too boring for you?"

She came forward, as he knew she would. "Come now, you're a toy of mine. I'd miss you terribly."

"Ah."

This time when she grabbed him, she dug her nails into his shaft. He held his gasp in by tightening his shoulders until his collarbones nearly snapped.

"So you wondered where I was?" she whispered as she leaned into him. Her mouth brushed his throat and the touch of her lips burned his skin. The lipstick she wore was made out of crushed peppers, carefully calibrated to sting. "You worried about me. Ached for me."

"Yeah. That's it," he said, because she would get off on the lie.

"I knew you did." The Princess sank down onto her knees and leaned in. The instant her lips met the head of his cock, the burning sensation from that lipstick made his balls squeeze up like fists. "Ask me."

"For what. A blow job or the why of the reschedule?"

"I'm thinking you need to beg for both." She took his arousal and pushed it up against his belly, then her tongue snaked out and teased the barb at the base of his erection. That barb was the part of him she liked best, the one that locked into place when he came and kept them linked. Personally, he hated the thing, but damn, it felt good to have it played with, even with the pain that came from what was on her mouth.

"Ask me." She let his cock fall back into place and took him deep into her mouth.

"Ah, shit, suck me," he groaned.

And holy hell, did she ever. She opened that throat of hers and took as much of him as she could. It was great, but the burning was a killer. To pay her back for her little Chanel No. Nightmare lipstick, he grabbed onto her hair and shoved his hips forward, making her choke.

In response, she dug one of her nails into his barb deeply enough to draw blood, and he cried out, tears spearing into his eyes. As one came out onto his cheek, she smiled, no doubt liking the color of the red against his face.

"You're going to say please," she said. "When you ask me to explain."

He was tempted to tell her to hold her breath for that, but instead he repeated the plunge into her mouth and she repeated the dig, and they did that back and forth for a while until they were both panting.

His sex was on fire at this point, raging with heat, pulsing with the need to come in that god-awful mouth of hers.

"Ask me why," she demanded. "Ask me why I didn't show."

He shook his head. "No . . . you'll tell me when you want to. But

I will ask if you're just wasting our time here, or are you going to let me finish?"

She lifted herself up from the floor, went over to the window, and braced herself on the sill with those horrible hands. "You can come. But only inside me."

The bitch always did that. *Always* with the inside.

And always with the window. Clearly, even though she couldn't know for sure that he'd come with backup, on some level she knew they were being watched. And if they fucked in front of the panes of glass, his sentry would be forced to see.

"Finish inside me, damn you."

The Princess arched her back and lifted her ass. The netting she wore ran up her legs and in between her thighs, and he was going to have to rip part of it open to get into her. Which was why she wore it. If her lipstick was bad, the mesh shit on her body was worse.

Rehvenge moved in behind her and dug the fore- and middle fingers of both his hands into the mesh at the small of her back. With a yank, he split the weave free from her ass and her sex.

She was glossy and swollen and begging for him.

Looking over her shoulder, she smiled, revealing perfect, boxy white teeth. "I'm hungry. I saved myself for you. As always."

He couldn't hide his wince. He couldn't stand the idea that he was her only lover—it would have been much better to be part of a grounds crew of males, so that what happened between them didn't loom so large. Plus the parity nauseated him. She was his only lover, too.

He shoved himself into her sex, knocking her forward until her head banged into the glass. Then he grabbed onto her hips and slid slowly out. Her legs quivered in a series of waves, and he hated that he was giving her what she wanted. So he pushed slowly back in, stopping halfway to home so she didn't get all of him.

Her red eyes spit fire over her shoulder. "More, thank you."

"Why didn't you show, my lovely bitch."

"Why don't you shut up and finish?"

Rehv leaned down and ran his fangs across her shoulder. The mesh was coated in scorpion venom, and he felt an instant numbing of his lips. That bad shit was going to be all over his hands and his body after the fucking was done, so he was going to have to shower at his safe house as soon as possible. It wasn't going to be fast enough. He was going to be viciously ill, as usual. Since she was a full-bred *symphath*, the venom didn't affect her; to her it was like perfume, an enhancement. To his vampire nature, which was especially susceptible, it was straight-up poison.

He slowly pulled out and eased back in a couple of inches. He knew he had her good when her three-knuckled fingers dug into the old, weathered wood of the sill.

God, those hands of hers, with their trio of joints and the fingernails that grew out red . . . they were something from a horror movie, the kind of thing that wrapped around the lip of a coffin before the undead came out and killed the good guy.

"Tell . . . me . . . why . . . bitch. . . ." He punctuated the words with his rhythm. "Or no finish for either of us."

God, he hated this and he loved it, both of them struggling to maintain the power position, both pissed at the concessions they had to make. It was eating her alive that she'd had to come around to see him jerking off, and he despised what he was doing to her body, and she didn't want to tell him why she was two nights late, but she knew she was going to have to if she wanted to get off. . . .

And around and around the merry-go-round went.

"Tell me," he growled.

"Your uncle grows strong."

"Does he." He rewarded her with a quick, nasty penetration, and she gasped. "Why's that?"

"Two nights ago . . ." Her breath sawed out of her mouth, as her spine torqued to accept him in the deepest way possible. "He was crowned."

Rehv lost his rhythm. *Shit.* A change in leadership was not good. The *symphaths* might be stuck in that colony, isolated from the real world, but any political instability there threatened what precious little control of them there was.

"We need you," she said, reaching behind her and sinking her nails into his ass. "To do what you do best."

No. Fucking. Way.

He'd killed enough relatives.

She glanced over her shoulder, and the scorpion in her ear stared at him hard, its spindly legs pinwheeling, reaching out to him. "I've given you the why. So get on with it."

Rehv put his brain on lockdown, focused on the scene of the beach, and let his body do its thing. Under his pounding rhythm, the Princess orgasmed, her body gripping him in a series of pulses that were like a fist twisting his cock in a vise.

Which was what made his sex catch hold of her inside and fill her up.

He pulled out as soon as he was able and started on the slide into hell. Already, he could feel the effect of the venom on that damn mesh. His body was tingling all over, the nerve endings in his skin blinking on and off in spasms of pain. It was only going to get worse.

The Princess righted herself and went to her gown. From a hidden pocket, she took out a long length of wide red satin, and with her eyes locked on him, she threaded the cloth between her legs and tied it in an elaborate series of bows.

Her ruby eyes gleamed with satisfaction as she made sure not a drop of him escaped her.

He hated that, and she knew it, which was why she never complained when he pulled out fast. She knew damn well he wanted to shove her in a bleach bath and make her wash until the sex was gone from her as if it had never been.

"Where is my tithe?" she said as she drew on her gown.

His vision was doubling up from the venom as he went over to

his jacket and took out a small velvet bag. He tossed it over to her and she caught it.

Inside were two hundred and fifty thousand dollars in rubies. Cut. Ready to be set.

"You need to come home."

He was too tired to play the game. "That colony is not my home."

"Wrong. So very wrong. But you'll come around. I guarantee it." On that she disappeared into thin air.

Rehv sagged, planting his palm onto the cabin's wall as a black wave of exhaustion shot through him.

As the door opened, he righted himself and picked up his pants. Trez said nothing, just came over and steadied him.

Sick as he was, and would become, he himself put his clothes on. That was important to him. He always did that himself.

When his jacket was back in place and his tie looped around his neck and his cane in his hand, his best friend and bodyguard scooped him up and carried him like a child back to his car.

THIRTY-SIX

Stress in a person was like air in a balloon. Too much pressure, too much shit, too much bad news . . . and the birthday party gets messy.

Phury ripped open his bedside table drawer even though he'd just looked in it. "Shit."

Where the fuck *was all his red smoke?*

He took his near-empty Baggie out of his breast pocket. Barely enough for a thin one. Which meant he'd better hightail it down to ZeroSum before the Reverend closed for the night.

He pulled on his light jacket so that he'd have someplace to hide the full bag when he came back, then jogged down the grand staircase. As he hit the foyer, his head was alive and writhing, swelling up with the wizard's Top Ten Reasons Phury, Son of Ahgony, Is a Shithead.

Number ten: Manages to get self kicked out of Brotherhood. Number nine: Drug addict. Number eight: Fights with twin when twin's preg-

nant shellan *is in a bad way. Number seven: Drug addict. Number six: Shits on female he wants to be with, driving her away. Number five: Tells lies to protect addictive behavior.*

Or did that fall under nine and seven?

Number four: Lets down parents. Number three: Drug addict. Number two: Falls in love with aforementioned driven-away female—

Shit.

Shit.

Shit.

Had he fallen in love with Cormia? How? When?

The wizard popped into his head. *To hell with that, mate. Finish the list. C'mon. Fine . . . I think we'll put "Drug Addict" as number one, shall we?*

"Where are you going?" Wrath's voice came down from above like some kind of conscience, and Phury froze with his hand on the vestibule's door.

"Where?" the king demanded.

Nowhere special, Phury thought without turning around. *Just fucking insane.*

"Out for a drive," he said, and held his car keys up over his head.

At this point, the lie didn't bother him in the slightest. He just wanted everyone to get out of his way. When he had his red smoke, when he was calm and his head was no longer a pipe bomb waiting to go off, he could go back to interacting.

Wrath's boots hit the stairs, the beat of his stride a countdown to one fuck of a bitch-slapping. Phury turned to face the king, a low-boil anger lighting off in his chest.

And what do you know, Wrath wasn't in a Hallmark mood either. His brows were behind his wraparounds, his fangs long, his body tense as hell.

Clearly there had been more bad news.

"What's happened now?" Phury bit out, wondering when in the

hell the current shit storm was going to move on to another group of people's lives.

"Four families from the *glymera* got hit tonight, and there were no survivors. I've got something awful to tell Qhuinn, but can't get hold of him or John Matthew at their stakeout at Blaylock's."

"You want me to go over there?"

"No, I want you to get your ass to the Sanctuary and do your fucking duty," Wrath snapped. "We need more Brothers, and you agreed to be the Primale, so stop putting the shit off."

Phury was itching to bare his fangs, but he stayed tight. "I've chosen another First Mate. She's being prepared, and I'm going there at nightfall tomorrow."

Wrath's brows flicked up. Then he nodded once. "Okay. Good. Now, what's Blaylock's number? I'm going to send the kid back over to his house. All the Brothers are busy, and I don't want Qhuinn hearing this over the phone."

"I can go—"

"The hell you can," the king shot back. "Even if you were still part of the Brotherhood, with the shit that's going down right now, I'm not losing the race's Primale, fuck you very much. Now what the good goddamn is Blaylock's number?"

Phury gave Wrath the digits, nodded a good-bye, and walked out through the vestibule. He didn't give a shit that he'd told Wrath he was going for a drive; he left his BMW where it was parked in the courtyard and dematerialized downtown.

Wrath knew he'd been lying anyway. And there was no reason to delay the trip to ZeroSum by taking his car just to live up to a falsity they were both well aware of.

When he came up to the club's entrance, Phury bypassed the wait line by simply walking up and having the bouncer get out of his way.

In the VIP section, iAm was standing at the door to Rehvenge's

office. The Moor didn't seem to be surprised to see him, but, then, it was hard to surprise either one of Rehv's private guards.

"Boss isn't here; you want to make a buy?" the guy asked.

Phury nodded, and iAm showed him the way in. Rally, the scale minion, scampered off after Phury flashed his open palm twice.

iAm leaned his hip against Rehvenge's desk and simply stared across the office, his black eyes impassive, calm. His brother, Trez, was the hothead of the two of them, so Phury had always thought that iAm was the one you needed to watch out for.

Although he supposed it was kind of like choosing between two different guns: a matter of degree.

"Word of advice," the Moor said.

"I'll pass."

"Tough. Don't jump to the harder stuff, my friend."

"I have no idea what you're talking about."

"Bullshit."

Rally came out from the hidden door in the corner, and as Phury looked at all those leaves in that clear plastic bag, his blood pressure dropped and his heartbeat eased up. He gave his thousand dollars over and got out of that office as fast as he could, ready for business back in his bedroom.

Just as he headed for the side exit, he saw Xhex standing by the VIP bar. Her eyes dropped to his arm, which was buried in his coat, and then she frowned and mouthed, *Fuck.*

As she came striding toward him, he had the bizarre impression she was going to try to snatch back his stash, and that was a no-go. He'd paid in good cash and bought what he had at a fair price. There was no reason for management to have beef with him.

He quickly ducked out the door and dematerialized. He had no fucking clue what the problem was, and he didn't care. He had what he needed and was going home.

As he traveled in a scramble of molecules back to the mansion, he thought about that druggie in the alley, the one who'd sliced up his dealer and then picked through the man's pockets while blood went everywhere.

Phury tried to believe that wasn't him. Tried not to see the desperation of the last twenty minutes as the stepping-stone to what that druggie had done with that switchblade.

The reality was, though, that nothing and no one was safe if they were between an addict and what he craved.

As John looked around Blay's backyard, he felt like he'd done this a thousand times. This waiting, this watching . . . this predatory pause, it all seemed second nature to him. Which was nuts.

Nah, something told him. *This is really just business as usual. You're only figuring that out now, though.*

Next to him in the shadows, Qhuinn was surprisingly still. Usually the guy was always moving, tapping his feet and hands, walking around, chattering. Not tonight, not in this stand of honeysuckle bushes.

Yeah, okay, they were hiding in honeysuckle. Not exactly as manly as standing behind a bunch of oaks, but the coverage was better, and besides, that was all they had for camouflage next to Blay's back door.

John checked his watch. They'd been waiting here for a good hour or two. Eventually they were going to have to get back to avoid the dawn, and didn't that suck. He was here to fight. He was prepared to fight.

If he didn't get a crack at another *lesser*, his inner ass-kicker was going to have a serious case of the blue balls.

Unfortunately all they had was an occasional late summer breeze to balance out the drone of crickets.

I didn't know about Blay, John signed for no particular reason. *How long have you known about . . . you know, how he felt?*

Now Qhuinn's fingers drummed on his thigh. "Pretty much since it started . . . which was a long time ago."

Wow, John thought. With all these secrets coming out, it was almost like they were going through their transitions again.

And like the changes that had taken over their bodies, the three of them would never be as they once were.

"Blay hid what he felt," Qhuinn murmured. "Although not because of the sex stuff. I mean, I don't have a problem being with guys, especially if there's chicks involved." Qhuinn laughed. "You look so shocked. You didn't know I went like that?"

Well . . . I . . . I mean . . .

Holy shit, if he'd ever felt like a virgin before, in the face of all of Qhuinn's . . . whatever it was . . . he realized now he was more like a VIRGIN.

"Look, if I make you uncomfortable—"

No, it's not that. Hell, I'm really not that surprised. I mean, you've gone into bathrooms with a lot of different . . .

"Yeah. I kind of just let what happens happen, you know. S'all good." Qhuinn rubbed his forehead. "I don't plan on being like this forever, though."

No?

"Someday I want a *shellan* of my own. In the meantime, though, I'm going to do anything and everything. That's how I know I'm living."

John thought about it. *I want a female, too. But it's hard because . . .*

Qhuinn didn't look at him, but the guy nodded in understanding— which was good. Funny, it was easier to talk about stuff, in a way, now that his friend knew exactly why certain shit would be difficult for him.

"You know, I see the way you look at Xhex."

John turned beet red. *Um . . .*

"It's cool. I mean, fuck . . . she's like off-the-chain hot. Partially because she's so damn scary. I think that one could make you eat your own teeth if you got out of line." Qhuinn shrugged. "But don't you suppose you might want to start off with someone who's a little . . . I don't know, softer?"

You don't get to pick who you're attracted to.

"Amen."

They heard the sound of someone coming around from the front of the house, and they both came to attention, upping the muzzles of their guns and swinging them to the east.

"It's me," Blay called out. "Don't shoot."

John stepped free of the honeysuckle. *I thought you were going with your parents?*

Blay stared at Qhuinn. "The Brothers have been trying to reach you."

"Why are you looking at me like that?" Qhuinn said, gun going down to his side.

"They want you to come back to the mansion."

Why, John signed even though Blay still had his eyes clamped on Qhuinn. *Wrath said it was okay for us to stay—*

"What's the news," Qhuinn said tightly. "You have news, don't you."

"Wrath wants you—"

"My family was hit, weren't they." Qhuinn's jaw tightened. "Weren't they."

"Wrath wants you—"

"Fuck Wrath. Talk!"

Blay's eyes flicked to John before returning to their friend. "Your mother, father, and sister are dead. Your brother is missing."

Qhuinn's breath left him on a wheeze, like someone had kicked him in the gut. John and Blay both reached out for him, but he shrugged them off and stepped away.

Blay shook his head. "I'm so sorry."

Qhuinn said nothing. It was as if he had forgotten English.

Blay tried to reach out again, and when Qhuinn only took another step back, he said, "Look, Wrath called me when he couldn't reach either one of you, and asked me to bring you both back to the mansion. The *glymera* is going into seclusion."

Let's get to the car, John signed to Qhuinn.

"I'm not going."

"Qhuinn—"

Qhuinn—

Qhuinn's voice was full of the emotion his face refused to show. "Fuck all of this. Fuck—"

A light went on inside of Blay's house, and Qhuinn's head whipped around. Through the glass of the kitchen's windows, they all saw a *lesser* walk into the room in plain sight.

There was no stopping Qhuinn. He was supersonic as he shot into the house through the back door with his gun up. And he didn't blow slow mo once he was inside, either. He leveled his H & K at the slayer and popped the trig over and over and over again, driving the pale bastard back against the wall.

Even as the *lesser* slumped and bled black, Qhuinn kept shooting, the wallpaper behind the thing going Jackson Pollock.

Blay and John rushed over and John threw an arm around his friend's neck. As he started hauling Qhuinn back, he grabbed the guy's gun hand in case he tried to swing around and shoot.

Another *lesser* came barreling into the kitchen, and Blay manned up, grabbing a carving knife from a butcher-block stand of Henckels. As he faced off at the pale bastard, the slayer palmed a switchblade from out of nowhere and the two circled each other. Blay was twitchy, his big body ready to engage, his eyes sharp. Trouble was, he was still bleeding from injuries he'd sustained before he left, his face white and drawn from everything that had gone down.

Qhuinn lifted up his gun muzzle in spite of John's lock hold on his arm.

As John shook his head, Qhuinn hissed, "Let me go. Right now."

The voice was so dead calm, John obeyed.

Qhuinn put one perfect bullet right between the *lesser*'s eyes, dropping the thing like a doll.

"What the fuck?" Blay snapped. "He was mine."

"Not going to watch you get sliced. Not going to happen."

Blay pointed a shaking finger at Qhuinn. "Don't ever do that again."

"I lost people I can't stand tonight. Not losing someone I actually give a shit about."

"I don't need you to be my hero—"

John stepped in between the two of them. *Home*, he signed. *Now.*

"There could be more—"

"There's probably more—"

All three of them went still as Blay's phone went off.

"It's Wrath." Blay's fingers flew over the keys. "He really wants us home. And John, check your phone, I think it's not working."

John took the thing out of his pocket. It was dead as a doornail, but now was not the time to figure out why. Maybe from the fighting?

Let's go, he signed.

Qhuinn went over to the stand of knives, pulled out a carver, and stabbed both the *lesser* he'd turned into a sieve and the one he'd bull's-eyed back to the Omega.

Moving quickly, they sealed up the house as best they could, triggered the alarm, and piled into Fritz's Mercedes, with Qhuinn behind the wheel and Blay and John in the backseat.

As they headed over to Route 22, Qhuinn started to put up the partition. "If we're going to go back to the mansion, you can't know where it is, Blay."

Which was, of course, only part of the reason that shield was going up. Qhuinn wanted to be alone. It was what he needed whenever he had a headfuck going on and why John had volunteered to Miss Daisy it.

In the dense darkness of the backseat, John glanced over at Blay. The guy was lying back in the leather seat as if his head weighed as much as an engine block and his eyes seemed to have sunk into his skull. He looked about a hundred years old.

In human terms.

John thought of the guy just nights ago, back at Abercrombie,

going through racks of shirts, holding one or another up for assessment. Staring at Blay now, it was as if that red-haired guy in the store were a distant, younger cousin of this person in the Mercedes, someone with the same coloring and height, but having nothing else in common.

John tapped his friend on the forearm. *We need to get Doc Jane to look you over.*

Blay glanced down at his white shirt and seemed surprised to find blood on it. "Guess this was what my mom was going on about. It doesn't hurt."

Good.

Blay turned and stared out of his window even though they were impossible to see through. "My dad said I could stay. To fight."

John whistled softly to bring the guy's head around again. *I didn't know your dad could throw the sword like that.*

"He was a soldier before he was mated to my mother. She made him stop." Blay brushed at his shirt even though the blood had sunk into the fibers and stained them. "They had a big argument when Wrath called me and asked that I find you two. My mom worries that I'll turn up dead. My dad wants me to be a male of worth when the race needs them. So there you go."

What do you want?

The guy's eyes flipped up to the partition and then scattered all around the backseat. "I want to fight."

John eased back against the seat. *Good.*

After a long silence, Blay said, "John?"

John turned his head to the side slowly, feeling as exhausted as Blay looked.

What, he mouthed, because he didn't have the strength to sign.

"Do you still want to be friends with me? Even though I'm gay."

John frowned. Then he sat up, made a fist, and nailed his buddy in the shoulder with a full-on punch.

"Ow! What the fuck—"

Why wouldn't I want to be friends with you? Other than the fact that you're a fucking idiot for asking that?

Blay rubbed where he'd been hit. "Sorry. Didn't know if it changed things or— Don't do it again! I've got a cut there!"

John settled back into the seat. He was about to sign another *Stupid idiot* at the guy, when he realized he kind of wondered the same thing after what had happened in the locker room.

He looked at his friend. *You're just the same to me.*

Blay took a deep breath. "I haven't told my parents. You and Qhuinn are the only ones who know."

Well, when you tell them or whoever, he and I will be right beside you. All the way.

The question John didn't have the balls to ask must have been in his eyes, because Blay reached over and touched his shoulder.

"No. Not at all. I don't believe there's anything that could make me think less of you."

The two of them let out identical sighs and closed their eyes at the same time. Neither said another word for the rest of the trip home.

Lash sat in the passenger seat of the Focus and had the frustrating sense that even with the hits he'd initiated on the aristocracy's houses, the Society was not getting the picture. The *lessers* were taking orders from Mr. D, not him.

Hell, they didn't even know he existed.

He glanced over at Mr. D, whose hands were at ten and two on the steering wheel. Part of him wanted to kill the guy just for spite, but his logical side knew he had to keep the bastard alive to be a mouthpiece—at least until he could prove who he was to the rest of his troops.

Troops. He loved that word.

It was second only to *his.*

Maybe he could cook himself up a uniform. Like a general's or something.

He sure as hell deserved it, given how tight his military strategy was. He was a straight-up genius—and the fact that he was using what the Brotherhood had taught him in training against them was goddamn glorious.

For the past however many centuries, the Lessening Society had been just picking away at the vampire population. With little intelligence to go on, and an uncoordinated soldier force, it was a hunt-and-peck strategy that had yielded minor successes.

He, however, was thinking big, and had the knowledge to rock his plans.

The way to eliminate vampires was to break the collective will of the society, and the first step was destabilization. The heads of four of the six founding families of the *glymera* had been wiped out. There were another two to go, and once they were hit, the *lessers* could start in on the rest of the aristocracy. With the *glymera* attacked and decimated, what was left of the Princeps Council would turn on Wrath as king. Competing factions would form. Power struggles would ensue. And Wrath, as a leader forced to deal with civil unrest, challenges to his authority, and an active war, would make compounding errors in judgment. Which would exacerbate the instability.

The fallout wouldn't just be political. More looting of homes meant fewer tithes to the Brotherhood due to erosions in the tax base. Fewer aristocrats meant fewer jobs for civilians, which would cause financial distress in the lower classes and an erosion of their support for the king. The whole thing would be a vicious circle that would inevitably lead to Wrath being deposed, killed, or relegated to a castrated figurehead—and to the vampire social structure going even further into the shitter. With everything in total shambles, that was when Lash would go in and broom up what was left.

Only thing better would be a vampire plague.

His plan was working so far, with this first night having been largely successful. He'd been pissed that that fucker Qhuinn hadn't been home when they'd raided his house, as he would have liked killing his cousin, but he'd learned something interesting. On his uncle's desk had been renunciation papers kicking Qhuinn out of the family. Which meant that poor wittle mismatched fuckup Qhuinn was out on the loose somewhere—although evidently not at Blay's, as that home had been hit as well.

Yeah, it sucked that Qhuinn hadn't been home. But at least they'd taken his brother alive. That was going to be fun.

There had been a number of Society losses, mostly at Blay's, house and Lash's own, but on the whole the tide was strongly in Lash's favor.

Momentum, however, was critical. The *glymera* would be running for their safe houses, and though he knew some of the areas those places were in, most of them were upstate, which meant travel time for his men. To expedite the killings, they had to hit as many addresses as possible here in town.

Maps. They needed maps.

As the thought occurred to him, Lash's stomach let out a whine.

They needed maps and food.

"Pull into that Citgo," he barked.

Mr. D didn't catch the left in time, so he swung a louie and backtracked.

"I need chow," Lash said. "And maps for—"

Across the street, the blue lights of a Caldwell Police Department squad car went off, and Lash cursed.

If the cop had tweaked to their moving violation, they were in deep shit. The Focus had guns and weapons in the trunk. Bloody clothes. Wallets, watches, and rings from dead vampires.

Great. Fucking great. The officer had evidently not been taking an emergency doughnut break, because he was gunning right for them.

"Fuck. Me." Lash looked at Mr. D as the guy pulled over. "Tell me you have a valid driver's license on you."

"Sure do." Mr. D put the car in park and rolled down the window as one of Caldie's protect-and-serves came up to them. "Hey, Officer. I gots my driver's license right chere."

"I need your registration as well." The cop leaned into the car and then grimaced as though he didn't like the smell of them.

God, that's right. The baby powder.

Lash eased back as Mr. D went for the glove compartment, cool as he could be. As he took out a piece of white paper the size of an index card, Lash quickly checked the registration out. Sure looked like it was official. Damn thing had the New York State crest on it, the name of Richard Delano, and an address of 1583 Tenth Street, apartment 4F.

Mr. D handed everything out the window. "I know I wasn't sup-posed to do that turn back there, sir. We just wanted something to eat and I missed the parking lot."

Lash stared at Mr. D, awed by the remarkable display of acting talent. D was just the right combo of rueful shame, earnest apology, and regular Joe as he stared up at the cop. Shit, he looked like his puss should be on the front of a cereal box as he flapped his gums and threw the word *sir* around like it was *amen* at a church. He was everything that was wholesome. Full of vitamins and fiber. Packed with vital, good old American nutrition.

The officer looked at the documentation and handed it back. As he flashed his light inside the car, he said, "Just don't do it—"

He frowned as he looked at Lash.

The cop's whatever-this-is-a-waste-of-my-time attitude was gone in a split second. Tilting the radio piece on his lapel toward his mouth, he called for backup, then said, "I'm going to have to ask you to get out of the car, sir."

"Who, me?" Lash said. Fuck, he had no ID on him. "Why?"

"Please get out of the car, sir."

"Not unless you tell me why."

The flashlight dipped to the dog chain around Lash's neck. "We received a complaint about an hour ago from a female at Screamer's concerning a white male, six-foot-six, blond crew cut, wearing a dog collar. So I need you to get out of the car."

"What was the complaint?"

"Sexual assault." Another cop car pulled up in front, then backed in tight to the Focus's headlights. "Please get out of the vehicle, sir."

That bitch back at the bar had gone to the police? She'd begged him for it! "No."

"If you do not get out of the car, I will take you out of it."

"Get out of the car," Mr. D said under his breath.

The second officer walked around the Focus and popped open Lash's door. "Get out of the car, sir."

This was so not happening. These fucking idiot humans? He was the Omega's son, for Christ's sake. He didn't follow vampire rules, much less ones that governed Homo sapiens.

"Sir?" the cop said.

"How about you fuck yourself with your Taser."

The officer leaned down and grabbed his arm. "You are under arrest for sexual assault. Anything you say can and will be used against you in a court of law. If you cannot afford an attorney—"

"You can't fucking be serious—"

"—one will be provided for you. Do you understand these rights—"

"Let go of me—"

"—as I've read them to you?"

It took both officers to drag Lash out of the car, and what do you know, a crowd gathered. *Shit.* Even though he could easily tear these men's arms off and feed them to both their asses, he couldn't make a scene. Too many witnesses.

"Sir, do you understand these rights?" This was said while Lash was pirouetted around, pushed face-first into the car's hood, and cuffed.

Lash looked through the windshield at Mr. D, whose face was no longer apple-pie innocent. The guy's eyes were narrowed, and one could only hope he was racking his brain for a way out of this.

"Sir? Do you understand these rights?"

"Yeah," Lash spat. "Fucking perfectly."

The cop on the left leaned in. "By the way, we're going to tack on a charge of resisting arrest. And that blonde? She was seventeen."

THIRTY-SEVEN

Out behind the Brotherhood's mansion, Cormia's bruised feet traveled across the cropped grass as fast as they would carry her. She ran to lose herself, ran in hopes of capturing some point of clarity, ran because there was nowhere she wanted to go and she could no longer stay where she was.

Her breath tore in and out of her lungs and her legs burned and her arms went numb and still she ran, racing down the flank of the retaining wall toward the edge of the forest, then turning around and heading back to the gardens.

Layla and the Primale. Layla laying with the Primale. Layla naked with the Primale.

She ran faster.

He was going to choose Layla. He was awkward in his role, so he would go for the one who he'd seen around and who had served his Brothers with discretion and grace. He would go for the familiar.

He would choose Layla.

With no warning, Cormia's legs dropped out from underneath her and she collapsed in an exhausted heap.

When she'd recovered enough to lift her head, she frowned as she panted. She'd fallen on an odd scratchy patch of the lawn, an imperfect stretch that was six feet in diameter. It was as if something had been burned there and the ground had yet to recover.

Seemed apt on a lot of levels.

Rolling over onto her back, she looked at the night sky. Her thighs burned and so did her lungs, but the real fire was in her brain. She didn't belong on this side. She couldn't stand the idea of going back to the Sanctuary.

She was like the summer air that stretched between the grassy green ground and the star-studded galaxy above. She was neither here nor there . . . and she was invisible.

Getting to her feet, she walked slowly back up to the mansion's terrace. Lamps glowed in the windows of the house, and as she looked around, she realized she was going to miss the palette of this world at night: The tea roses' reds and pinks and yellows and purples were muted, as if the blooms were feeling shy. Inside the library, the deep red of the drapes was like banked fire, and the billiards room appeared to have been constructed out of emeralds, with its vivid deep green.

So lovely. It was all so lovely, this feast for the eyes.

To put off the leaving a little longer, she went to the pool.

The black water spoke to her, its shimmering surface whispering in the lilting sighs and beckoning sparkles of moonlight on gentle waves.

Dropping her robe, she plunged into the soft darkness, penetrating the weave of the pool's surface, going deep and staying there as she stroked through the water.

When she came up at the far end, resolve entered her body on the gasping inhale of air she took. She would leave word with Fritz that she was going and ask him to tell Bella. Then she would go to the

Sanctuary and seek an audience with the Directrix Amalya—wherein she would put forward a request to become a sequestered scribe.

She knew that in the course of her duties as scribe she was going to have to keep track of the Primale's offspring, but better to deal with them in the land of letters than have to set her eyes upon legions of young with multicolored hair and lovely yellow eyes.

And there would be young. Though she had challenged him on his strength, the Primale was going to do what he needed to do. He was struggling ever harder now with his role, but his sense of duty would override his sense of self.

Bella was so very right in her assessment of him.

"Well, hello, there."

Cormia sputtered and looked straight into a pair of gigantic, metal-toed boots. With a start, she ran her eyes up the long, rangy body of a male dressed in what they called blue jeans.

"And who are you?" he asked, settling down on his haunches, his voice smooth and warm. His eyes were arresting—deeply set and mismatched, with lashes the color of his thick black hair.

Before she could answer, John Matthew came up from behind him and whistled loudly to get his attention. As the male at the edge of the water looked over his shoulder, John shook his head and signed frantically.

"Oh . . . shit, sorry." The dark-haired male rose to his full height and lifted his hands as if calling a stop to himself. "I didn't know who you were."

Another male came out of the house through the library's doors. This redheaded one had bloodstains on his shirt and an air of utter exhaustion about him.

They were soldiers who fought with John, she thought. Young soldiers.

"Who are you?" she asked the one with the odd, lovely eyes.

"Qhuinn. I'm with him." His thumb jogged in John Matthew's direction. "The redhead's—"

"Blaylock," the other one cut in sharply. "I'm Blaylock."

"I'm just going for a swim," she said.

"So I see." Qhuinn's smile was friendly, no longer sexual.

Still, he was attracted to her. She could sense it. And that was when she realized that with the path she was on, she would remain untouched forever. As a sequestered scribe she would never be among the ones whom the Primale visited sexually.

So that gathering storm that had been called from her in such a glorious way would never be summoned and relieved again.

Ever.

As the great stretch of her years of life unfurled before her, some restless, desperate chord was struck, and the vibrations of its dissatisfaction carried her through the warm water over to the ladder. Grasping the handrails and pulling herself out, she felt the cool air on her body and knew all three of the soldiers were looking at her.

The knowledge depressed and emboldened her. This was the last time any male would see her body, and it was hard to think that she was locking down all that was female about herself forever. But she wasn't going to be with anyone save the Primale, and she couldn't bear to be with him as things stood with all her sisters. So this was the end.

In a few moments, she would close her robing around herself and bid good-bye to something that had never really gotten started.

So she would not apologize for her nakedness nor hide her body as she stepped free of the water's gentle embrace.

Phury rematerialized in the gardens at the back of the Brotherhood's mansion because he had no interest in running into anyone. With what was in his head, marching through the front door and running the risk of—

His feet stopped and his heart stopped and his breath stopped.

Cormia was rising from the pool, her resplendent female form dripping with water . . . while three newly transitioned males stood about ten feet from her with their tongues hanging down to their navels.

Oh . . . hell . . . no.

The bonded male in him came out like a beast, breaking free of the lies he'd fed himself about how he felt, roaring out of the cave of his heart, stripping him of everything that was civilized.

All he knew was that his female was standing naked and being coveted by others.

That was all that mattered.

Before he was aware of what he was doing, Phury let out a growl that broke through the air like a crack of thunder. John Matthew's and his buddies' eyes shot his way, and then the three of them moved back as one. Big-time. Like the pool had caught fire.

Cormia, on the other hand, didn't look in his direction. She didn't scramble to cover up, either. Instead, she deliberately picked up her robe and slid it slowly onto her shoulders, all latent defiance.

Which powered him up like nothing else. "Come into the house," he demanded of her. "Now."

As she glanced at him, her voice was as level as her eyes. "And if I choose not to?"

"I will put you over my shoulder and carry you inside." Phury turned to the boys. "This is our business. Not yours. Get gone if you know what's good for you. *Now.*"

The trio hesitated until Cormia said, "It's going to be all right. Don't worry."

As they turned away, Phury had a feeling they weren't going to go far, but Cormia didn't need protection. Bonded males were mortally dangerous to everyone but their mates. He was out of control, yes, but she held his remote.

And he suspected she knew this.

Cormia reached up and wrung out her hair calmly. "Why do you want me inside?"

"Are you walking on your own or being carried?"

"I asked you why."

"Because you are going to my bedroom." The words were pushed out of his mouth by his sawing breath.

"Your bedroom? Don't you mean mine? Because you told me to get out of yours five months ago."

His cock was the seat of his beast, straining to be let out so it could let out into her. And the arousal was undeniable: His train was on the tracks. His ticket was punched. The journey had already started.

For Cormia as well.

Phury stepped up close to her. Her body was roaring with so much heat, he could feel it against his own skin, and her jasmine scent was as thick as his blood.

He flashed her his fangs and hissed like a cat. "We're going to my room."

"But I have no reason to go to your bedroom."

"Yes. You do."

She casually tossed her thick twist of hair over her shoulder. "No, I'm afraid I don't."

With that, she turned her back on him and strolled into the house.

He tracked her like prey, following on her heels through the library, up the grand staircase, and to her room.

She opened the door a fraction and slipped inside.

Before she could shut him out, he slapped his palm around the wooden panel and pushed his way in. He was the one who shut the door. And locked it.

"Take your robe off."

"Why?"

"Because if I do it, I'm going to shred it."

Her chin lifted and her lids dropped, so that even though she had to look up to meet his eyes, she was still staring down her nose at him. "Why do I need to disrobe?"

With every territorial bone in his body, he growled, "I'm going to mark you."

"Are you? You realize that would be for no reason."

"It is for every reason."

"You didn't want me before."

"The hell I didn't."

"You compared me to the other female you tried to be with, but ultimately couldn't."

"And you didn't let me finish. She was a whore I bought for the sole purpose of getting rid of my virginity. Not a female I wanted. Not you." He inhaled her scent and let it out on a purr. "She was not you."

"And yet you accepted Layla, did you not?" When he didn't answer, she sauntered into her bathroom and turned the shower on. "Yes, you did. As First Mate."

"This is not about her," he said from the doorway.

"How can it not be? The Chosen are a whole and I am still one among them." Cormia turned, faced him, and dropped her robe. "Am I not."

Phury's cock slammed against the backside of his zipper. Her body positively glowed under the recessed lights of the ceiling, her breasts tight and peaked, her thighs slightly parted.

She got into the shower, and he watched as she arched her back and washed her hair. With every move she made, he lost more of what little was left of his civilized side. On some dim lower shelf in his brain, he knew he should leave, because he was about to make a complicated situation downright untenable. But his body had found the food it needed to survive.

And the instant she stepped free of that fucking shower he was going to eat her alive.

THIRTY-EIGHT

Yes, she was going to let him.

As Cormia rinsed the suds from her hair, she knew the moment she left the shower, she was going to end up under the Primale.

She was going to let him take her. And in the process she was going to take him.

Enough with the *almost*s and the *nearly*s and the *are they or aren't they*s. Enough with the twisted destiny they were both caught in. Enough with doing what she'd been told she had to.

She wanted him. She was going to have him.

To hell with her sisters. He was hers.

Although only for tonight, an inner voice pointed out.

"Fuck you," she said to the marble wall.

She slammed the spigot to the left and threw open the door. As the rush of water was cut off short, she confronted the Primale.

He was naked. Erect. Fully fanged.

The roar he let out was that of a lion, and as the sound reverberated off all the marble in the bathroom, she got even wetter between her legs.

He came at her, and she didn't fight him as he grabbed her around the waist and popped her off her feet. He wasn't gentle, but she didn't want gentle—and to make sure he knew it she bit him in the shoulder as they came into the bedroom.

He roared again and dumped her on her bed, her body bouncing once. Twice. She flipped onto her stomach and started to scramble away just to make him to work for it. She had no thought of saying no, but damn it, he was going to have to chase her—

The Primale leaped onto her back and pinned her hands up over her head. As she tried to twist around under him, he kneed her legs apart and held her in place with his hips. His arousal slipped down and probed at her, making her arch up.

He gave her just enough slack in her arms so she could turn her shoulders and look at him.

He kissed her. Deep and long. And she held her own, finished with being trapped in the Chosen's yielding tradition.

With a sudden shift, he pulled back, moved a little, and . . .

Cormia moaned as he penetrated her body in one smooth stroke. And then there was no time for talking or thinking or lingering on what pain there was as his hips became a driving force. It felt so good, so right, the whole thing, from the smell of his dark spices and the weight of him to the way his hair fell down into her face to the gasps that left both of their parted mouths.

As his strokes deepened, she moved her legs even farther apart and echoed his rhythm in her own hips.

Tears sprang to her eyes, but she didn't think twice about them as his relentless momentum carried her away, a knot of fire taking hold where he was pumping in and out of her until she thought she would be burned alive—and didn't find that a bad thing in the slightest.

They both seized up at the same time, and in the midst of her

own climax she caught a vision of him from over her shoulder, his head rearing back, his jaw clenching, the great muscles in his arms standing out against his smooth skin. But then she was too lost to see anything at all as her own body corded and released, corded and released, the greedy pulls on his sex making him moan and twitch as she drew the marking out of him.

And then it was done.

In the aftermath, she thought of the summer thunderstorms that swept over the mansion from time to time. When they receded, the quiet was all the more dense for the fury they'd wrought. This was the same. With their bodies stilled and their breath easing and their hearts slowing, it was hard to recall the vivid urgency that had propelled them here to this now-resonant moment of silence.

She watched as dismay, then abject shock, took the place of his single-minded marking urge.

What had she expected? That this dance of bodies was going to make him renounce his Primale status, forsake his vow, and declare her his one and only *shellan*? That he would be overjoyed that right before her departure they had done on a passionate impulse what they should have completed with reverence and forethought all those months ago?

"Please get out of me," she said in a choked voice.

Phury could not comprehend what he had done, and yet the proof was there. Cormia's slender body was under his heavy one, her cheeks were wet with tears, and there were bruises on her wrists.

He had taken her virginity from behind, like she was a dog. Held her down and made her submit because he was stronger. Plowed into her without regard for the pain she definitely had felt.

"Please get out of me." Her words were shaky, and the word *please* killed him. She could only request it of him, as she was completely overpowered.

He pulled free of her and got off the bed, stumbling like a drunk.

Cormia turned onto her side and tucked her legs into her body. Her spine seemed so fragile, the delicate column of bones utterly breakable under her pale skin.

"I'm sorry." God, those two words were such empty buckets.

"Please just go."

Considering how he'd already forced himself on her, honoring her request now seemed significant. Even though leaving her was the last thing he wanted to do.

Phury went into the bathroom, put his clothes on, and headed for the door. "We need to talk later—"

"There is no later. I'm going to put in to be a sequestered scribe. So I will record your history, but not be a part of it."

"Cormia, no."

She looked over her shoulder at him. "It's where I belong."

Her head went back down on the pillow.

"Go," she said. "Please."

He had no conscious awareness of walking out of her door or going through his own. He just realized sometime later that he was back in his room, sitting on the edge of his bed, smoking a blunt. In the silence, his hands were shaking and his heart was a broken drum machine and his foot was tapping on the floor.

The wizard was front and center in Phury's mind, standing with black robes waving in the wind, his silhouette jagged against a vast gray horizon. In his hand, balanced on his palm, was a skull.

Its eyes were yellow.

I told you that you would hurt her. I told you.

Phury looked at the tight roll of red smoke in his hand and tried to see anything other than ruination. He couldn't. He'd been a beast.

I told you what was going to happen. I was right. I've been right all along. And by the way, your birth wasn't the curse. It wasn't that you were born after your twin. You are *the curse. Whether there had been five babies born with you or none, the outcome of all the lives around you would have been the same.*

Reaching for the remote, Phury turned on his Bose system, but the instant one of Puccini's luscious, beautiful operas flooded through the room, tears boiled up into his eyes. So lovely, the music, and so unbearable as he contrasted the magical lilt of Luciano Pavarotti's voice with the grunting he'd uttered when he'd been on top of Cormia.

He'd held her down. Pinned her arms. Mounted her from behind—

You *are the curse.*

As the voice of the wizard continued to pound at him, he felt the ivy of the past overtaking him once again, all the things he had failed to do, all the differences he hadn't made, all the care he'd tried to take, but had fallen short on . . . and now there was a new layer. Cormia's layer.

He heard his father's last wheezing breath. And the crackle of his mother's body going up in flames. And his twin's anger at having been rescued.

He heard Cormia's voice, worst of all: *Please get out of me.*

Phury covered his ears with his hands even though that did nothing to help.

You *are the curse.*

With a moan, he pushed his palms into either side of his skull so hard his arms shook.

You don't like the truth? the wizard spat. *You don't like my voice? You know how to make me go away.*

The wizard dropped the skull into the tangle of bones at his feet. *You know how to do it.*

Phury smoked with desperation, terrified of everything that was in his head.

The blunt wasn't even touching the self-hatred or the voices.

The wizard put his black claw-toed boot on top of the yellow-eyed skull. *You know what to do.*

THIRTY-NINE

Up north in the Adirondacks, deep in a cave in Black Snake State Park, the male who had collapsed at the coming of the dawn two days ago could not understand why the sun was shining on him and he wasn't up in flames. Unless he was in the Fade?

No . . . this couldn't be the Fade. The aches and pains in his body and the screaming in his head were too much like what he felt on Earth.

Except, what about the sun? He was bathed in its warm glow, and yet he breathed.

Man, if all that vampire-no-daylight shit was a lie, the race was an idiot as a whole.

But, wait, wasn't he in a cave? So how were the rays reaching him?

"Eat this," the sunshine said.

Okay, going with the idea, however improbable it was, that he remained alive, clearly he was hallucinating. Because what was

shoved in his face looked like a McDonald's Big Mac, and that was impossible.

Unless he actually was dead, and the Fade had the Golden Arches instead of the golden gates?

"Look," the sunshine said, "if your brain's forgotten how to eat, just open that mouth of yours. I'll cram this fucker in and we'll see if your teeth remember what to do."

The male parted his lips, because the smell of the meat was waking his stomach up and making him drool like a dog. When the hamburger was stuffed into him, his jaw went on autopilot, clamping down hard.

As he tore a hunk off, he moaned. For a brief moment, the tingling approval of his taste buds replaced all of his suffering, even the mental shit. Swallowing brought another whimper out of him.

"Take more," the sunshine said, pressing the Big Mac back against his lips.

He ate it all. And some fries that were lukewarm, but a godsend nonetheless. Then his head was lifted and he sucked back some slightly watery Coke.

"The nearest Mickey D's is twenty miles away," the sunshine said, like it was looking to fill the silence. "That's why it's not as hot as it could be."

The male wanted more.

"Yup, I got you seconds. Open wide."

Another Big Mac. More fries. More Coke.

"I've done the best I can with you, but you need blood," the sunshine told him, like he was a child. "And you need to go home."

As the male shook his head, he realized he was lying on his back with a slab of rock for his pillow and a dirt floor as his mattress. He wasn't in the same cave as before, though. This one smelled different. It smelled like . . . fresh air, fresh spring air.

Although . . . maybe that was the sunshine's scent?

"Yeah, you need to go home."

"No . . ."

"Well, then we got a problem, you and me," the sunshine muttered. There was a shuffling like someone big was sitting down on their haunches. "You're the favor I need to return."

The male frowned, dragged in a breath, and croaked, "Nowhere to go. No favor."

"Not your call, buddy. Or mine." The sunshine seemed to be shaking its head, because the blurry shadows it created in the cave shifted like waves. "Unfortunately, I gotta deliver your ass back to where you belong."

"I'm nothing to you."

"In a perfect world, that would be true. Unfortunately, this ain't heaven. Not by a long shot."

The male couldn't agree more, but the whole going-home thing was bullshit. As the energy from the food seeped into him, he found the strength to sit up, rub his eyes, and—

He stared at the sunshine. "Oh . . . shit."

The sunshine nodded grimly. "Yeah, that's pretty much how I feel about it. So here's the deal, we can do this the hard way or the easy way. Your pick. Although I would like to point out that if I have to find your place without your help, it's going to require some effort on my part, and that's going to crank my shit out."

"I'm not going back there. Ever."

The sunshine put a hand through his long blond-and-black hair. Golden rings glinted on his fingers and flashed from his ears and winked from his nose and glittered around his thick neck. Brilliant white, pupil-less eyes flashed with a boatload of pissed off, the bright blue ring around those moonlike irises flashing navy.

"Right. The hard way. Say good night, Gracie."

As everything went black, the male heard the fallen angel Lassiter say, "Mother. Fucker."

FORTY

"Did you see the look on Phury's face?" Blay said.

John glanced across the island in the kitchen and nodded in total agreement. He and his buddies were sucking back relief beers. At a dead run.

He had never seen any male look like that. Ever.

"That was some bonded-male shit, for real," Qhuinn said as he went over to the refrigerator, opened the door, and took out another three bottles from the queen's Sam Adams stable.

Blay took the one he was offered, then winced and prodded at his shoulder.

John cracked open his freshie and took a slug. Putting down the bottle, he signed, *I'm worried about Cormia.*

"He won't hurt her." Qhuinn sat down at the table. "Nah, no way. He might have planted us in early graves, but not her."

John peeked out into the dining room. *There were doors shutting. Loudly.*

"Well, there are a lot of people in this house. . . ." Qhuinn looked around like he was tackling a bad math problem in his head. "Including the three of us. Go fig."

John stood up. *I have to go check. I won't . . . you know, interrupt anything. I just want to make sure everything's cool.*

"I'll go with you," Qhuinn said as he started to get up again.

No, you'll stay here. And before you gum-flap, fuck you. This is my home, and I don't need a shadow all the time.

"Okay, okay, okay." Qhuinn's eyes shifted to Blay. "Then we'll hit the PT suite. Meet us there?"

"Why are we going to the PT suite?" Blay asked without looking at the guy.

"Because you're still bleeding and you don't know how to get to the first-aid shit from here."

Qhuinn stared hard at Blay. Blay stared hard at his beer.

"Why don't you just tell me how to get there," Blay muttered.

"And how are you going to handle your back?"

Blay took a long suck on his Sam. "Fine. But I want to finish my beer first. And I have to have something to eat. I'm starved."

"Fine. What kind of food do you want."

The two were a pair of Joe Fridays, stiff and staying to the facts.

I'll meet you guys down there, John signed, and turned away. Man, the two of them not getting along upset the whole world order in a way. It was just wrong.

John left through the dining room and was all but jogging by the time he made it to the top of the grand staircase. Up on the second floor, he smelled red smoke and heard opera coming from Phury's room—the poetic-sounding one he usually played.

Hardly the accompaniment for hard-core marking. Maybe they'd just gone to their separate bedrooms after an argument?

John crept up to Cormia's room and listened. Nothing. Although the draft drifting out into the hall was perfumed by a lush, flowery fragrance.

Figuring it couldn't hurt just to see if Cormia was okay, John lifted his knuckles and rapped on her door softly. When there was no answer, he whistled.

"John?" her voice said.

He opened the door because he assumed he was meant—

John froze.

Cormia was lying across her bed on a tangled mess of duvet covers and sheets. She was naked, with her back to the door, and there was blood . . . on the insides of her thighs.

She lifted her head over her shoulder, then scrambled to cover herself. "Dearest Virgin!"

As she snapped the duvet up to her neck, John stood stock-still, his brain trying to process the scene.

He'd hurt her. Phury had hurt her.

Cormia shook her head. "Oh . . . damn."

John blinked and blinked again . . . only to see his younger self in a grungy hallway after what had been done to him had finished.

There had been things on the insides of his thighs, too.

Something in his face must have alarmed the hell out of her, because she reached for him. "John . . . oh, John, no . . . I'm okay . . . I'm okay—trust me, I'm—"

John turned and walked calmly out her door.

"John!"

Back when he'd been small and helpless, there had been no vengeance to be had against his attacker. Now, as he stalked the ten feet to Phury's door, he was in a position to do something about his past and Cormia's present. Now he was big enough and strong enough. Now he could stand up for someone who'd been at the mercy of a person stronger than they were.

"John! No!" Cormia came rushing out of her room.

John didn't knock. No, there was no knocking. At this moment, his fists were not meant for wood. They were meant for flesh.

Throwing open Phury's door, he found the Brother sitting on his bed with a blunt between his lips. As their eyes met, Phury's face had guilt and pain and regret in it.

Which sealed the deal.

On a soundless roar, John launched himself across the room, and Phury did absolutely nothing to stop the attack. If anything, the Brother opened himself up to the pounding, falling back against his pillows as John punched him in the mouth and the eyes and the jaw over and over again.

Someone was screaming. A female.

People came running.

Yelling. Lot of yelling.

"What the _fuck_!" Wrath boomed.

John heard none of it. He was focused only on pounding the bloody hell out of Phury. The Brother was no longer his teacher or his friend, he was a brute and a rapist.

Blood ran on the sheets.

Which was only fucking fair.

Eventually someone peeled John off—Rhage, it was Rhage—and Cormia ran to Phury. He held her off, though, rolling away.

"Jesus fucking Christ!" Wrath bit out. "Can we get a break around here?"

The opera in the background so didn't match the scene: The majestic beauty was at total odds with Phury's wrecked face, and John's shaking rage, and Cormia's tears.

Wrath wheeled on John. "What the fuck is wrong with you?"

"I deserved it," Phury said, wiping off his bloody lip. "I deserved it and worse."

Wrath's head whipped toward the bed. "What?"

"No, he didn't," Cormia said, holding the lapels of her robe close to her throat. "It was consensual."

"No, it wasn't." Phury shook his head. "It was not."

The king's whole body stiffened. In a low, tight voice, he said to the Chosen, "What was consensual?"

While the convention in the room looked back and forth between the two of them, John kept his eye on Phury. In the event Rhage's hold loosened, he was going after the Brother again. No matter who was ringside.

Phury sat up slowly, wincing, his face already starting to swell. "Don't lie, Cormia."

"Take your own counsel," she snapped. "The Primale did nothing wrong—"

"Bullshit, Cormia! I took you by force—"

"You did not—"

Someone else started arguing. And another. Even John got into the act, mouthing filthy things at Phury while he strained against Rhage's deadweight.

Wrath reached over to the bureau, picked up a heavy crystal ashtray, and fired it at the wall. The thing shattered into a thousand pieces, leaving a dent the size of a head in the plaster.

"Next person who says one more *fucking* word, I do that with their skull, feel me?"

Everyone went quiet. And stayed that way.

"You"—Wrath pointed at John—"get out of here while I sort this."

John shook his head, not caring about the ashtray. He wanted to stay. He needed to stay. Someone had to protect—

Cormia came up and took his hand, squeezing it hard. "You are a male of worth, and I know you believe you are protecting my honor, but seek my eyes and see the truth of what happened."

John stared into Cormia's face. There was sadness, but it was of the poignant variety, the kind you got when you were in an unhappy situation. There was also resolve and a forthright strength.

There was no fear. No choking despair. No horrible shame.

She was not as he had been afterward.

"Go," she said softly. "All is well. Truly."

John looked at Wrath, who nodded. "I don't know what you

walked in on, but I'm going to find out. Let me deal with this, son. I'll do right by her. Now everyone, out."

John squeezed Cormia's hand and left with Rhage and the others. The second he was out in the hall, the door was shut and he heard quiet voices.

He didn't go far. Couldn't. He made it to just outside of Wrath's study when his knees took a TO and he collapsed in one of the antique chairs that dotted the hall. After reassuring everyone he was okay, he let his head hang and breathed slowly.

The past was alive in his head, reanimated by the lightning strike of what he'd seen in Cormia's room.

Closing his eyes didn't help. Trying to talk himself down didn't help.

While he struggled to get the slipcovers back on his sofa, he realized it had been weeks and weeks since he and Zsadist had had one of their walks in the woods. As Bella's pregnancy had progressed and become more of a concern, his and Z's once-nightly sojourns where they traipsed through the forest in silence had become more and more infrequent.

He needed one now.

Lifting his head, he glanced in the direction of the hall of statues and wondered whether Zsadist was even in the house. Probably not, as he hadn't been in the room when the drama had rolled out. Given all the killings that had gone down tonight, the Brother no doubt had his hands full in the field.

John stood and went to his room. After he shut himself in, he stretched out on his bed, texted Qhuinn and Blay, and told them he was crashing. They'd get the messages when they came back out of the tunnel.

Staring up at the ceiling, he thought . . . of the number three. Bad things did come in that number, and did not always involve death.

Three times he had lost it within the last year. Three times his temper had snapped and he'd attacked someone.

Twice Lash. Once Phury.

You're unstable, a voice said.

Well, except he'd had his reasons, and they had all been good ones. The first time, Lash had gone after Qhuinn. The second time Lash had more than deserved. And this third time . . . the circumstantial evidence had been overwhelming, and what kind of male walked in on a female like that and didn't take action?

You're unstable.

Closing his eyes, he tried not to remember that stairwell in that grungy apartment building where he'd lived by himself. He tried not to remember what those boots on the steps had sounded like as they'd rushed at him. He tried not to remember the old mold and the fresh urine and the sweaty cologne that had tunneled into his nose when what had been done to him had been going down. . . .

He couldn't shake the memories. Especially of the smells.

The mold had been from the wall he'd been pushed face-first into. The urine had been his own and had run down the insides of his thighs to the pants that been ripped down from his hips. The sweaty cologne had been his attacker's.

The scene was as fresh as where he was now. He felt his body then as clearly as he knew it now, saw the stairwell as he did the room he was currently in. Fresh . . . fresh . . . fresh . . . and there appeared to be no expiration date on the horrible episode's milk carton.

It didn't take a psychology degree to know that this explosive temper of his was rooted in all he kept inside.

For the first time in his life, he wanted to talk to someone.

No . . . not exactly.

He wanted back the one who was his. He wanted his father.

After John's Oscar de la Hoya routine, Phury's face felt as if it had been spit-broiled and put on a bed of fresh-cut I've-hit-bottom. "Look, Wrath . . . don't get angry with John."

"It was a misunderstanding," Cormia said to the king. "Nothing more."

"What the hell happened between you two?" Wrath asked.

"Nothing," Cormia replied. "Absolutely nothing."

The king so wasn't buying it, which proved their fearless leader had half a brain, but at the moment Phury didn't have enough left in him to argue for the truth. He just kept mopping up his busted mouth with the back of his forearm as Wrath kept talking and Cormia kept defending him, God only knew why.

Wrath glowered from behind his wraparounds. "Look, do I need to break something else to get you two to cut the shit? The hell it was nothing. John's a hothead, but he's not a—"

Cormia cut the king off. "John misinterpreted what he saw."

"What did he see?"

"Nothing. I say it was nothing and therefore it is as such."

Wrath gave her the once-over, as if checking for bruises. Then he looked hard at Phury. "What the fuck do you have to tell me?"

Phury shook his head. "She's wrong. John didn't misunder—"

Cormia's tone was sharp. "The Primale is clothing himself in blame that is unnecessary. My honor was not impeached in any fashion, and I do believe that is my call to make, is it not."

After a moment, the king inclined his head. "As you wish."

"Thank you, Your Highness." She bowed deep and low. "Now, I shall be taking my leave of you."

"Would you like me to send Fritz with some food—"

"No. I am taking my leave of this side. I am returning home." She bowed again, and as she did, the blond hair that was still drying from her shower slipped off her shoulder and brushed the floor. "I wish you both the very best and proffer my kindest regards to the rest of the household. Your Majesty." She bowed again to Wrath. "Your Grace." She bowed to Phury.

Phury leaped up off the bed and rushed forward in a panic . . . but she disappeared into the thin air before he reached her.

Gone. Just like that.

"Will you excuse me," he said to Wrath. It wasn't a request, but he didn't give a shit.

"I really don't think you should be alone right now," Wrath said in a dark tone.

There was conversation at that point, some sort of back-and-forth, which must have reassured Wrath on some level, because the king left.

When he was gone, Phury stood in the middle of his room, still as a statue, staring at the imprint of that ashtray on the wall. On the inside he writhed, but on the outside he was utterly motionless: The choking ivy was growing underneath his skin, instead of over it.

With a flick of his eyes, he checked the clock. Only an hour before dawn.

As he headed into the bathroom for a cleanup, he knew he was going to have to be quick about this.

FORTY-ONE

The Caldwell Police Station had two separate faces to it: the front entrance on Tenth, with all the steps, which was where the TV crews filmed the shit you saw on the evening news, and the back one, with the iron bars, where business was taken care of. In truth, the Tenth Street facade was only marginally better-looking, because the 1960s-era building was like the profile of an aging, ugly woman. There were no good sides.

The squad car Lash was in the back of pulled to a stop right behind the rear entrance.

How the fuck had he ended up here?

The cop who'd arrested him came around and popped the door. "Step out of the car, please."

Lash stared up at the guy, then shifted his legs, unhinged his knees, and towered over the human. Fantasies of ripping the man's throat open and turning his jugular vein into a soda fountain were all but undeniable.

"This way, sir."

"No problem."

He could tell he made the SOB jumpy by the way the cop's hand drifted over to the butt of his gun in spite of the fact that they were in full view of the CPD home team.

Lash was led through some double doors and down a linoleum hallway that looked like it had been installed when the shit had first been invented. They stopped at a Plexiglas window that was thick as an arm, and the cop yammered into a circular metal patch that was mounted on the wall. The woman on the other side was all business in her navy blue uniform, and about as attractive as the male cop.

But she took care of the paperwork quickly. When she was satisfied that she'd pulled together enough forms for them to fill out, she slid the stack under the window to the cop and nodded. The door next to them let out a *beeeeeeep* and a clunk, as if it had burped open its lock, and then it was another beat-to-shit linoleum stretch that ended in a little room with a bench, a chair, and a desk.

After they were seated, the officer took out a pen and clicked it. "What's your full name?"

"Larry Owen," Lash said. "Just like I told him."

The guy bent over the papers. "Address?"

"Fifteen eighty-three Tenth Street, apartment four-F for right now." He figured he might as well go with the addy from the registration on the Focus. Mr. D was going to bring the fake driver's license Lash had used when he'd lived with his parents, but he couldn't remember exactly what was on it.

"Do you have any identification to prove you live there?"

"Not on me. But my friend will bring my ID."

"Date of birth?"

"When do I get my phone call?"

"In a minute. Date of birth?"

"October thirteenth, 1981." At least, he thought that was his fake one.

The officer shifted an ink pad across the desk, got up, and freed one of Lash's cuffs. "I need to fingerprint you now."

Good luck with that, Lash thought.

He let the guy take his left hand and pull it forward, watched as the pads of his fingertips were rolled and pressed onto a white piece of paper with ten squares in two rows.

The policeman frowned at what he saw and tried another finger. "Nothing's coming up."

"I was burned as a child."

"Sure you were." The guy did the roll and press a couple more times, and then gave up and redid the cuffs. "Over to the camera."

Lash went across the room and stood still as a flash went off in his face. "I want my phone call."

"You'll get it."

"What's my bail?"

"Don't know yet."

"When will I be out?"

"Whenever the judge sets the bail and you pay it. Probably this afternoon, given how early in the a.m. it is."

Lash was recuffed with his hands in front of him and a phone was pushed over to him. The officer hit a button for speakerphone and dialed Mr. D's cell phone as Lash recited the digits.

The cop stepped back as the *lesser* answered.

Lash didn't waste time. "Bring my wallet. It's in my jacket in the back of the car. They haven't set bail, but find some cash ASAP."

"When do you want me to come?"

"Get the ID here now. Then it's whenever the judge sets the bail." He looked at the officer. "Can I call him again to let him know when to pick me up?"

"No, but he can dial our precinct line, ask for the jail, and find out when you'll be released that way."

"You hear that?"

"Yup," Mr. D said through the tinny speaker.

"Don't stop working."

"We're not."

Ten minutes later, Lash was in a holding cell.

The thirty-by-thirty cinder-block room was standard-issue with its bars across the front and its anti-Kohler stainless-steel toilet and sink setup in the corner. As he went over to the bench and sat with his back to the cell wall, five guys checked him out. Two were clearly druggies, because they were greasy as bacon and had evidently had their brains pan-fried earlier in the night. The other three were his peeps, even though they were just humans: a guy with massive biceps and a good dozen prison tats in the opposite corner, away from everyone; a gangbanger with a blue do-rag doing the rat-in-a-cage pace at the bars; and a skinhead psycho who was twitching by the cell door.

Naturally, the druggies didn't care that someone had been added to the mix, but the other ones sized him up like he was a lamb shank at a deli counter.

He thought of the number of *lessers* who had been lost tonight.

"Hey, asshole," Lash said to the sw'old-up one, "your boyfriend give you those p-tats? Or was he too busy fucking you in the ass?"

The guy's eyes narrowed. "What'd you say to me?"

The gangbanger shook his head. "Gotta be out ya damn mind, white boy."

Skinhead laughed like a blender, high and fast.

Who knew recruiting would be this easy, Lash thought.

Phury did not dematerialize to ZeroSum. He went to Screamer's instead.

As it was nearly the end of the night, there was no wait line outside the club, so he just walked right in the front door and went back to the bar. While hard-core rap thumped, the dregs of the party set were hanging on to their buzzes with death grips, drooping over each other in the dark corners, too blitzed even to have sex.

As the bartender approached, the guy said, "We're last-calling it."

"Sapphire martini."

The guy came back with the drink and flipped a cocktail napkin out flat before putting the triangle glass down. "That'll be twelve dollars."

Phury slid a fifty across the black bar and kept his hand on the bill. "I'm looking for something. And it's not change."

The bartender looked down at the green. "Whatchu after?"

"I like to ride horses."

The guy's eyes started cruising the room. "Do you. Well, this is a club, not a stable."

"I don't wear blue. Ever."

The bartender's eyes drifted back, and he gave Phury the once-over. "Clothes as expensive as the ones you've got on . . . you could wear any color you like."

"I don't like blue."

"You from out of town?"

"You could say that."

"Your face is a mess."

"Is it. I hadn't noticed."

There was a pause. "You see that guy in the back? With the eagle on his jacket? He might be able to help you. *Might* be able. I don't know him."

"Of course you don't."

Phury left the fifty and the drink and walked through the thinned-out, spaced-out crowd with a single-minded focus.

Just before he got within range, the guy in question sauntered off, leaving out of the side door.

Phury followed him into the alley, and as they stepped outside, something fired off in his mind, but he ignored it. He was interested in one and only one thing . . . was so locked in that even the wizard's voice was gone.

" 'Scuse me," he said.

The dealer turned on his heel and gave Phury the same kind of head-to-toe the bartender had. "I don't know you."

"No, you don't. But you know my friends."

"Do I." When Phury flashed a couple hundred dollars, the guy smiled. "Ah, yeah. What you looking for?"

"H."

"Perfect timing. I'm almost out." The guy's class ring flashed blue as he put a hand into his coat.

For a split second, Phury had an image of that dealer and the druggie in that alley, the ones he and the *lesser* had walked up on all those nights ago. Funny, that encounter had started the great slide, hadn't it, the slope taking him here, to this moment, in this alley . . . where a little envelope full of heroin landed in his hand.

"I'm here"—the dealer nodded in the direction of the club's door—"pretty much every night—"

Lights hit them from every direction—courtesy of the unmarked police cars parked at the foot and the head of the alley.

"Hands up!" someone yelled.

Phury stared into the dealer's panicked eyes and felt no sympathy and no complicity. "I gotta go. Later."

Phury wiped the memory of himself from the four cops with the guns and the dealer with the aw-fuck-me expression and dematerialized with his buy.

FORTY-TWO

Qhuinn led the way through the tunnel that ran underground from the Brotherhood's mansion to the training center's office. Blay stayed behind him, and the only sound was their boots. The meal they'd shared had been the same, only silverware on silverware and an occasional, Could you please pass the salt?

Dinner's great conversational drought had been broken only by a rainstorm of some kind of drama upstairs. When they'd heard shouting, they'd both put their forks down and run into the foyer, but Rhage had looked over the balcony and shaken his head, telling them to stay out of it.

Which was cool. The two of them had plenty of their own shit to deal with.

When they got to the door that led into the office closet, Qhuinn punched 1914 into the security pad so Blay could see the numbers.

"Year the house was built, evidently." As they stepped through the

closet and came out next to the desk, he shook his head. "I always wondered how they got here."

Blay made a noise that could have been anything from "Me, too," to "Fuck you with a chain saw, you rat bastard."

The route to the PT suite didn't require a leader, and once they got into the gym, it was hard not to count the yards Blay put between them as soon as he could.

"You can go now," Blay said as they came up to the door marked EQUIPMENT ROOM/PT. "I'll manage the cut on my back."

"It's between your shoulder blades."

Blay gripped the knob and went again with the noise in the back of his throat. And this time it was definitely not a me-too kind of thing.

"Be reasonable," Qhuinn said.

Blay's eyes stared straight ahead. After a moment, he opened the door. "Wash your hands first. Before you touch me, I want you to wash your hands."

As they went in, the guy made a beeline for the gurney that Qhuinn had been operated on the night before last.

"We should get a time-share on this bitch," Qhuinn said as he glanced around the tiled room with its stainless-steel cabinets and medical equipment.

Blay popped himself up on the table, shrugged out of his shirt, and winced as he looked down at the barely closed bleeders on his chest. "Shit."

Qhuinn let out all the breath in his lungs and just stared at his friend. The guy's head hung off his neck as he examined where he'd been cut, and he was beautiful like that, his shoulders wide, the pads of his pecs thick, his arms corded with muscle. What made him all the more appealing, though, was his self-contained reserve.

Hard not to wonder what was underneath all that modesty.

Qhuinn got on with the nurse shit, grabbing some gauze, tape, and antiseptic wash from the cabinets, then putting it all on a push tray and scooting the lot over to the gurney.

With the supplies gathered, he went over to the stainless-steel sink and pressed the foot pedal to get the water running.

While he washed his hands, he said quietly, "If I could, I would."

"Excuse me?"

Qhuinn pumped some suds into his palms and scrubbed all the way up his forearms. Which was overkill, but if Blay wanted him superclean, then that was what he was going to be. "If I could love a guy like that, it would be you."

"Yeah, on second thought, I'll work on myself and to hell with my back—"

"I'm serious." He released the pedal to stop the water running, and shook his hands over the sink. "You think I haven't thought about it? Being with you, that is. And not just for the sex shit."

"You have?" Blay whispered above the dripping.

Qhuinn dried his hands on a stack of blue surgical towels to the left and took one with him as he went over to Blay. "Yeah, I have. Hold this under the wounds, would you?"

Blay did as he was told, and Qhuinn squeezed some wash over the gash on the guy's sternum.

"I didn't know— Mother*fucker!*"

"Stings, huh." Qhuinn went around the table, to his buddy's back. "I'm going to do this one now, and I think you'd better brace yourself. It's even deeper."

Qhuinn put another towel under the wound and hit it with shit that smelled like Lysol. As Blay hissed, he winced. "It'll be over in a second."

"Bet you say that to all the—" Blay stopped right there.

"Nah. I don't say that to anyone. They take me as I come. They can't handle it, it's their problem."

Picking up a sterile pack of gauze, Qhuinn tore the thing open and pressed the white weave against the wound between Blay's shoulder blades. "I've absolutely thought about us . . . but I see myself with a female long-term. I can't explain it. It's just the way it's going to be."

Blay's rib cage expanded and compressed. "Maybe because you don't want another defect?"

Qhuinn frowned. "No."

"You sure about that."

"Look, if I cared what people thought, do you think I'd do what I do already?" He went around and blotted the slice on Blay's chest, then tended to the wound on his shoulder. "Besides, my family's dead. Who've I got to impress anymore?"

"Why were you so cruel?" Blay asked in a dignified voice. "Back in the tunnel at my place."

Qhuinn picked up a tube of neomycin and went around to his buddy's back again. "I was pretty sure I wasn't coming back, and I didn't want you ruining your life over me. Figured it was better for you to hate me than miss me."

Blay laughed for real, and the sound was nice. "You are so arrogant."

"Duh. But it's true, isn't it." Qhuinn smoothed the milky ointment onto the break in Blay's skin. "You would have."

As he came back around in front, Blay lifted his head and his eyes. Their stares met, and Qhuinn reached out and put his palm on his friend's cheek.

Rubbing his thumb gently back and forth, he whispered, "I want you with someone who's going to be worthy of you. Treat you right. Be only with you. I'm not that guy. Even if I settled with a female . . . shit, I tell myself I could be with just her, but in my heart of hearts, I don't really believe that."

The yearning in the blue eyes staring up at him broke his heart. It totally did. And he couldn't imagine what it was that Blay saw in him that made him so special.

"What is wrong with you," he whispered, "that you care so much about me?"

Blay's sad smile added about a million years to his age, lining his face with the kind of knowledge that came only after life kicked you

in the nuts a number of times. "What is wrong with you that you can't see why I would?"

"We're going to have to agree to disagree on that."

"Promise me something?"

"Anything."

"Leave me if you want, but don't do it for my own good. I'm not a child, and I don't break easily, and what I feel is none of your god-damned business."

"I thought I was doing the right thing."

"You weren't. So promise me?"

Qhuinn exhaled hard. "Fine, I promise. As long as you swear you'll look for someone real, okay?"

"You're real to me."

"Swear to it. Or I'm going to do that I-am-an-island bit again. I want you open to meeting someone you can really have."

Blay's hand crept up Qhuinn's forearm and squeezed his wrist, the pact becoming solid on both sides. "Okay . . . all right. But it's going to be a guy. I've tried females, and it just doesn't feel right."

"As long as you're happy. Whatever makes you happy."

As the tension eased between them, Qhuinn wrapped his arms around his friend and held him close, trying to absorb the male's sadness, wishing there were another way for them.

"I suppose this is for the best," Blay said into his shoulder. "You can't cook."

"See? I'm so not Prince Charming."

Qhuinn could have sworn Blay whispered, "Yes, you are," but he wasn't sure.

They pulled apart, looked into each other's eyes . . . and something shifted. In the silence of the whole training center, in the vast privacy of the moment, something changed.

"Just once," Blay said softly. "Do it just once. So I'll know what it's like."

Qhuinn started to shake his head. "No . . . I don't think—"

"Yes."

After a moment, Qhuinn slid both his hands up Blay's thick neck and captured the male's sturdy jaw in his palms. "You sure?"

When Blay nodded, Qhuinn tilted his friend's head back and to the side and held it in place as he slowly closed the distance. Just before their mouths touched, Blay's eyelashes fluttered down and he trembled and—

Oh, it was sweet. Blay's lips were incredibly sweet and soft.

The tongue probably wasn't supposed to be part of it, but there was no helping that. Qhuinn licked inside and then sank deep as his arms slipped around Blay and held him hard. When he finally lifted his head, the look in Blay's eyes said he would let anything happen between them. Let it all happen.

They could take this spark between them all the way home until they were both naked and Qhuinn was doing what he did best to his buddy.

But things would never be the same after that, and that was what stopped him, in spite of the fact that he suddenly wanted exactly what Blay did. "You're too important to me," he said roughly. "You're too good for the kind of sex I have."

Blay's eyes lingered on Qhuinn's mouth. "At this moment, I would so disagree with that."

As Qhuinn let go of the guy and stepped back, he realized it was the first and only time he'd ever turned someone down. "No, I'm right. I'm so fucking right about this."

Blay took a deep breath, then braced his arms against the gurney and seemed to try to collect himself. He laughed a little. "I can't feel my feet or my hands."

"I'd offer to rub them, but . . ."

Blay's glance under his lashes was damned sexy. "You'd be tempted to rub something else of mine?"

Qhuinn grinned. "Fucker."

"Fine, fine. Be that way." Blay reached over for the antiseptic, put some on his chest, then covered the wound with gauze, which he taped in place. "Will you take care of covering up the one in back?"

"Yeah."

As he hit the raw patch with some gauze, Qhuinn imagined someone touching Blay's skin . . . running their hands over him, easing the kind of ache a male got between his thighs.

"One thing, though," Qhuinn murmured.

"What?"

The voice that came out of his throat was unlike anything he'd ever heard from himself before. "If any guy breaks your heart or treats you like shit, I will bust him apart with my bare hands and leave his broken, bloody body for the sun."

Blay's laughter rumbled around the tiled walls. "Of course you will—"

"I'm dead fucking serious."

Blay's blue eyes shot over his shoulder.

"If there are any who dare to hurt you," Qhuinn growled in the Old Language, *"I shall see them staked afore me and shall leave their bodies in ruin."*

At his great camp in the Adirondacks, Rehvenge was desperately trying to get warm. Bundled in a thick terry cloth robe, with a mink blanket over his body, he was stretched out on a couch a mere five feet from the flames of a crackling fire.

The room was among his favorites in the huge, barny house, its grumpy Victorian décor of garnet and gold and deep blue often suiting his mood. Funny, he'd always thought a dog would look good by the massive stone fireplace. A retriever of some sort. God, maybe he would get a dog. Bella had always liked dogs. Their mother hadn't, though, so there had never been one in the family house in Caldwell.

Rehv frowned and thought of his mother, who was staying at another of the family homes about a hundred and fifty miles away. She hadn't recovered yet from Bella's abduction. Probably never

would. Even all these months later, she didn't want to leave the country, although given the state of Caldwell, that wasn't a bad thing.

She was going to die in the house she was in now, he thought. Likely within the next couple years. Old age was upon her, her biological clock starting to race to the finish line, her hair already having gone white.

"Got more wood," Trez said as he came in with an armload of logs. The Moor went over to the fireplace, moved the screen out of the way, and stoked the blaze until it roared even brighter.

Which was pretty whacked for August.

Ah, but this was August in the Adirondacks. Plus he was double-loaded on dopamine, so he had about the same sensory perception and core temperature as petrified wood.

Trez put the screen back in place and looked over his shoulder. "Your lips are blue. You want me to make you some coffee?"

"You're a bodyguard, not a butler."

"And we've got how many people standing around here with silver trays?"

"I can get it." Rehv went to sit up, and his stomach lurched. "Fuck."

"Lie back down before I knock you out."

As the guy left, Rehv resettled against the cushions, hating the aftermath of what he did to the Princess. *Hating* it. He just wanted to forget the whole thing, at least until next month. Unfortunately, the shit was on an endless play loop in his head. He saw what he'd done in that cabin tonight over and over again, saw himself jerk off to seduce the Princess and then fuck her at that windowsill.

Variations on that perversion had been his sex life for how long now? *Shit . . .*

He wondered briefly what it would be like to have someone he cared about but he shelved that fantasy pretty damn quick. The only way he could have sex was if he was off his meds—so the only person he could be with was a *symphath*, and there was no way in hell he was going to warm up to one of those females. Sure, he and Xhex had tried it out, but that had been a disaster on a lot of levels.

A coffee mug was shoved under his nose. "Drink this."

Reaching for the thing, he said, "Thanks—"

"Oh, shit, check you out."

Rehv quickly switched hands, tucking his bad forearm back under the blankets. "Like I said, thank you."

"So that's why Xhex made you go to the clinic, huh." Trez parked it in an oxblood club chair. "And, no, I won't be holding my breath for a confirm on that. I'll just take it as self-evident."

As Trez crossed his legs, he looked like a perfect gentleman, a real example of royalty: In spite of the fact that he was wearing black cargo pants, combat boots, and a muscle shirt—and was fully capable of tearing a male's head off and using it as a soccer ball—you'd have sworn he was just one visit to the closet away from ermine robes and a crown.

Which, actually, just happened to be true.

"Good coffee," Rehv murmured.

"Just don't ask me to bake. How's the antivenom doing?"

"Jim-dandy."

"So your stomach's still off."

"You should be a *symphath*."

"I work with two of them. That's close enough, fuck you very much."

Rehv smiled and took another monster drag from the mug's lip. The lining of his mouth was probably getting burned given how much steam was rising from what was inside, but he didn't feel a thing.

On the other hand, he was all too conscious of Trez's unwavering black stare. Which meant the Moor was about to say something Rehv wasn't going to like. As opposed to most people, when the guy told you what you didn't want to hear, he looked right into you.

Rehv rolled his eyes. "Just get it over with, why don't you."

"You're worse each time you're with her."

True. Back when it started, he could be with the Princess and go back to work right away. After a couple years had passed, he'd needed a quick lie-down. Then a nap for a couple of hours. Now he was on his ass for a good twenty-four hours. Thing was, he was developing an allergic reaction to the venom. Sure, the antivenom serum Trez pumped into him afterward kept him from going into shock, but he wasn't recovering well anymore.

Maybe one day he wouldn't recover at all.

As he considered the number of medications he needed to have regularly, he thought, *Shit, better living through chemistry. Kind of.*

Trez was still looking at him, so he took another drink and said, "Quitting with her is not an option."

"You could blow out of Caldwell, though. Find another place to live. If she doesn't know how to find you, she can't turn you in."

"If I leave town, she'd just go after my mother. Who won't relocate because of Bella and the young."

"This is going to kill you."

"She's too addicted to risk that, though."

"Then you need to tell her to cut the shit with that scorpion rub-down she gives herself. I understand your wanting to look strong, but she's going to be fucking a cadaver if she doesn't give that up."

"Knowing her, necrophilia would be a turn-on."

Behind Trez, a lovely glow pierced the horizon.

"Oh, shit, is it that late," Rehv said, diving for the remote that closed the steel shutters on the house.

Except it wasn't the sun. At least, not the sun that pinwheeled in the sky.

A figure of light was coming up the lawn toward the house, walking with a saunter.

There was only one thing that Rehv could think of that could get that effect.

"Fan-fucking-tastic," he muttered, sitting up. "Man, is this night over yet?"

Trez was already on his feet. "You want me to let him in?"

"Might as well. He'd just walk through the glass anyway."

The Moor slid one of the doors back and stood to the side as Lassiter came into the den. The guy's gliding walk was the physical manifestation of a drawl, all smooth and slow and insolent.

"Long time, no see," the angel said.

"Not long enough."

"Always with the hospitality."

"Listen, GE." Rehv blinked hard. "Mind if you dim your disco ball?"

The brilliant glow drifted away until Lassiter appeared normal. Well, normal for someone with a serious-ass piercing fetish and aspirations for being some country's gold currency standard.

Trez shut the door and stood behind it, a wall of you-fuck-with-my-boy-and-angel-or-not-ima-show-your-ass-a-beatdown.

"What brings you onto my property?" Rehv said, cradling his mug with both hands and trying to absorb its warmth.

"Got a problem."

"I can't fix your personality, sorry."

Lassiter laughed, the sound ringing through the house like church bells. "No. I like myself just as I am, thank you."

"Can't help your delusional nature, either."

"I need to find an address."

"Do I look like the phone book?"

"You look like shit, as a matter of fact."

"And you with the compliments." Rehv finished his coffee. "What makes you think I'd help you?"

"Because."

"You want to toss in a couple of nouns and verbs there? I'm lost."

Lassiter grew serious, his ethereal beauty losing its SOP fuck-yourself smirk. "I'm here on official business."

Rehv frowned. "No offense, but I thought your boss pink-slipped your ass."

"I've got one last shot at being a good boy." The angel looked hard at the coffee mug between Rehv's hands. "If you help me, I can pay you back."

"Can you."

When Lassiter tried to take a step forward, Trez was on him like paint. "No, you don't."

"I'll heal him. If you let me touch him, I'll heal him."

Trez's brows came down, and he opened his mouth like he was about to tell the angel to heal himself right out of the goddamn house.

"Hold up," Rehv said.

Shit, he was so tired and achy and miserable, it was hard not to imagine himself feeling like this when night fell. A week from to-morrow.

"Just what kind of address is it."

"The Brotherhood's."

"Ha. Even if I knew it—and I don't—I couldn't tell you that."

"I have something they've lost."

Rehv was about to laugh again when his *symphath* side fired up. The angel was an asshole, but he was totally serious. And, shit . . . could it be true? Could he have found—

"Yes, I have," Lassiter said. "Now, are you going to help me help them? And in return, 'cause I'm a stand-up guy, I'll take care of your little problem."

"And what problem would that be?"

"The MRSA infection in your forearm. And the fact that, at the moment, you're about two more exposures away from anaphylaxis with that scorpion venom." Lassiter shook his head. "I'm not going to ask any questions. On either account."

"You feeling okay? Usually you're nosier than that."

"Hey, if you want to share—"

"Whatever. Rock out if you want." Rehv extended his gutted forearm. "I'll do what I can for you, but I can't make any promises."

Lassiter shot Trez a smile. "So, big guy, you going to take a breather and step aside? Because your boss has consented—"

"He's not my boss."

"I'm not his boss."

Lassiter inclined his head. "Your colleague, then. Now, you mind getting out of my way?"

Trez bared his fangs and clapped his jaws together twice, the Shadow way of telling someone they were walking a thin trail on the edge of a very tall cliff. But he did step back.

Lassiter came forward, his glow resurfacing.

Rehv met the guy's sterling-silver, pupil-less eyes. "You fuck with me, and Trez will damage you till your packaging can't even be taped back together. You know what he is."

"I know, but he's wasting his hard-on. I can do no harm to the righteous, so you're safe."

Rehv barked a laugh. "He should still be worried, then."

When Lassiter reached out and made contact, current licked into Rehv's arm, making him gasp. As a wondrous healing started to pour into him, he shuddered and lay back in his nest of blankets. *Oh, God* . . . His exhaustion was lifting. Which meant the pain he didn't feel was backing off.

In that gorgeous voice of his, Lassiter murmured, "You've got nothing to worry about. The righteous do not always do right, but their souls remain pure. You are untainted at your core. Now close your eyes, numb nuts, I'm about to light up like a bonfire."

Rehv squinted and had to look away as a blast of pure energy slammed through his body. It was like an orgasm on steroids, a huge rush that carried him away, splintering him apart until he drifted down in a shower of stars.

When he came back into his body, he sighed long and hard.

Lassiter let go and rubbed his hand on the low-slung jeans he wore. "And now for what I need from you."

"It's not going to be easy to get to them."

"Tell me something I don't know."

"I'm going to have to verify what you have first."

"He's not in his happy place."

"Well, of course not, he's hanging with you. But I don't fly the flag until I see the sights."

There was a pause. And then Lassiter inclined his head. "Fine. I'll come back at nightfall and take you to him."

"Fair enough, angel, fair enough."

FORTY-THREE

On the cusp of dawn, Phury went to his bedroom and packed an L.L. Bean bag with workout supplies, such as a towel, his iPod, and his water bottle . . . and drug paraphernalia that included a spoon, a lighter, a syringe, a belt, and his stash of red smoke.

He left his crib and headed down to the hall of statues, walking like he was all about healthy purpose. He didn't want to be too close to Bella and Z, so he chose one of the empty guest rooms that was nearer to the grand staircase. Slipping in through the door, he almost went back out to pick another: The color of the walls was a dusty lavender, just like the roses Cormia had enjoyed.

Voices of *doggen* passing by outside in the hall made him stay put.

He went into the bath, shut that door as well, and dimmed the lights until they glowed like a banked fire. As the shutters came down for the day, he sat on the marble floor with his back against the Jacuzzi and got out the things he was going to use on himself.

The reality of what he was about to do didn't seem like any big deal.

It was kind of like immersing yourself in cold water. Once the shock was over, you got used to where you were.

And he was encouraged by the quiet in his head. Since he'd started down this road, the wizard hadn't said a goddamned thing.

Phury's hands didn't shake at all as he tapped out some white powder into the belly of a sterling-silver spoon and added a little water from his bottle. Flipping open the top of his lighter, he struck up a flame and brought it under the mix.

For no apparent reason, he noted that the silver spoon's pattern was Gorham's Lily of the Valley. From the late nineteenth century.

After the sauce had boiled, he put the spoon down on the marble floor, loaded up the syringe, and reached for his Hermès belt. Extending his left arm, he looped the leather through its shiny gold buckle, pulled the thing tight, and tucked the end under his arm so he could hold it in place.

His veins popped at the crook of his elbow and he prodded them. He chose the thickest one, then frowned.

The shit in the needle's belly was brown.

For a moment, panic flickered. Brown was a bad color.

He shook his head to clear it, then pierced his vein with the needle and drew up the plunger to make sure he was in properly. When he saw a flash of red, he pushed his thumb down, emptied the syringe's load, and let the belt go loose.

The effect was so much faster than he'd imagined. One second he was letting his arm fall lax, and the next he was viciously sick to his stomach and crawling for the toilet in a bizarre, rushing slow motion.

This shit was definitely not red smoke. There was no mellow easing, no polite knock on the door before the drug stepped into his brain. This was an all-guns-blazing assault with a battering ram, and as he threw up, he reminded himself that what he'd gotten was what he'd wanted.

Dimly, in the far background of his consciousness, he heard the wizard start laughing . . . heard his addiction's cackling satisfaction get rolling, even as the heroin took over the rest of his mind and body.

As he passed out while throwing up, he realized he'd been cheated. Instead of killing the wizard, he was left only with the wasteland and its master.

Good job, mate . . . excellent job.

Shit, those bones in the wasteland were the leftovers of the addicts the wizard had worded to death. And Phury's skull was front and center, the newest casualty. But certainly not the last.

"Of course," the Chosen Amalya said. "Of course you may be sequestered . . . if you are sure that is what you wish?"

Cormia nodded, then reminded herself that, as she was in the Sanctuary, she was back in the land of the bowing. Lowering her upper body, she murmured, "Thank you."

As she straightened, she looked around the Directrix's private quarters. The two rooms were decorated in the tradition of the Chosen, which was to say that they had no decor at all. Everything was simple, sparse, and white, with the only difference from the other Chosen quarters being that Amalya had a seating arrangement for audiences with the sisters.

Everything was so white, Cormia thought. So . . . *white.* And the chairs they were both sitting on were stiff backed and without cushions.

"I suppose this is timely," the Directrix said. "The last remaining sequestered scribe, Selena, stepped down with the advent of the Primale's ascension. The Scribe Virgin was pleased to have her relinquish the duty, given our change in circumstance. No one, however, has come forward to replace her."

"I'd like to suggest that I function as a primary recording scribe as well."

"That would be very generous of you. It would free up the others for the Primale." There was a stretch of silence. "Shall we proceed?"

When Cormia nodded and knelt on the floor, the Directrix lit some incense, and performed the ceremony of sequestering.

When it was through, Cormia stood and walked over on the far side to an open expanse in the wall that she would have called a window.

Across the white expanse of the Sanctuary, she saw the Temple of the Sequestered Scribes. It was annexed to the entry into the Scribe Virgin's private quarters and had no windows. Inside its white confines, there would be no one else but herself. Herself and licks of parchment scrolls and pints of sanguinary ink and the unfolding history of the race, hers to record as a viewer, not a participant.

"I can't do this," she said.

"I'm sorry, what did you—"

There was a knock on the jamb. "Enter," Amalya called out.

One of their sisters came in and bowed low. "The Chosen Layla is readied from the baths for His Majesty, the Primale."

"Ah, good." Amalya reached for an incense burner. "Let us install her at his temple, and then I shall summon him."

"As you wish." While the Chosen bowed her head and backed out of the room, Cormia caught the smile of anticipation on the female's face.

She probably hoped to be next in line for a trip to the temple.

"Will you excuse me?" Cormia said, heart beating erratically, an instrument that couldn't find its beat. "I'm going to retire to the Scribes' Temple."

"Of course." Abruptly, Amalya's eyes grew shrewd. "Are you sure about this, my sister?"

"Yes. And this is a glorious day for all of us. I'll be sure to record it properly."

"I shall have meals delivered unto you."

"Yes. Thank you."

"Cormia . . . I am here for you should you need counsel. In a private capacity."

Cormia bowed and left in a hurry, going directly to the solid white temple that was now her home.

When she shut the door behind herself, she was enveloped by a dense pitch-black darkness. At her will, candles positioned at the four corners of the high-ceilinged room lit, and, in their glow, she looked at the six white desks with their white quill pens standing at attention and their pots of sanguinary ink and their crystal bowls of seeing water. In baskets on the floor, sheaves of parchment were rolled and tied with white ribbon, ready to accept the symbols of the Old Language that would preserve the race's progress.

Against the far wall, there were three double-layered bunks, each set with a single pristine pillow and made up with sheets that were precisely folded. No blankets were bundled at the feet of the beds, as the temperature was too perfect for extra covers to be required. Off to one side, there was a curtain that led into the private bath.

Over to the right there was an ornate silver door that led into the Scribe Virgin's private library. The sequestered scribes were the only ones to whom Her Holiness dictated her private diary, and when they were summoned, they used that door to take the audience they were granted.

The slot in the center of the portal was used to slip parchments generated by both recording and sequestered scribes back and forth during the editing process. The Scribe Virgin read and approved or edited all history until she found it appropriate. Once accepted, a scroll was either cut to size and bound with other pages to become one of the volumes in the library, or it was rolled and placed in the Scribe Virgin's sacred archives.

Cormia went over to one of the desks and sat down on the back-less stool.

The silence and the isolation were as agitating as a teeming crowd, and she had no idea how long she sat there, struggling to get control of herself.

She'd assumed she could do this—that the sequestering solution was the only one that would work. Now she was screaming to get out.

Maybe she just needed something else to focus on.

Taking the white-plumed quill into her hand, she opened the pot of ink to her right. To warm up, she began by composing some of the simpler characters of the Old Language.

She couldn't keep it up, though.

The letters became geometric designs. The designs turned into rows of boxes. The boxes turned . . . into building plans.

Back in the Brotherhood's mansion, John's head lifted from his pillow as he heard a knock on his door. Shifting off his bed, he went over and answered the knuckle-rap. Out in the hall, Qhuinn and Blay were standing side by side, shoulder-to-shoulder, just like they always did.

At least one thing had apparently gone right.

"We need to find Blay a room," Qhuinn said. "You got any idea where we should stuff him?"

"And I should get some of my things at nightfall," Blaylock tacked on. "Which would mean a trip back to my house."

No problem, John signed.

Qhuinn was in the room that adjoined his, so he went down one farther and opened the door into a pale lavender guest room.

We can change the decor, John signed, *if it's too girlie.*

Blay laughed. "Yeah, I'm not sure I can rock this."

As the guy went over and tested out the bed, John walked to the bathroom's double doors and pushed them open—

Phury was passed out with his head next to the toilet, his huge body lax, his face the color of candle wax. At his feet were a needle and a spoon and a belt.

"Fuckin' hell!" Qhuinn's curse echoed around all the creamy marble.

John wheeled around. *Get Doc Jane. Right now. She's probably in the Pit with Vishous.*

Qhuinn tore off as John rushed over and rolled Phury onto his back. The Brother's lips were blue, but not because of all the bruising John's fists had done. The male wasn't breathing. Hadn't been for a while.

Against all odds, Doc Jane came in with Qhuinn literally a split second later. "I was on my way to see Bella— Oh . . . shit."

She came over and did the fastest vitals check John had ever seen. Then she popped open her doctor's bag and took out a needle and a vial.

"Is he alive."

All four of them looked toward the bathroom's doorway. Zsadist was standing there, feet planted, scarred face pale.

"Is he . . ." Z's eyes drifted over to what was on the floor next to the Jacuzzi. "Alive."

Doc Jane looked at John and hissed, "Get him the fuck out of here. Now. He doesn't need to see this."

John's blood went cold from what he saw in her face: She wasn't sure she could bring Phury back.

With shock rolling through him, he stood up and went over to Z.

"I'm not leaving," Zsadist said.

"Yes, you are." Doc Jane held up the syringe she'd filled and pressed the plunger. As a hair-width stream of something shot out the tip, she turned back to Phury's body. "Qhuinn, you stay with me. Blaylock, go with them and shut the door."

Zsadist opened up his mouth, but John just shook his head.

It was with the oddest calm that he stepped to the Brother's face, put his hands on both the guy's arms and pushed backward.

And it was in stunned silence that Z let himself get walked out of the room.

Blay shut the doors and stood in front of them, blocking the way.

Z's bleak eyes held on to John's.

All John could do was stare right back into them.

"He can't be gone," Zsadist said hoarsely. "He just can't be. . . ."

FORTY-FOUR

"What do you mean, work?" the guy with the prison tats said.

Lash put his elbows on his knees and looked his new best friend in the eyes. How the two of them had gone from loudmouth loggerheads to cozy as kittens was a testament to the powers of seduction. First you hit head-on to establish equality. Then you showed respect. Then you talked about money.

The other two, the 'banger with *Diego RIP* around his collarbone, and Mr. Clean with the chrome dome and the combats, had inched in and were listening, too. Which was another part of Lash's strategy: Draw the toughest one in and the others will follow.

Lash smiled. "I'm looking for help with enforcement."

Prison Tat's stare was full of dirty deeds done dirt cheap. "You run a bar?"

"Nope." He glanced at RIP. "Guess you could say it's territorial."

The 'banger nodded like he knew all the rules of that board game.

Prison Tat flexed his arms. "What makes you think I'd carry on anything wichu? I don't know you."

Lash leaned back so his shoulders were against the cinder blocks. "Just thought you'd like to make some green. My bad."

As he closed his eyes like he was going to sleep, he heard voices that popped open his lids. An officer was bringing another offender down to the holding cell.

Well, what do you know. The guy with the eagle jacket from Screamer's.

The newbie was let in, and the three hard-asses pulled their glaring, watch-yer-ass welcome wagon. One of the junkies looked up and offered a watery smile like he knew the guy in a business capacity.

Interesting. So the guy was a dealer.

Eagle Man sized up the crowd and nodded to Lash in recognition before taking a seat on the other end of the bench. He looked more annoyed than scared.

Prison Tat leaned into Lash. "Didn't say I weren't interested."

Lash shifted his eyes over. "How do I find you to talk terms?"

"You know Buss's Bikes?"

"It's that Harley rehab place on Tremont, right?"

"Yeah. Me and my bro own it. We ride."

"Then you know more people who could help me."

"Maybe. Maybe not."

"What's your name?"

Prison Tat's eyes narrowed. Then he pointed to a depiction of a Harley low-rider that was inked on his arm. "You call me Low."

Diego RIP's foot started tapping, like he was holding something in, but Lash wasn't ready to tango with the gangs or the skinheads. Not yet. Starting small was safer. He'd see if he could add a couple of bikers to the Lessening Society mix. If that worked out, then he'd go trolling. Maybe even get his ass arrested again as an entrée.

"Owens," a cop called out at the door.

"Laters," Lash said to Low. He nodded at Diego, the skinhead, and the dealer and left the druggies to their conversations with the floor.

Out in central processing, he waited while an officer explained page after page of "here are the charges against you," "this is the public defender's office number—you need to call them if you want to get assigned an attorney," "your court date is in six weeks," "if you fail to show, your bail will be forfeited and an arrest warrant will be issued," blah, blah, blah . . .

He signed the name Larry Owens a couple of times, and then he was let out into the hall he'd been led down while handcuffed eight hours ago. At the end of the linoleum stretch, Mr. D was sitting in a grotty plastic chair, and as he got to his feet he seemed relieved.

"We're going for food," Lash said as they headed toward the exit.

"Yes, suh."

Lash walked out of the front of the CPD's building, too distracted by the things he needed to do to think about the time. When the sunshine hit him square in the face, he reared back with a scream and slammed into Mr. D.

Covering his face, he scrambled back for the building.

Mr. D caught him by the upper arms. "What—"

"The sun!" Lash was almost back through the doors when he realized . . . nothing was happening. There was nothing up in flames, no great ball of fire, no horrible burning demise.

He stopped . . . and turned around to face the sun for the first time in his life. "It's so bright." He shielded his eyes with his forearm.

"You're not supposed to look straight into it."

"It's . . . warm."

Falling back against the building's stone facade, he couldn't believe the warmth. As the rays beat into him, they radiated through his skin into his muscles.

He'd never envied humans before. But, God, if he'd known how this felt, he would have all along.

"You okay?" Mr. D asked.

"Yeah . . . yeah, I am." He closed his eyes and just breathed in and out. "My parents . . . they never let me go out. Pretrans are supposed to be able to handle sunlight up until the change, but my mom and dad never wanted to risk it."

"Can't imagine not havin' no sun."

After this, neither could Lash.

Tilting his chin up, he closed his eyes for a moment . . . and vowed to thank his father the next time he saw him.

This was . . . magnificent.

Phury woke up with a burning, foul taste in his mouth. Actually it was all over, like someone had sprayed the inside of his skin with oven cleaner.

Eyes were glued shut. Stomach was a lead ball. Lungs were inflating and deflating with all the enthusiasm of a pair of stoners the day after a Grateful Dead binge. And leading the charge on going absolutely nowhere was his brain, which evidently had flatlined and not been resuscitated along with the rest of his body.

Actually, his chest was pretty much a closed shop as well. Or . . . no, his heart must have still been beating, because . . . well, it had to be, didn't it? Or he wouldn't have thoughts, right?

An image of the gray wasteland came to him, the wizard silhouetted against that vast gray horizon.

Welcome back, sunshine, the wizard said. *That was such bloody fun. When can we do it again?*

Do what again, Phury wondered.

The wizard laughed. *Oh, how easily they forget the fun times.*

Phury groaned and heard someone move.

"Cormia," he croaked.

"No."

That voice, that deep, male voice. So like the one that came out of his own mouth. In fact, it was identical.

Zsadist was with him.

As Phury turned his head, his brain sloshed in his skull, his bone dome nothing but a fish tank that had water and plants and a little treasure chest with bubbles, but nothing with fins in it. Nothing that actually lived.

Z looked as bad as Phury had ever seen him, with dark shadows under his eyes and his lips drawn tight and that scar more visible than ever.

"I dreamed of you," Phury said. God, his voice was just a rasp. "You were singing to me."

Z's head slowly went back and forth. "That wasn't me. Not up for singing anymore."

"Where is she?" Phury asked.

"Cormia? The Sanctuary."

"Oh . . ." *That's right.* He'd driven her there after having sex with her. And then he'd . . . Shot. Up. With. Heroin. "Oh, God."

That happy little realization brought his eyes into proper focus and had him looking around.

All he saw, everywhere, was pale lavender, and he thought of Cormia coming through the closet in the office in her white robe with that rose in her hand. The rose was still there, he thought. She'd left it behind.

"You want something to drink?"

Phury turned back to his twin. Across the way, the guy looked like he felt, worn-out and empty.

"I'm tired," Phury murmured.

Z stood and brought over a glass. "Lift your head up."

Phury did what he was told, even though it made the water level in his tank shift and threaten to spill over. As Zsadist held the glass to his lips, he took one pull, then another, and then he was gulping with desperate thirst.

When it was gone, he let his head fall back down on the pillow. "Thank you."

"More?"

"No."

Zsadist put the glass back on the bedside table and then settled once more in the pale lavender chair, his arms crossing, chin resting almost on his chest.

He'd been losing weight, Phury thought. His cheeks were beginning to stand out again.

"I had no memory," Z said softly.

"Of what?"

"You. Them. You know, where I came from before I was stolen, then bought."

Whether it was the water or what Z had just said, one of the two brought Phury into full consciousness. "You wouldn't have remembered our parents . . . our house. You were just an infant."

"I recall the nursemaid. Well, I have one memory. It was of her putting jam on her thumb and letting me nurse on it. That's about all I have. Next thing . . . I was up on the block with all these folks looking at me." Z frowned. "I grew up as a kitchen boy. I washed a lot of dishes, cleaned a lot of vegetables, fetched ale for the soldiers. They were good to me. That part of it was . . . okay." Z rubbed his eyes. "Tell me something. What was it like for you? The growing-up part."

"Lonely." Okay, that sounded selfish. "No, I mean—"

"I was lonely, too. I felt like I was missing something, but didn't know what it was. I was half of a whole, except there was only me."

"That's how I felt. Except I knew what was missing." The *you* went unsaid.

Z's voice went utterly flat. "I don't want to talk about what happened after I went through the change."

"You don't have to."

Zsadist nodded and seemed to retreat into himself. In the silence that followed, Phury couldn't even imagine what he was remembering. The pain and the degradation and the rage.

"Remember before we joined the Brotherhood," Z murmured, "when I took off for three weeks? We were still in the Old Country and you had no idea where I'd gone?"

"Yeah."

"I killed her. The Mistress."

Phury blinked, surprised at the admission of what everyone had always guessed at. "So it wasn't her husband."

"Nope. Sure, he was violent, but I was the one who did it. See, she'd taken another blood slave in. Put him down in that cage. I . . ." Z's voice wobbled, then became rock solid again. "I couldn't let her do that to someone else. I went back there . . . found him . . . Shit, he was naked and in the same corner I used to . . ."

Phury held his breath, thinking this was everything he had wanted and feared knowing. Odd that they were having the conversation now.

"You used to what?"

"Sit. I used to sit in that corner when I wasn't being . . . Yeah, I sat there, because at least I knew what was coming at me. The kid, he had his back to the wall and his knees up, too. Just exactly how I'd done it. He was young. So young, like just out of his transition. He had pale brown eyes . . . and they were terrified. He thought I was there for him. You know . . . like, there for him. As I came in, I couldn't speak, and that scared him even worse. He shivered . . . he shivered until his teeth rattled, and I still remember what the knuckles of his hands looked like. He was holding on to his skinny calves, and the knuckles were nearly popping out of his skin."

Phury clamped his teeth down, remembering when he'd gotten Zsadist out, recalling the sight of him chained naked to the bedding platform in the middle of that cell. Z hadn't been afraid. He'd been used too much and for too long to be rattled by anything that could be done to him.

Zsadist cleared his throat. "I said to the kid . . . I told him that I

was going to get him out. He didn't believe it at first. Not until I pushed up the sleeves of my coat and showed him my wrists. After he saw my slave bands, I didn't have to say another word. He was with me all the way." Z took a deep breath. "She found us while I was taking him through the castle's lower level. He was having trouble walking, because I guess the day before had been . . . busy. I had to carry him. Anyway, she came up on us . . . and before she could call for the guards, I took care of her. That boy . . . he watched as I snapped her neck and let her fall to the ground. After she was down, I cut off her head because . . . see, neither of us really believed she was dead. Shit, man, I was in that rabbit warren of tunnels, where anyone could have caught us, and I couldn't move. I just stared down at her. The boy, he asked me whether she was truly dead. I said I didn't know. She wasn't moving, but how could I be sure?

"The boy looked up at me, and I'll never forget the sound of his voice. 'She'll come back. She always comes back.' Way I figured it, he and I were living with enough shit, we didn't need to worry about that. So I cut off her head, and he held it by the hair as I got us the fuck out of there." Zsadist rubbed his face. "I didn't know what to do with the kid when I got him free. That's what those three weeks were about. I took him way down to the tip of Italy, as far away as I could get him. There was a family there, one Vishous knew from his years working for that merchant in Venice. Anyway, that household needed help, and they were good people. They took him in as a paid servant. Last thing I heard, about a decade ago, was that he'd had his second young with his *shellan*."

"You saved him."

"Getting him out didn't save him." Zsadist's eyes drifted over. "That's the point, Phury. There isn't any saving him. There isn't any saving me. I know that's what you keep waiting for, living for. But . . . it's never going to happen. Look . . . I can't thank you, because . . . as much as I love Bella and my life and where I am now, I still go back there. I can't help it. I still live it every day."

"But—"

"No, let me finish. This whole drug thing with you . . . Look, you didn't fail me. Because you can't fail at the impossible."

Phury felt a hot tear ease out of his eye. "I just want to make it right."

"I know. But it's never been right and it's never going to be, and you don't have to kill yourself because of that. Where I ended up is where I am."

There was no promise of joy in Z's face. No potential for happiness. The lack of homicidal mania was an improvement, but the absence of any sustainable satisfaction in being alive was hardly cause for celebration.

"I thought Bella had saved you."

"She's done a lot. But right now, with the way the pregnancy's going . . ."

He didn't have to finish. There were no words adequate to describe the horrible what-ifs. And Z had made up his mind he was going to lose her, Phury realized. He'd decided that the love of his life was going to die.

No wonder he didn't want to throw around the thank-yous for being rescued.

Z went on, "I kept the Mistress's skull with me all those years not out of some sick attachment. I needed it for when I had nightmares that she was coming back for me. See, I'd wake up, and the first thing I'd do is check and make sure she was still dead."

"I can understand that—"

"You want to know what I've been doing for the last month or two?"

"Yes . . ."

"I wake up and panic whether you're still alive." Z shook his head. "See, I can reach out through the sheets for Bella and feel her warm body. But you, I can't do that with you . . . and I think my subconscious has figured out that both of you are probably not going to be around a year from now."

"I'm sorry . . . shit . . ." Phury put his hands to his face. "I'm sorry."

"I think you should go. Like, to the Sanctuary. You're going to be safer there. If you stay here, you may not even make it for a year. You need to go."

"I don't know whether that's necessary—"

"Let me be a little clearer. We had a meeting."

Phury dropped his hands. "What kind of a meeting."

"The closed-door kind. Me and Wrath and the Brotherhood. The only way you stay here is if you quit using and become a friend of Bill W.'s. And no one thinks you're going to do that."

Phury frowned. "I didn't know there were vampire NA meetings."

"There aren't, but there are human ones at night. I looked it up on the Web. But that doesn't matter, does it. Because even if you said you'd go, no one believes you would, and I don't think . . . I don't think you believe you would, either."

That was hard to argue, considering what he'd brought into the house and put into his arm.

As he thought about quitting, Phury's palms grew sweaty. "You told Rehv not to sell red smoke to me anymore, didn't you." Which was why Xhex had gone after him when he'd dropped in for that last buy.

"Yeah, I did. And I know it wasn't him who sold you the H. There was an eagle on the package. He marks his with a red star."

"If I go to the Sanctuary, how do you know I won't keep using?"

"I don't." Z stood up. "But I won't have to watch it. And neither will the rest of us."

"You're so damn calm," Phury murmured, almost as an after-thought.

"I saw you dead next to a toilet, and I've had the last eight hours to watch over you and wonder how in the fuck to turn this all around. I'm exhausted and my nerves are shot, and if you haven't tweaked to it, we're all washing our hands of you."

Zsadist turned away and slowly went to the door.

"Zsadist." Z stopped, but didn't turn around. "I'm not going to thank you for this. So I guess we're even."

"Fair enough."

As the door shut, Phury had a strange, disassociative thought that considering all that had just been said was arguably inappropriate.

With Zsadist no longer singing, the world had lost a treasure.

FORTY-FIVE

At the other end of the Brotherhood's compound, about forty feet underground, John sat at the desk in the training center's office and stared at the computer in front of him. He felt like he should be doing something to earn his money, but with classes on hiatus indefinitely, there wasn't a lot of paper pushing to do.

He liked paperwork, so he liked his job. Usually he spent his time recording grades, updating files with training injury reports, and keeping track of the curriculum's progress. It was nice to make order out of chaos, to have everything where it needed to be.

He checked his watch. Blay and Qhuinn were working out in the weight room and they'd be in there for another half hour, minimum.

What to do . . . what to do . . .

On a random impulse, he went through the computer directory and found the folder marked *Incident Reports.* Opening it, he called up the one Phury had filed about the attack on Lash's house.

Jesus . . . Christ. The dead bodies of the parents had been seated around the dining room table, moved there from the sitting room where they had been killed. Nothing else was touched in the house, except for a drawer up in Lash's room, and Phury had jotted down a side note: *personal effect? but of what value as jewelry remained?*

John called up the other reports from the houses that had been attacked. Qhuinn's. Blay's. Three other classmates'. Five other aristo-crats'. Total death toll: twenty-nine, including *doggen.* And the loot-ing had been extensive.

Evidently it had been the most successful series of raids since the sacking of Wrath's family's estate back in the Old Country.

John tried to imagine what Lash had been put through to have those addresses come out of his mouth. He'd been a shit, but he'd had no love for the *lessers.*

Tortured. He had to be dead.

For no particular reason, John went into the guy's computer file. Phury, or someone, had already filled out the death certificate. *Name: Lash, son of Ibix, son of Ibixes, son of Thornsrae. DOB: March 3, 1983. Date of death: approx. August 2008. Age at time of death: 25. Cause of demise: Unconfirmed; assumption torture. Location of body: Unknown, assumption—Lessening Society disposed. Remains released to: N/A.*

The rest of the file was extensive. Lash had had a lot of disci-plinary issues, not just at the training program, but at *glymera* re-treats. It was a surprise to see them in the record at all, given how secretive the aristocracy was with imperfections, but then again, the Brotherhood had required full disclosure of all trainees' histories be-fore you could enter the program.

The guy's birth certificate had been scanned in as well. *Name: Lash, son of Ibix, son of Ibixes, son of Thornsrae. DOB: March 3, 1983, 1:14 a.m. Mother: Rayelle, blooded daughter of the soldier Nellshon. Certification of live birth signed by: Havers, son of Havers, MD. Young released from clinic: March 3, 1983.*

Too weird that the guy was gone.

The phone rang, making him jump. When John picked up the call, he whistled, and V's voice said, "Ten minutes, Wrath's study. We're meeting. You three be there."

The line went dead.

After a moment of *holy shitting*, John ran into the weight room and got Qhuinn and Blay. The two of them pulled the same kind of *whoa* pause, and then they all raced for Wrath's study, even though his buddies were still in their workout sweats.

Up in the king's pale blue digs, all the Brotherhood was there, filling out the room until everything dainty and proper about it was overpowered: Rhage was unwrapping a Tootsie Pop over by the mantel, a grape one going by the purple wrapper. Vishous and Butch were together on an antique couch, the spindly legs of which you had to worry about. Wrath was behind the desk. Z was in the far corner, arms crossed over his chest, eyes staring straight ahead into the middle of the room.

John shut the door and stayed put. Qhuinn and Blay followed his lead, the three of them barely in the room.

"Here's what we got," Wrath said, putting his shitkickers up on the paper-covered desk. "The heads of five of the founding families are dead. Most of what's left of the *glymera* is scattered around the eastern seaboard and in safe houses. Finally. Total losses of life are in the high twenties. Although there's been a massacre or two throughout our history, this is a hit of unprecedented gravity."

"They should have moved faster," V muttered. "Damn fools didn't listen."

"True, but did we really expect anything different? So here's where we are. We should expect some kind of negative response from the Princeps Council in the form of a proclamation against me. My guess is they're going to try to marshal up a civil war. Granted, as long as I'm breathing no one else can be king, but they could make it damn hard for me to rule properly and keep things together." As the Brothers muttered all kinds of nasty things, Wrath held up his hand to stop the chatter. "Good news is, they've got organizational problems, which will give us some time. The Princeps Council's charter says that it must be physically seated in Caldwell and convene its meetings here. They created the rule a couple of centuries ago to make sure the power base didn't go elsewhere. As none of them are in town, and—hello—conference calling didn't exist in 1790 when they drafted the current charter, they can't convene a meeting to change their bylaws or elect a new *leahdyre* until they drag their asses back here, at least for an evening. Given the deaths, that'll be a while, but we're talking weeks, not months."

Rhage bit down on his Tootsie Pop, the crack ricocheting around the room. "Do we have an idea of what hasn't been hit yet?"

Wrath pointed to the far edge of his desk. "I made copies for everyone."

Rhage went over, picked up the stack of papers, and handed them out . . . even to Qhuinn and John and Blay.

John looked at the columns. First was a name. Second was an address. Third was an estimate of the number of folks and *doggen* in the household. Fourth was an approximate value of what was in the place based on the tax roll. Final was whether or not the family had vacated the premises and how much looting had or had not occurred.

"I want you to divvy up the list of the ones we haven't heard from," Wrath said. "If there's anyone still in those houses, I want you to get them out, even if you have to drag them by the hair. John, you and Qhuinn go with Z. Blay, you're going with Rhage. Any questions?"

For no good reason John found himself looking over at the ugly-ass avocado green chair that was behind Wrath's desk. It was Tohr's.

Or had been.

He would have liked Tohr to see him with the list in his hand, ready to go out and defend the race.

"Good," Wrath said. "Now get the fuck out of here and do what I need you to do."

On the other side, in the Temple of the Sequestered Scribes, Cormia rolled up the parchment she had been sketching houses and buildings on and placed it on the floor next to her stool. She had no idea what to do with the thing. Maybe burn it? Wastepaper baskets didn't exist in the Sanctuary.

As she moved a crystal bowl that was full of water from the Scribe Virgin's fountain in front of her, she thought of the ones Fritz had brought her with her peas in them. She missed that hobby of hers already. Missed the butler. Missed . . .

The Primale.

Palming the bowl, she began to rub the crystal, creating ripples in the surface of the water that caught the light of the candles. The warmth of her hands and the subtle movement created a swirling effect, and from out of the gentle waves came the vision of exactly who she wanted to see. Once the image appeared, she stopped agitating the water and let the surface smooth out so she could watch and then describe what she saw.

It was the Primale, and he was dressed the way he'd been that night he'd met her at the top of the stairs and looked at her as if he hadn't seen her for a week. But he wasn't in the Brotherhood's mansion. He was racing down a corridor that was marked with streaks of blood and black heel prints. Bodies were crumpled on the floor on either side, the remains of vampires who had been living just moments before.

She watched as the Primale gathered a small group of terrified males and females and put them into a supply closet. She saw his face as he locked them in, saw the dread and the sadness and the anger in his features.

He'd scrambled to save them, to find a way to safety, to take care of them.

When the vision dimmed, she palmed the bowl once more. Now that she had seen what had transpired, she could call it up again, and she watched his actions once more. Then again.

It was as the movie had been back on the far side, only this was real; this was past that had transpired, not a constructed fictional present.

And then there were other things she saw, scenes tied to the Primale and the Brotherhood and the race. Oh, the horror of the killings, of those dead bodies in luxurious houses . . . the corpses too numerous for her to comprehend. One by one, she saw the faces of those who had been killed by the *lessers*. Then she saw the Brothers out fighting, their numbers so small that John and Blay and Qhuinn were being forced too early into the war.

If this continued, she thought, the *lessers* would win. . . .

She frowned and bent down closer to the bowl.

On the surface of the water, she saw a blond *lesser*, which was not unusual . . . but it had fangs.

There was a knock, and as she jumped from being startled, the image disappeared.

A muffled voice came from the other side of the temple door. "My sister?"

It was Selena, the previous sequestered scribe.

"Greetings," Cormia called out.

"Your meal, my sister," the Chosen said. There was a scraping sound as a tray was slid through a trapdoor. "May it please you."

"Thank you."

"Have you any inquiries of me?"

"No. Thank you."

"I shall come back for the tray." The excitement in the Chosen's voice lifted it nearly an octave. "After his arrival."

Cormia inclined her head, then remembered that her sister couldn't see her. "As you wish."

The Chosen left, no doubt to prepare herself for the Primale.

Cormia leaned back over the desk and looked at the bowl, instead of into it. Such a fragile thing, so thin, except at its base, where it was heavy and solid. The lip of the crystal was sharp as a knife.

She wasn't sure how long she stayed like that. But eventually she shook herself out of her numb trance and forced her palms back onto the bowl.

When the Primale came to the surface again, she wasn't surprised—

She was *horrified*.

He lay sprawled out on a marble floor, unconscious by a toilet. Just as she was about to leap up to do only the Virgin knew what, the image changed. He was in a bed, a pale lavender bed.

Turning his head, he looked straight out of the water at her and said, "Cormia?"

Oh, dearest Virgin Scribe, the sound made her want to weep.

"Cormia?"

She shot to her feet. The Primale was standing in the temple's doorway, dressed in whites, the medallion of his station around his neck.

"Verily . . ." She could go no further. She wanted to rush forward and put her arms around him and hold on. She'd seen him dead. She'd seen him . . .

"Why are you here?" he asked, looking around the barren room. "All by yourself."

"I'm sequestered." She cleared her throat. "As I said I would be."

"So I'm not supposed to be here?"

"You're the Primale. You can be anywhere."

As he walked around the room, she had so many questions, none of which she had any right to ask.

He looked over at her. "No one else is allowed in here?"

"Not unless one of my sisters joins me as a sequestered scribe. Although the Directrix may come in if she is granted leave by me."

"Why is the sequestering necessary?"

"In addition to recording the races's general history, we . . . I see the things the Scribe Virgin wishes to keep . . . private." As the Primale's yellow eyes narrowed, she knew what he was thinking. "Yes, I've seen what you did. In that bathroom."

The curse he let out echoed up to the white ceiling.

"Are you all right?" she asked.

"Yeah. I'm fine." He crossed his arms over his chest. "Are you going to be okay here? All by yourself?"

"I'll be fine."

He stared at her. Long and hard. The sorrow was in his face, in its deep grooves of pain and regret.

"You didn't hurt me," she said. "When we were together, you didn't hurt me. I know you think you did, but you didn't."

"I wish . . . things were different."

Cormia laughed sadly, and on a whim murmured, "You're the Primale. Change them."

"Your Grace?" the Directrix appeared in the open doorway, looking confused. "Whatever are you doing here?"

"Seeing Cormia."

"Oh, but . . ." Amalya seemed to shake herself, as if remembering that the Primale could go wherever he chose and see whomever he wished, as *sequestered* was a term that restricted all but him. "But of course, Your Grace. Ah . . . the Chosen Layla is prepared for you and in your temple?"

Cormia looked down at the bowl in front of her. As Chosen had very short fertility cycles here on this side, it was very likely Layla was either fertile or about to become fertile. No doubt there would be words of the pregnancy to record very soon.

"Time for you to go," she said, glancing up at the Primale.

His eyes positively bored into hers. "Cormia—"

"Your Grace?" the Directrix cut in.

In a hard voice, he said over his shoulder, "I'll be there when I'm good and damned ready."

"Oh, please forgive me, Your Grace, I didn't mean to—"

"That's all right," he said wearily. "Just tell her . . . I'll be there."

The Directrix quickly ducked out, and the door shut.

The Primale's eyes refocused on Cormia, locking in. And then he came across the room with a grave expression on his face.

As he sank down on his knees in front of her, she was shocked. "Your Grace, you shouldn't—"

"Phury. You call me Phury. Never 'Your Grace' or 'Primale.' Starting now, I don't want to hear anything but my real name from you."

"But—"

"No buts."

Cormia shook her head. "All right, except you shouldn't be on your knees. Ever."

"In front of you, I should only be on my knees." He put his hands lightly on her arms. "In front of you . . . I always should be bowed." He looked over her face and her hair. "Listen, Cormia, I need you to know something."

As she looked down at him, his eyes were the most amazing thing she'd ever seen, hypnotic, the color of citrines in firelight. "Yes?"

"I love you."

Her heart clenched. "What?"

"I love you." He shook his head and eased back so he was sitting cross-legged. "Oh, Christ . . . I've made such a mess out of everything. But I love you. I wanted you to know it because . . . well, shit, because it matters, and because it means I can't be with the other Chosen. I can't be with them, Cormia. It's you or it's nobody."

Her heart sang. For a split second, her heart was flying in her chest, soaring on gusts of joy. This was what she had wanted, this pledge, this reality—

Her brilliant happiness dimmed as quickly as it flared.

She thought of the images of the fallen, of the tortured, of the cruelly killed. And the fact that there were now how many fighting Brothers left? Four. Just four.

Centuries ago their numbers had been in the twenties and thir-
ties.

Cormia glanced at the bowl in front of her and then at the quill
she'd used. There was a very real possibility that at some point in the
not-too-distant future there would be no more history to write.

"You need to go to her, to Layla," she said in a voice that was flat
as the parchment she was going to write on. "And you need to go to
them."

"Didn't you hear what I said?"

"Yes. I did. But this is bigger than you and me." She stood up,
because if she didn't move around she was going to go mad. "I'm not
a Chosen anymore, not in my heart. But I've seen what's happening.
The race is not going to survive like this."

The Primale rubbed his eyes with a grimace. "I want you."

"I know."

"If I'm with the others, can you handle that? I'm not sure I can."

"I'm afraid . . . I can't. That's why I chose this." She swept her
hand around the room. "Here I can have peace."

"I can come see you, though. Can't I?"

"You're the Primale. You can do anything." She paused by one of
the candles. Staring into the flame, she asked, "Why did you do what
you did?"

"About becoming the Primale? I—"

"No. The drug. In the bathroom. You almost died." When there
was no response, she looked over at him. "I want to know why."

There was a long silence. And then he said, "I'm an addict."

"An addict?"

"Yeah. I'm proof positive you can come from the aristocracy and
have money and position and you can still be a junkie." His yellow
eyes were brutally clear. "And the truth is, I want to be a male of
worth and tell you I can stop, but I just don't know. I've made promises to myself and to others before. My words . . . they don't hold
water any longer with anyone, including myself."

His word . . .

She thought of Layla waiting, the Chosen waiting, the whole of the race waiting. Waiting for him.

"Phury . . . my dearest beloved Phury, live up to one of your promises now. Go and take Layla and bind yourself to us. Give us history to write and to live and to prosper in. Be the strength of the race, as you should be." As he opened his mouth, she held up her hand to stop him. "You know this is right. You know I am right."

After a tense moment, Phury got to his feet. He was pale and unsteady as he straightened his robe. "I want you to know . . . if I'm with anyone else, it's you in my heart."

She closed her eyes. She had been taught all her life to share, but letting him go to another female was like throwing something precious on the ground and stomping it to dust.

"Go in peace," she said softly. "And come back with the same. Even if I cannot be with you, I will never deny your company."

Phury walked up the knoll to the Primale's Temple with a foot that felt like it was wrapped in chains. Chains and barbed wire.

God, along with feeling weighed down, his real foot and ankle were burning like he'd stepped into a bucket of battery acid. He'd never thought he'd be glad he was missing half a leg, but at least he didn't have to feel that shit in stereo.

The double doors to the Primale Temple were closed, and as he opened one side, he caught the scent of herbs and flowers. Stepping inside, he stood in the vestibule, sensing Layla in the main room beyond. He knew she would be as Cormia had been: lying on the bed with bolts of white cloth falling from the ceiling and pooling at her throat so that only her body was visible.

He stared at the white marble steps that led up to the great swath of drapery he would push aside to get at Layla. There were three steps. Three steps up, and then he would be in the open room.

Phury turned around and sat down on the shallow stairs.

His head felt odd, probably because he hadn't had a blunt in like twelve hours. Odd . . . as in strangely clear. Christ, he was actually lucid. And the byproduct of the clarity was a new voice in his mind talking to him. A new and different one that wasn't the wizard's.

It was . . . his own voice. For the first time in so long, he almost didn't know what it was.

This is wrong.

He winced and rubbed the calf he still had. The burn seemed to be traveling upward from his ankle, but at least when he massaged his muscle it seemed a little better.

This is wrong.

It was hard to disagree with himself. All his life he had lived for others. His twin. The Brotherhood. The race. And the whole Primale thing was right out of that playbook. He'd spent his whole life trying to be a hero, and now not only was he sacrificing himself, he was sacrificing Cormia as well.

He thought of her in that room, alone with those bowls and the quills and all that parchment. Then he saw her up against his body, warm and alive.

Nope, his inner voice said. *I'm not doing this.*

"I'm not going to do this," he said, rubbing at both his thighs.

"Your Grace?" Layla's voice came from the other side of the drapery.

He was about to answer her, when in a rush, the burning sensation swept throughout his body, taking him over, eating him alive, consuming every inch of him. With shaking arms, he reached out to keep himself from falling backward as his stomach knotted.

A strangled sound bubbled up his throat, and then he had to work to draw his breath in.

"Your Grace?" Layla's voice was worried—and closer.

But there was no replying to her. Abruptly, his whole body turned into a snow globe, the inside of him shaking and sparking with pain.

What the . . .

DTs, he thought. It was the fucking DTs, because for the first time in, like, two hundred years his system was without red smoke.

He knew he had two choices: Poof it back to the other side, find a dealer other than Rehvenge, and keep the addict cord plugged into its current socket. Or bite the fucking bullet.

And stop.

The wizard blinked into his mind's eye, the wraith standing at the forefront of the wasteland. *Ah, mate, you can't do it. You know you can't. Why even try?*

Phury took a moment to retch. Shit, he felt like he was going to die. He truly did.

All you have to do is go back to the world and get what you need. You can feel better with the strike of a lighter. That's all. You can make this go away.

The shaking was so bad, Phury's teeth started to knock together like ice cubes in a glass.

You can stop this. All you need to do is light up.

"You lied to me once already. You said I could get rid of you, and you are so not gone."

Ah, mate, what's a wee fib between friends?

Phury thought about the bathroom of that lavender bedroom and what he'd done there. "It's everything."

As the wizard started to get pissed and Phury's body milk-shaked it something fierce, he stretched out his legs, lay down on the vestibule's cool marble floor, and got ready for a whole lot of going-nowhere.

"Shit," he said as he gave himself over to the withdrawal. "This is going to suck."

FORTY-SIX

John and Qhuinn were a couple of yards behind Zsadist as the three of them approached a low-slung modern house. The place was number six on the list of yet-to-be-hit properties, and they stopped in the shadows of a couple of trees at the edge of the lawn.

Standing there, John had a serious case of the creeps. With its sprawling elegance, it was too much like the home he'd had for such a short time with Tohr and Wellsie.

Zsadist looked over his shoulder. "You want to stay here, John?"

When John nodded, the Brother said, "Figured. Creeping me out as well. Qhuinn, you hang with him."

Zsadist strode through the darkness, checking windows and doors. As he disappeared around the back of the house, Qhuinn glanced over.

"Why is this creeping you out?"

John shrugged. *I used to live in something like it.*

"Wow, you had it good as a human."

It was after that.

"Oh, you mean with . . . Right."

God, the house must have been built by the same builder, because the facade and the arrangement of rooms were basically the same. Looking at all the windows, he thought of his bedroom. It had been navy blue with modern lines and a sliding glass door. The closet had been barren when he'd arrived, but it had gotten filled with the first new clothes he'd ever had.

Memories came back, memories of the meal he'd had the night Tohr and Wellsie had taken him in. Mexican food. She'd cooked Mexican food and put it all out on the table, big platters of enchiladas and quesadillas. Back then, when he'd been a pretrans, his stomach had been very delicate, and he could remember feeling mortified that he'd only be able to push the food around his plate.

Except then Wellsie had put a bowl of white rice with ginger sauce in front of him.

As she'd taken her chair, he'd wept, just curled his fragile little body into itself and cried for the kindness. After having spent all his life feeling as if he were different, from out of nowhere he'd found someone who knew what he needed and cared enough to give it to him.

That was a parent, wasn't it. They knew you better than you knew yourself, and they took care of you when you couldn't care for yourself.

Zsadist came back up to them. "Empty and unsacked. Next house?"

Qhuinn looked at the list. "Four Twenty-five Easterly Court—"

Z's phone went off with a soft chime. He frowned as he checked the number, then put the thing up to his ear. "What's up, Rehv?"

John's eyes shifted back to the house, but then returned to Z as the Brother said, "What? Are you kidding me? He showed up where?" Long pause. "You are fucking serious? You're sure, you're one hundred percent sure?" When the Brother hung up, Z stared at the phone. "I have to go home. Right now. Shit."

What is it? John signed.

"Can you guys cover the next three addys?" As John nodded, the Brother looked at him strangely. "Keep your phone close, son. You hear me?"

When John nodded, Z disappeared.

"Okay, clearly whatever that is, it's not our biz." Qhuinn folded up the list and put it in his jeans pocket. "Shall we outtie?"

John glanced back at the house. After a moment, he signed, *I'm sorry about your parents.*

Qhuinn's reply was a while in coming. "Thanks."

I miss mine.

"I thought you were an orphan?"

For a while I wasn't.

There was a long silence. Then Qhuinn said, "Come on, John, let's get out of here. We need to hit Easterly."

John thought for a minute. *You mind if we stop somewhere else first? It's not far.*

"Sure. Where?"

I want to go to Lash's house.

"Why?"

I don't know. I guess I want to see where this all started. And I want to look in his room.

"How're we going to get inside, though?"

If the shutters are still on autotimer, they'll be up, and we can dematerialize through the glass.

"Well . . . hell, if that's where you want to go, okay."

The two of them dematerialized to the side yard of the Tudor. The shutters were up for the night, and in a blink they were standing inside the sitting room.

The smell was so bad, John felt like someone had taken steel wool to the inside of his nose and used the shit like a Q-tip . . . all the way to his frontal lobe.

Covering his mouth and nose, he coughed.

"Fuck," Qhuinn said, doing the same.

The two of them looked down. There was blood all over the car-pet and the sofa, the stains brown from having dried.

They followed the streaks out into the foyer.

"Oh, Jesus . . ."

John lifted his head. Through the lovely archway of the dining room was a scene right out of a Rob Zombie movie. The bodies of Lash's mother and father, seated in what were no doubt their regular chairs, were facing a beautifully set table. Their pallor was that of sidewalk pavement, a pale matte gray, and their fine clothes were like the rugs, streaked in brown.

There were flies.

"Man, those *lessers* are sick, for real."

John swallowed down the bile in his throat and walked over.

"Shit, do you really need a close-up there, buddy?"

Peering into the room, John forced himself to ignore the horror and note the details. The platter that the roasted chicken was on had blood marks on the edges.

The killer had put it on the table. After he'd arranged the bodies, most likely.

Let's go up to Lash's room.

Walking upstairs was totally freaky, because they were alone in the house—but not really. Somehow, the dead downstairs filled the air with something close to sound. Certainly the smell followed John and Qhuinn up the stairwell.

"His crib's on the third floor," Qhuinn said when they got to the second-floor landing.

They walked into Lash's bedroom, and it was such a nonevent compared to the shock of the living room. Bed. Desk. Stereo. Com-puter. TV.

Bureau.

John went over and saw the drawer with the bloody prints. These were too smudged to tell whether or not a swirl pattern had been left.

He picked up a random shirt and used it to open the thing, because that was what they did on the TV shows. Inside, more bloody marks, too smudged to read.

His heart stopped beating and he bent down closer. There was one print that was especially clear, on the corner of a Jacob & Co. watch box.

He whistled to bring Qhuinn's head around. *Do* lessers *leave fingerprints?*

"If they come into contact with something, sure."

I mean, do they leave prints, prints. Not just blanks, but, like, stuff with lines.

"Yeah, they do." Qhuinn came over. "What are you looking at?"

John pointed to the box. On the corner was a perfect reproduction of a thumb . . . that had no discernible ridges. Like a vampire's would.

You don't suppose—

"No. No way. They've never turned a vampire."

John took out his phone and snapped a picture. Then, on second thought, he took the box itself and put it inside his jacket.

"We done?" Qhuinn asked. "Make my night and say yes."

I just . . . John hesitated. *I need a little longer up here.*

"Okay, but I'm going to go through those second-floor bedrooms, then. I can't . . . I can't be in here like this."

John nodded as Qhuinn left, and felt bad. Jesus, maybe it had been cruel even to ask the guy to come here.

Yeah . . . because this was fucked-up. Standing around all this shit of Lash's, it was like he was still alive.

Across town, behind the wheel of the Focus, Lash was not a happy camper. The car was a piece of shit, for real. Even though they were in residential traffic, the beater still had no pickup. For chrissakes, it was zero to thirty in three days.

"We need to upgrade."

In the passenger seat, Mr. D was checking his gun, his slim fingers flying over the weapon. "Yeah . . . um, 'bout that."

"What."

"I think we gonna need to wait 'til the money comes in from the looting."

"What the fuck?"

"I gots me the bank statements, you know, from the last *Fore-lesser*? That Mr. X? They was in his cabin. And there's not a ton in there."

"Define 'not a ton.'"

"Well, it's all gone, basically. I don't know where and I don't know who. But there's about five thousand left."

"Five? Are you fucking kidding me?" Lash let the car decelerate. Which was like taking a vegetable off life support.

Out of money? What the hell? He was like the Prince of Darkness or some shit. And his army's net worth was five grand?

Sure, he had his dead family's money, but as much as that was, he couldn't wage an entire war with it.

"Man, fuck this . . . and I'm going back to my old house. I'm not driving this tin-can piss box anymore." Yeah, he was *so* over the whole mommy/daddy thing all of a sudden. He needed a new car ASAP, and there was a spank Mercedes parked in that Tudor's garage. He was going to get in the damn thing and drive it around, and he wasn't going to feel guilty.

Fuck the whole vampire thing.

As he hung a rightie and shot over toward his neighborhood, though, he started to feel sick to his stomach. Except he wasn't going inside the house, so he wouldn't have to see the bodies, assuming they were still where he'd left them—

Shit, he was going to have to go in for the keys.

Whatever. He needed to grow the fuck up.

Ten minutes later, Lash pulled up by the garages in back and got out of the car. "Take this to the farmhouse. I'll meet you there."

"You sure I shouldn't wait?"

Lash frowned and looked down at his hand. The ring the Omega had given him the night before was warming up on his finger and starting to glow.

"Looks like your sire done wants ya," Mr. D said, getting out of the passenger seat.

"Yeah." *Shit.* "How does this work?"

"You need somewheres private. You gets quiet and he will come to you or take you to him."

Lash looked up at the Tudor and figured that it would do. "I'll see you at the farmhouse. And then I want you to take me to that cabin where all the records are."

"Yes, suh." Mr. D touched the brim of his cowboy hat and slid behind the wheel.

As the Focus wheezed its way back down the drive, Lash went inside through the kitchen. The house smelled really bad, the fruity-nauseating stench of death and decay nearly a solid, it was so strong.

He had done this, he thought. He was responsible for what was stinking up the fine house.

He took out his phone to call Mr. D back, but then hesitated, focusing on his ring. The gold was burning to such a degree, he was surprised it didn't take his finger off.

His sire. His *sire*.

The dead people here were not his.

He had done the right thing.

Lash walked through the butler's door and into the dining room. With his ring glowing, he stared at the people he'd thought were his parents. The truth was in the lies, was it not. All through his life, he'd had to cover up his real nature, camouflage the evil in him. Minor flashes of his true self had come out, sure, but the core that was his engine had been kept hidden.

Now he was free.

Staring at the murdered male and female before him, he abruptly

felt nothing. It was as if he were looking at ghoulish posters hanging off a cinema lobby wall, and his mind accorded them with appropriate weight.

Which was no weight at all.

He touched the dog chain at his neck and felt stupid for the silly feelings that had made him take it. He was tempted to whip it off, but no. . . . The animal it reminded him of had been strong and cruel and powerful.

So it was as a symbol, not from sentiment, that he left it around his neck.

Man, the dead smelled bad.

Lash walked into the foyer and figured the marble floor was as good a place as any to see his true father. Copping a seat, he pulled his legs into himself and felt like an idiot just sitting there. Closing his eyes, he couldn't wait to get this over with and cop the keys to the—

A humming started to displace the silence in the house, the sound emanating from no particular direction.

Lash flipped his eyes open. Was his father coming here? Or taking him somewhere else?

From out of nowhere, a current began to swirl about him, warping his vision. Or perhaps it warped what was around him. In the middle of the maelstrom, though, he was rock steady, struck by an odd confidence. The father would never harm the son. Evil was as evil did, but the blood tie between him and his sire meant he was the Omega.

And, if for self-interest only, the Omega wouldn't hurt itself.

Just as Lash was about to be carried away, when the rush had nearly consumed his corporeal form, he looked up.

John Matthew was on the stairs before him.

FORTY-SEVEN

"My sister," came the hiss from the other side of the temple's door. "My sister."

Cormia looked up from the parchment on which she had been recording the scenes she'd watched of the Primale saving those civilians. "Layla?"

"The Primale is ill. He is calling for you."

Cormia let the quill fall from her hands and flew to the door. Sweeping it open, she stared at her sister's pale, frantic face. "Ill?"

"He is abed, shivering in coldness. Verily, he is unwell. He wouldn't let me help him for the longest time, I dragged him from the vestibule when he lost consciousness."

Cormia put the hood of her robe up. "Are the others—"

"Our sisters are at meal. They are all at the meal. There is no one who will see you."

Cormia hurried out of the sequestered temple, but was blinded by the brilliant light of the Sanctuary. She took Layla's hand until

her eyes adjusted, and the two of them raced for the Primale's temple.

Cormia slipped in through the golden door and swept aside the drapery.

The Primale was lying on the bed with nothing but the silken bottoms of his Sanctuary dress on him. His skin had an unhealthy glow to it and a sheen of sweat. Racked with the shakes, his big body seemed horridly frail.

"Cormia?" he said, reaching out with a palsied hand.

She went over to him, shucking her hood. "I'm here." He strained at the sound of her voice, but then she touched his fingertips and he calmed.

Good God, he was on fire.

"What's wrong?" she said, sitting by him.

"I th-th-th-think th-this is d-detox."

"Detox?"

"N-n-no . . . d-drugs . . . n-n-nnno mo-mo . . . d-d-d-drugsss . . ."

She could barely make out what he was saying, but knew on some level the last thing she should do was offer to get him any of the hand-rolled he'd always smoked.

"Is there anything I can do to ease you?" When he began to lick his dry lips, she said, "Would you like some water?"

"I shall get it," Layla said, heading for the bath.

"Thank you, my sister." Cormia looked over her shoulder. "Bring cloths as well?"

"Yes."

As Layla disappeared behind a curtain across the way, Phury closed his eyes and started turning his head back and forth on the pillow, his speech abruptly evening out. "The garden . . . the garden is full of weeds . . . oh, God, the ivy . . . it's everywhere . . . the statues are covered in it."

When Layla returned with a pitcher and a bowl and some white cloths, Cormia said to her, "Thank you. Now please leave us, my sister."

She had a feeling things were going to get much worse, and that Phury wouldn't want to be seen by others in his delusional state.

Layla bowed. "What shall I speak unto the Chosen when I appear at the meal?"

"Tell them that he is resting after your mating, and that he has requested time to himself. I shall care for him."

"When shall I return?"

"Does the sleep cycle begin soon?"

"Following Thideh prayers."

"Right. Come back after all are settled. If this persists . . . I'll need to go over to the far side and fetch Doc Jane, and you'll have to stay with him."

"Fetch who?"

"A healer. Go. Now. Extol the virtues of his body and your station. Be loud about it." Cormia smoothed Phury's hair back. "The louder you are, the better for him."

"As you wish. And I shall return."

Cormia waited until her sister left, then tried to give him something to drink. He was too out of it to take water, though, unable to focus on what she held to his lips. Giving up, she wetted a cloth and pressed it to his face.

Phury's feverish eyes flipped open and clung to her while she blotted his forehead. "The garden . . . is full of weeds," he said urgently. "Full of weeds."

"Shhh . . ." She dipped the cloth in the bowl again, getting it cool for him. "It's all right."

On a desperate breath, he moaned, "No, it's covered them all up. The statues . . . they're gone . . . I'm gone."

The terror in that yellow stare made her blood run cold. He was hallucinating, clearly out of his mind, but whatever he was seeing

was very real to him—he was getting more agitated by the second, his body twisting and turning in the white sheets.

"The ivy . . . oh, God, the ivy is coming for me . . . it's all over my skin—"

"Shh . . ." Maybe she couldn't handle this on her own. Maybe . . . Except if his mind was the problem, then— "Phury, listen to me. If there is ivy overgrowing things, then we shall clean it up."

His thrashing slowed, his eyes focusing a little. "We . . . will?"

She thought of the landscapers she'd watched on the far side. "Yes. We are going to get rid of it."

"No . . . we can't. It will win. . . . It will—"

She leaned down, getting right in his face. "Says. Who." Her forceful voice seemed to get his attention. "Now tell me, where should we start cutting it back?"

When he began to shake his head, she clamped her hand on his jaw. "Where do we start."

He blinked at her command. "Ah . . . it's worst at the statues of the four stages . . ."

"Okay. Then we go there first." She tried to picture the four stages . . . infancy, youth, middle age, and the eve of passing. "We will start with the infant. And what tools shall we use?"

The Primale closed his eyes. "The shears. We will use the shears."

"And what shall we do with the shears."

"The ivy . . . the ivy is growing all over the statues. You can't . . . see the faces any longer. It . . . chokes the statues. They are not free . . . they can't see. . . ." The Primale started to weep. "Oh, God. I can't see anymore. I've never been able to see . . . past the weeds of that garden."

"Stay with me. Listen to me—we're going to change that. Together we're going to change that." Cormia took his hand and pressed it to her lips. "We have shears. Together, we're going to cut free the ivy. And we're going to begin with the statue of the young." She was encouraged, as Phury took a deep breath, as if he were approaching a big job. "I'm going to peel the ivy from the face of the young and you are going to cut it. Can you see me?"

"Yes . . ."

"Can you see you?"

"Yes."

"Good. Now I want you to cut the piece of ivy I'm holding. Do it. Now."

"Yes . . . I will . . . yes, I am."

"And you place what you've cut on the ground at our feet." She brushed his hair back from his face. "And now you cut again . . . and again. . . ."

"Yes."

"And again."

"Yes."

"Now . . . can you see some of the statue's face?"

"Yes . . . yes, I can see the young's face. . . ." A tear ran down his cheek. "I can see it. . . . I can see . . . me in it."

In Lash's house on the far side, John stopped on the stairs and thought maybe the creep factor in the Tudor had shorted his brain out.

Because that couldn't possibly be Lash down below, sitting cross-legged on the floor of the foyer, a warping blur swirling around him.

While John's brain tried to tease out what was reality and what couldn't possibly be real, he noticed that the sweet smell of baby powder permeated the air, nearly turning the shit pink. God, it didn't eclipse the nauseous bouquet of death—it enhanced that godawful rotting stench. The reason the scent had always made him sick was because it was just like the bouquet of death.

At that moment, Lash looked up. He seemed as shocked as John was, but then he gradually smiled.

From out of the malestrom, the guy's voice drifted up the stairs, seeming to come from a distance greater than the number of yards between them.

"Well, hello, John-boy." The laugh was familiar and bizarre at the same time, echoing strangely.

John palmed his gun, steadying it with both hands as he trained it on whatever was down there.

"I'll see you soon," Lash said as he went two-dimensional, becoming an image of himself. "And I'll give your regards to my father."

His form blinked on and off and then disappeared, swallowed up by the warping rush.

John lowered his weapon, then holstered it. Which was what you did when there was nothing around to shoot.

"John?" The beat of Qhuinn's boots came from behind him on the stairwell. "What the hell are you doing?"

I don't know. . . . I thought I saw . . .

"Who?"

Lash. I saw him right down there. I . . . well, I thought I saw him.

"Stay here." Qhuinn took his gun out and hit the stairs, doing a sweep of the first floor.

John slowly went down to the foyer. He'd seen Lash. Hadn't he?

Qhuinn came back. "Everything's tight. Look, let's go back home. You don't seem right. Did you eat tonight? And while we're at it, when was the last time you slept?"

I . . . I don't know.

"Right. We're leaving."

I could have sworn . . .

"Now."

As they dematerialized back to the mansion's courtyard, John thought maybe his buddy was right. Maybe he should grab some food and—

They didn't make it into the house. Just as they arrived, the Brotherhood filed out of the grand double doors one by one. Collectively, they were wearing enough weapons to qualify as a full-on militia.

Wrath pegged him and Qhuinn with a hard stare through his

wraparounds. "You two. In the Escalade with Rhage and Blay. Unless you need more ammo?"

When they both shook their heads, the king dematerialized along with Vishous, Butch, and Zsadist.

When they got into the SUV, with Blay riding shotgun, John signed, *What's going on?*

Rhage stomped on the gas. As the Escalade roared and they shot out of the courtyard, the Brother said dryly, "Visit from an old frenemy. The kind you wish you never saw again."

Well, wasn't that the theme for the evening.

FORTY-EIGHT

The dream . . . hallucination . . . the whatever-it-was felt real. Totally and completely real.

Standing in the overgrown garden of his family's house in the Old Country, beneath a brilliant full moon, Phury reached up to the face of the third-stage statue and pulled the ivy vines free of the eyes and nose and mouth of the male who so proudly bore his own young in his arms.

By now, Phury was an old pro at the cutting, and after he'd worked the shears' magic, he tossed another green tangle to the tarp that lay on the ground at his feet.

"There he is," he whispered. "There . . . he is. . . ."

The statue had long hair just like him, and deep-set eyes just like him, but the radiant happiness on its face was not his. Nor was the young cradled in his arms. Still, there was liberation to be had as Phury continued to strip off the ivy's messy layers of overgrowth.

When he was finished, the marble underneath was streaked with the green tears of the weeds' demise, but the majesty of the form was undeniable.

A male in his prime with his young in his arms.

Phury looked over his shoulder. "What do you think?"

Cormia's voice was all around him, in stereo, even though she stood right next to him. "I think he is beautiful."

Phury smiled at her, seeing in her face all the love he had for her in his heart. "One more."

She swept her hand around. "But look, the last one's already done."

And so the final statue was; its weeds gone, along with any stains of neglect. The male was old now, seated with a staff in his hands. His face was still handsome, though it was wisdom, not the bloom of youth, that made it so. Standing behind him, tall and strong, was the young he had once cradled in his arms.

The cycle was complete.

And the weeds were no more.

Phury glanced back at the third stage. It too was magically clean, and so were the youth and the infant statues as well.

In fact, the entire garden had been righted and now rested beneath the warm, dulcet night in full, healthy bloom. The fruit trees beside the statues were heavy with pears and apples, and the walkways were bordered with neat boxwood hedges. Inside the beds, the flowers thrived in graceful disorder, as all fine English gardens did.

He turned to the house. The shutters that had hung cockeyed from their hinges were righted, and the holes in the tile roof were no more. The stucco was smooth, its cracks having disappeared, and every glass pane was intact. The terrace was free of leaf debris, and the sinking spots that had gathered rain were level again. Potted arrangements of thriving geraniums and petunias sprinkled white and red among woven wicker chairs and tables.

Through the living room window, he saw something move—could it be? Yes, it was.

His mother. His father.

The pair came into view, and they were as the statues had become: resurrected. His mother with her yellow eyes and her blond hair and her perfect face . . . His father with his dark hair and his clear stare and his kind smile.

They were . . . impossibly beautiful to him, his holy grail.

"Go to them," Cormia said.

Phury walked up onto the terrace, his white robing clean in spite of all the work he had done. He approached his parents slowly, afraid of displacing the vision.

"Mahmen?" he murmured.

His mother put her fingertips to her side of the glass.

Phury reached out and mirrored the exact position of her hand. As his palm hit the pane, he felt the warmth of her radiating through the window.

His father smiled and mouthed something.

"What?" Phury asked.

We are so proud of you . . . son.

Phury squeezed his eyes shut. It was the first time he'd ever been called that by either of them.

His father's voice continued. *You can go now. We're fine here now. You've fixed . . . everything.*

Phury looked at them. "Are you sure?"

Both of them nodded. And then his mother's voice came through the clean glass.

Go and live now, son. Go . . . live your life, not ours. We are well here.

Phury stopped breathing and just stared at them both, drinking in what they looked like. Then he placed his hand over his heart and bent at the waist.

It was a farewell. Not a good-bye, but a fare . . . well. And he had the sense they would.

Phury's eyes flipped open. Looming over him was a dense cloud cover . . . no, wait, that was a lofty ceiling made of white marble.

He turned his head. Cormia was seated beside him and holding his hand, her face as warm as the feeling in his chest.

"Would you like something to drink?" she said.

"Wh . . . at?"

She reached over and lifted a glass off the table. "Would you like a drink?"

"Yes, please."

"Lift your head up for me."

He took a test sip and found the water all but ephemeral. It tasted like nothing and was the exact temperature of his mouth, but swallowing it felt good, and before he knew it he'd polished off the glass.

"Would you like more?"

"Yes, please." Evidently that was the extent of his vocabulary.

Cormia refilled the glass from a pitcher, and the chiming sound was nice, he thought.

"Here," she murmured. This time she held his head up for him, and as he drank, he stared into her lovely green eyes.

When she went to take the glass from his lips, he clasped her wrist in a gentle hold. In the Old Language he said, *I would wake like this always, bathing in your stare and your scent.*

He expected her to pull away. Get flustered. Shut him down. Instead she murmured, "We cleaned up your garden."

"Yes . . ."

There was a knock upon the temple's double doors.

"Wait before you answer that," she said, looking around.

Cormia put the glass down and padded across the marble. After she took cover in some yards of white velvet draping across the way, he cleared his throat.

"Yeah?" he called out.

The Directrix's voice was kind and respectful. "May I enter, Your Grace?"

He pulled a sheet over himself even though he had his pants on, then double-checked that Cormia wasn't visible. "Yes."

The Directrix pulled back the vestibule's curtain and bowed low. There was a covered tray in her hands. "I have brought you an offering from the Chosen."

As she straightened, the glow in her face told him that Layla had lied, and lied well.

He didn't trust himself to sit up, so he beckoned her with his hand.

The Directrix approached the bedding platform and knelt before him. As she lifted the gold top, she said, "From your mates."

Lying on the tray, folded as precisely as a map, was an embroidered neck scarf. Made of satin, and inlaid with jewels, it was a spectacular work of art.

"For our male," the Directrix said, bowing her head.

"Thank you." *Shit.*

He took the scarf and splayed it out in his palms. Citrines and diamonds spelled out in the Old Language *Strength of the Race.*

As the gems sparkled, he thought they were like the females here in the Sanctuary, held so tightly in their platinum settings.

"You have made us very happy," Amalya said with a tremor in her voice. She got up and bowed again. "Is there anything we may get you to repay this joy of ours?"

"No, thank you. I'm just going to rest."

She bowed once more, and then was gone like a gentle breeze, departing in a silence that was tragically full of anticipation.

Now he sat up, but only with help from his arms. On the vertical, his head was a balloon, light and full of nothing, bobbing on his spine. "Cormia?"

She stepped out from behind the drapery. Her eyes went down to the scarving, then returned to him. "Do you need Doc Jane?"

"No. I'm not sick. It was the DTs."

"So you said. I'm not clear on what that is, though."

"Withdrawal." He rubbed at his arms, thinking it wasn't over yet. His skin was itching and his lungs were burning as if they needed air, even though they had it.

What they wanted, he knew, was red smoke.

"Is there a bathroom through there?" he said.

"Yes."

"Will you wait for me? I won't be long. I'm just going to wash."

It will be longer than her lifetime before you return cleansed, the wizard said.

Phury closed his eyes, abruptly losing the strength to move.

"What is it?"

Tell her your old mate is back.

Tell her your old mate is never leaving.

And then let's get over to the real world and get what will take care of that tight feeling in your lungs and that itching all over your skin.

"What is it?" Cormia asked again.

Phury took a deep breath. He didn't know much at the moment, barely his own name, and certainly not who the president of the United States was. But he was sure about one thing: If he listened to the wizard anymore, he was going to be dead.

Phury focused on the female before him. "It's nothing."

That didn't go down well in wasteland. The wizard's robes blew up as a wind came barreling in over the field of bones.

You lie to her! I am everything! I am everything! The wizard's voice was high-pitched and getting higher. *I am—*

"Nothing," Phury said weakly, hefting himself to his feet. "You are nothing."

"What?"

As he shook his head, Cormia reached out to him, and he steadied himself with her help. Together, they walked into the bath, which was kitted out like any other save for the fact that there wasn't a logo on the toilet. Well, that and there was a stream running right through the back of the room—which he presumed served as the bath.

"I'll be right outside," Cormia said, leaving him to it.

After using the loo, he waded into the stream with the help of a set of marble stairs. The water rushing by was as it had been in the

glass, a current precisely the temperature of his skin. Over in a dish in the corner, there was a bar of what he assumed was soap, and he picked it up. It was soft, shaped in the form of a crescent; he cradled the bar in his palms and submersed his hands in the water. The suds that formed were tight and small, a froth that smelled of evergreens. He used it on his hair and his face and his body, breathing in so the scent went down into his lungs—and hopefully could cleanse them of the centuries of self-medication he'd been sucking in deep.

When he was done, he just let the water run past his itching skin and his aching muscles. Closing his eyes, he shut the wizard off as best he could, but it was tough because the guy was throwing a tantrum of nuclear proportions. In his old life, he would have put opera on, but now he couldn't—and not just because Bose didn't exist on this side. That particular kind of music reminded him too much of his twin . . . who wasn't singing anymore.

Still, the sound of the stream was lovely, its soft, musical chiming echoing up from the smooth stones as if the noise were skipping from one to another.

Not wanting to keep Cormia waiting, he planted his soles on the riverbed and lifted his upper body out of the rush. The water sluiced off his chest and down his stomach, like soothing hands, and, lifting his arms up, he felt it drop from his fingers and his elbows.

Running down . . . pouring down . . . easing down . . .

The wizard's voice tried to rise up and take over. Phury heard it in his head, fighting for airtime, fighting to find purchase in his inner ear.

But the chiming of water was louder.

Phury drew in a great breath, smelling the evergreen and feeling a freedom that had nothing to do with where his body was, and everything to do with where his head was at.

For the first time, the wizard was not bigger than he was.

Cormia paced around the Primale temple. Not ill. In withdrawal. Not ill.

She stopped at the foot of the bedding platform.

She remembered being strapped down and hearing a male enter and being utterly terrified. Unable to see, unable to move, and not permitted to say no, she'd lain there at the mercy of tradition.

Each virgin female, after she went through her transition, was presented to the Primale like that.

Surely others must have felt the fear she had. And more would, in the future.

God . . . this place was dirty, she thought, looking around at the white walls. Dirty with lies both spoken and left to lie intrinsic in the hearts of the females who breathed the still air.

There was an old saying among the Chosen, the sort of ancient stanza that one never knew when one had first heard it. *Rightful is the cause of our faith, serene be our countenance of duty, nothing shall harm we the believers, for purity is our strength and our virtue, the parent to guide our child.*

There was a wild roar from the bath.

Phury screaming.

Cormia wheeled around and raced into the other room.

She found him naked in the stream, rearing back, his fists clenched, his chest craning upward, his spine straining. Except he wasn't screaming. He was laughing.

His head came around, and when he saw her he dropped his arms, but didn't stop his laughter. "Sorry . . ." As more of the wild joy bubbled up out of him, he tried to keep it in, but he couldn't. "You must think I'm crazy."

"No . . ." She thought he was beautiful, his golden skin slick from the water, his hair falling in thick ringlets down his back. "What's funny?"

"Pass me a towel?"

She handed him a bolt of cloth, and didn't look away as he emerged from the stream.

"You ever hear of *The Wizard of Oz*?" he said.

"Is it a story?"

"Guess not." He secured the wrap by tucking it into itself. "Maybe someday I'll show you the movie. But that's what I was laughing at. I got it wrong. It wasn't an all-powerful Ring-wraith in my head. It was the Wizard from Oz, nothing but a frail old man. I only thought he was terrifying and stronger than I am."

"Wizard?"

He tapped his temple. "Voice in my head. Bad one. The one I smoked to get away from. I thought he was this huge, overwhelming Ring-wraith. He wasn't. He isn't."

It was impossible not to join in Phury's happiness, and as she smiled at him, a sudden warmth suffused her from heart to soul.

"Yeah, it was a big, loud voice that is nothing special." His palm went to his upper arm, and he rubbed at his skin as if it had a rash—except there was nothing that she could see marring its smooth perfection. "Big . . . loud . . ."

Phury's stare abruptly changed as he looked at her. And she knew the cause. Heat flared in his eyes as his sex thickened at his hips.

"Sorry," he said, reaching down for another long cloth and holding it in front of himself.

"Did you lay with her?" Cormia blurted.

"Layla? No. I got as far as the vestibule when I decided I couldn't go through with it." He shook his head. "It's just not going to happen. I can't be with anyone but you. The question is what to do now—and for better or worse I think I know the answer. I believe that all this"—he motioned his hand around, as if encompassing everything in and about the Sanctuary—"this can't go on any longer. This system, this way of life, it's not working. You're right, it's not just about us, it's about everyone. It's not working for anyone."

As his words sank in, she thought of the place in the race she had been born into. Thought of the white rolling lawns and the white buildings and the white robes.

Phury shook his head. "There used to be two hundred Chosen,

right? Back when there were thirty or forty Brothers, right?" When she nodded, he stared down into the rushing water of the stream. "And now how many are left? You know, it's not just the Lessening Society that's killing us. It's these damn rules we live under. I mean, come on. The Chosen aren't protected here, they're imprisoned. And they're mistreated. If you hadn't been attracted to me, it wouldn't have mattered. You still would have had to have sex with me, and that's cruel. You and the sisters are trapped here, serving a tradition I wonder how many of you actually believe in. Life as a Chosen . . . it's not about choice. None of you has any. Take your own case—you don't want to be here. You came back because you had no options, didn't you?"

Three words came out of her mouth, three impossible words that changed everything: "Yes, I did."

Cormia lifted up her robing and let it fall back into place, thinking of that scroll that was on the floor back at the Temple of the Sequestered Scribes, the one with her sketches of buildings on it, the one she had nowhere to go with.

Now she was the one shaking her head. "I never knew how much I didn't know about myself until I went over to the far side. And I have to believe the others are the same. They must be . . . it can't just be me who has talents undiscovered or interests unrevealed." She paced around the bath. "And I don't think any one of us doesn't feel like a failure—if only because the pressures are so great that everything elevates to a level of supreme and total importance. One small error, either in a word written incorrectly or a note off-pitch in a chant or a stitch done wrong in a bolt of cloth, and you feel like the whole of the race is disappointed in you."

Suddenly, she couldn't stop the words falling from her lips. "You are so right. This is *not* working. The purpose of us is to serve the Scribe Virgin, but there's got to be a way of doing that while honoring ourselves." Cormia looked across at Phury. "If we are her Chosen children, doesn't that mean that she wants the best for us? Isn't that

what parents want for their young? How is this . . ." She looked around at the all-pervasive, stifling white of the bath. "How is this the best? For most of us, it's more like a deep freeze than a life. We're in suspended animation even though we move. How . . . is this best for us?"

Phury's brows went down. "It's not. It's fucking not."

He wadded up the long cloth in his hands and slammed it to the marble floor. Then he grabbed the Primale medallion and tore it off his neck.

He was going to step down, she thought, both elated and disappointed for the future. He was going to step down—

Phury lifted up the heavy weight of gold, the medallion swinging on its length of leather, and she lost her breath completely. The expression on his face was one of purpose and power, not of irresponsibility. The light in his eyes was about ownership and leadership, not ducking or shirking. Standing before her, he was the whole landscape of the Sanctuary, all the buildings and the land and the air and the water: He was not of this world, but the world here itself.

After a lifetime of watching history unfold in a bowl of water, Cormia realized as she measured the medallion being held aloft that for the first time she was seeing history made right in front of her, in live time.

Nothing was ever going to be the same after this.

With that emblem of his exalted station waving back and forth under his fisted grip, Phury proclaimed in a hard, deep voice, "I am the strength of the race. I am the Primale. *And so shall I rule!*"

FORTY-NINE

On the outskirts of Caldwell, in the temperate summer night, the Brotherhood was gathered together under a fat, heavenly moon—and wondering what the hell was going on. As the Escalade pulled up next to their tight group, John was amazed to be among them. Popping his seat belt free, he got out as Rhage shut the SUV down. Blay and Qhuinn fell in side by side, and together, the three of them walked over to the Brothers.

The meadow up ahead stretched out between a collar of pine trees, the grass marked by stands of goldenrod and the occasional frothy-mopped milkweed.

Vishous lit one of his hand-rolls, the scent of Turkish tobacco drifting over. "Fucker is late."

"Easy, V," Wrath said under his breath. "I will relieve your ass if you can't stay tight."

"Fucker. Not you, him."

"Butch, chain your boy, would you? Before I muzzle him with a goddamn pine tree."

The glow came from the east, starting out small as the flick of a lighter, then growing big as the sun. As it gathered in the forest, the light was filtered by trunks and branches, and John thought of the nuclear bomb test films he'd seen in school, the ones where the trees and everything were leveled flat after the great burst of illumination.

"Please tell me that shit isn't radioactive," Qhuinn said.

"Nah," Rhage replied. "But we're all going to have tans in the morning."

Butch put his arm up to shield his eyes. "And me without my Coppertone."

Except none of their weapons were drawn, John noted. Although they were tense as cats.

Suddenly, from out of the trees came a man . . . a glowing man, the source of the light. And there was something draped over his arms, a tarp or a rug or—

"Son of a bitch," Wrath breathed as the figure stopped twenty yards away.

The glowing man laughed. "Well, if it isn't good King Wrath and his band of merry-merry happy-happy. I swear you boys should do kiddie shows, you're so fucking cheery."

"Great," Rhage muttered, "his sense of humor's still intact."

Vishous exhaled. "Maybe I can try to beat it out of him."

"Use his own arm to do it, if you can—"

Wrath glared at the two of them, who shot him back a pair of *who-us?* stares.

The king shook his head and addressed the lit figure. "Been a while. Thank God. How the hell are you?"

Before the man could answer, V cursed. "If I have to hear all that Keanu Reeves, *Matrix*, 'I am Neo' kind of shit, my head's going to explode."

"Don't you mean Neon?" Butch shot back. " 'Cause he reminds me of the Citgo sign."

Wrath's head turned. "Shut the fuck up. All of you."

The glowing figure laughed. "So do you want your early Christmas present? Or you going to keep dissing my shit until I decide to take off."

"Christmas? I believe that's your tradition, not ours," Wrath said.

"So, is that a no? Because it's something you've been missing for a while." With that, the glow dissipated, like someone had unplugged the light source.

Standing in the clearing now was a man like any other . . . well, sort of like any other, given that he was draped in gold chains. There was someone in his arms, a bearded male with a streak of white running through his dark hair. . . .

John's whole body tingled.

"Don't recognize your brother?" the figure said, then looked down at the male he held. "How soon they forget."

John was the one who broke ranks and ran through the long grass. Someone shouted his name, but he wasn't stopping for anyone or anything. He ran as fast as his legs would carry him, the wind roaring in his ears, his blood pounding through his veins.

The meadow lashed against his jeans, and the cool August night slapped at his cheeks, and the straining fists his hands had cranked into beat at the air.

Father, he mouthed. *Father!*

John bounced to a halt and then covered his mouth with his palm. It was Tohrment, but it was a shrunken version of the Brother, as if he had been left out in the sun for months. His face was gaunt, the skin hanging loose from the bones, the eyes sunk deep into the skull. The beard was long and dark, the shaggy hair nothing but a black tangled nest except for the brilliant, snowy white stripe at the front. His clothes were the exact same ones he'd been wearing the

night he had disappeared from the training center, all tattered and filthy.

John jumped as a hand landed on his shoulder.

"Easy, son," Wrath said. "Jesus Christ—"

"Actually it's Lassiter," the man said, "in case you forgot."

"Whatever. So what's the price?" the king asked, reaching out to take Tohr.

"I like how you assume there is one."

John wanted to be the person who took Tohrment back to the car, but his knees were knocking so badly he probably needed to be carried too.

"Isn't there a price?" As Wrath accepted his brother's body, the king shook his head. "Shit, he doesn't weigh a thing."

"He's been living off deer."

"How long have you known about him?"

"Found him two days ago."

"Price," Wrath said, still looking at his brother.

"Well, here's the thing." As the king cursed, the man, Lassiter, laughed. "It's not a price, though."

"What. Is. It."

"We're a two-for-one deal."

"Excuse me?"

"I come with him."

"The fuck you do."

The man lost any levity in his voice. "It's part of the arrangement, and believe me, I wouldn't choose this either. Fact is, he's my last chance, so yeah, I'm sorry, but I go with him. And if you say no, by the way, I'm going to level us all like that."

The man snapped his fingers, a brilliant white spark flaring against the night sky.

After a moment, Wrath turned to John. "This is Lassiter, the fallen angel. One of the last times he was on earth, there was a plague in central Europe—"

"Okay, that was *so* not my fault—"

"—that wiped out two-thirds of the human population."

"I'd like to remind you that you don't like humans."

"They smell bad when they're dead."

"All you mortal types do."

John could barely follow the conversation; he was too busy staring into Tohr's face. Open your eyes . . . open your eyes . . . please God . . .

"Come on, John." Wrath turned back to the Brotherhood and started walking. When he came up to them, he said softly, "Our brother is returned."

"Oh, Christ, is he alive," someone said.

"Thank God," someone else groaned.

"Tell them," Lassiter demanded from behind. "Tell them he comes with a roommate."

As one, the Brothers' heads snapped up.

"Fuck. Me," Vishous breathed.

"I will so pass on that," Lassiter muttered.

FIFTY

Phury walked through the glowing white expanse of the Sanctuary, going over to the Scribe Virgin's private entry. He knocked once and he waited, willing a request for an audience.

When the doors opened, he expected the Directrix Amalya to be the one who greeted him, but there was nobody on the other side. The Scribe Virgin's white courtyard was empty save for the birds in their white-blossomed tree.

The finches and canaries were out of place, and all the more lovely for it. Their colors were bright against their background of white branches and leaves, and hearing their calls, he thought of the number of times Vishous had come over here with one of the fragile things cupped in his palms.

After the Scribe Virgin had given them up for her son, the son had returned them to her.

Phury went over to the fountain and listened to the water fall into its marble basin. He knew when the Scribe Virgin appeared behind him, because the hair on the back of his neck stood up.

"I thought you were going to step down," she said to him. "I saw the path of the Primale unfolding for another's footfalls. You were supposed to just be the transition."

He looked over his shoulder. "I thought I was going to step down as well. But, no."

Odd, he thought. Beneath the black robes that shielded her face and hands and feet, the glow of her seemed dimmer than he remembered.

She drifted over to her birds. "I would have you greet me properly, Primale."

He bent down low and said the proper words in the Old Language. Also paid her the service of staying in a bow, waiting for her to release him from the supplication.

"Ah, but that is the thing," she murmured. "You have already released yourself. And now you want the same for my Chosen." He opened his mouth, but she cut him off. "You need not explain your reasoning. Think you I know not what is in your head? Even your wizard, as you call him, is known unto me."

Okay, that made him uncomfortable.

"Rise, Phury, son of Ahgony." When he did, she said, "We are all products of our upbringings, Primale. The constructions that result from our choices are laid upon the foundation set by our parents and their parents before them. We are but the next level in the house or paver in the path."

Phury shook his head slowly. "We can choose a different direction. We can move ourselves along a different heading of the compass."

"Of that I am not sure."

"Of that I must be sure . . . or I'm not going to make anything of this life you've given me."

"Indeed." Her head turned toward her private quarters. "Indeed, Primale."

In the silence that stretched, she seemed saddened, which surprised him. He'd been prepared for a fight. Hell, it was hard not to think of the Scribe Virgin as anything other than an eighteen-wheeler in black robes.

"Tell me, Primale, how do you intend to handle this all?"

"I'm not sure yet. But those who feel more comfortable here can stay. And those who want to venture forth to the far side will find a safe haven with me there."

"You are abandoning this side for good?"

"There is something I need on the far side, something I have to have. But I will be back and forth. It's going to take decades, maybe longer, to change everything. Cormia is going to help."

"And you shall take only her, as a male does?"

"Yes. If the others find mates of their choosing, then I will accept all their female offspring into the traditions of the Chosen and urge Wrath to take their males into the Brotherhood, whether they are born here or on the far side. But I will have only Cormia."

"What of the purity of the blood? The strength that comes of it? Are there to be no standards? The breeding was deliberate, to beget strength from strength. What if a Chosen chooses one not of a Brotherhood line?"

He thought of Qhuinn and Blay. Strong boys who would be stronger males over time. Why shouldn't they be in the Brotherhood?

"It would be up to Wrath. But I would encourage him to accept the worthy regardless of lineage. Courage of heart can make a male taller and stronger than he is physically. Look, the race is failing, and you know it. We're losing ground with every generation, and not just because of the war. The Lessening Society isn't the only thing killing us. The traditions are, too."

The Scribe Virgin drifted over to the fountain.

There was a long, long, long silence.

"I feel as though I have lost," she said softly. "All of you."

"You haven't. Not at all. Be a mother to the race, not a warden, and you will win everything you want. Set us free and watch us thrive."

The sound of the chiming fountain seemed to swell, growing louder, as if catching the drift of her emotions.

Phury looked at the falling water, seeing it catch the light and twinkle like stars. The rainbows in each of the droplets were impossibly beautiful, and as he watched the flashing gems in every fragment of the whole that fell back down, he thought of the Chosen and whatever individual gifts they possessed.

He thought of his brothers.

He thought of their *shellans*.

He thought of his beloved.

And he knew the whys of her silence. "You won't lose us. We will never leave you behind and forget you. How could we? You birthed us and squired us and strengthened us. But now . . . now is our time. Let us go and we will be closer to you than ever before. Let us take the future into our hands and shape it as best we can. Have faith in your creation."

In a rough voice, she said, "Have you the strength for this, Primale? Can you lead the Chosen even after all you have been through? Your life has not been easy, and the road you are contemplating is neither level nor well of surface."

As Phury stood on his one leg and his prosthesis, and thought about the days of his existence, and weighed the mettle of his marrow, he came up with only one reply.

"I'm here, aren't I," he pronounced. "I'm still standing, aren't I. You tell me whether I have the fucking strength or not."

She smiled a little then—though he couldn't see her face, he knew she smiled.

The Scribe Virgin nodded once. "So be it, then, Primale. So it shall be as you wish."

She turned and disappeared into her private quarters.

Phury exhaled as though someone had pulled a stopper out of his ass.

Holy. Shit.

He'd just blown apart the whole spiritual fabric of the race. As well as its biological one.

Man, if he'd known where the night was going to lead, he'd have had a bowl of Wheaties before getting off that bedding platform.

He turned and headed back to the Sanctuary. First stop would be Cormia; then the two of them would go to the Directrix and—

He froze as he threw open the door.

The grass was green.

The grass was green and the sky was blue . . . and the daffodils were yellow and the roses were a Crayola rainbow of colors . . . and the buildings were red and cream and dark blue. . . .

Down below, the Chosen were spilling out of their living quarters, holding their now colorful robes and looking around in excitement and wonder.

Cormia emerged from the Primale temple, her lovely face stunned as she looked around. When she saw him, her hands clamped to her mouth and her eyes started to blink fast.

With a cry, she gathered her gorgeous pale lavender robe and ran toward him, tears streaming down her cheeks.

He caught her as she leaped up to him and held her warm body to his.

"I love you," she choked out. "I love you, I love you . . . I love you."

In that moment, with the world that was his in transformation, and his *shellan* safely in his arms, he felt something he never would have imagined.

He finally felt like the hero he had always wanted to be.

FIFTY-ONE

Back on the far side, in the Brotherhood's mansion, John Matthew sat in a stuffed chair across from the bed where Tohr lay sleeping. The Brother hadn't moved since they'd gotten home hours and hours ago.

Which seemed to be the SOP for tonight. It was like everyone in the house was asleep, a collective, pervasive exhaustion overwhelming them all.

Well, everyone except John. And the angel who was pacing in the guest room next door.

Tohr was on both their minds.

God, John had never expected to feel bigger than the Brother. He'd never expected to be physically stronger. He'd certainly never thought about taking care of the male. Or being responsible for him.

He had all of that going on and more, now, because Tohr had lost sixty pounds, easy. And had the face and body of a male who'd gone to war and been mortally injured.

It was weird, John thought. At first, he'd wanted the Brother to wake up right away, but now he was scared to see those eyes open. He didn't know if he could handle being shut out. Sure, it would be understandable, given all that Tohr had lost, but . . . it would kill him.

Besides, as long as Tohr was still asleep, John wasn't going to break down and sob.

See, there was a ghost in the room. A beautiful, red-haired ghost with a rounded pregnant belly: Wellsie was with them. In spite of her death, she was with them, and so was her unborn child. And Tohr's *shellan* was never going to be far. There was no looking at Tohr without seeing her. The two had been inseparable in life, and they were in death as well. Sure as shit, Tohr might have been breathing, but he wasn't alive anymore.

"Is that you?"

John's eyes shot to the bed.

Tohr was awake and looking across the dim stretch that separated them.

John slowly stood up and straightened his T-shirt and jeans. *It's John. John Matthew.*

Tohr didn't say anything, just kept looking him up and down.

I went through the transition, John signed like a fool.

"You're D's size. Big."

God, that voice was exactly like he remembered it. Deep as the bass note of a church organ and just as commanding. There was a difference, though. There was a new hollowness in the words.

Or maybe that was coming from the blank space behind those blue eyes.

I had to get new clothes. Jesus Christ, he was an idiot. *Are you . . . are you hungry? I got roast beef sandwiches. And Pepperidge Farm Milanos. You used to like—*

"I'm good."

Can I get you something to drink? I got a thermos of coffee.

"Nah." Tohr glanced over at the bathroom. "Shit, indoor plumbing. Been a while. And no, I don't need help."

It was painful to watch—something out of a future John didn't think would come for hundreds and hundreds of years: Tohrment as an old male.

The Brother put a shaking hand on the edge of the sheets and dragged them off his naked body inch by inch. He paused. Then slid his legs out so they dangled to the floor. There was another pause before he heaved himself up, his once-wide shoulders straining to bear weight that was little more than that of a skeleton.

He didn't walk. He shuffled like the advanced elderly did, head down, spine curving toward the floor, hands up as if he expected to fall at any moment.

The doors shut. The toilet flushed with a gurgle. The shower came on.

John went back to the chair he'd been in, his gut empty, and not just because he hadn't eaten since the night before. Worry was all he knew. Concern the breath he drew into his chest. Anxiety the very beat of his heart.

This was the flip side of the parent/child relationship. Where the son worried about the father.

Assuming he and Tohr still had that whole connection going on.

He wasn't sure. The Brother had stared at him like he was a stranger.

John's foot ticked off the seconds, and he rubbed his palms on his thighs. Strange, everything else that had happened, even the stuff with Lash, seemed unreal and unimportant. There was only the now with Tohr.

When the door opened nearly an hour later, he went still.

Tohr was wearing a robe, and his hair was mostly detangled, though the beard was still ragged.

In that loose, unreliable shuffle, the Brother went back to the bed and stretched out with a groan, settling awkwardly into the pillows.

Is there anything I can—

"This is not where I wanted to end up, John. I'm not going to front. This is not . . . where I want to be."

Okay, John signed. *Okay.*

As silence stretched, in his mind, he had the conversation he wanted to have with Tohr: *Qhuinn and Blay ended up here, and Qhuinn's parents are dead, and Lash is . . . I don't know what to say about him. . . . There's a female I like, but she's out of my league, and I'm in the war and I missed you and I want you to be proud of me and I'm scared and I miss Wellsie and are you all right?*

And most important . . . *Please say you're not leaving again. Ever. I need you.*

Instead, he rose to his feet and signed, *I guess I'll leave you to rest. If you need anything—*

"I'm tight."

Okay. Yeah. Okay . . .

John pulled at the hem of his T-shirt and turned away. As he walked to the door, he couldn't breathe.

Oh, please let him not run into anyone on the way to his room—

"John."

He stopped. Pivoted back around.

As he met Tohr's weary navy blue stare, John felt like his knees were having an out-of-socket experience.

Tohr closed his eyes and opened his arms.

John ran to the bed and grabbed on to his father for everything he was worth. He buried his face in what was once a broad chest and listened to the heart that still beat inside of it. Of the two of them he held on harder, not because Tohr didn't care, but because he hadn't the strength.

They both cried until there was no more breath with which to wail.

FIFTY-TWO

Triggers didn't have to be on guns to be trouble, Phury thought as he stared at ZeroSum's glass-and-steel facade.

Shit, detox was about the body banging through a shift in chemistry. It didn't do jack dick for the cravings that were in your head. And, sure the wizard was smaller than him, but the bastard still hadn't left. And Phury had the sense it was going to be a long while before the voice did.

With a kick to his own ass, he walked up to the bouncer, who gave him an odd look, but let him in. Inside, he didn't pay any attention to the crowd, which as usual parted to make way for him. He didn't nod at the bouncer standing at the velvet rope in front of the VIP section. He didn't say anything to iAm, who let him into Rehv's office.

"To what do I owe this pleasure," Rehvenge said from behind his desk.

Phury stared at his dealer.

Rehv was wearing a standard-issue black suit about which there was nothing standard. The fit was gorgeous, even though the male was sitting down, and the fabric gleamed under the low lights, a clear indication that there was a bit of silk in the weave. The lapels lay perfectly flat on a powerful chest, and the sleeves showed precisely the right amount of shirt cuff.

Rehv frowned. "I can feel your emotions from here. You've done something."

Phury had to laugh. "Yeah, you might say that. And I'm on the way to Wrath's now, because I have some serious 'splainin' to do. I came here first, though, because my *shellan* and I need a place to stay."

Rehvenge's brows shot up over his amethyst eyes. "*Shellan*? Wow. Not Chosen anymore?"

"No." Phury cleared his throat. "Look, I know you have houses. Like, multiples. I want to know if I can rent one for a couple of months. I need a lot of rooms. A lot."

"Brotherhood mansion too full?"

"No."

"Mmm." Rehv tilted his head to the side, the shaved parts of his mohawk smooth. "Wrath has other places, doesn't he? And I know your brother V does. I've heard he's got a BDSM pad somewhere. Hafta admit I'm surprised you came to me."

"Just figured I'd start with you."

"Mmm." Rehv stood up and relied on his cane as he went over and opened a sliding panel behind his desk. "Nice outfit, by the way. You get it at Victoria's Secret? 'Scuse me for one sec."

As the male went into the bedroom that was revealed, Phury glanced down at himself. No wonder those people had been giving him strange looks. He was wearing his white satin robing from the other side.

Rehv came out a moment later. In his hands, he had a pair of black alligator-skin loafers with telltale bridle bit links.

He dropped the Guccis at Phury's feet. "You might want to slip your bare soles into these. And I'm sorry, I don't have anything you can rent."

Phury took a deep breath. "Okay. Thanks—"

"But you can live in my great camp in the Adirondacks for free. For as long as you want."

Phury blinked. "I can p—"

"If you're about to say you can pay me, fuck you. Like I said, I don't have anything you can rent. Trez can meet you up there, give you the codes. You'll see me right before dawn after the first Tuesday of every month, but other than that you'll have the place to yourselves."

"I don't know what to say."

"Maybe someday you'll return a favor. And we'll just leave it at that."

"My honor is yours."

"And my shoes are yours. Even after you get your own back."

Phury arranged the pair, then slid into them. They fit perfectly. "I'll bring them—"

"Nope. Consider it a mating gift."

"Well . . . thank you."

"You're welcome. I know you like Gucci—"

"Not for the loafers, actually, although they are fabulous. I meant . . . for putting me on the no-buy list. I know Z talked to you."

Rehv smiled. "So you're getting clean, huh."

"I'm going to do my best to stop."

"Mmm." That amethyst stare narrowed. "I think you're going to make it, too. You've got that kind of resolve I've seen in the eyes of people who come into my office a lot, and then one night, for what-

ever reason, they decide never to come again. And that is that. It's good to see."

"Yeah. You're not going to catch me around here anymore."

Rehv's phone went off, and as he checked the caller, he frowned. "Hold up. You might be interested in this. It's the de facto head of the Princeps Council." As he picked up, the male's voice was part impatience, part boredom. "I'm doing all right. You? Yeah. Yeah. Terrible, yeah. No, I'm still in town, call me a stalwart."

Rehv leaned back in his chair and played with his envelope opener, the one that was shaped like a dagger. "Yup. Uh-huh. Right. Yeah, I know, the vacuum in leadership is— Excuse me?" Rehv let the opener fall onto the blotter. "What did you say? Oh, really. Well, what about Marissa? Ah. Indeed. And I'm not surprised. . . ."

Phury had to wonder exactly what kind of bomb had just been dropped.

After a while, Rehv cleared his throat. Then a slow smile spread across his face. "Well, then, considering how you feel . . . I'd love to. Thank you." He hung up and his eyes lifted. "Guess who the new *leahdyre* of the Council is?"

Phury felt his mouth fall open. "You can't. How the hell can you—"

"Turns out I'm the oldest surviving member of my line, and there is a rule that females may not serve as *leahdyre*. As I'm the only male of the Council, guess who's coming to dinner." He eased back in his leather chair. "They need me."

"Holy . . . crap."

"Yeah, if you live long enough, you can get to see just about anything. Tell your boss it's going to be a pleasure doing business with him."

"I will. I absolutely will. And listen, thank you again for this. For everything." He went over to the door. "You need me, ever, just call."

Rehvenge dipped his head once. "I will, vampire. Sin-eaters always collect on favors."

Phury smiled a little. "The politically correct term is *symphath*."

As he left the office Rehv's low, slightly evil laughter rolled like thunder.

Phury materialized in front of the Brotherhood mansion and straightened his robe. In his desire to make a good impression, he felt like he didn't live under its roof anymore.

Which he supposed made sense: His head had had a change of address.

It felt awkward as hell to walk up to the house, go into the vestibule, and ring the video screen like a stranger would. Fritz seemed likewise surprised as he opened the door.

"Sire?"

"Could you let Wrath know I'm here and that I'd like to talk to him?"

"Of course." The *doggen* bowed and bounced quickly up the grand stairs.

While he waited, Phury looked around the foyer, thinking of how his brother Darius had built the place . . . how many years ago?

Wrath appeared at the top of the stairwell, and there was wariness on his face. "Hey."

"Hey." Phury lifted his hand. "Mind if I come up for a few?"

"Sure."

Phury ascended slowly. And the closer he got to his room, the more his skin tingled, because he couldn't help thinking of all the red smoke he'd done there. Part of him wanted some so badly he was nearly wheezing for a draw, and his head began to pound.

Wrath's tone was hard. "Listen, if you came here for your drugs—"

Phury held up his hand and in a hoarse voice said, "Nope. Can we do this in private."

"Fine."

When the study door was shut, he did his best to throw off the cravings and start talking. He wasn't completely sure what came out

of his mouth. Primale. Cormia. Scribe Virgin. Future. Chosen. Brothers. Change.

Change.

Change.

When he finally ran out of gas, he realized Wrath hadn't said a thing.

"So that's where I'm at," Phury tacked on. "I've already addressed the Chosen and told them that I'm going to get us a place over here."

"And where's that going to be?"

"Rehv's great camp upstate."

"Really?"

"Yup. It's safe up there. Secure. Not too busy, not a lot of humans. I can protect the ones who come over here more easily. This whole thing, it's going to have to be gradual. A couple of them are already interested in visiting. Exploring. Learning. Cormia and I are going to help them assimilate to the extent they want. But it's all voluntary. They get to choose."

"And the Scribe Virgin was *okay* with this?"

"Yeah. She was. Of course, the Brotherhood side of things is up to you."

Wrath shook his head and stood up.

Phury nodded, not blaming the guy for doubting the plan. Phury had said a lot of words. Now he could only hope to prove some with action. "Okay, well, like I said, that's up to—"

Wrath came over and put out his palm. "I'm totally on board. And whatever you need for the Chosen on this side you have. Anything."

Phury could only look at what was being offered. When he took hold of his brother's hand, his voice was rough. "Good . . . deal."

Wrath smiled. "Anything you need, I'll give you."

"I'm fine right . . ." Phury frowned and glanced at the king's desk. "Um . . . can I use your computer for a moment?"

"Absolutely. And when you're done, I'm going to share some good news with you. Well, sort of good news."

"What is it?"

Wrath nodded to the door. "Tohr's back."

Phury's throat seized. "He's alive?"

"Sort of . . . sort of. But he's home. And we're going to try and keep him that way."

FIFTY-THREE

Sitting at the Brotherhood's table in ZeroSum's VIP section, John Matthew was drunk off his ass. Drunk off his motherfucking ass. Totally shwasted.

So as soon as he finished whatever number beer he'd been working on for all of five minutes, he ordered a Jäger bomb.

Qhuinn and Blay, to their credit, were saying absolutely nothing.

It was hard to explain what was driving all the bottle pounding and the shot sucking. The only thing he kept coming back to was that his nerves were decimated. He'd left Tohr back at the house sleeping in that bed like the thing was a coffin, and though it was great that they had reunited, the Brother was not home free, not by any stretch.

John couldn't go through losing him again.

And then there was that bizarre Lash sighting and the fact that John was kind of convinced he was losing his ever-loving mind.

When the waitress came over with the shot, Qhuinn said, "He'd like another beer."

I love you, John signed to his buddy.

"Well, you're going to hate both of us when you get home and throw up like a golf course sprinkler, but let's just live in the here and now, shall we?"

Roger that. John threw back the shot and it didn't burn, didn't land in his stomach in a burning rush. But, then, really. Would a forest fire give two shits about a Zippo lighter?

Qhuinn was right: He was probably going to hurl. As a matter of fact—

John lurched to his feet.

"Oh, shit, here we are," Qhuinn said, getting up as well.

I go alone.

Qhuinn tapped the chain around his neck. "Not anymore."

John planted his fists into the table, leaned across, and bared his fangs.

"What the fuck?" Qhuinn hissed as Blay frantically looked around at the other banquettes. "What the *fuck* do you think you're doing?"

I go alone.

Qhuinn glared like he was going to argue, but then he parked his ass again. "Fine. Whatever. Just keep that grille to yourself."

John walked away, amazed that no one else in the club seemed to notice that the floor was shifting back and forth like a funhouse. Just before he got to the hall of private bathrooms, he changed his mind, louied, and snuck out past the velvet rope.

On the other side, he navigated the packed crowd with the grace of a buffalo, sideswiping people, knocking into walls, pitching forward, then leaning back to keep from yard-sale-ing.

He took the stairs to the mezzanine floor and punched his way into the men's bathroom.

There were two guys at the urinals, one by the sinks, and John met none of their eyes as he went all the way back to the end of the stalls. He opened the handicapped one, then pulled back because he felt bad, and stepped into the second-to-last one. As he locked the door, his stomach cement-mixered on him, churning like it was collecting a care package for immediate airmailing.

Shit. Why hadn't he just used the private bathrooms in the back of the VIP section? Did he really need those three Joes hearing him tribute-band a plumber strong-arming a drain?

God . . . damn. He was wicked faced.

On that note, he turned and looked down at the toilet. The thing was black, as almost everything in ZeroSum was, but he knew it was clean. Rehv kept a clean house.

Well, except for the prostitution. And the drugs. And the booking.

Okay, it was clean by Spick-and-span standards, not according to the penal code.

John let his head fall back against the metal door and closed his eyes, the true reason for all the drinking bubbling up.

What the hell was the measure of a male? Was it fighting? Was it how much you could bench-press? Was it revenge carried out?

Was it staying in control of your emotions when the whole world seemed funhouse-unstable? Was it loving someone even when you knew there was a risk they could walk away from you forever?

Was it sex?

Okay, big mistake to close his eyes. Or start thinking. He cracked his lids and focused on the black ceiling with its recessed, starlike lights.

The sink shut off. Two urinals flushed. The door to the club opened and shut, then opened and shut.

There was a sniffing noise from a couple stalls down. And another. Then a whiffling and an *ahhhhh*. Footsteps. Running water. Laughter of the manic kind. Another open and shut with the door to the outside again.

Alone. He was alone. Except it wouldn't last long, because some-one would come in again soon.

John looked down to the black toilet and told his stomach to get with the program if it wanted to spare him embarrassment.

Evidently it didn't. Or maybe . . . yes. No? Shit . . .

He was staring at the toilet, waiting for his gag reflex to make up its mind, when he forgot about his stomach and realized where he was.

He'd been born in a toilet stall. Brought into the world in a place where people threw up after having had too much to drink . . . left to fend for his infant self by a mother he'd never known and a father who'd never known him.

If Tohr took off again . . .

John wheeled around and couldn't make his fingers work the lever so he could get out. With increasing panic, he clawed at the black mechanism until finally it sprang free. Bursting into the bathroom, he beelined for the door and didn't make it.

Over each of the six copper sinks, there was a gold-framed mirror.

Taking a deep breath, he picked the mirror that was the closest to the door and stepped in front of it, meeting his grown-up face for the first time.

His eyes were the same . . . his eyes were exactly the same blue and the same shape. Everything else he didn't recognize, not the hard cut of the jaw or the thickness of the neck or the broad forehead. But the eyes were his.

He supposed.

Who am I, he mouthed.

Peeling his lips off his front teeth, he leaned in and looked at his fangs.

"Don't tell me you've never seen those before?"

He spun on his boot. Xhex was standing against the door, effectively closing them in together.

She was wearing exactly the same thing she always did, but to him

it was as if he'd never seen the tight muscle shirt or the leathers before.

"I saw you tumble in here. Just thought I'd make sure you were okay." Her gray eyes didn't waver, and he bet they never did from anything. The female had a stare like a statue's, direct and unflappable.

An incredibly sexy statue's.

I want to fuck you, he mouthed, not caring that he was making a fool out of himself.

"Do you."

Clearly, she read lips. Either that or cocks, because God knew his had its hand raised and waving in his jeans.

Yeah, I do.

"Lot of women in this club."

Only one you.

"I think you'd be better off with them."

And I think you'd be better off with me.

Where the fuck the confidence was coming from, he didn't care. Whether it was an ego-gift from God or just bottle-born stupidity, he was going with it.

Fact, I know you would.

He deliberately slipped his thumbs under the waistband of his jeans and gave the fuckers a slow jack up. As his arousal showed plain as siding on a house, her eyes dipped down, and he knew what she was seeing: He was hung fit for the size of his six-foot-seven body. And that was without an erection. With one, he was tremendous.

Ah, not so statuelike, are we, he thought as her stare didn't return to his face, but flared ever so slightly.

With her eyes on him, and an electrical sizzle between them, he wasn't his past anymore. He was just now. And now was her locking that goddamn door and letting him go down on her. Then the two of them fucking while standing up.

Her lips parted, and he waited for her words like he waited for God's arrival.

Abruptly, she jerked her hand up to her earpiece and frowned. "Shit. I've got to go."

John whipped out a paper towel from the wall dispenser, took his pen from his pocket, and wrote some bold words. Before she could take off, he went over and forced what he'd scribbled on into her hand.

She looked down at it. "You want me to read now or later."

Later, he mouthed.

As he pushed through the door, he was a lot more sober. And he had a big-ass, I'm-the-man smile on his face.

When Lash reappeared in his parents' foyer, he kept still for a little bit. His body felt as though it had been pressed between two sheets of waxed paper and hit with an iron, a fallen leaf captured and preserved artificially, and not without some pain.

He glanced at his hands. Flexed them. Cracked his neck.

The lessons from his father had begun. They were going to meet regularly. He was ready to learn.

Curling his hands into fists and releasing them, he counted the tricks he had now. Tricks that were . . . not tricks, actually. Not tricks at all. He was a monster. A monster just beginning to understand the usefulness of the scales on his body and the flames in his mouth and the barbs on his tail.

It was kind of like it had been after his change. He had to figure out who he was again and how his body worked.

Fortunately the Omega was going to help him. As any good parent should.

When he could stand it, Lash turned his head and looked up the stairs, picturing where John had been standing.

It had been so good to see his enemy again. Positively heartwarming.

Hallmark really needed to start up a line of revenge cards, the kind that let you reach out to those you were going to come after with a vengeance.

Lash stood up carefully and did a slow turn and review, taking in the grandfather clock in the corner by the front door and the oil paintings and the generations of family shit that had been carefully stewarded.

Then he looked toward the dining room.

The shovels, he thought, were in the garage.

He found a pair of them lined up against the wall beside the peg-board that had the garden trowels and shears hanging on it. The shovel he chose had a wooden handle and a broad red-enameled palm.

When he stepped outside, he was amazed to see it was still dark, as he felt like he'd been with the Omega for hours and hours. Unless this was tomorrow? Or even the day after?

Lash went around to the side yard and picked a spot under the oak tree that offered shade to the study's wide windows. As he dug, his eyes occasionally flicked up to the panes of glass and the room beyond them. The couch still had bloodstains on it, although what a ridiculous thing to notice. What, like they would evaporate out of the silk fibers?

He dug one grave that was five feet down into the earth, seven feet long, and four feet across.

The resulting pile of dirt was bigger than he'd thought, and it smelled like the lawn did after a heavy rainstorm, musky and sweet. Or maybe he was the sweet part.

The gathering glow in the east had him tossing the shovel out of the hole and leaping up to level ground. He had to move fast before the sun came up, and he did. He put his father in first. His mother was second. He angled them so they were spooning, with his father doing the holding.

He stared down at the two of them.

He was surprised that he needed to do this before he could get another squadron of men in here to try and empty the place, but whatever. These two had been his parents for the first part of his life, and though he'd told himself he didn't give a shit about them, he did. He wasn't going to have those *lessers* desecrating their rotting bodies. The house? Fine, fair game. But not the bodies.

With the sun rising, and golden rays spearing through the oak's leafy arms, he made a phone call and then put the dirt back where it had been.

Holy shit, he thought when he'd finished. The thing really looked like a grave, with its domed bread-loaf top from all the displacement.

He was returning the shovel to its home in the garage when he heard the first of the cars pull up to the front door. Two *lessers* got out just as a second sedan eased onto the driveway, followed by a Ford F-150 and a minivan.

The bunch of them smelled as sweet as the sunshine while they filed into his parents' house.

The U-Haul moving truck, driven by Mr. D, was the last to arrive.

As the *Fore-lesser* took charge and the looting commenced, Lash went up and took a quick shower in his old bathroom. While he was drying off, he went over to his closet. Clothes . . . clothes . . . somehow, what he'd been wearing lately didn't strike the right note anymore, and he took out a spank Prada suit.

His military minimalist-chic stage was so over. He wasn't the Brotherhood's good little soldier-in-training anymore.

Feeling all sexy beast and shit, he went over to his bureau, opened up his jewelry drawer, and—

Where the fuck was his watch? The Jacob & Co. with the diamonds?

What the hell had . . .

Lash looked around and sniffed the air of his room. Then he flipped his vision to blue so that the prints of anyone who had been touching his shit showed up pink, just as his father had taught him.

Fresh, characterless prints, ones more vivid than those he'd left days ago, were on the bureau. He inhaled again. John had . . . John

and Qhuinn had been here . . . and one of those miserable mother-fuckers had taken his fucking *watch*.

Lash picked up the hunting knife on his desk and, with a roar, pitched it across the room, where it landed blade-first in one of his black pillows.

Mr. D appeared in the doorway. "Suh? What's wrong—"

Lash wheeled around and pegged the guy with his finger, not to make a point but to use another one of his real father's gifts.

But then he took a deep breath. Dropped his arm. Straightened his suit.

"Make me . . ." He had to clear the rage out of his throat. "Make me breakfast. I want to take it in the sunroom, not at the dining table."

Mr. D left, and about ten minutes later, when Lash wasn't seeing double anymore from fury, he went downstairs and parked it in front of a nice spread of bacon, eggs, toast with jam, and OJ.

Mr. D had squeezed the oranges himself, evidently. Which, considering how good the shit tasted, was justification enough for not having blasted the fucker right out of his combat boots.

The other slayers ended up all gathered in the sunroom's entryway, watching him eat like he was pulling off a magic trick and a half.

Just as he took a good last long suck from his cup of coffee, one of them said, "What the fuck are you?"

Lash wiped his mouth with his napkin and calmly removed his jacket. As he stood up, he undid the buttons down the front of his pastel pink shirt.

"I am your motherfucking king."

With that, he opened the shirt and willed his skin to slit down the sternum. With his ribs cranked wide, he bared his fangs and exposed his black, beating heart.

As a group, the *lessers* jumped back. One even crossed himself, the fucker.

Lash calmly closed up his chest and rebuttoned his shirt and sat back down. "More coffee, Mr. D."

The cowboy blinked stupidly a couple of times, doing an excellent impression of a sheep confronted with a math problem. "Yes . . . yes, suh."

Lash picked up his cup again and met the pale faces in front of him. "Welcome to the future, gentlemen. Now get your asses moving. I want the first floor of this place empty before the mailman comes at ten thirty."

FIFTY-FOUR

The East Caldwell Community Center was located between Caldie Pizza & Mexican and the Caldwell Tennis Academy, over on Baxter Avenue. Housed in a big old farmhouse that had been built way back when the surrounding acreage had been used to grow corn, the place had a nice front lawn and a flagpole and some swing sets out back.

When Phury materialized behind the facility, all he could think about was getting gone again. He checked his watch. Ten minutes.

Ten minutes of having to make himself stay.

God, he wanted a red smoke. His heart was doing laps in his ribs and his palms felt like dripping washcloths and his itchy skin was driving him *nuts*.

Trying to get out of his body, he looked at the parking lot. Twenty cars were in it, with no pattern in the makes or models. There were trucks and Toyotas and a Saab convertible and a pink VW Bug and three minivans and a MINI Cooper.

He put his hands in his pockets and walked over the grass to the sidewalk that ran around the building. When he reached the asphalt stretch that made up the drive and the parking lot, he took it over to the double doors under the aluminum-sided porte cochere.

Inside, the place smelled like coconut. Maybe from the floor wax on the linoleum.

Just as he was thinking seriously of taking off, a human man stepped out of a doorway, the sound of a toilet flushing fading as the door marked MEN eased shut behind him.

"Are you a friend of Bill W's?" the guy asked as he dried his hands with a paper towel. He had kind brown eyes, like a retriever, and a tweedy jacket that looked heavy for summer. His tie was knit.

"Ah, I don't know."

"Well, if you're looking for the meeting, it's down in the basement." His smile was so natural and easy, Phury nearly returned it before he remembered the dental differences between species. "I'm going there now if you want to come with me. If you want to wait a little, that's fine too."

Phury looked down at the man's hands. He was still drying them, going back and forth, back and forth.

"I'm nervous," the guy said. "Hands are sweaty."

Phury smiled a little. "You know . . . I think maybe I'll come with you."

"Good. I'm Jonathon."

"I'm Ph—Patrick."

Phury was glad his hands didn't shake. He didn't have a paper towel, and his pockets were making his own sweaty palms worse.

The ECCC's basement had cement-block walls that were white-washed in cream; a floor carpeted in low-napped, high-traffic dark brown; and a lot of fluorescent lights in the low ceiling. Most of the

thirty or so chairs that were arranged in a fat circle had someone parked in them, and when Jonathon headed to a vacancy at the center, Phury nodded a see-you-later and took one as close to the door as he could.

"It's nine o'clock," a woman with short black hair said. Getting to her feet, she read off a piece of paper: "Everything that's said here, remains here. When someone is talking, there is no side conversation or cross talk. . . ."

He didn't hear the rest of it because he was too busy checking out who was there. No one else was wearing Aquascutum like he was, and they were all humans. Each one of them. Age range was early twenties to late forties, maybe because the time of day was convenient for folks who worked or went to school.

Staring at the faces, he tried to figure out what each one had done to end up here, in this coconut-smelling, stark basement with their butts planted on black plastic.

He didn't belong here. These were not his people, and not just because none of them had fangs and a problem with sunlight.

He stayed anyway, because he had nowhere else to go, and he wondered whether that could be true for some of them as well.

"This is a speaker group," the woman said, "and tonight Jonathon is going to talk."

Jonathon stood up. His hands were still working the remnants of the paper towel, rubbing back and forth over what was now an impacted Bounty cigar.

"Hi, my name is Jonathon." A pattering of hellos bounced around the room. "And I'm a drug addict. I . . . I, ah, I used cocaine for about a decade and lost just about everything. I've been to jail twice. I've had to declare bankruptcy. I lost my house. My wife . . . she, ah, she divorced me and moved out of state with my daughter. Right after that, I lost my job as a physics teacher because I just was going from bender to bender.

"I've been clean since, yeah, last August. But . . . I still think about using. I live in transitional housing right now because I got through rehab and I have a new job. Started two weeks ago. I'm teaching in a prison, actually. The prison I was an inmate in. Math, it's math." Jonathon cleared his throat. "Yeah . . . so, ah, one year ago tonight . . . one year ago tonight I was in an alley downtown. I was making a buy from a dealer and we got caught. Not by the cops. By the guy whose territory we were in. I got shot in the side and the thigh. I . . ."

Jonathon cleared his throat again. "As I lay there bleeding, I felt my arms get moved around. The shooter took my coat and my wallet and my watch, then he pistol-whipped me in the head. I really . . . I really shouldn't be here right now." There were a lot of *uh-huh*s murmured. "I started coming to meetings like this because I had nowhere else to go. Now I choose to come here because I want to be where I am tonight more than I want the high. Sometimes, sometimes that's only by a slim margin, so I don't look into the future any further than next Tuesday at nine o'clock. When I come here again. So, yeah, that's where I've been and where I am."

Jonathon sat back down.

Phury waited for people to pile on with the questions and the comments. Instead, someone else stood up. "Hi, my name is Ellis. . . ."

And that was it. Person after person testifying about their addiction.

When it was nine fifty-three, according to the clock on the wall, the black-haired woman stood up. "And now for the Serenity Prayer."

Phury rose to his feet with the rest of them and was shocked when someone reached for his hand.

His palm wasn't wet anymore, though.

He didn't know whether he was going to make it long-haul. The wizard had been with him a lot of years and knew him like a brother. The one thing he did know was that next Tuesday at nine p.m. he was going to be here again.

He left with the others, and as the night air hit him, he nearly doubled over from the need to light up.

As everyone else scattered to their cars and engines started and headlights came on, he sat on one of the swings with his hands on his knees and his feet planted on the patch of raw earth.

For a second, he thought he was being watched—although maybe paranoia was an offshoot of recovery, who the hell knew.

After about ten minutes, he found a dark shadow and dematerialized upstate to Rehv's place.

As he took form behind the Adirondack-style great camp, the first thing he saw was a figure at the sliding glass doors of the den.

Cormia was waiting for him.

Slipping outside, she quietly closed the slider and crossed her arms for warmth. The bulky Irish knit sweater she had on was his, and the leggings had been borrowed from Bella. Her hair was long and loose, down to her hips, and the lights from the house's diamond-pane windows made it glow like gold.

"Hi," she said.

"Hi."

He came forward, moving up the lawn and onto the stone terrace. "You cold?"

"A little."

"Good, that means I can warm you." He opened his arms, and she stepped into them. Even through the sweater's thick heft, he felt her body against his. "Thank you for not asking how it went. I'm still trying. . . . I don't know what to say, really."

Her hands went from his waist up to his shoulders. "You'll tell me if and when you're ready."

"I'm going back again."

"Good."

They stood one to the other in the cool night, and they were warm, very warm.

He shifted his lips to her ear and breathed, "I want to be in you."

"Yes . . ." she replied, drawing out the word.

They would not be alone inside, but they were alone here in the quiet, dark lee of the house. Moving her backward, even deeper into the shadows, he slipped his palms under the lip of his sweater and onto the skin of his *shellan*. Smooth, warm, vital, she arched under his touch.

"I'll let you keep your top on," he said. "But those tights are going down."

Hooking his thumbs into the waistband, he took them to her ankles and slipped them off her feet.

"You're not cold, are you?" he asked, even though he could feel and catch the scent of the answer.

"Not at all."

The side of the house was stone, but he knew that heavy Irish knit would mattress her shoulders. "Lean back for me."

As she did, he put his arm around her waist to give her more cushioning, and found her breast with his free hand. He kissed her deep and long and slow, and her mouth moved under his in ways that were both familiar and mysterious—but, then, that was making love with her, wasn't it. By now, he was well acquainted with her from the inside out—there was nothing of his that hadn't been inside her in one form or another. And yet being with her was as wondrous as the first time.

She was the same, yet she was always new.

And she was aware what this was about. She knew he needed to be in control of them right now, knew he needed to be the driver. At this moment, he wanted to do something that was right and beautiful and do it well, because after that meeting all he could think about was how much ugliness he'd done to himself and to others, and, nearly, to her.

He took his time, with his tongue dipping in and out of her

mouth and his hand caressing her breast, and the investments had a dividend that left his erection nearly punching the way out of his pants: Cormia melted in his hold, getting fluid and hot.

His hand drifted downward. "I think I should make sure you're not catching a draft."

"Please . . . do," she groaned, her head falling to the side.

He wasn't sure whether she exposed her throat on purpose, but his fangs didn't care. They instantly readied for penetration, dropping down from his upper jaw, sharp and hungry.

His hand went between her thighs, and the welling heat he found buckled his knees. He'd meant to keep going slowly, but there would be no more of that.

"Oh, Cormia," he moaned, slipping both his hands around the contours of her hips and picking her up. His body split her thighs wide open. "Undo my pants. . . . Let me out. . . ."

As his bonding scent roared, she released his arousal and linked them up in a glide that was at once effortless and full of power.

Her head fell back as he held her up and worked her body on and off of his. He took her vein as well in a feat of coordination that was easy as pie.

Just as his fangs breached the sweet skin of her neck, her arms tightened on his shoulders, her fists balling up his shirt.

"I love you. . . ."

For a split second, Phury froze.

The moment was so clear to him, everything from the feel of her weight in his palms and her core around his sex and her throat at his mouth to the scent of them coming together and the smell of the forest and the crystal-clear air. He knew the balance between his whole leg and his prosthesis and exactly how his shirt pinched under his arms from her gripping the thing. He knew the pumping of her chest against his own, the beat of both her blood and his, the gathering of erotic tension.

Mostly, though, he knew the cradle of their love for each other.

He couldn't remember anything being this vivid, this real.

This was the gift of recovery, he thought. The ability to be here in this moment with the female he loved and be fully aware, fully awake, fully present. Undiluted.

He thought of Jonathon and the meeting and what the guy had said: *I want to be where I am tonight more than I want the high.*

Yes. Damn it . . . *yes.*

Phury started moving again, taking and giving by turns.

Breathless and straining, he lived as they came together . . . lived vividly.

FIFTY-FIVE

Ehex left the club at four twelve a.m. The cleaning staff were doing their suck, buff, and shine thing, and would be responsible for shutting the doors, and she had the alarms ready for automatic activation at eight o'clock. The cash registers were empty, and Rehvenge's office was not just locked but impenetrable.

Her Ducati was waiting for her in the private garage slip where the Bentley was parked when Rehv didn't need his wheels. She rolled the black bike out, mounted it as the door trundled shut, and started the bitch with a kick.

She never wore a helmet.

She always wore her leather chaps and her biker jacket.

The motorcycle roared between her legs, and she took the long way home, weaving in and out of downtown's maze of one-ways, then opening the Ducati up on the Northway. She was going well over a hundred when she blew past a cop car parked under the pines in the median.

She never put her lights on.

Which explained why, assuming she'd tripped the guy's radar and he wasn't asleep behind his badge, he didn't come after her. Hard to chase what you couldn't see.

She had two places in Caldwell to lay her head: a basement apartment downtown for when she found herself needing privacy stat, and a secluded two-bedroom cabin on the Hudson River.

The dirt road to her waterfront property was nothing but a footpath, thanks to her having let the underbrush grow in over the past thirty years. On the far side of the tangle, the 1920s-era fishing cabin sat on a seven-acre lot, the house built solidly but without grace. The garage was detached and over to the right, and that had been a major value-add when she'd looked at the property. She was the kind of female who liked to keep a lot of firepower around, and storing the ammo outside of the house reduced the likelihood of her getting blown up in her sleep.

The bike went into the garage. She went into the house.

Walking into the kitchen, she loved the way the place smelled: old pine boards from the ceiling and walls and floors, and sweet cedar from the closets that had been built for hunting gear.

She didn't have a security system. Didn't believe in them.

She had herself. And that had always been enough.

After a cup of instant coffee, she went into her bedroom and stripped out of her leathers. In her black sports bra and panties, she lay down on the bare floor and braced herself.

Tough as she was, she always needed a moment.

When she was ready, she reached down to her thighs, to the barbed metal bands she had clamped into her skin and muscles. The locks on the cilices released with a pop, and she groaned as blood rushed to the wounds. With her vision flickering, she curled onto her side, breathing through her mouth.

This was the only way she could control her *symphath* side. Pain was her self-medication.

As her skin went slick with her blood, and her body's nervous system recalibrated, a tingling went through her. She thought of it as her reward for being strong, for keeping it together. Sure it was chemical, nothing except garden-variety endorphins racing around in her veins, but there was magic to the spacey, racy, ringing sensation.

It was times like this when she was tempted to buy herself some furniture for this place, but the impulse was easy to resist. The wooden floor was easier to clean up.

Her breath was easing and her heart was slowing and her brain was starting to turn over again when something popped into her head that reversed the trend toward stabilization.

John Matthew.

John Matthew . . . that bastard. He was, like, twelve, for god-sakes. What the hell was he thinking, trying to sex her up?

She pictured him standing underneath those lights in the mezzanine bathroom, his face that of a fighter, not a young boy, his body that of a male who could deliver, not a wallflower with self-esteem issues.

Reaching to the side, she pulled over her leathers and took out the folded paper towel he had given her. Unfurling it, she read what he had written.

Next time say my name. You'll come more.

She snarled and wadded up the damn thing. She had half a mind to get up and burn it.

Instead, her free hand went between her legs.

As the sun came up and light spilled into her bedroom, Xhex pictured John Matthew on his back beneath her, thrusting what she had seen in his jeans up to meet her riding surges. . . .

She couldn't believe the fantasy. Resented the hell out of him for it. Would have cut the shit if she could have.

But she said his name.

Twice.

FIFTY-SIX

The Scribe Virgin had control issues.

Which was not a bad thing when you were a goddess and had created a whole world within the world, a history within the universe's history.

Really. It was not a bad thing.

Well, mayhap it was a good thing . . . in measure.

The Scribe Virgin floated over to the sealed sanctum in her private quarters, and at her will, the double doors eased open. Mist poured out of the room beyond, billowing like satin cloth in a wind. Her daughter was revealed by the condensation's recession, Payne's powerful body suspended inanimate in the air.

Payne was as her father had been: aggressive and calculating and powerful.

Dangerous.

There had been no place among the Chosen for a female such as Payne. No place in the vampire world, either. After that final act of

hers had come to pass, the Scribe Virgin had isolated here the daughter who would not fit anywhere, for everyone's safety.

Have faith in your creation.

The Primale's words had been ringing e'er since he had spoken them. And they exposed a truth that had been buried in the deep earth of the Scribe Virgin's inner thoughts and fears.

The lives of the males and females whom she had called forth from the biological pool by a single gift of will could not be shelved in separate sections like books in the Sanctuary's library. The order was appealing, true, as there was safety and security in order. Nature, however, and the natures of living things, was messy and unpredictable and not subject to binding.

Have faith in your creation.

The Scribe Virgin could see many things to come, whole legions of triumphs and tragedies, but they were mere grains of sand within a vast shore. The larger whole of fate, she could not envision: As the future of the race she had borne was tied too closely with her own destiny, the thrive or demise of her people was unknown and unknowable to her.

The only totality she had was the present, and the Primale was right. Her beloved children were not flourishing, and if things stayed as they were, soon there would be none of them left.

Change was the only hope they had for the future.

The Scribe Virgin lifted her black hood off her head and let it fall down the back of her robing. Extending her hand, she sent a warm rush of molecules scampering through the still air toward her daughter.

Payne's ice white eyes, so like her twin brother Vishous's, snapped open.

"Daughter," the Scribe Virgin said.

She was not surprised at the reply.

"Fuck you."

FIFTY-SEVEN

ore than a month later, Cormia woke up in the way she was becoming accustomed to greeting the night's fall.

Phury's hips were pushing at hers, his body nudging a rock-hard erection against her. He was likely still asleep, and as she rolled over onto her stomach and made room for him, she smiled, knowing what his response would be. Yup, he was on her in a heartbeat, the blanket of his heavy weight warm and grounding and—

She moaned as he pushed inside.

"Mmmm," he said into her ear. "Good evening, *shellan*."

She smiled and tilted her spine so he could go even deeper. "*Hellren* mine, how fare thee—"

They both groaned as he surged, the powerful stroke going right into the very soul of her. As he rode her slow and sweet, nuzzling at her nape, nipping at her with his fangs, they held hands, their fingers intertwined.

They hadn't been officially mated yet, as there had been too much

to do with the Chosen, who wanted to see what this world was like. But they were together every moment, and Cormia couldn't imagine how they had lived apart.

Well . . . there was one night a week that they were separated for a little while. Phury went to his NA meeting every Tuesday.

Quitting the red smoke was hard on him. There were a lot of times when he would get tense or his eyes would lose focus or he would struggle not to snap at something in annoyance. He'd had day sweats for the first two weeks, and though they were lessening, his skin still went through periods when it was hypersensitive.

He hadn't had one single relapse, though. No matter how bad it got, he didn't cave. And there had been no alcohol for him, either.

They had been having a lot of sex, however. Which was fine with her.

Phury pulled out and rolled her over on her back. As he settled into place at her core again, he kissed her with urgency, his palms going to her breasts, his fingertips brushing over her tight nipples. Arching into him, she slipped her hands between them, took his arousal, and stroked it just as he liked it, from base to tip, base to tip.

Over on the bureau, his cell phone went off with a beep, and they ignored it as she smiled widely and guided him back inside. When they were one again, the firestorm took off and took over them, their rhythm becoming urgent. Holding on to her love's surging shoulders and mirroring his thrusts, she was carried away by him, with him.

After the rush had passed and faded, she opened her eyes and was greeted by the warm yellow stare that made her glow from the inside out.

"I love waking up," he said, kissing her on the mouth.

"Me, too—"

The stairwell fire alarm went off, its shrill cry the kind of thing that made you want to be deaf.

Phury laughed and rolled to the side, tucking her into his chest. "Five . . . four . . . three . . . two—"

"Soooooooooorrrrrrrrrrrrrrrrrrrrrryyy!" Layla called out from the foot of the stairs.

"What was it this time, Chosen?" he hollered back.

"Scrambled eggs," she yelled up.

Phury shook his head and said softly to Cormia, "See, I'd have figured it was the toast."

"Can't be that. She broke the toaster yesterday."

"She did?"

Cormia nodded. "Tried to put a piece of pizza in it. The cheese."

"Everywhere?"

"Everywhere."

Phury spoke up. "That's okay, Layla. You can always clean the pan and try again."

"I don't think the pan's going to work anymore," came the reply.

Phury's voice dropped. "I'm so not going to ask."

"Aren't they metal?"

"Should be."

"I'd better go help." Cormia shifted upright and called out, "I'm coming down, my sister! Two secs."

Phury tugged her back to him for a kiss, then let her go. She had a quick shower, as in lightning quick, and came out wearing loose blue jeans and one of Phury's Gucci shirts.

Maybe it came from years of wearing robes, but she didn't like tight clothes. Which was fine with her *hellren*, because he liked her in his.

"That color looks perfect on you," he drawled as he watched her plait her hair.

"You like the lavender?" She did a little twirl for him and his stare flashed brilliant yellow.

"Oh, yeah. I like. Come here, Chosen."

She put her hands on her hips as the piano started playing down below. Scales. Which meant Selena was up. "I have to go downstairs before Layla burns the house down."

Phury smiled that smile he sported when he was picturing her very, very naked. "Come here, Chosen."

"How about I go and come back with food?"

Phury had the audacity to throw the tangled sheet away and put his hand on his hard, heavy sex. "Only you have what I'm hungry for."

A vacuum cleaner joined the chorus of noise coming from down-stairs, so it was clear who else was up and about. Amalya and Pheonia drew straws every day to see who got to use the Dyson. Didn't matter whether the carpets in Rehvenge's great camp needed it or not—they always got vacuumed.

"Two secs," she said, knowing that if she got within range of his hands, they were going to be all over each other again. "Then I'll come back and you can feed my mouth, how about that."

Phury's massive body trembled, his eyes rolling back into his skull. "Oh, yeah. That's . . . Oh, *yeah*, that's a very good plan."

His phone let out a reminder beep, and he reached over to the bedside table with a groan. "Okay, go on now, before I don't let you out of here for another hour. Or four."

She laughed and turned for the door.

"Dear . . . God."

Cormia turned around. "What is it?"

Phury sat up slowly, his hands holding the phone as if it were worth more than the four hundred dollars he'd paid for it the week before.

"Phury?"

He held it out to her screen-first.

The text was from Zsadist: *Baby girl, two hours ago. Nalla. Hope you're good. Z.*

She bit her lip and then gently put her hand on his shoulder. "You should go back to the house. You should see him. See them."

Phury swallowed hard. "Yeah. I don't know. Not going back there . . . I think it's maybe a good thing. Wrath and I can do what we need to over the phone and . . . Yeah. Better not to."

"Are you going to return the text?"

"I am." He covered his hips with the sheet and just stared at the phone.

After a moment, she said, "Would you like me to do it for you?"

He nodded. "Please. Make it from both of us, 'kay?"

She kissed the top of his head and then texted, *Blessings upon you and your* shellan *and your young. We are with you in spirit, love, Phury and Cormia.*

The following evening, Phury was tempted not to go to the NA meeting. Very tempted.

He wasn't sure what made him go. Didn't know how he did it.

All he wanted was to light up so he didn't have to feel the pain. But how messed up was it that he was hurting? The fact that his twin's young had come into the world healthy, that Z was now a father, that Bella had lived through it, that the young was all right . . . you would figure he'd be thrilled and relieved. It was what he and everyone else had been praying for.

No doubt he was the only one who was fucked in the head over it all. The rest of the Brothers would be busy toasting Z and his new daughter and pampering Bella. The celebrations would be going on for weeks, and Fritz would be ecstatic with all the special meals and ceremonies.

Phury could just see it. The grand entrance of the mansion would be draped in bolts of brilliant green, the color of Z's bloodline, and purple, the color of Bella's. Wreaths of flowers would be hung on every single door in the house, even the closets and cabinets, to symbolize that Nalla had come through to this side. The fireplaces would stay lit for days with sweet logs, those slow-burning, treated pieces of wood whose flames would burn red for the new blood of the darling one.

At the start of the twenty-fourth hour following her birth, every person in the house would bring unto the proud parents a tremendous ribbon bow woven of their family colors. The bows would be

tied on the spindles of Nalla's crib, as pledges to oversee her through her life. By the end of the hour, the place where she laid her precious head would be covered with a cascade of satin bows, their long ends reaching the floor in a river of love.

Nalla would be gifted with priceless jewelry and draped in velvet and held in gentle arms. She would be cherished for the miracle she was, and ever would her birth be rejoiced in the hearts of those who had waited with hope and fear to greet her.

Yeah . . . Phury didn't know what got him to the community center. And he didn't know what helped him through that door and into that basement. And he didn't know what made him stay.

He did know that when he returned to Rehvenge's house, he couldn't go inside.

Instead he sat on the back terrace, in a woven wicker chair, under the stars. There was nothing on his mind. And absolutely everything.

Cormia came out at some point and put her hand on his shoulder, as she always did when she sensed he was deep in his head. He kissed her palm, and then she kissed his mouth and went back inside, likely to get back to work on the plans for Rehv's new club.

The night was quiet and downright cold. Every once in a while the wind would come and brush through the treetops, the autumnal leaves rustling together with a cooing sound like they enjoyed the attention.

Behind him in the house, he could hear the future. The Chosen were stretching their arms out into this world, learning things about themselves and this side. He was so proud of them, and he supposed he was the Primale of old tradition in that he would kill to protect his females and would do anything for any of them.

But it was a fatherly love. His mated love was for Cormia and her alone.

Phury rubbed the center of his chest and let the hours pass as they would, at their own speed, while the wind gusted as it did, at its own strength. The moon drifted up to its apex in the sky and began its descent. Someone put opera on inside the house. Someone changed it to hip-hop, thank God. Someone started a shower. Someone vacuumed. Again.

Life. In all its mundane majesty.

And you couldn't take advantage of it if you were sitting on your ass in the shadows . . . whether that was in actuality, or metaphorically because you were trapped in an addict's darkness.

Phury reached down and touched the calf of his prosthesis. He'd made it this far with only part of a leg. Living through the rest of his life without his twin and without his brothers . . . he would do that, too. He had much to be grateful for, and that would make up for a lot.

He wouldn't always feel this empty.

Someone in the house went back to the opera.

Oh, shit. Puccini this time.

"*Che Gelida Manina.*"

Of all the choices they had, why pick the one solo guaranteed to make him feel worse? God, he hadn't listened to *La Bohème* since . . . well, forever, it seemed. And the sound of what he had loved so much squeezed his ribs so tightly, he couldn't breathe.

Phury gripped the arms of the chair and started to stand. He just couldn't listen to that tenor's voice. That glorious, soaring tenor reminded him so much of—

Zsadist appeared at the edge of the forest. Singing.

He was singing. . . . It was his tenor in Phury's ear, not some CD from inside the house.

Z's voice surfed the aria's peaks and valleys as he came forward over the grass, moving closer with each perfectly pitched, resonant word. The wind became the Brother's orchestra, blowing the spectacular sounds that breached his mouth out over the lawn and the trees and up into the mountains, up into the heavens, where only such a talent could have been born.

Phury got to his feet as if his twin's voice, not his own legs, had

lifted him from the chair. This was the thanks that had not been spoken. This was the gratitude for the rescue and the appreciation for the life that was lived. This was the wide-open throat of an astounded father, who was lacking the words to express what he felt to his brother and who needed the music to show something of all he wished he could say.

"Ah, hell . . . Z," Phury whispered in the midst of the glory.

As the solo reached its zenith, as the tenor of emotions was struck most powerfully, the Brotherhood appeared one by one from out of the darkness, pulling free of the night. Wrath. Rhage. Butch. Vishous. They were all dressed in the white ceremonial robing they would have worn to honor the twenty-fourth hour of Nalla's birth.

Zsadist sang the last delicate note of the piece right in front of Phury.

As the final line, "*Vi piaccia dir!*" drifted into the infinite, Z held up his hand.

Waving in the night wind was a tremendous bow made of green-and-gold satin.

Cormia came to stand close at just the right time. As she put her arm around Phury's waist, she was all that kept him steady.

In the Old Language, Zsadist said, "*Wouldst both thou honor my birthed daughter with the colors of thy lineages and the love of thy hearts?*"

Z bowed deeply, offering the bow.

Phury's voice was hoarse as he took the streaming lengths of satin. "*It would be the honor of the ages to pledge our colors unto your birthed daughter.*"

As Z straightened, it was hard to say who stepped forward first.

Most likely they met in the middle.

Neither said anything while they embraced. Sometimes words didn't go far enough, the vessels of letters and the ladles of grammar incapable of holding the heart's sentiments.

The Brotherhood started to clap.

At some point, Phury reached out and took Cormia's hand, drawing her close.

He pulled back and looked at his twin. "Tell me, does she have yellow eyes?"

Z smiled and nodded. "Yeah, she does. Bella says she looks like me . . . which means she looks like you. Come meet my little girl, brother mine. Come back and meet your niece. There's a big empty place on her crib, and we need the two of you to fill it."

Phury held Cormia close and felt her hand rub the center of his chest. Taking a deep breath, he swiped his eyes. "That's my favorite opera and my favorite solo."

"I know." Z smiled at Cormia and referenced the first two lines, "*Che gelida manina, se la lasci riscaldar.*" "And now you have a little hand to warm in your own."

"Same can be said of you, my brother."

"So true. So blessedly true." Z grew serious. "Please . . . come see her—but also, come see us. The Brothers miss you. I miss you."

Phury narrowed his eyes, something sliding into place. "It's you, isn't it. You've come to the community center. You've watched me sit on that swing afterward."

Z's voice grew hoarse. "I'm so damned proud of you."

Cormia spoke up. "Me, too."

What a perfect moment this was, Phury thought. Such a perfect moment with his twin before him and his *shellan* beside him and the wizard nowhere in sight.

Such a perfect moment that he knew he was going to remember for the rest of his days as clearly and as poignantly as he lived it now.

Phury kissed his *shellan*'s forehead, lingering against her, giving thanks. Then he smiled at Zsadist.

"With pleasure. We'll come to Nalla's crib with pleasure and reverence."

"And your ribbons?"

He looked down at the green and the gold, the lovely satin lengths

intertwined, symbolizing the union of him and Cormia. Abruptly, she tightened her arms around him, as if she were thinking exactly the same thing he was.

Namely, that the two went perfectly together.

"Yes, my brother. We're absolutely coming with our ribbons." He looked deeply into her eyes. "And, you know, if we have time for a mating ceremony, that would be great because—"

The hooting and hollering and back slapping of the Brotherhood cut off the rest of what he was going to say. But Cormia got the gist. He'd never seen any female smile as beautifully and broadly as she did then while looking up at him.

So she must have known what he meant.

I love you forever didn't always need to be spoken to be understood.